Geoffrey Spinks was educated in London and Scotland and became a dairy technologist in 1970. The following years were involved in consultancy, working in most of Europe, Scandinavia, Russia, America, and South Africa. Geoffrey was the founder and chairman of GR Spinks & Company Ltd, a fruit processing business based in the UK. He is a fellow of the Institute of Food Science and Technology. Since retirement in 2021, he has turned his attentions to painting, writing, and playing golf.

Donald J Martin—Former chief at IBM—USA.

Thank you for your support and advice.

Christopher Spinks—for your young mind and AI comments.

Geoffrey Spinks

2084

AUSTIN MACAULEY PUBLISHERS™

LONDON • CAMBRIDGE • NEW YORK • SHARJAH

A CIP catalogue record for this title is available from the British Library.

ISBN 9781035853076 (Paperback)
ISBN 9781035853083 (Hardback)
ISBN 9781035853090 (ePub e-book)

www.austinmacauley.com

First Published 2024
Austin Macauley Publishers Ltd®
1 Canada Square
Canary Wharf
London
E14 5AA

Table of Contents

Prologue

"Last night at 21.00 Eastern time, 10 March 2004, a NASA Rover perfected the first landing on the planet Mars. It will conduct tests over the next two years that will be the first step of a long-term mission to understand the conditions that prevail, and what science needs to be developed if we are to send humans to this planet. Their media spokesman was quoted as saying that this was one of the most important steps taken by our planet to further our understanding of the universe."

This broadcast by the BBC Radio in London took place on 18 February 2021.

In 2022, a Chinese agency advised that they are to launch a satellite that will arrive, and orbit around the planet Mars in 2023.

In an article in the Telegraph newspaper on 15 September 2021, printed in a small section on the fourth page, you could have read the following extract.

"The University of California has announced that two of its chemists, Dr Suits, and Professor Parker, have developed a system that can convert CO_2 into oxygen by exciting the carbon dioxide, using what is to be known as a 'high-energy vacuum ultraviolet laser'. By this means, they claim to have been able to turn carbon dioxide back into oxygen and a single carbon atom."

"There have been regular sightings of UFOs in our skies for the last 70 years, all dismissed as being due to unusual weather patterns, shooting stars, or other rare occurrences that could be partly explained."

"Professor Sagan stated in 2020 that any life that is out there in the universe will either be very far behind us in their scientific development, or extremely far ahead."

"Today, just 3 months after the Mars Rover landed, we are delighted to announce that we are going ahead with the building of a new Biosphere in the Arizona desert that will allow us to speed up our research and development of the planet Mars. For the sceptics in our world who wonder why we are spending so much of tax payer's money on these space programmes, we would like to assure you that, as with the moon programmes, we are constantly obtaining information and developing new ideas that have been, and will be, of great value to the planet Earth. Just look at your smartphones for just one simple example of progress that is being made by the finding of new materials, and new science." NASA space research spokeswomen, May 2021.

A God created heaven and earth, but surely the whole universe for these things to exist. **Are there more gods, or are those that have taken that title really the angels of the only God?**

"It is naïve of us, here on the planet Earth, to not believe that there is other life existing in our universe, and that beyond." Extract from lecture by Professor George Williams to the Imperial College in London, April 1978.

Part One

Earth—Biosphere 1, Arizona Desert, September 2061

Josh Devonshire awoke with a happier feeling than he had experienced for some time. For the last 2 years, he had been living in a 100,000 sq. ft 'bubble' known as Biosphere 1. Where he and a team of research scientists, had continued the challenge of understanding the universe, developing new technology, space transport, and new weaponry to meet those challenges. The Biosphere had also been designed to house the experienced and future astronauts who, apart from normal space training, were being subjected to the experience of living and surviving in a hostile atmosphere.

Today, however, was a special day. The space programme was ready to move on. The research of the last two years had been productive, and it was time to analyse some of the results.

An experienced research medical scientist, his mind had wandered back to the start of this adventure, for that was certainly what it was. As a young qualified medical doctor, he had studied hard and achieved his next aim, that of being a surgeon. By the time, he was 30 he was specialising in his field, and subsequently had developed groundbreaking success in gamma ray brain tumour surgery. This work had earned him a Professorship from the University of Arizona.

On his 38th birthday, he had been approached by the ISPEG, the International Space Exploration Group, to lead a team that would further research medical advancements, radiation, and gamma ray technology that he had developed through his surgery work. They had seen the potential for their space research programme.

Today, he was speaking as the Head of the Biosphere team. The last few years had been demanding, but at the same time, he felt the adrenalin running every time that they discovered something new. He had no regrets on his decision to take on this job.

"Professor—*good morning. I am already printing your programme text for today's programme—Please collect it from me before leaving.*"

"Well, good morning to you Zikky, you caught me dreaming. Have you already called my wife?"

"*She said to tell you that she will be finished breakfast early as she is going down to check out the lecture hall before everyone arrives.*"

"OK Zikky, tell her I shall be going down for breakfast soon, and will be ready for the lecture at 10.00 hours."

"*Do I have permission to enter the lecture hall, Professor?*"

"I shall call ahead to ensure you can gain entry. You will be pleased to know that we are soon going to add our special robot team to our working group, and good news, Zikky, we are looking at a face lift for you!"

"*Well Professor—I am surprised you think I need a face lift—However I am as vane as any of the robot team—look forward to it. I shall leave you now—as usual you will find me in the administration room if you need me today.*"

The professor's wife was a research scientist and professional psychiatrist, as well as the head of the health and safety team in the Biosphere. They had met first at university, and had not taken long to both realise that they had similar goals and ambitions. Josh had no doubts that he had chosen the right mate. Dr Ruth Devonshire had shown great skill in developing the younger members of the ISPEG team, and with them, she had established a research programme for artificial intelligence.

This team were now being recognised as leaders in that field. Her experience in psychiatry had been a major factor, particularly as they continued towards one of their main ambitions, that of building human robots. Zikky was one of four candidates for the programme, the robot having already shown remarkable progress towards 'humanisation'.

****

"Good morning, ladies, and gentlemen, I am so pleased to be speaking to you today, the 30th Anniversary of our Biosphere programme."

"I am Professor Joshua Devonshire, head of the ISPEG space research team. Today, my senior team and I are going to outline our programme for the next revolution, that of the Space Age."

"It is over two hundred years since our world experienced the first real modern day technical advance, aptly named the Industrial Revolution. The second was less than 80 years ago, when we saw the second, the Technical Revolution, and of course we are still in that period. Some of you may say, what about the Egyptians, Greeks and Romans and their contributions to science, astronomy, culture, law, and of course architecture, which in turn created what we know today as civilisation. Yes, some of that progress was huge, and we should all be thankful for those contributions, which over several centuries, has taken us, albeit slowly, into the 21st century, and soon the challenge of the 22nd."

"However, with improved learning techniques, and rapidly improving computer capability, the human mind has been able to develop faster in the last 20 years, and all of you here today are living proof of that. Together with you, and with the experience of our existing senior scientists, we are ready to accelerate up to the next stage. A programme that will not only give us better means of safeguarding our own planet, but, following our successful trips to the moon, and our early exploration of the planet Mars, provide the knowledge that takes us to the goal of landing and returning humans and robots on other planets in our galaxy, and hopefully to find new life and resources that will take our planet forward to a new era."

Josh paused, and was pleased to see the anticipation on the faces in the audience.

"How do we start? We are all aware of the wars and attacks on the civilised world over the past decades. Fortunately, we have been able to not only identify terrorist cells more easily with our satellite technology, but also our work with quantum computing has helped us to improve identify of cyber warfare origins. So today, we have one major enemy; that of extreme communist groups who have developed their ideology over the last twenty years, following our peace agreements with former communist countries, for example Russia and China. These groups have become a real threat to the general world peace that we surely all wish to see. Apart from these concerns, we also must take into account the continuing deterioration of the Earth's atmospheres. By seeking new answers in space, we hope to find some better solutions for our future."

"ISPEG space research is our major science centre for the civilised world, working with governments, as well as the USAF, RAF, and UNPTO, our new formation of the old NATO alliance that now includes our new friends, China, and Russia. Our aims are related to not only the advance of our knowledge of the universe, but to discovery of new and improved methods of creating energy, new and more efficient transport, including space travel. Our scope is wide, it will even include developing a new generation of protective and aggressive armoury, that will be our future guarantee against major conflicts in the future."

"You are all here today because we believe you are now qualified to help take this programme forward."

"OK, enough of me for now. Major Phillip Somester, our head of the astronaut and intelligence sectors, is now going to take you through a rough outline of your programme for the next few years."

Phillip moved up to the Roster, his imposing figure, together with his impeccable USAFA uniform, immediately taking the audience's attention. He was just a year younger than Josh, and had arrived at the Biosphere headquarters via a background with the USAF and ISPEG astronaut programme.

"Thanks Professor; good morning, everyone. You will be meeting more with me and our senior team over the next few days, but right now, we want to share with you some of our exciting plans;"

"First, you may be surprised to know that we are close to manufacturing a second international space station that will be assembled in orbit, and then moved to deeper space. This will become a staging post for our future spacecraft and advanced satellites. We aim to increase our use of our robots in this area, working closely with our senior astronauts. The governments of USA and Europe are financing and building this huge development, working closely with our ISPEG Space Centre in Florida. ISPEG will be developing and preparing the necessary spacecraft for this project."

"To give you a quick idea of the immensity of this task, the present ISS was made in 9 parts, the total weight on Earth being about 450 tonnes. We are now talking about production of a unit that will have 30 parts, using our new lighter, but tougher materials, many of these incidentally a result of our findings on the moon, and in meteorite waste. This will limit the weight to approximately 1000 tonnes, still a massive operation. The source of the ISS manufacturing site is for the moment being treated as strictly confidential, but at some stage some of you will be involved."

Phillip paused a moment for them to take that information in before continuing, he could see that he had now their full attention.

"The next project is no less ambitious and as confidential. However, as you have now been cleared by our Intelligence examiners for top secret work, I can announce that we are working on the creation of a new powerful weapon that will in due course supersede the present missile programmes. We shall be selecting some of you who have skills in the area of monochromatic light, photons, gamma ray technology, etc."

"In another sector, we shall be working with those of you with service backgrounds. I am delighted to see in the enrolment list that we have some graduates from the USAFA in Colorado Springs where I spent many happy and productive years. The team that is selected will be trained over the next two years with our Astronaut and Robot team, who will be undertaking our next major missions into space, following our recent successes with the Moon Orbiter, and the planet probes."

"Over the years, here in Biosphere 1, many of our scientific teams have been subjected to living in conditions that may be expected if we learn to live on Mars, or any other planet with atmospheres or conditions that are hostile. Those years of research and experiences have all contributed to the building of Biosphere 2.

Therefore, it is with pleasure that we can announce to you today that most of our main work will move into that new base on October 7."

"Over the next months we shall be internally re-constructing the current Biosphere to be our new chemical and material research labs, and great news for us, we shall install an advanced spacecraft and space station simulator centre. Apart from the simulator, where we can achieve any type of gravity or atmosphere required for trials, all other areas of Biosphere 1 will be returned to normal levels, thus making that area more comfortable for every day work by our administration personnel."

"So, to conclude for today. If you look through the glass wall at the side of this hall, you will now see our fantastic new Biosphere 2 where most of you will be based. 400,000 square feet of latest in building techniques, and advanced scientific facilities. That is over 37,000 square metres for our friends from overseas. Access to this will be via a tunnel air-lock system, and changing and functional facilities will be situated in this area. The area will be under the usual very strict security, and personnel will be issued with ID codes. You will be briefed on all health and safety measures that will be required, and undertake the usual pre-entry medical checks."

"We shall be speaking to you more in the next few days regarding your individual programme. Our psychology and medical teams will make themselves known to you before you leave the hall, and I shall remain here, together with the professor, for the next 30 minutes as you may have some immediate questions."

"Congratulations to you all for making this very special team. You will shortly be joining up with the rest of our research teams that have been working here for the last few years, and their experiences will I feel sure help you to get up to speed more quickly."

"Finally, I want to thank those who have graduated to us from other countries for the time they gave to learning our language. As you were advised we shall conduct all our discussions and writing in English-American is also welcome!"

He waited a few seconds while some refreshing light laughter met this announcement.

"We look forward to working together in the coming years. It will be an exciting journey in more ways than one—good luck!"

****

Phoenix, Arizona, January 2062

Josh was having his first major meeting with the senior ISPEG team since they moved into Biosphere 2. He first turned to Phillip. They had both started on this venture some years ago, and now, with both their wives also heavily involved in the ISPEG projects, and each having young sons, they had become inseparable.

"How are the new team settling in Phillip?"

"Great so far, Josh. We have split up the teams to concentrate on specific subjects and sectionalised the Biosphere to allow for each group to have some autonomy to improve focus. They all have signed the OSA forms and understand that anyone breaking the rules will be expelled, and electronically monitored after departure. All communications are now in English, and there have been no dissentions, even from our French crew!"

"Good, are there any more questions, team?"

Lt. Tom Lancs raised a hand. "As the Major says we have had a smooth transition to the new areas, and now I am concentrating, together with Ruth, Li Chun Woo and Lt. Cumber on the laser programme."

"Thanks Tom, good to hear from you, and yes you are right that we need to move soon on that project following research on the findings we had from the work that we undertook last year. The accident we had with the space vehicle on the last orbit run around Jupiter indicates that we need to provide armoury to the future spacecraft, and the work we are doing on the laser development seems to be pertinent. I am particularly thinking of micrometeorites, and of course any

27

future enemy situation. Now, before we break up for the day, can we discuss the robot programme?"

Ruth now intervened, "OK, apart from the work we have completed with Zikky's team, we are of course continuing our research into human tasking, and eventually humanisation. It is certain now that we shall have the space vehicles that will be able to travel to and from the new ISS Venus, and beyond, and it would be great if we can develop a robot team who can assist in the projected landings on Mars. We are a long way behind the Chinese who have already established a good base there."

"Phillip has been in touch with some old contacts in the hospital where we did our first training. They are very keen to advance the technology on 3D prosthetics and are already using robotic simulation. Shall we ask them up to talk this through? It would be great if we could also bring better identity to the robots."

"I like that thinking, Ruth, it is exciting. OK, let us make contact, and can you ask our Intelligence section if they would undertake the usual checks on the company and the personnel before we meet."

****

ISPEG Arizona Office—August 2062

Josh, Phillip, and Ruth were back at their desks in the Phoenix office. The co-operation between the company Proactive AI Future Ltd and the ISPEG space team had been remarkable over the last few months.

"Josh, apart from what you see in the initial sketches, they were suggesting that they continue to work on achieving a more 'live' image, and had ideas related to limbs and some kind of facial work. These ideas seem very advanced, but it would certainly bring some humanity to our robots, and thus we could start to think of them in more comforting terms if we eventually get to live with them on these new terrestrial areas of the universe. I have put a picture up on the computer for you to see the projected model."

"That's great you two, it does look ambitious at this stage, but as I told Zikky, she may be having a new face lift soon, I feel committed."

"Ruth and I are looking at ordering two models that we can both work on with Proactive, and that will give them some confidence in continuing the research with our team. I am particularly keen for them to work on the limb and facial structures while we continue to improve the human technology. As you can see from the latest photograph, Zikky has progressed really well."

"She and her small team have developed good voice and translation abilities in the sound boxes, and we are now working on raising their IQ to next levels. Ruth told me she had been warned of a theory that had been established some years earlier regarding the danger of letting loose on this subject, as the development of IQ could multiply very rapidly once they reached IQ200. Therefore, at this time we have opted to take the IQ to a maximum 170. We can review this in a few years. We are measuring IQ by involving them in computer competitive games, chess, and bridge, playing against our best brains. We already are having difficulty defeating some of the team, particularly in the game 'Counter-strike-Global Offensive'; the robots seem to be having a big advantage when we play this."

"Well, both of you, that is all fine with me. The robot programme is moving rapidly, and good income is coming into the ISPEG space programme as our government, and indeed the industrial private sectors, see the huge advantages of using robotic intelligence and labour."

Josh then turned to the others in the meeting.

"I think that is all for now, we have to concentrate next on the laser tests that we shall be conducting in the next few days. Phillip and Ruth, can you just stay for a few more minutes."

Phillip and Ruth moved their chairs to the head of the table as the rest of the team exited.

"While we are progressing on these matters, and while we are together, I was thinking of our own boys. They are both of an age now when they want to know more and are very interested in science and our work here. I think they already have said they want to get into the USAFA school, and to do that we have to find a new school for them to enter after their time at the Archway, which I think ends soon. One where they will hopefully progress onto the university, as we did, here in Phoenix."

"I am sure that they both want to eventually be astronauts. In that respect, and to get them totally enthused, I am asking General Worcester in the Florida control centre if we may take them, just for a day or two into our Biosphere 1. We shall have to sign something I am sure, but he is someone I have worked with in the past and think he may be supportive. It would be great if they could understand the objectives of this space programme, and maybe it will help them make firmer plans for their futures."

****

Biosphere 1, Arizona Desert, March 2063

"Today, we are ready to test the stage 3 laser that has been under research now for the last two years. Apart from the regular occurrence of small Asteroids, we also now know that there are micrometeorites flying through space at ultra-high speeds. We need a means of dispersing or deflecting this debris during longer space flights. We also have certainly not ruled out other risks, including enemy attack, as experience has taught us that when we make any significant advance in technology, we become a target for the factions wanting to hurt us, or steal from us. This latter concern is a prime motivator for WPO and all civilised governments, and ISPEG do not underestimate the importance of these tests."

"You should also know that the test has been put on higher priority following the recent destruction of Stellarship2, which was hit by large space debris during its investigative flight toward the planet Venus, sadly resulting in the loss of 6 lives."

Josh was addressing the team of 25 selected scientists and trainee astronauts. Included in this team were senior personnel representing ISPEG's partner space agencies. They had all been briefed about the research to date related to energy mass needed for improved laser weaponry, as well as for laser use in advancing technologies for heavy industry.

"This new laser is being tested to check its potential as an armoury for the new 'Stellarship5' spacecraft that is being prepared for the latest mission that is to meet up with our US base team working on the moon. It is also being tested in other areas of defence, which detail is still classified. We are also close to establishing our first mission to erect a revolutionary space station, which has been named Venus. Work is in progress as I speak to manufacture structural parts, and discussion is ongoing as to how they will be assembled and maintained in outer space. Up to now it has only been possible to use orbital paths with satellites using centrifugal force versus magnetic gravity to ensure they do not fall back to Earth."

"All these huge developments are ambitious and somewhat dangerous, as they are tackling new ground in space exploration. We know that to succeed, we not only have to travel in secure vessels, but eventually go into unknown territory to achieve our final goal of being able, to not only survive on another planet, but be able to move to and from these new territories on a regular basis."

He stopped for a moment to allow them to absorb this information.

"Now, to those who have joined us today, may I now introduce Dr Ruth Devonshire. Ruth is our leading authority on health and safety matters. Please listen carefully to her and she will take you through the procedures and important information related to this upcoming simulator test."

"Welcome to you all; For these laser tests, we shall adopt normal atmosphere in the simulator, so we can make that trip more comfortable for our untrained visitor friends, and not least, to help us all to be fully focused throughout. As the professor has said, we shall be conducting other tests later with our astronaut team relating to spacecraft and ISS operations in varying atmospheres, but you will be duly warned and prepared. I look forward to working with you on this project."

Biosphere 2—Simulator Chamber, April 2063

The new simulator was elaborate. It had been constructed as a complete interior replica of the Stellarship5, which, unknown to most, was the latest craft built for long distance space travel.

Josh and Phillip spent a few minutes giving the crew details of their duties and observation requirements needed during this 'trip'. Josh was feeling confident as they moved into their seats in front of the console, and quickly switched on the controls. All checked out. The 'flight' was soon on its way to the target which today had been set as a rogue Asteroid that was speeding through space towards the Earth and needed to be attacked well before reaching the gravitational pull of the planet. This was an exercise to just test the pilot control and work out any problems that may arise.

Initial flight data showed that the spacecraft was making good progress. The signal had now come up on the huge computer face that the laser was to be set to standby mode as the target had been recognised by the craft's early warning systems. Josh and the team knew that the GRD laser, that was not simulated, was waiting some miles away in the Nevada desert, and he needed radar tracking data, and trigger confirmation for firing. The laser had been set up to 'beam' to the target approximately a mile further away in the desert.

Operators in the simulator were calculating the exact spot where the target would be at a certain time. They understood that later there would be further tests that would take place in space where there was no wind, but further into space it was possible that solar winds would be present, and they had to allow for all contingencies that may occur on a longer space voyage.

The laser was using solar plate cells, but technology had enabled them to increase the heat from the sun's rays x300 by means of giant titanium and sapphire crystals, built similarly to the huge telescopes developed in earlier years, but with the lenses inverted. The combination of mass and light created electromagnetic waves, known as gamma rays, that when released under controlled direction, sent a beam of such intensity that anything in its path could be destroyed, or very severely damaged. This was the first time that they had tried to achieve accuracy at such a distance as the beam had now to allow for curvature of the Earth.

The team now prepared for the final step in the test. For security reasons, the laser beam could only be activated by two personnel on the spacecraft, and as the two senior officers on this project, Josh, and Phillip, were standing by, and checking the codes provided to them by their employers, the ISPEG HQ.

The simulator's console would show the whole process on the screen as an attack on the artificial Asteroid, and if successful they had been advised that there would be a small, controlled explosion in the target. Both were now looking intently for the signals on the console. It briefly came into their minds that this was rather like the early computer games that they both had experienced as children, except this was for real! The crew were now alerted to action stations and made aware of their tasks.

The security co-ordinates were entered on the two computer consoles in front of them. The operations crew had all advised systems were OK to go.

Josh then turned to Phillip, "Be ready to press code entry keys."

The target had been suspended by a steel cable, held in position about 300 metres from the ground by a USAF controlled mini-drone. All of this had been noted, and location established prior to this final firing instruction.

They both pressed the entry keys and the beam line could be clearly seen on their monitors as having been activated precisely to the instruction. However, the crew who were closely following the screens were alerting them to a slight loss of power to the laser box at the firing time. They watched the monitors carefully to see what this meant, but so far so good, the beam was working and aimed towards the target. Normally this would be reached in seconds.

However, it was soon clear to them all that the target had not been destroyed, and indeed on checking the data on the computers it was evident that the laser had only 'reached' about two thirds of its target, before dying. However, the console pictures did not show any sign of damage to the laser or target.

"What happened, Josh?"

Phillip was also looking at the target on his screen.

Josh looked up, disappointment on his face.

"Some kind of malfunction in the energy mix it would seem. We need to close down the operation, and get out there to investigate."

He turned on the control microphone, "Ladies and gentlemen, attention please. Sorry to advise that the test has apparently not been totally successful. We are closing down the simulator, and preparing for analysis and inspection. Please make your way back to the Biosphere 1 as soon as possible. However, the following names should be prepared to meet with me and Major Somester in the ops room immediately."

****

There was a distinct buzz back in the Operations room. The five names that Josh had called were mainly those who had been directly involved in the early development of this project, and they were now assembled in his office. Josh turned first to his wife.

"Ruth, I would like you to accompany us—can you ensure health and safety measures are in place, and get Tom, Leon, Li Chun and Pete up to speed. Oh, and bring the post mortem camera please. Phillip, can you call up the desert wagon for us, and stay with the rest of the team a while so we can start the investigation. We need to get a report ready for ISPEG and the USAF space labs teams."

"OK Josh, will do, take care out there."

The transport arrived as they were speaking. It was designed to handle the hostile desert terrain, and had been built similarly to the vehicles that were now in investigative work on the moon and Mars. It could handle all conditions of terrain, and specifically built cabins on its 8 rotor wheels enabled a research team to travel in controlled conditions. After quick checks, they were under way. It was less than an hour since the test run.

They soon crossed the border from the Arizona desert into the sparser Nevada desert.

Some 30 miles away they came upon the laser compound, and after checking that there was no physical damage to the laser or the site, they called in to the ISPEG centre to advise them they were now moving onto the target site. Ruth took a few photos, and then they secured the laser site for further post-operation checks by the space research team.

****

On arrival at the target site, they could see clearly in the desert air that the 'asteroid star' was still in suspension, although it did appear to be out of alignment. The drone was still operating above the target so obviously no real damage could have taken place. It was now confirmed that the laser beam had not reached its target.

Josh got on his satellite phone to the ISPEG space centre. He was in weekly contact with Major Hank Fife.

"Morning, Hank, have you got us on screen, what do you think has happened here."

"Hi Josh, our commiserations, but it looks as if we need to do some more work. Can you let the target down so we can just take a quick examination, we believe there may be some minor damage."

"OK, look out for the drop. We shall lower the drone down and then release the target close to the ground. We then will take our bird back to Phoenix USAF base. We can pick up the target later after your first inspection on the ground. Hey, and keep clear of the landing area as it may throw up a little dust!"

"Thanks, Hank, see you back at base; you, Major Somester and I need to get together urgently if we are going to get this project back on track."

They all watched as the drone started its descent, the target moving gradually into clear sight. They could now see that the damage was real. Suddenly, a huge shout from Li Chun, their fission expert.

"Stop the drop, stop!—it is out of control!"

Josh reached for his phone again, but too late! What Li Chun had seen was that the cable was releasing too early, and the target was in free fall.

"Everyone down in protect mode."

It was Ruth now shouting to them through the headsets.

The explosion as the target fell out of the sky was devastating, sand and debris, and sharp shrapnel like pieces were flying through the air. It was hitting the ground all around them, and the noise was incredible. They had not enough time to drop to ground level. The target had indeed been set up to explode mildly in the air when hit by the laser, but now, with the increased velocity, the explosion had been multiplied several times.

It was Tom who recovered first, he was groggy but intact.

"Shout and account guys!" he bellowed into his headset.

No response. The sand and dust were clearing, and as he looked down, he saw that the rest of the team were not moving. He snatched the satellite phone from Josh's pocket.

"Major, Lieutenant Tom Lancs here, we have an emergency. The target has exploded when hitting the ground, and we have been hit. I am recovered enough to move, but so far, I can see no signs of movement in the rest of my team here—instructions please?"

Hank was unbelieving at first, what could have gone wrong to create such chaos from what appeared to be a normal controlled test run. His brain whirled into action.

"Lieutenant, we shall have someone with you shortly, our helicraft is being prepared right now. Please re-check all personnel for any signs of life, and advise as soon as possible. Do not go near the target site until we arrive. I am calling in our top medical guy so he will be with you soon with his emergency gear. Look out on your watch receptor for a call number and code for you to speak directly to him."

"Copy that sir, thank you." Tom started the unwelcome task of checking the bodies of his comrades, but he did not like what he was seeing.

Earth, Krulandistan, May 2063

Dr Ho Chi Dae was in his office, situated in a six-storey modern building on a huge airfield some thirty miles from the city. He could clearly see the airfield from his top floor office where there were regular satellite rocket flights sponsored by various agencies around the world. The site was used for space programmes, but mainly it was used by various countries who used it as a base for satellite launches. Their politicians had found it not only useful to have a site outside of their own country where there was less concern about the potential contamination of the atmosphere, but also as important to many, operations were considerably cheaper to operate.

Ho Chi and his Satnova.inc. team had also quietly built up a team of scientists and astronauts from Russia, China and the Korean Republic that were mainly dedicated to the cause, which was clearly that of bringing extreme communist ideals back into the world and defeating the so-called 'Western Culture'. They had been looking intensely at the possibility of developing a new generation of communist idealistic young people, who would create a new power in the world.

For a true communist looking in, it would seem strange that someone who followed their cause could run a business that was not only very commercial, but where the chairman of the company appeared to have many properties, and a private yacht. However, this was mainly overlooked by most of his followers, many of whom had been brainwashed in their youth. They saw Ho Chi as the brains to take them to the new world, and the pay they received now was well above the sums they had been used to receiving in their former occupations in communist territories. Most of the other scientists on the base were unaware of Ho Chi's aims, and were only there to fulfil their countries need to have satellite technology and launching abilities.

This centre, situated on the edge of Asia and the West was perfect for his long-term plans that were being gradually put into play. Here, they could monitor most of the rocket, missile, and space programmes as they unfolded. His team, despite assuring the Satnovo company clients to the contrary, and signing anything put in front of them, were gradually putting together drawings and plans that would enable them to build their own superior rocket programme.

The chairman turned from the view, and looked across the office towards the computer wall.

"Kim Jong, how are things? Are you ready to give me the latest news from our cell contacts and from the CRV23 satellite?"

Kim Jong Woo was his right hand in intelligence matters, and he ran a small team of 'workers' who had access to the airfield, but had also been trained in espionage and cyber warfare.

"We have some good news, Comrade Chairman, and a little bad news. Our spy satellite picked up pictures of the ISPEG trials in Nevada and they showed that the laser tests were only partly successful. Their new laser is still not perfected due to our agent's intervention. They also lost some of their key people in the explosion. However, unfortunately, we also lost our agent, and my cousin, Li Chun in the fall-out. She had managed to alter the beam strength which resulted in the test failure, but had not envisaged that there also was a problem with the target site. That was not down to us."

"OK comrade, I am sad to hear about Li Chun, she was very clever, very beautiful, and a good agent. We have lost one of our key people that we had managed to get into the ISPEG programme."

Kim Jong continued, "I think from the intelligence we have that they are very close to an answer, and this setback, particularly if they have lost key people, will push them to greater efforts in the next few years."

Ho Chi looked thoughtful. "I think that may be right, we must make more effort to steal this technology, and then destroy their next trial, otherwise we may see our future spacecraft and missiles being detected and destroyed by such a lethal weapon. Please start investigating how we can replace Li Chun. Is there anyone of her calibre in our US cells that may have sympathies for our cause?"

He continued before his henchman could respond, "On another subject, but very important to us, what have we done to monitor the building of the new space station that we have heard about, can we arrange an accident to delay that development? Alternatively, we may start to think about allowing them to build and erect it, and then plan to take it over. To do this, we would have first to ensure we have control of the laser and their other advanced weapons systems."

"I shall start investigation of possibilities, including training of some of our supporters to be capable of astronaut duties, to see if we can infiltrate the ISS programme. They are accepting trained people from all countries, so we may have to change ID. I shall also talk to our major contacts around the world. However, Chairman, this is a long-term programme."

"Thank you, Kim Jong, I appreciate that this will be a long-term project, but move with some urgency in finding the new recruits. However, I agree we should tread carefully, and be extra careful with sharing of information during these years ahead, only make direct contact with me and our cell leaders. I do not trust the computer transfer system. When you have some news, let me know and we can make our next plan—in the meantime, do ensure our income from our business is strong, we shall have some heavy expenditure soon. With the increase in countries wishing to launch satellites, and with our good contacts, perhaps it is time to increase the rates? I appreciate that we are being partly subsidised, but I would like us to greatly increase our inflow of cash. We are, after all, very competitive, and I believe we can maintain that advantage."

"Thank you, Chairman for your understanding. You are of course correct, and I shall go now to talk to our company administrators at the airfield regarding some adjustments to certain rental and take-off rates."

Kim Jong saw this as one of his easier tasks in the years ahead.

****

Biosphere 1, Early January 2064

Dr Li Chun Woo and Lieutenant Peter Cumber had indeed died from wounds inflicted by the bullet like shrapnel, but Tom and the ISPEG doctor had been able to save Josh and Ruth. They had been knocked unconscious, and had many wounds, but not critical. The three survivors had now been debriefed, and were recovering from the tragic experience.

Some nine months had now passed since the tragedy in the Mojave Desert. The subsequent enquiries had found that, first, there had been a malfunction in the laser start-up which had, as the scientists had expected, affected the strength of the beam. However, the final blow, leading to the deaths, had definitely been caused by a simple but fatal fault, when the cable had released from the target too early, due to what was described as a 'computer error', possibly started by an attack on the ISPEG systems, but that was still being investigated by the US government authorities. The deaths of Dr Li Chun, and Lieutenant Peter Cumber, were recorded as 'killed in line of duty'.

****

Major Phillip Somester, and his wife, Dawn, were taking some time out at their home, as they were still feeling the loss of their friends and colleague. They looked across to their son Robert, who like many teenagers was engrossed in his computer and school work. Today, he was playing a computer game.

Phillip distracted him, "Robert, are you playing against Christopher again?"

His son indicated yes by a quick nod, as obviously he was not going to be distracted for long.

"OK, that is good, when you finish ask him if he wants to come over. We are going to speak to Uncle Josh and Auntie Ruth to check if we can have dinner together, how does that sound?"

Another quick nod.

"We shall have to put you and Chris up against our new robots to see how good you really are at those games."

Robert now finally looked up, "Really Dad, that would be really cool, any chance?"

"OK, we shall see, in meantime, keep up the good results from school."

He turned again to his wife. "Dawn, give Ruth a call will you, and see if they all free tonight. We do have to get back to work next week, as we are ready to begin our next stage of testing on the new laser, and I understand from the AI team that they are ready to discuss the robot prosthetics after their meeting with the company that I introduced to them—Another thing, I was thinking about our present robot ability. Next time we do an investigation we must take the robots with us, I hate to say it, but I think I could have saved our colleagues if I had thought this out earlier."

"Honey, I am not sure that you would have saved them, it was an accident that could not be predicted, and I know they would want us to move on. Perhaps we can also talk to Ruth about the ideas we have for Robert's schooling; she may have the same ambitions for Chris."

"We did have some good news that came back from General Worcester. Permission has been granted for Robert and Chris to attend the Biospheres for two days under our guidance, to allow them to learn more about the long-term objectives of the ISPEG space programmes."

"Good, when they go, I may be able to fulfil the boy's hopes of playing against the new robot generation? I would not mind having a game myself."

Dawn was laughing at him. "There is always a boy inside you guys!"

****

Phoenix, Arizona, September, 2067

Some 4 years had passed since the tragic events in the desert. Chris and Robert were having one of their regular meetings in Chris' room, situated in the halls of residence at the University of Arizona. They had both developed well at the boarding school and were progressing with their educational targets. Chris was studying Astro sciences and Physics, and Robert had chosen Applied Mathematics and Artificial Intelligence. They saw these subjects as helpful to meeting their ambitions. They still had a common goal of wanting to follow their parent's careers, eventually being part of the ISPEG space research and astronaut teams. Their enthusiasm had been increased by the fact that they had so much enjoyed the trip to see their parents in the Biospheres a few years ago, and had learnt much about what was needed if they were to qualify for working with the space programmes.

Chris, who was always the leader in these regular chats, poured them both some home-made ginger beer from the large decanter that he kept on in the fridge, it seemed to be always full. Then he looked up, and unusually, surprised Robert with his opening subject.

"Rob, I have seen a lovely girl in the Physics section. She also seems to have an amazing brain, and would love to get closer to her if I can. She seems really different; apart from her outstanding interest in the sciences, she speaks languages, and has a mutual interest in the future of our planet. I hope to get a meeting with her next week, and as she has already advised me that she has a friend at the same college of similar age, I wondered if we should ask them if we can all meet?"

Robert looked a little stunned, this was so unusual for Christopher to be talking about anything other than school work, or their interests in sport, or not least, computer games.

"Chris, you certainly must have been smitten with this girl, you really caught me off guard for once! I guess we have been mostly dedicated to our schooling, and girls have not been much in our thoughts before, but, yes, why not, we should try to find partners eventually. Of course, I want to meet this dream of yours, so happy to take pot luck on my date!"

"OK Rob, I shall make contact with Helena, and her friend, I think her name is Athena, and see if we can make a first date to go to the concert that the university are running for a month starting next week. The first week is Tchaikovsky, and we just love the Piano concerto and his ballet music; let us hope that interests them as well."

"Don't forget the wonderful symphonies as well, Chris, I think they would find the 6th really exhilarating."

"We can investigate all that later this week after I am able to confirm the meetings. Hey, I guess we would go anyway. I am very keen though to have some time with this girl and let us hope Athena is as interesting as your girl."

"Well Chris, we are lucky so far. We both have maintained our friendship through our teens, and have mutual goals, and I am sure you know you always have my strong support. However, I agree that if Aunty Ruth, I still like to call your mother by that name, and my mother are anything to go by, that is another kind of support, but significant for our lives ahead."

"OK, will come back to you in a few days."

****

Earth, Krulandistan, May 2068

Ho Chi Dae was back in his huge office after spending some six months on his private yacht. He, and his Korean cell friends had however not only enjoyed the life on the Indian Ocean but had been looking at various strategies for future advances to their cause. He was now looking out over the familiar views of the airfield. Without turning he called out to his young but trusted right-hand man.

"Kim Jong, time is moving on, and it is some time since we evaluated our position. Please update me on our progress with the ISPEG laser project, and our plans for replacement agents. I have also seen that over the last three years the ISS Venus is being constructed in Canada, and during the next few years they are going to assemble the parts in a new area in space, the code name is Gateway. This will give them further ability to send spacecraft on regular missions to Mars and beyond in the next decade. They already have been testing the moon orbital transfer unit that they sent up two years ago."

"Good morning, Comrade Chairman, as you know we have not been too idle in the last few years since we looked at this venture. First, let us look at the bad news. According to our local cell sources, the ISPEG laser programme has developed since we lost our Li Chun in the biosphere complex, and it is certain that this will now be commercially viable. Therefore, we must assume they will soon be setting up the next tests, which could be in space. To ensure we have some presence again in the ISPEG camp, I chose two of our young, but academically brilliant contacts from our Russian cell, namely Irina Ivanov and Lara Gorinski, and had them fast tracked by our science and cyber computer team."

"I am pleased to advise that we managed to obtain places for them at the University of Arizona to study astronomy sciences and Physics. It did cost us several thousand dollars for the visa applications, and for creating the necessary clean background information for the US authorities. However, this move I believe is significant for us, as I anticipate, with the high IQ's and scientific knowledge that they have, that they will mix with other students who are in line for future work in the ISPEG research and space units. They are of course also fully trained in combat, and have been successfully indoctrinated with our cause.

They could be quite dangerous should their cover be blown; we have given them access to our local cell contact, and to the tools required for any activity they feel fits the situation."

"That sounds very good comrade, I am of course disappointed that we could not stop the laser project, but your thinking is sound; we must be present in the enemy's camp if we are to stop further acceleration of their plans. Now, regarding the ISS, any better news?"

"Not yet, we badly need the new agents to be active. We do know that there is to be a launch of the first parts of the new ISS in the next few years. The finished unit is evidently to be trialled, firstly orbiting around the moon, and then later if all successful, they plan to move the complete unit into mid-space. With the new technology they have added to this unit, the newly developed spacecrafts, some of which we have already seen at this station, will be able to use the ISS Venus, for that is, what they are calling it, as a staging station for what they hope will be their eventual regular journeys to Mars."

Kim Jong paused, before continuing.

"A positive is that we have located where the parts are being manufactured in Canada. As we understand it, the space agency's plan is to assemble these parts gradually in space. The structure will be ten times the size of the present ISS. It is very creative, and it would be a large setback for them if we can stop this project, or at least slow it down significantly. Alternatively, we can re-consider the possibility of earlier thoughts about infiltrating the ISS with one of our own people when it is in the early stages of tests, for instance the moon orbiting trial."

"So, Comrade Chairman, let us talk again about this in a few months' time, and in the meantime, I shall be in contact with my new young agents in Arizona, as when they graduate, which I do expect, I may be able to assist their selection with help from our US contact; then we can ensure that they can be active in the ISPEG camp."

"OK Kim Jong, we still have a long way to go, but as usual you have followed up our plans well, and we must now be patient while we wait for developments from our on-site comrades."

"On another subject, congratulations on the new deals you and the team have managed regarding the new terms. The airfield is now bringing in good money in dollars, and in fact that has, as we expected, been necessary as per your costs in getting our new agents into the USA."

Ho Chi did not mention of course the amount that was needed to finance his lifestyle!

****

Phoenix, University of Arizona, March 2069

Chris and Robert were sitting in Chris's room, and as usual, drinking the ginger beer concoction he called 'Gunners', and having a catch up on events.

"Well Rob, we are ready to take our finals in June, how are you feeling? Have we done enough do you feel? It has been more difficult since we met Helena and Athena?"

"I must say Chris, things have moved on very fast from our meeting them back in September. The concert was a great idea, they really appeared to enjoy that. However, I think I have been pretty good at keeping my head on my shoulders despite the many times when I would have liked to be with Athena."

"It is quite strange how well they seem to understand everything. Their academic knowledge is remarkable, and honestly, I think you would agree, beyond our own IQ. They also seem to understand that we need to be single minded in our ambitions and learning, and have not put us under any stress to spend more time with them socially or sexually, unfortunately!"

"No, kidding, but it is true they do not try to divert us in any way, despite, I think you will agree, that they both seem to be very happy with our company. I know they are very attractive, although their faces are rather larger than we have seen with our American girls. The dark hair and eyes, and darker skin all point to a Greek background. I hope as we get to know them more, they will tell us more about their parents and their earlier lives. Someone in the family must have super brains for them to be so well educated and advanced."

"I noticed the same thing with Athena, but boy, I just feel I want to be near her, so let us see how this develops. It certainly would be great if we graduate together and maybe even eventually work together. Their knowledge is certainly remarkable."

"Could not agree more. On another subject Rob, something else that Helena shared with me. There are two new intakes to the university, from I think, the Russian Republic, and evidently, they are also very bright. They evidently have been asking forward questions relating to how they can get into ISPEG research positions at the Biosphere. She just thought that they were a little strange and

44

wanted to mention it. Anyway, we shall no doubt meet them if they graduate, and see what that is all about. They may just be feeling isolated in view of their country background, and trying to make friends."

****

University of Arizona, August 2069

Irina Ivanov and Lara Gorinski were on their way to the university forum. The hall was filling with students all keen to see their results. They pushed forward through the crowd, and were clearly upsetting a few of the students as they tried to get nearer to the board.

"Hey, you two, who do you think you are, you may be pretty, but we are all equal on this day. Don't you think we are all as anxious as you to know our grades."

The young man who spoke was tall and good-looking, but had a severe look on his face. The students around him all stopped talking. Hank Blackburn was well known and well liked in the university, even if he was not recognised as the most academic of the students. He ran a musical DJ programme every Friday night for them, and had a great following.

Irina and Lara had got to the board. They hesitated, but Irina quickly sized up the situation. She was angry and ready to attack this guy, and almost without thought her hand had moved to the small concealed knife that she always carried, but in those seconds her mind had quickly returned to their main mission, and she could see that this was not the time to make any enemies. Their time would come! She turned to face them.

"We are so very sorry all of you, we were too excited, and please forgive us this time."

They all looked to Hank, they could see that his expression had changed.

"OK girls, we understand perhaps that you are used to different ways in your homeland. We thank you for your response, let us take our time, and good luck. I am not too sure I need to get there in a hurry, I shall be surprised if I am excited with my results."

Chris and Robert had been watching this as they entered the hall a little late, and were surprised at the uproar. However, it seemed harmless, and all had now quietened down. Students were now taking notes of their results, and either

45

looking excited, or downright glum. They had noted that the two Russian girls had evidently started the row, but it seemed that they had been forgiven.

****

Chris and Robert had both achieved firsts in their subjects, and were now sitting with Helena and Athena and several other happy students in the university common room. Chris looked up at Helena, who for some reason were not showing any great emotion after the recent results.

"Well, as good as our results were, it was nothing compared with yours, you and Athena easily topped the honours, congratulations, you were terrific."

"Well Chris, we were lucky to have had a really good education before we came here, and the university has been great in getting us information that we needed to support our efforts. Are you both going to apply for a job, or are you, as you mentioned once, going to apply to join the USAFA? Athena and I are now both keen to apply to work at the ISPEG science centre in California."

Before they could respond, Athena added, "Yes, although you have said you want to be with us as friends, Helena and I both want to stay together if possible, and with our scientific backgrounds it would be wonderful if we can work in the new Biosphere that you have told us about, and where your parents worked. It does not mean we cannot remain good friends as we understand that the USAFA centre is also in Arizona?"

Chris and Robert were surprised at the disappointment they felt that the girls were not concerned that they would not be with them on a regular basis, but at the same time they could see sense in their thoughts. They knew that they would certainly apply for the USAFA, as they needed the training, and flying experience, before they could apply for an astronaut and spacecraft programme. This was still their final aim, and they could see that having Helena and Athena working at the Biosphere, it could possibly lead to them being back together again, which somehow was there in their thoughts.

Both of them tried to speak first, it was Robert this time.

"You are right that Chris and I wish to pursue positions at the USAFA, as we see that as our first goal, one that eventually may lead to joining the ISPEG and USAFA teams."

"Chris' father, Professor Devonshire, is still in charge of the Biosphere programme, and my father, Colonel Somester, is the Head of the USAFA

Astronaut programme. He is also the second in command at the Biosphere. Anyway, to the point, it is Dr Dawn Somester—yes, my mother, who conducts intelligence interviews for those seeking a future in the ISPEG Biosphere organisation. We can certainly ask her if she will agree to see you, and if she does, we feel sure you would be selected. If that happens, you would then be assigned to tasks in the Biosphere sectors. We both are certainly sure that our parents will recognise your remarkable knowledge, and that you will be a welcome addition to their team."

****

Irina and Lara were also studying their results, and it was now clear that they had achieved good grades. This task completed, they would now both look forward towards their target of infiltration, and upsetting of the ISPEG space programmes.

"Lara, now we have the credentials, we are ready to plan our next move. First, I am concerned about those two Greek girls. They appear to be watching us very closely. After the recent explosion in Canada, when our Canadian cell managed to damage part of the manufacturing area for the ISS structures, we can expect anyone with a former communist country background to come under suspicion. The West is still suspicious of Russia and China, despite the changes they have made in the social system. Of course, we know that there are still many of us who wish to return to real communist ideals and that is what ECAW is all about."

"OK Irina, but our main aim now is to get selected for the ISPEG Biosphere work so we can follow up on the late Li Chun's work. We should work on those two guys who are obviously closely connected to the ISPEG senior administrators. They seem to be smitten with those two Greek girls, and those two are really our main rivals for the few openings that ISPEG make available to overseas graduates. At the moment, their graduation results indicate that they would be favourites for any positions that become available."

"If we can remove them without tracing it back to us, we surely would have a better chance of being selected. I have some ideas on that subject."

"Great, this is the Lara that I know, I had thought earlier that maybe you were going a little soft. I was also thinking, you remember that guy who I nearly was going to attack yesterday? His name is Hank Blackburn. He is running a 2020s

47

music evening on Friday night and I shall go and put our names down for tickets. It will be a chance to put ourselves in the limelight, be at our most seductive, and remove any anti-feeling about us. At the same time, we can study those two girls more, and decide how we can deal with them. It will also be good to dress up a little, maybe something a little lower cut, that should get the guys looking and forgetting anything bad about us, even the two we had our eyes on."

****

Planet Attica—Earth Time, November 2069

Chairman Isis Parapoulis was watching, together with several other Attican dignitaries, live action on the huge 'space' wall in the chamber, situated in a grand pillared hall in the New Parthenon, headquarters of the assembly. The members were in session with one of their regular 'Universe' meetings.

Isis, and ten of the senators in the chamber, represented the Planet Cabinet who were in turn elected by the assembly every 10 years. Ninety other prominent leaders were in the hall, all elected by the Attica citizens. The members had varied backgrounds, representing law, sciences, administration, space exploration and health.

It was still fascinating to them all to be able to see the amount of activity that was taking place in the universe millions of miles from their little planet, although they had been watching scientific developments on the other planets, and in outer space, for some time now. Today, the satellite known as 'CRV23', that was launched by the Chinese in earth year 2060 was recording picture and sound data that they had captured by cyber intervention with their sophisticated systems. They had considered this was easier than showing an alien presence at this stage, although the necessary technology was available, and they could make a presence in the Earth's orbit if they deemed it necessary.

As they all studied the data, Isis was going over the progress that the planet had made since the Attica team had sent their first spacecraft out into the universe over 200 years ago. It had taken another 60 years for them to perfect a spacecraft that would travel through the universe with their own trained scientists, ready to study other planets, and check for other life. The new spacecraft were named Rotoships due to their ability to rotate outer rims at very high speeds and yet maintain a direct course.

Isis was one of the descendants of the founders of the planet, who were believed to be spirits from the former Greek kingdoms; their natural language was ancient Greek. His ancestors had named it Attica, which was the historic area of Athens in ancient Greek times. The planet was about one tenth the size of the planet Earth, was close to a bright star named Euclipse, and had 66% of the Earth's gravity at ground level.

The first generations had developed with the intelligence of the ancient Greeks, and this had been a great asset over time, so that today they were a very advanced people in scientific and cultural matters.

During the last century they had also realised that they had to remove warring factions between their peoples as it would soon destroy the population. However, an infertility threat that had arisen over the last 30 years had made that task so much easier, as citizens pulled together to research means of solving this problem. All wars had ended, and now they were looking outward to new horizons for their people.

In recent times, they had also managed to perfect a new inter-person communication system involving telepathy. All young adults had undergone a minor surgery procedure to implant a miniature recorder in their head, that could not only take messages, but also translate languages that they have heard from their spying trips to other planets.

Like Isis, most of the people in Attica had olive coloured skin, and slightly larger heads than those they had seen on the Earth. The other difference was that as they needed to compensate for the lower gravity in their atmosphere, their arms had been lengthened and strengthened with evolution to enable them to feel comfortable when moving or when standing.

Isis was now looking out over the eager faces in the assembly. His large arms were lifted towards them as he started his address.

"My dear senators and assembly members, this is a rather special meeting. As most of you know we have been travelling the universe for some time now, and we have learnt many things that may help us preserve our people in the future."

"The current fertility problem is certainly going to become worse in the next twenty years. It has already affected our male population but also is now prevalent in our animals. We must speed up our plans to find some solutions."

Panis Odysseus, the senior magistrate present in the chamber had stood up and indicated he would speak.

"Chairman, Senators, although the people have been united by the fact that they see the population decreasing, do we want to emphasise the problem at this stage? Shall we be able to calm the situation if we wait until there is a definite plan for survival? What is your advice, and that of the cabinet senators?"

"Thank you, Panis, as usual you are right to ask these questions. You will all be pleased to know that our intelligence centre has already consulted on this subject, and after much consideration we think it is not the time to advise them. When we have made our plan for solving this problem, we shall arrange, after final approval from this assembly, to produce a bulletin for all to understand our aims and progress to date. So, before I continue, are you all in favour of that position?"

The assembly chamber had a unique voting system, whereby the question was posted on a huge screen behind the chairman. The assembly members had only had to point a red or green gloved hand at the screen.

The voting was anonymous, the screen would only advise how many votes for or against the motion. There were 50 senators in the chamber, plus senior members of the space centre. The chairman could have a deciding vote if required.

Isis looked up at the screen which had turned totally green—all had agreed to wait for the bulletin. His vote was certainly not needed.

"Thank you all for your supportive votes. We wish to move on now. General Dimitris Hermes will outline the plans that we have to endeavour to solve this problem, and our progress to date."

Dimitris rose from his bench, and moved to the dais next to Isis. When upright, he was a commanding figure some 7 feet tall. He had a very large imposing face, and when he started to speak, it carried easily through the large assembly chamber so that it was not even necessary to use the head monitors.

"Dear Chairman, Senators, I salute you."

"May I start with our first objectives that we feel we have to address before we can get to the final goal, that of recovering our ability to breed future generations."

Our Senate Cabinet has confirmed that I can now reveal to you that we have successfully landed two of our subjects onto the planet Earth. Excuse us for not sharing this news earlier as it was considered we should wait to see the outcome, as frankly we were not that confident of success. The two brave scientists that made this mission have not only survived, but have established a firm base on Earth. They are Dr Helena Poulakis and Dr Athena Balakakis.

He was interrupted by sounds in his head recorder as members started to get excited. He raised his large hands.

"I know this is sudden news for you, but as I said, please excuse us for holding that information from you for so long. However, if you will let me continue, you will see where we are with the project, and then you may of course, cross examine me and my space team at the end of the presentation."

To his surprise they all stood and started patting their chests with green gloved hands, an assembly sign of high approval.

"Thank you, Members, your trust is much appreciated, and now I can give you much more detail. You will know that 10 years ago we developed spacecraft that would cope with any gravitational problems on long journeys and that are very much faster than the old space vehicles. As importantly, they are very difficult to detect in space."

"One of these new spacecrafts was used to enter the Earth's atmosphere in the Earth year 2062, and our two young scientist agents, who were using specially designed suits that we had trained them to use, were able to exit the spacecraft in the upper atmosphere of the Earth, and then literally fly down to the ground level in the area of the Earth's territory known as Arizona. The new suits gave them the ability to fly-dive in the air. A retro charge-wing system had been built into the suit to slow down their drop, and this relatively new invention has proved that we shall be able to use such a system on a regular basis if required. For the record, you may be amazed to know that their flight time from the moment they departed our Rotoship 1, to the time they landed, was just over five minutes in our time."

"When they landed, their health monitors were checked by our Rotoship medical crew. These proved to be very satisfactory considering the ordeal. The two agents were then able to unlock the suits, and step out dressed in clothes that we had been researching on our screens for some time. The procedure had been rehearsed many times prior to this trip."

The General paused and was delighted to see that he had full attention. He continued…

"The difference in oxygen levels and gravity were a factor for a few days, but they had not found any difficulty in finding shelter. They were in possession of local credentials that we had reproduced here prior to their trip. In the first few days they were therefore able to arrange credit facilities with a local Bank, the equivalent of our Trapeza. We had asked them to obtain credit cards or money chips as soon as possible, as these appear to still be extensively used for trading on that planet."

"Within days of landing, they had found accommodation, they are called motels, and had recovered from the minor sickness that they experienced in the new gravitational atmosphere."

"You will also be interested to know that we had made a surgical change to their arms some time before their departure, so that they would not be too different in appearance when they finally met the Earth's people. The telepathy and recording devices all worked at about three quarters of their strength within days of landing, and although it is taking some time to relay messages, we are in regular communication. The two scientists know that they will have to adapt to life on Earth for some time if we are to achieve our goals."

Dimitris looked around, and could see that the assembly were now totally entranced, and before they could stop him to start questions, he quickly continued…

"So, dear Senators, what is the aim of this long-term project? In the last 10 years, we have made many trips to the orbital areas of the Earth, and at the same time our work on securing a link to the Chinese satellites has enabled us to obtain information that leads us to believe that the Earth is also in some crisis."

"Our studies of the planet and their moon, indicate that they have many problems with future climate effects on their planet, and are still in an age when terrorist activity, particularly related to what we all knew in our planetary studies as extreme communism, is prevalent."

"They are still looking for answers to their present and future problems. We know that they have started exploration of the planets to see if they can find other mineral substances, or even make a human habitat for future generations; They have also been researching means of slowing climate change problems that may put their planet at risk, hence the increased interest in these matters. They already have sent regular trips to the moon, and have sent reconnaissance vehicles and drones to Mars. Shortly, they are starting to build a new space station which they evidently intend to use as a staging post for future ventures."

Dimitris paused again to allow that to be absorbed, and no doubt recorded in the head units.

"We could, of course, infiltrate the Earth and transfer some of our people to that planet. However, we have noted that the Earth is vastly over-populated already, and in any case, we then become part of the problems relating to the Earth's existence for the long term. Yes, we have the technology that would help them, but maybe there is a better way."

"From the information that we are now receiving from Earth directly through our two brave young women, we can look at another scenario."

"The good news coming back is that generally the people on Earth are similar in intellect, but several years behind us in technology. The language problem has been adequately solved by the Brain Units that we had the sense to install in our adult people in recent years. Our two astronauts are conversing in the local language already, even if with a slight Greek accent."

"There people are built differently to us to some degree, as their arms are shorter and so balance easily on two limbs. Unlike our planet, their gravity levels are such that this is quite feasible. We do not see that as a problem. There is a small risk that they may fear us when we finally meet, but we shall address that problem later because we believe there is a solution. Our two representatives have already undergone certain physical changes as I mentioned earlier, they will be our guide as to our ability to develop and grow our population on Mars, creating a partnership if you will with the Earth's citizens."

"As you will now see on the space wall in the chamber, we do have regular surveillance set up so we can monitor their future movements, and from time to time, our chairman will call you to the chamber so that we can share new information with you."

"The Earth is still unaware of our presence due to our advanced systems of stealth, and although their news agencies reported that a few people had seen 'flying saucers' in the sky, they were not believed, and we were not static long enough in the lower atmospheres for anyone there to make more of the news."

"Chairman Isis, I realise that I have been speaking for some time, and there is much to digest. May I suggest a short break before I go onto the discussion re our further plans?"

"Dimitris, as you say, there is so much for the assembly to absorb. I will ask that the robots bring some watered wine and some vegetable nuts. However, I see that the senators are getting very excited; they are obviously anxious to hear all our news and plans. Perhaps we should re-start in 30 minutes."

Dimitris moved back for a moment from the dais, and gratefully took some watered wine from his serving robot.

****

University of Arizona, Phoenix, November 2069

Irina and Lara had a plan. They had observed that the Greek girls seemed to only eat non-meat and non-dairy products, and in fact mainly oats and nuts and some vegetables. They also had seen them drink watered down white wine.

"Why do you think they only eat these type of foods Lara? Maybe they are vegetarians, it is a strange mixture."

"Possibly an intolerance of other foods, some allergies?"

"Studying them over the last week I noted that they had eaten many nut dishes, but did not see peanuts in the mix. As there are several million people here who cannot eat or even be near to peanuts without suffering severe allergenic reaction, we should look at that possibility. In fact, it would be easy to test that one out very quickly."

"OK Irina, I shall find a way of getting some ground peanut extracts into one of their dishes. It certainly would be a clean exit if that works. If it does not work, we can then think of another strategy."

****

Attica Planet—Earth Time, November 2069

Dimitris rose again as they all settled after the drinks break. There was complete silence as he again started to speak.

"What is certain is that we do not want to see the terrorist wars on the Earth continue, they could easily lead to more hostile thinking in their space programme. I believe it is far better for us if we help them eliminate the threats from terrorism, and in particular, this extreme communism that is so averse to our own ideas of democracy, so that when they eventually find us, we may be able to develop a civilisation that our forebears, and theirs, would have admired."

"Hopefully we may find a peace together, and integrate our peoples to ensure future mixed blood generations on a new planet."

"You are all aware in this chamber that we have already established a base on Mars, and that is progressing well. Our astronaut team and the human robots

54

have been able to build a village that we have named Acropolis. A power hub has also been established using the regular wind storms to feed turbines that we landed two years ago, and our robots managed to erect in the top end of the volcano known to astronauts as Olympus Mons. As we see things at this stage, we consider that our living areas will actually be within the many long extinct volcanoes and craters, for not least, we can now develop an atmosphere that would allow both our own people and the Earth people to survive. We have also found the ice caps that had been predicted, and now with power available from the turbines we shall safely develop a water source for human and plant development."

As he paused, he heard a little muttering starting in the chamber, but he continued, "I know there is a lot to absorb, but before we start questions, can I just move onto the most daring aspects of the plan we have considered, that will get us to base one as outlined above, but much more importantly for our future, the ability to reproduce on a new planet. The plan is to be taken in three stages. First phase, our continued study of Earth's people, infiltrating their ISPEG research centre with our two representatives, who with their vast knowledge will help them develop the necessary technology to advance their plans to be able to send humans to Mars."

"Secondly, the increased intelligence we can offer will assist them to move towards the extinction of the extreme communist terrorists known as ECAW, who have been active in delaying or preventing their people fulfilling their plans for further exploration of the planets. This form of terrorist activity does not fit our plans, and we cannot allow that to continue."

"The third phase, which is our final goal, is to persuade their governments to help us with our fertility problems. We do have our 'Moro Birth Banks' preserved, but as our female population are experiencing difficulties in developing the samples, we need to look for means of surrogation, or preferably, in due course, develop marriages between our younger people. We are hopeful that by our offer of help to them, we can create a partnership, one that can live and survive together on Mars. This is going to be possibly the biggest challenge we have faced in our history."

Dimitris stood back, and now waited for some reaction from the assembly.

First to indicate that they wanted to respond was Astronaut Captain, Efi Panomosis. She now rose to address the assembly. Efi was dressed in her full uniform which added to her striking figure. She was only 30 years old, but she had developed her career through the APSP, the Attica Planetary science Programme, which had been founded some 200 years ago. She knew that her team had been, and would be in the future, very involved in the plans outlined by the General, and wanted to be sure that her concerns were voiced.

"Chairman, Senators, I trust you will allow me to speak as I shall be very involved in these plans."

Isis waved to her to signify acceptance.

"I am sure that the chamber are delighted to hear this news from our General, as we had been concerned about the two young scientists since we dropped them from the craft, and had not been able to discuss this until now…"

"May I just add some thoughts? Although we have learnt to speak many languages, we shall have to conquer perfection in their language in the coming years, so that when we meet them, they should feel more at ease. The Greek accents that we have inherited are fine for now, and they suit the present situation for our two agents, Helena, and Athena. My other observation is that Earth people may have some concerns about appearance. We do have similar looks, but slightly larger heads and faces. Our biggest difference is that we all have evolved and adapted to using four limbs due to the gravitational differences on our planet…"

"My main concern is that unless we make changes to our appearance, aliens may conceive us as something ancient and weird when we finally meet. The danger then being that they have always tried to eliminate anything that they do not understand. My point is that, although we want to create a new world and would welcome new contacts, we should be prepared to acknowledge that there may be some hostility towards our own population on the new planet."

Efi only hesitated a few seconds before continuing, "Maybe we can continue our research into how we can overcome the possibilities I have just outlined. The surgery on the two scientists was remarkable, but do we need to go that far? I think we should take some time to consider after we have more news from Earth."

Isis watched the reaction from the room. Senator Gregori Poppoloukis was indicating he was ready to speak. He was one of the elder statesmen, now 104 Attica years old, and a member of the Senate Cabinet. He was always considered a wise man, and the assembly noise dropped as he rose to speak.

"My dear fellow Senators, Captain Panomosis has made some excellent points for us to consider as we move forward with our plans. The General outlined our main objectives, and there will be priorities. We must not lose sight of the fact that our population is decreasing, and despite our superior scientific knowledge, we have not been able to solve that problem. The success of the two young scientists is paramount in our objective. I trust you will all agree to support the Cabinet with our plans, and continue to assist us with your contributions. If our two representatives can survive on the Earth, then we could be ready to increase our numbers on that planet, and begin the task of developing closer relationships, that could eventually lead to expansion of our population both here and on Mars. I particularly support the idea of helping the Earth advance in their efforts to bring a peace to their planet, and to ensure that when we do eventually see them arrive on Mars, we do not import any factions that will upset our plans for peace."

Now Senator Takis Fotopoulis, the assembly Speaker rose and ambled across to the dais.

"Fellow Senators, following these wise words from our revered Senator Poppaloukis, we must now vote on the above suggestions and advice in the form of a legislator. Your tablets will be live in the next few minutes, and our secretariat will send you the questions that we shall vote on today. Please place your coloured voting responses on your tablet by night time. I shall send the results through to you all tomorrow."

"The meeting is now closed, my thanks to you all. I shall just pass you over to Spiros for a final word."

Spiros Artemis was the head of the planetary intelligence section. He now rose and looked over the assembly.

"Thank you, Senators, we shall, as always, feed any arising important information to the Cabinet, and Senator Spiros will I am sure arrange for transfer of any news affecting this programme. In the meantime, may I remind you all that the information relating to the Mars and Earth programmes that have been clearly set out today, and any discussion regarding our representatives on the planet Earth are strictly confidential. We do not want our citizens to be alarmed by mis-reading our intentions at this stage. Thank you for your co-operation."

****

University of Arizona, January 2070

The music evening had indeed gone well for Irina and Lara. They had, as expected, caused quite a stir with not only the men, but many of the girls. Someone had been heard to say that they were looking like girls from the old romance films. The dresses had certainly helped attract a lot of attention to them. The music was strange to them, but they liked the Americans choice of 20s and 30s music which had certainly got the groups dancing. In particular, the songs of some girls called Lady Gaga and Roxanne. They must be old ladies by now!

They were now back in the halls of residence, feeling elated that they were now part of the party groups, and was sure many invites would soon follow.

"Lara, there is a message in the mail box from the Chancellor to us all. Evidently our plan for the Greek girls has had some good results. He has advised the students that they are in the hospital and in a state of coma, and that they suspect food poisoning and are making an investigation. He has asked anyone who shows any symptoms to report to his office as soon as possible."

They were quietly exultant that apparently the first plan had worked. Adding the peanut meal to the breakfast mix had been quite easy.

"Well, Irina, let us get our applications in for the jobs at the ISPEG Biospheres as soon as possible, we have to move quickly before there is any further investigation as to what has happened to those girls."

"I have an address, and a Dr Dawn Somester is evidently the senior contact, so let's get on it."

****

Krulandistan, October 2070

"I have just had some strange but good news from Arizona." Kim Jong was looking all excited as he entered the chairman's office.

"Do sit down comrade, and calmly tell me what is so strange. It is unlike you to be so excited; it must be good news."

"I have just received news that our agents in Arizona, Irina and Lara, have managed to get rid of the Greek girls that they felt were going to get in their way with the objectives we have set. They now have a contact to write to regarding their application to the ISPEG space operations in Northern Arizona, and expect that with their credentials intact, and the degrees they both attained from the university, they should be successful."

"On another subject, although the authorities do believe that they know who made the attack on the Canadian company making the new ISS units, they have no proof, and therefore, although we should be cautious, I think we have managed this operation very well."

"That is great news, Kim Jong, do keep me updated if you hear that the girls have been successful in joining the ISPEG. Another thing, we are preparing some new rocket space missiles that we shall test in a year or so now, and the need for finding out more regarding the ISPEG laser and space weapons programme has become more of a priority. We are hoping to use one of these missiles to destroy, or at least damage, the moon orbit unit that they are using as an assembly platform for the new ISS Venus."

"OK Chairman, will pass that news onto our two agents in Arizona."

****

Phoenix, Arizona—January 2070

Chris and Robert were now both sitting with their mothers in Ruth's Phoenix home.

Chris was explaining the recent events at the university, and their next plans.

"We were devastated when we first heard the news from the university regarding Helena and Athena, and of course rushed down to the hospital immediately. When we arrived, the girls were indeed in the ICU, and the doctors advised that they seemed to be in a coma."

"We asked to sit with them, and when the nurses had left the room, they both suddenly opened their large eyes, and made signs to stop us making any noise, we were so surprised."

His mother looked baffled, "What are you both saying, they were not in a coma?"

"Yes Mother, we both saw that they were not suffering, and what we are going to share with you now is extremely confidential. Rob, would you add your version of these events and how it has led to our next plans."

"As Chris says, we were both so surprised by this sudden change, but of course exceedingly happy to see the rapid improvement in their health. The girls told us that they had suspected that there was a problem with the food that morning. Their senses had picked up the aroma of some peanut meal, they evidently call it Fistiki. However, although they did not normally eat this for other reasons, they knew they were not allergic to any form of nut, as nuts and seeds were a major part of their diet in Attica. They suspected that this meal had been added to their normal dish for other reasons. However, they decided to eat the mix and pretend to be affected, hoping that they would be able to trace anyone who may have been related to this incident."

"We did know that they had been suspicious of two Russian girls that had been making a bit of a scene in the last year at the university. They said that before they were rushed out to the hospital, they had seen the girls in the breakfast room, and as they passed by on the stretchers, they both thought they saw them smiling."

Chris then picked up the story…

"So, they explained the situation in confidence to the hospital doctors, and asked them if they would continue the façade by advising any callers that they were still in a coma. We have emphasised to them that this is probably a case of attempted murder, and we need full co-operation in catching the culprits."

"After we recovered from the shock and had established the truth of the incident, we planned for them to be moved quietly into an apartment in Phoenix. We are not advising anyone of that fact, and have explained that to the doctors who have agreed to parry any questions for now."

"Our plan now is to ask you both if you can help to get them into the Biosphere programme. We know it is a difficult request for you, as you are, first and foremost our mothers, and you may think we are only asking because we have a crush on them, but believe us when we say we have not seen or heard of anyone, including our fathers, with such advanced scientific brains. It is uncanny sometimes how much they know."

Ruth and Dawn looked amazed. It was Ruth who recovered first.

"This is truly some story boys, but knowing you both we are sure you have the best interests of us all in mind." She paused a moment, and then continued, "Let us see; we shall of course have to see the application papers first. Dawn, are you ready to go ahead with seeing these girls as soon as possible if we can get the papers signed by next week?"

Dawn Somester was listening intently.

"Ruth, what a story. I am a little concerned about the fact that if the Russian girls are indeed trying to injure Helena and Athena then we must surely try to find out why. It is very strange. Shall we also look at the original applications from Irina Ivanov and Lara Gorinski, I think that is the names? If they are approved then we obviously need to keep an eye on them, and maybe we should not allow them to meet Helena and Athena for some time."

"So, Chris and Robert, you can see we are ready to take things to the next step. Get those applications in to me and I will discuss them with Ruth, and then we can meet again when we have completed the interviews."

"Thanks Dawn, that is a good summing up of the situation. As you are the leader on this one, I am standing by if you need any help, or want to share any thoughts. Now, Chris and Rob, we know you also have some plans to join up with the NASAF team, and you need to pursue this and not be too distracted by these events. If you get accepted you will of course be parted from Helena and Athena for some time, but California and Arizona are not too far apart! If you do go, is there anyone in the Biosphere programme now that we all can fully trust? I am thinking we shall need someone if we are to be watchful of all the girl's activities, and hopefully spot any potential problems before they happen? Josh and Phillip are of course in charge there now, but they will be so busy with the Laser and Astronaut programmes these next two years or so, and in any case, we really need someone who is closer to everyday events."

Chris was listening intently and now could see how to proceed.

"Mother, Aunty Dawn, I know I speak for both of us, thanks for your understanding. Could we ask one more favour. Obviously, you also will both continue to be highly involved in the Biosphere programmes, so if they are all approved, you will see and hear about Helena and Athena from time to time. It would be good to hear directly how they are progressing."

He saw the mothers both smile and he was confident that the girls would be in good hands. He now continued, "On another subject, I heard from Dad that Tom Lancs is now a Captain, and he is evidently very heavily involved in the latest laser work. We all remember, and are thankful for his quick actions in saving you and Dad in that terrible day in 2062. If he would agree, he would be someone we could all trust to keep an eye on suspects. He has a great relationship with both our fathers and is, of course, close to the confidential stuff at the Biosphere."

It was Dawn who responded first, "We both know Tom very well, and agree with you that he would be a great asset to us all if he can keep an eye on the girls. We meet often, so we would be able to transfer any news to you, and more importantly deal with anything that comes up in a professional way. Let us put him in the picture, and we shall let you know his decision."

They all agreed that was the next move, and after thanking their mothers once more, Chris and Robert drove back to the campus. They felt so much better and more confident concerning the future of the girls after this conversation.

****

Krulandistan, October 2070

Kim Jong had just received a message, and he almost shouted across the room at his boss.

"Dear Comrade Chairman, we have some more good news. The Russian girls have been accepted for the ISPEG Biosphere programme, and they believe the Greek girls maybe dead as they have not heard more about them in the last few months. Their plan with the contaminated peanut meal seems to have had the best results. There is no doubt that removing them must have helped our two to get the few openings left in the ISPEG programme for graduates, as their grades, although good, were evidently nowhere near those that the two Greek girls achieved."

"I can understand your excitement comrade, are we sure the source of this news is reliable? If so, we must give our agents some tasks as soon as they settle in the Biosphere. It would be great if they can get involved in the ISS programme, and give us regular updates, as well as getting any copies of plans that may be useful to us. Ask them to ensure they contact the Canadian cell so that they have the latest news on launch times. In the next year or so we want to make an impact on that programme, and really slow the whole activity, maybe even destroy the parts when they are being sent out to space."

"I shall advise them to speak to our agents in Canada, Ho Chi, and between them they should get some information regarding the new assembly site for the ISS. Then I shall personally talk to Irina regarding her next tasks."

"OK, I shall look forward to being kept informed, let us agree to push our plans further in the next year or two."

They both turned to look out again over the airfield and the increased activity. It would not be long now.

****

Following the assembly's unanimous approval of the plan at the last meeting, an extraordinary meeting had been called by Chairman Isis. There was silence as he walked up to the dais.

"My esteemed council, we have some more news now regarding our representatives, and we wish to move on to our next phase of the plan. General Hermes and Senator Artemis have been busy."

The General was first to rise.

"Thank you, Chairman Isis. We can now give you confirmation that our representatives on the planet Earth have been accepted into the Earth's space research programmes known as ISPEG, which is their International Space and Energy Group. This is great news as they will be working with the Earth's top scientists, and meeting more people, who may make an influence on decisions that need to be taken in the next few years if we are to make progress to our final goal. They have also met two Earth men who have shown much interest in being close friends. These two men are due to join the Earth's prominent Air Force and astronaut training centre in a County known as California very shortly. Our representatives will maintain regular contact with them as they may be key to final plans for both our planets. I will now step down so Senator Artemis may add some more news from his sector."

Spiros rose and moved to the dais.

"Salutations to you all. During the last year there was we believe, an attempt on our representatives lives by two girls who appear to be from a terrorist group known as ECAW, which evidently is a terrorist group trying to impose its communist doctrine on other countries on the Earth. You may not be conversant with the word communism as we have not experienced any other forms of our own doctrine in our history. To explain for your understanding of how different the Earth's systems are compared with our own, here is a quick review. I am raising this subject because I see it as being significant as we move towards our goals."

"If we are to attain a closer bond with their people, then it may be necessary to remove these extremists. On investigation with my colleagues at AIHQ, we discover that several wars, and much terrorism over several hundred years have come and gone, but at great cost to the overall wealth and health of many of the Earth's countries. This led to the religious group leaders joining with the governments of their various countries to agree to help remove these extremist religious groups. Over twenty Earth years ago, there was a significant change in understanding between the ethnic groups due to the gradual integration of these different cultures in each Earth country."

"However, communism is not really a religion. It is a way of government that controls all the people in all their activities, from labour, property ownership, land distribution, communication and even banking. In the Earth years of their period known as the 20th century, there were bloody revolutions by the people against those who had power and money. These attacks were led by prominent communist figures who became revered by the working classes, who saw a chance to share in the wealth of the country. Millions of people were evidently killed, imprisoned, or tortured during their next 100 years."

"Today, the former communist countries are mainly trading as most other countries on the planet, and many of their citizens are very wealthy, but also many are still very poor. However, the extreme element wishes to return pure communism to the whole planet. Whereas this appears to be a reasonable objective, that of equal rights for all, and sharing of wealth, it has proved already that the system does not actually work, and many countries became very poor following this kind of doctrine. It is now obvious that the extremists have other plans; to become dictators, and divert wealth to themselves and their supporters."

"To summarise, senators, if we are to make a pact with the Earth's countries and governments, we surely need to eliminate any potential threat from these extremists."

"Together with General Hermes' team, we are discussing a plan of campaign that, together with our two brave scientists and astronauts, will enable us to solve this difficult situation."

General Hermes walked back to the dais, and then his voice as usual thundered through the assembly.

"The chairman and Cabinet have given Senator Spiros Artemis and my team permission to take this project to the next step. As we have said earlier, it is not a short programme, we have to receive your trust in us to plan a good course of action that will eventually meet the assembly's targets, and at that stage we can share the plan with our people."

The Elder Senator, Gregori Poppoloukis now rose to speak.

"Dear assembly members, we should all be thankful that we have such a brave and dynamic space team, and an intelligence sector that in our opinion is remarkable. I would urge all of us here today to continue to show our support by voting green when the proposal is presented at the end of this session."

Now the chairman moved over to the dais, and turned to the assembly.

"We have heard today a remarkable account and short history of a planet that we wish to, not conquer, but find a way of working and living with on another planet. However, I am sure you will all agree, it is imperative that the Earth people must play their part, and if we do see any treachery, we shall of course retaliate with all the superior power that we know we possess."

"In the meantime, the Mars programme is progressing well, and with our closer proximity to the planet, we shall make more regular flights, and continue to increase supplies to our existing small team."

"We continue to learn more every day, and in our opinion, we shall be prepared for a much larger population of the planet within the next 10 years."

He stopped a few seconds for the assembly to quieten.

"I shall watch for the results of your votes tonight, and l shall make a call to assembly if there are dissentions, so that we may discuss these and arrive at a quick solution. It is imperative we now move forward."

****

California, USAFA Headquarters, 2073

Chris and Robert had been taken into the test pilot training programme, and were settled in their new home in the Edwards Air Base in California They had already been accepted for first real flights after showing their ability in the simulator tests. As fully trained airman they were now members of the 461st Test Squadron, which was known best for testing Joint Strike Fighters, but was also the headquarters of the astronaut training centre.

The Commander of the base, Edward Glen, had been a good colleague of Robert's father, and was very pleased to see the next generation making such great strides. Although he saw Robert as the more talented flyer, he was more than impressed with Christopher's organisation ability, and saw him as probably a future Commander. He had certainly heard much about Professor Devonshire, and there was no doubt that his lad was also going far.

Robert was now sitting in the mess sipping the ginger drink concoction that Chris had introduced on his first day at the base.

"What is today's programme, Chris? We have a meeting with the Commander's team tomorrow, and I have heard that there is something important going on with the new Gateway orbiter."

Chris put his glass of the ginger beer brew down and turned to his friend and colleague.

"Rob, first, just heard from Helena, and they have both settled well in the new biosphere astronaut training section, and she and Athena wanted to send us both good luck with our new roles. As agreed, they have not made any contact with the Russian girls, who are now working in another sector. However, they say that they have reported to Captain Lancs that they suspect there is something going to happen to try and delay or hurt one of the ISPEG programmes. They could not tell me more than that, and maybe we should ask the Commander if he knows any more about this. We know from previous experience in the university that the girls seem to have some sixth sense about this kind of thing."

"Anyway, we can discuss later, but regarding today, I see our log has us down to test fly the F95S, the latest stealth bomber. We shall be taking over for part of the trip, but under the eye of a senior Captain, Gary Westmorland. It will be a hairy flight I think, hope we picked up all the key points in the simulator. We are evidently taking the flight to edge of the thermosphere and testing the new laser weapon on a target which we shall only know when we are in flight, as it is coded for the trip."

"The laser is the latest model and far advanced from the first prototype that my father developed in 60s. The discovery of gallium nitride with its ability to form high voltage transmission has revolutionised our ability to strike over longer distances."

"OK Chris, I think I understand, the Biosphere team should be proud of this advance. Regarding the other news that we received from the girls, it is a little bit of a mystery how they detect these things, but we shall see what is said tomorrow."

"Anyway, I am ready to go up to the base, see you up there. Incidentally, I like the new uniforms."

"Cheers Rob, be with you in 30 minutes or so, but as you say we need to maintain vigilance on what is happening down there."

Krulandistan, March 2074

"Comrade Chairman, we are now ready to make our planned attack on the ISS assembly unit that is currently in the moon orbit, which incidentally is orbiting very much closer to the moon than ever achieved before."

"I have selected the team who will take over the French spacecraft that is due to be sent into orbit on Friday. The plan is to capture the French astronauts at the last moment and take them off the site and imprison them for a period until the heat comes of any investigation. We may have to dispose of them later if we have any problems."

"Then, our astronaut team, who incidentally I have personally vetted, and who are from our very reliable source, the Chinese Academy of Sciences in Nanjing, will appear in the stolen French uniforms on Friday morning, and be fully briefed for this mission. We already have intelligence from our agents in Canada to advise the co-ordinates for the Gateway orbiter's position at that time. We may attempt to strike just before the docking procedure to the Gateway orbiter that they evidently plan to use as an assembly unit."

"That is good news, Kim Jong, it is time to make the West suffer some setbacks. I shall be here over the weekend before leaving for the Black Sea resort. I shall then take a few weeks on my yacht to be away from any backlash. You will be invited there for a few days break after this attack. I assume you have personally vetted the missile rocket team. Our enemies must see this as a French missile experiment that went wrong. They will investigate with the French I am sure, but if we get our men back quickly, we can hide all evidence and keep them guessing."

"I have every confidence in the team Ho Chi. Thank you for your invitation to join your yacht after the mission, it would be very good for me to get away from here for a few days. I shall now concentrate on the weekend programme."

****

Biosphere HQ, Arizona, March 2074

Helena and Athena had indeed settled in well at the Biosphere HQ, and Captain Tom Lancs and a Lt. Gary Kent had been very keen to hear the girls discussing their ideas with them. They were also amazed at the expertise of these younger scientists.

The girls had maintained a regular dialogue with their Attica contact. They found it was taking about 12 minutes for messages to transfer to and from the planet. The head recorders were working at about 75% of their usual strength, but that was not a worry. The skills that they had attained over the years before leaving for this venture had put them in a strong mental position, and they were coping well with all the daily life and routines.

"Athena, are you also receiving some telepathy murmurs? I cannot get a real reading of the full message, but my brain unit is picking something up. I am concerned that it may relate to one of the ISPEG adversaries. I wonder if the vibes are coming from those two young Russian women again? I am most concerned as I think most of the Biosphere personnel know now that some major parts of the ISS Venus structure have been manufactured and transferred from Canada to the Florida launch site. Therefore, the ISPEG Stellarship7 should be ready to take the parts to the Moon Orbiter for assembly very shortly."

"Apart from crew, two astronaut engineers, together with two robot engineers, will be aboard. I understand that the space craft will then return to the California base. The whole operation will be completed in two days. If the Russian girls are not to be trusted, then this news will almost certainly be transferred to enemy groups."

"Yes, I agree, Helena, but should we share these concerns with Tom and Gary yet? We don't have real proof, also we may be giving ourselves away as to our mission if they start wondering why we know so much. Let us continue to watch and wait, like you, I would like to explain our position first to Chris and Robert. It is only fair as they obviously care very much about us."

"Agreed, Athena, we shall wait. Are you on the robot work today? I am sure we both can take them to the next steps for the creation of a copy of our humanised robots."

"You are right, we should concentrate on moving them all on with this project if we are to get their people to Mars in the foreseeable future. I have met Ziggy and the advanced robot team and am working with her on the next stages of development. Professor and Dr Devonshire were both in favour of you also working on this project. They have had a company called Proactive AI Future Ltd from a country called England working on the limbs and other factors to upgrade the robots, so you could help with that, and at the same time your experience on powering the robots by advanced electric activators, and of course your work on Autonomous robot revolution, will all take them to the next generation."

"I shall enjoy that Helena, where are you working?"

"I am working mainly at the moment with Captain Lancs on the astronaut programme and hope to gradually introduce to him our progress on the 'fly suits' that we both used so successfully on our voyage here. After that meeting, I shall meet up with you in the AI research quarters. We should then review what news we wish to send back to General Hermes."

****

Attica—Earth time—March 2074

General Hermes had just received an intelligence report from Senator Artemis that was disturbing. Following information that they had received from their representatives only today regarding the potential terrorist cells that may be active on the planet, their satellite cameras had captured pictures of unusual activity on the Earth's Russian border. A new spacecraft was spotted that appeared ready to be launched from the adjoining country, namely Krulandistan, and although at first it appeared a normal operation, the intelligence team were interested as it was a new craft, and after making closer surveillance, they considered that something was strange relating to not only the voyage co-ordinates, but also the crew. Although they were dressed in a uniform that represented the French craft, the sophisticated listening devices had heard the astronauts speaking a dialect that they translated as Chinese Mandarin.

He called Spiros on his telepathy unit.

"Spiros, please come over to the Cabinet room. This report indicates that there may be a problem approaching."

Spiros only had to take the very short hyperlink journey from his home in the suburbs of Atlantis, the Attica capital, and was in the office within 10 minutes. They both now transferred to the assembly chamber to watch the pictures unfolding on the huge space screens.

"Spiros, I think we should advise Helena and Athena that as they suspected, there is a potential problem, but unfortunately, we are four weeks journey away, even with our new Rotoship craft, so we must just wait and continue our surveillance, and ask them to report any further activity at their end."

****

Biosphere 2—March 2074

Helena and Athena were trying to relax after their working day. However, they had just received the news from Attica that appeared to confirm their own concerns.

"Athena, this does look very suspicious now. Do you think it definitely relates to the ISS launch? Do you think they would actually attack the craft in orbit? I think we should share our concerns with Chris and Robert and hope they don't question us too far as to our source at the moment. Maybe they can make some suggestions for a closer surveillance of the latest spacecraft and missile activity to see if they also have any concerns."

"Yes, I think we must tell them, and very soon. It may be necessary to actually outline our whole story, and hope that they still trust us. I have a meeting with Captain Lancs shortly regarding the astronaut suits, but first let us try to contact the California USAFA base."

****

USAFA base, California, March 2074

Chris, Robert and some of the crew had just been briefed by Commander Glen and were all dressed in the 5G suits that had been designed for this new F95S test flight to the edge of space. They expected a call within the next thirty minutes to alert them for take-off time.

They were all ready to leave when suddenly a USAF senior administrator, Corporal Bert Edwards rushed into the briefing room, saluted, and then passed over a document to Chris.

"Commander, sorry for the intrusion at this late hour, but this message is from the ISPEG Biosphere in Arizona, and they were asked to ensure Lt. Devonshire or Lt. Somester received it urgently."

Chris quickly read the note and passed it to the Commander.

"Commander, looking at this information, we should discuss this urgently as it may affect some of our ISPEG colleagues."

"OK, I am not sure what this all about Lieutenant but let us ask Captain Westmorland to join us in the anti-room right now. Corporal, would you be so kind as to call Captain Westmorland and advise him something important has cropped up, and we need to talk before departing this trip."

****

Chris had disclosed the message from Helena to Robert, and they were both stunned. How did they get this information, and how true is it? Certainly, they had shown an uncanny ability to detect things that were a little strange.

"Rob, we have to take a chance that the Commander and Captain Westmorland will believe this, and at least look into the possibility of there being a problem. We do know now that the ECAW group did make that attack on the ISS Venus assembly plant in Canada fairly recently, whereby we had to move the plant, but we have had nothing to report since."

"I agree, let us hope he does not push us too hard on the source of this information, but just will go on alert. We do have to take the F95S up today that is for sure. The crew are due to be off duty this weekend. Anyway, first things first, let us get into the anti-room, they are waiting."

The Commander and Captain Westmorland were listening carefully, and they seemed at first to be suspicious of the news. However, the Captain was first to respond, "Thanks to you both for sharing this news with us. I am not sure if your source is reliable yet, but for sure we must always be on alert. So, please return to the briefing room, we are to reset the take-off time for this test flight, and in the meantime, I shall talk to the Commander to see if we want to make any other plans, or at least put the ISPEG team in Florida on full alert."

"Thank you, Captain, we shall await your new instructions."

****

Captain Westmorland had returned to the briefing room.

"Gentlemen, take-off time is now 11.30 hours. We have a change in our flight plan that does leave room for some uncertainty and risk. However, the F95S has been designed to handle extreme heights and speeds, and we do have robotic ability for certain tasks on board. If any of you should feel really uncomfortable with this new demand, then we shall of course understand your withdrawal."

As Gary had rather expected there were no hands going up. It was all systems go!

****

ISPEG HQ, Florida, March 2074

Following the news from California, Major Lancs was now at the Florida ISPEG headquarters, and talking to their intelligence control team. He was advised that they were monitoring the spacecraft/missile launches in Krulandistan, and they would advise the NASAF team if they detected anything strange in the flight trajectories. They had also been in touch with French ESA authorities to advise them of the situation, but emphasised that this news was just precautionary, and had not received any specific threats from terrorists, but were on orange alert due to recent incidents which they could not disclose at this time.

The French had been able to confirm that they were due a test flight soon, but the Krulandistan control centre had not advised them of an exact date at this time.

The Major looked up at the monitors and noted that the Stellarship was on the launch pad and ready to go. He could not see any reason to delay. He picked up the transmitter.

"Lt. Dorsett, we have green to go here, finalise the count-down."

****

Gateway Moon Orbiter—March 2074

Commander Norman Hunter was into his second month on the Orbiter. He had been the first to take command of the unit and would stay another four months before returning to Earth duties.

He was briefing his team of four visiting astronauts regarding the upcoming events, and alerting the onboard working robots to the programme that was due to unfold in the next few days.

Captain Ann Broxborne, Dr Rosalind Ware, Lt. Jez Cambridge and Lt. Barry Keynes were all listening carefully as they were aware of the importance of this latest task. It was so exciting to know that they were to be involved in the new space station and were going to actually assist in the assembly here at the Gateway. They had waited so long for this moment.

"We are expecting the Stellarship to arrive from HQ tomorrow at 15.00 GMT. Please ensure all the time pieces are checked and you are on Median time for this exercise. After docking, you will take a team of two robots to assist in the unloading of the ISS Venus parts. Then, after taking a rest break, you will, together with the onboard engineers from ISPEG, start the outside work. Over the next few weeks, more parts are due to arrive, so we need to keep well on our schedule for this first important assembly work. Any questions?"

Captain Broxborne spoke up, "OK Commander, I believe we are all ready. Can you confirm that the robot team have also been advised of the mechanical procedures? They are going to have to manage the movement of pretty heavy parts."

"The robots were trained at the Biosphere 2 by Dr Ruth Devonshire and Dr Dawn Somester, and therefore they will surely have been trained and programmed for this occasion. You will find that you can converse with them due to the recent voice improvements, you can have total confidence in their ability. So, get some rest, and be ready for this important day tomorrow."

Dr Rosalind Ware stopped sipping her tonic drink, "Commander, I understand Colonel Somester has taken charge of the Stellarship and is to be part of the supervising team. Please advise who is our main contact during this operation? I worked with Phillip for some years at ISPEG and he has been very involved in this major development."

"Thanks Rosalind, for bringing that up. I have agreed with the Colonel that I am your main contact. He will be an observer and advise me if he sees anything that needs more of my attention. So, now all have a good rest, see you in the morning."

****

Krulandistan Space Launching Centre, March 2074

The plan to kidnap the French astronauts had gone well, and they were safely under guard at the ECAW centre. The two Chinese astronauts had been fitted out and given last instructions and were already in the spacecraft.

"Chairman, do come and look through the window, we have set the filter as usual so you can watch the take-off. The original co-ordinates show that this journey is taking the two French astronauts to the ISS-1 as part of the European Space Agency's programme of rotating the astronauts regularly and bringing in new qualified teams. Our agents have been primed on the changes they need to make in flight so as to reach the Moon Orbiter."

"Good, well done, Kim Jong. This will be very interesting. Set the space monitors so we can track its orbit out and the return journey. I assume we are returning the spacecraft to another base as there will surely be some repercussions if we are successful, we just don't want them to trace anything to us."

"Yes, Comrade Chairman, our Chinese friends have set aside their private site in the Paracel Islands. The spacecraft will land via the Sea of China, and then be towed by our people's tug to be concealed on the island site. They will probably then convert it to one of their craft for future use in a year or so."

The sound of the take-off was normal, but this one somehow had a more satisfying sound!

In flight, over Pacific Ocean, March 2074

Captain Gary Westmorland was speaking over the headphones as they cruised at 70,000 feet above the sea.

"The Stellarship has arrived at the Gateway orbiter, and news is good so far. Work is due to start very shortly on the assembly. It will involve working outside in their newly prepared suits, but all confident that together with Zikky's help, the crane setup on the Orbiter will soon be ready for the next stage. We are getting really close to reality on this important project."

He paused before continuing, "We are now going to test the F95S at a new record height of 100,000 feet, which as you know, is the edge of space. We shall be testing the new engines for their power in this very light atmosphere. I am also able to advise you now, that we have the latest laser equipment on board that is to undertake its first test as we return from the high atmosphere. A target has been set for us. I want you all to look at the monitors and you will see a full task manual for the next few hours work. Please be ready in a few minutes' time because as you can see from your manual, the first step is that we are going to ascend to the target height at a speed of 2.4 Mach. Please all confirm you are in your G-force suits and ready to go to the next stage?"

He received quick confirmation from them all, and now reset the computer. He knew this trial was far more dangerous than he was willing to share at the moment. They were all trained and as ready as they could be.

****

Gateway Moon Orbiter, March 2075

Colonel Phillip Somester had decided he needed to be in charge of the Stellarship in view of the recent rumours, but also this was an historic occasion, and he wanted to be in at the beginning of this mammoth feat of engineering. He had borrowed Josh's assistant, Robot Zikky, and was now in constant communication with the Orbiter and the Florida and Biosphere teams.

The Stellarship had performed well, and was now approaching the docking station on the Orbiter.

"Commander Hunter, we are ready to dock. I assume you have briefed everyone on my role, and look forward to working with you on this massive project."

The speakers in his cabin came over loud and clear.

"Thank you, Colonel, the programme is already registered and we are ready for you. I have briefed them all on our roles, and we shall be ready to start tomorrow after all involved have had a night's rest."

The next day had started with a breakfast reunion between the Orbiter and Stellarship crews. They were all now prepared for their roles, and the Orbiters crane was working under the direction of one of the robot team. This was going to be like a jig-saw puzzle being assembled, except the pieces weighed several tonnes, but the pieces were clearly marked as to their destination. First was the framework of the whole station, which in itself would need engineering expertise to prepare and secure it in the space allocated below the Orbiter.

There was already a little tension in the crew as to how this extra weight would affect the Orbiter before being released into a new orbit, but they had been assured by the scientists at the Biosphere that the power circuits on Orbiter could correct any shift in movement that may take place as the extra weight was added.

The robots were now being asked to undertake the initial outside work, ensuring connections and power lines were secure before moving to the next stages.

Captain Broxborne turned to Zikky, who was now the leading robot for this project. "Zikky, we need you to take some outside checks later, so will you ensure you have the master plan on your arm phone monitor, and everyone has the necessary tools. We shall of course make sure all security arrangements are in place for you and your team, and you will have contact with us at all times."

"Thank you, Captain, however, Dr Ruth had already given me advance warning of the project, and she also took the liberty of fitting me with a fast reaction panic button if we need help."

"OK Zikky, good to hear, please now brief your engineers, and be ready to go out to start the assembly programme."

****

F95S Flight—Karmer Line, January 2075

Captain Westmorland and the crew had been pleased with the new engines, and had achieved the targets for speed and height without any major problem.

They were now getting ready for the laser test and then they were all thinking of a quick return to their Californian base.

"Captain, Captain Westmorland, come in please, this is Commander Glen, we have an emergency!"

Gary and his crew were quickly taken out of their immediate thoughts for the day.

"I hear you, Commander. We were just getting ready to run the laser test and then return to base. What is the problem?"

"Gary, listen to this, and advise if you feel you can help. Our Orbiter base has received an attack by a missile from a spacecraft which apparently is the French craft that was due to arrive at the ISS-1, but not today. Missiles were fired from this craft that hit the assembly area outside of the Orbiter. There is some damage, and we have lost one of our robots, but mainly the new ISS parts are not affected. WE shall know more when Colonel Somester has investigated. In the meantime, we need to track this craft, obviously something is not right."

"We have managed to detect the spacecraft on our monitoring system and it appears to have returned into original orbit. We are watching to identify when it will leave the orbit and return to Earth. My question is whether you are able to track it when it returns into atmosphere if we are able to give you the estimated position?"

"Well Commander, we can certainly move this plane fast, but do you know where to. The new nuclear power source has given us abilities that we did not have ten years ago, and the new engines are working really well. I shall cancel the laser test for now and alert the team. We shall watch for your messages."

"Thanks Gary, we shall be back to you shortly. Will you also advise Lt Devonshire and Lt Somester that the Major is not hurt, and they now have things under control at the Orbiter. However, it may have set our Venus ISS programme back."

****

Josh and Ruth had just called Dawn to advise of the attack, and to confirm Phillip was unhurt. There was damage which they were evaluating, but confirmed that they had lost one of Zikky's team.

"Josh, this is so uncanny, Helena and Athena had told our boys that they suspected something was not right, and to expect an attack, but had no real

77

evidence. They just wanted us to be careful. We really need Chris and Robert to have a talk with them to understand where all this is coming from. The two Russian girls are still doing well in the Biosphere, but they are obviously still not trusted by the Greek girls. It is all very strange."

"You are right Ruth, our boys are on a very confidential test flight at the moment, but we are in touch with them, and as soon as possible we shall have a chat with them to see if we can get to the bottom of all this. I am just going to call Phillip to see what plans he has to return, and then when we have seen the full report, we can take this further."

"Josh, I must also see if Zikky is returning to base soon, she will be very upset at loss of one of her own. Her feelings are so close to human now, we must respect that."

"I understand Ruth, will check her programme with Phillip. I certainly do think of her as a colleague."

★★★★★★★★★★★★

On Board F95S, February 2075

"Gary, we now have a trace on the spacecraft, it is in orbit but as we think it was sent from the space rocket site in Krulandistan, it may be headed back. However, in view of this serious incident we have to assume that it is not manned by the French, and that it may divert. Can you get that plane as fast as possible over to the Russian border area, maybe in the vicinity of the Black Sea, and we shall keep you informed of any new development."

"OK Commander, we are coding in the new destination, and if we can keep up the present speed and height, we expect to be in the area within two hours. We shall, however, have to be aware of fuel requirements if we are to up here for more than six hours."

★★★★★★★★★★★★★★

Krulandistan, March 2075

Song Jing To, and Li Sue Kwang were happy that they had completed their main task, but a little disappointed that the missiles had not fired as well as expected. They had to be content that they had hit part of the structure and they hoped they had also hit one or more of the engineers.

"FS2.046 calling base, we require co-ordinates for our return destination. We are now in orbit again, but need to return quickly if we are to avoid detection."

"Well done, comrades, you can give us full report after landing, we agree that we need to get you down here as fast as possible. Take the following codes and repeat. 16 degrees N. 112 degrees E. You are going to land your shuttle craft in the sea just off the Vietnamese coast where we shall arrange to collect you and take you to final safe destination from that point."

"Acknowledged. We shall be making descent after our next orbit."

****

Edwards Air Base, California, March 2075

"Commander Glen calling Captain Westmoreland. Gary, we have new destination details for the suspect shuttle craft."

"OK Commander, we are now close to the Russian/Chinese border. We are in stealth mode so hopefully we are not being spotted on the satellite yet? Go ahead with new co-ordinates. Do we know who is in control of the craft, and are we to make contact?"

"Negative, Gary. Your task is to follow the spacecraft when it returns to the atmosphere without detection, and then advise the final destination. We shall make another decision after we have your report."

"May I also recommend that we make contact with our friends in Korea regarding having you stop over to check the plane, and make your report, they have the runway facility, and have ESA security clearance. I can make arrangements if you agree."

"Thanks, I think we are all going to need some break, we are very happy with the plane's performance but it has been a little hairy for my young crew. I shall come back to you when we have tracked the spacecraft."

****

Krulandistan, March 2075

"Comrade Chairman, I can advise you that the French shuttle spacecraft has landed. We have not been able to detect anything that may concern us. I believe the West are still investigating what has happened."

"Thank you, comrade, Get the spacecraft into hiding as soon as possible. After we get the Chinese astronauts report, ensure they get back to the cell destination without suspicion. We then shall lie low for a while. I shall arrange to go to my yacht, and as promised I shall send for you in a few days."

"That is kind, Chairman. I shall bring you full details of the operation, and advise if we have any news on possible retribution. It was a good idea of yours to return them to a Chinese island, the security will be sound."

****

On Board F95S Flight—March 2075

"Commander, we have the spacecraft on our monitors, and we are at 80,000 ft over the South China Sea. No sign that we have been detected, but we are in dangerous area, despite our new accord with them, the Chinese do not like our planes being in this airspace."

He was suddenly aware that Lt Devonshire was trying to catch his eye.

"Captain, I have just received another communication from our base contacts, who advise that the French spacecraft has evidently reached its destination, which is in the Paracel Islands, owned by China, and just off the Vietnamese coast. They are sending the data to you now. Can you advise the Commander that we have this news?"

"Chris, how has that news been extracted? Commander, are you aware of this latest information? It does seem strange that this news did not come from our usual intelligence source?"

"Commander here Gary, heard all that. We shall investigate, but in the meantime, forget the laser test for now. You do not have enough fuel to take this further at this stage, so make a new course to our Korean base. I shall make contact now with Colonel Sang-Hoon, and will be sending over the codes for entry to the base runway shortly. Let us then have a good night, and we shall all discuss again in the morning after we have investigated more in relation to these incidents."

Biosphere 2—April 2075

Professor Devonshire had now received all the detail of the recent Orbiter incident, and was ready to talk to his close colleague, Colonel Somester, who had just arrived back at the Biosphere base.

"Phillip, welcome back, my friend, it is good that at least you and your colleagues are all safe. Very sorry to hear about robot engineer Marie-Ann, Zikky will be very affected. What is the final position regarding the damage?"

"Thanks Josh, it was very scary for a while, but apparently the two missiles that were fired did not make full impact, and although we have certainly sustained some damage, we can recover, and anticipate we shall be able to add more parts in two weeks or so. We managed to get the other engineers back into the Orbiter. They were slightly injured, but mostly shocked. They have clearly said that they wish to stay and continue as soon as possible."

"Good, thank them for us. However, we must investigate with Florida HQ what has happened here. I have just had news from our California USAFA base, and it is very worrying. Captain Westmorland was on a test flight in the new F95S, and they were going to test not only the new engines, but as you know we also had installed the new GR laser, and they had a target that we had set up based on recent trials. Before they could get to this test, they received an urgent message from the base, that apparently had been given them by our two Greek scientists that befriended Chris and Robert. Everyone was in doubt as to what to do, but Commander Glen made a decision to take the apparent threat seriously, and low and behold, we now know the result."

"Josh, I did not know the boys were on that flight, I hope they are OK, what happened after they had news regarding the attack on us?"

"Captain Westmorland was instructed to follow the spacecraft after we picked it up on the orbiter satellite detection unit. To cut a long story short, before they could follow this craft's track, they received a message from here that advised that the craft had landed and was somewhere on an island owned by the Chinese, just off the Vietnam coast."

"So, what do we do now? I assume we decided not to attack the spacecraft in this location as we were not sure what was happening? We need to know more, for instance how did we know about the final destination of this craft if we did not follow it?"

"Yes, it may have been easy to destroy it with the laser system, but we must wait. We are talking to the French ESA before making final decision, and making intelligence enquiries regarding the set up in Krulandistan. We shall, however need to talk to Helena and Athena very shortly because we need to know more about how they are able to give us this information ahead of our own intelligence!"

"I agree, but we should wait for Chris and Robert to return, as they can possibly find out more than we can, and it will be a chance for them to meet again."

****

Attica, Earth time, May 2075

The news had been confirmed to the Cabinet. Their detection unit was correct, and there had been an attack on the ISPEG property. They were assessing the news from Helena and from the satellite readings, which had followed the French spacecraft attack. Helena and Athena had confirmed that the ISPEG people had sent a plane under cover to track the final destination of the spacecraft.

Chairman Isis turned to the Cabinet members. "We have seen and heard the results of this particular incident on the Earth. It must stop if we are to obtain our goals in the time frame we have set. This is exactly the type of incident where we have to assist the ISPEG authorities. General Hermes, I am giving you and Senator Artemis permission to go ahead with a full search for the sites being used by this so-called ECAW group. I also think it is time to advise our representatives that they may discuss our goals with the people that they feel they can trust. In the meantime, General Hermes and Senator Artemis will put the astronaut team on full alert and have the Rotoships readied for action."

Dimitris was the first to respond. "Thank you, chairman, I am sure that we are all so pleased to hear that decision. I shall meet with Spiros immediately after the meeting, and we shall send the Cabinet the full plan after speaking to our two representatives."

****

Krulandistan, June 2075

"Comrade Chairman, you will be pleased to hear that Son Ji To and Li Sue Kwang have arrived safely in China. The attack on the Orbiter was partly successful, and we believe that we have put the ISS programme back several weeks. They had to continue on their orbit after firing missiles so they had only brief seconds to assess the final detail, but are sure they made hits. We are going to release the French astronauts now as they cannot identify us, and, in any case,

82

it may be more difficult to dispose of them without the local security being more suspicious."

"OK Kim Jong, that all sounds fine, are we ready now to push our Russian agents to get us more information on the new laser? Also, we have not stopped the ISS progress, only slowed it. What do you think the next step should be now? Do you believe our operations should still lie low for a while, or as we apparently have managed this exercise without detection, shall we continue attacks?"

"Let us instruct Irina and Lara regarding the laser, we do need this info as soon as possible, I can see some bigger problems if they get ahead of us on weapon development. Advise our Cuba and Canada cells that we are to keep close surveillance on the ISS project, but to continue to keep a low profile for the rest of this year. They can just advise us of any significant events."

****

Korea, USAFA base, June 2075

Chris and Robert had returned from Korea after the extraordinary events of the last month or so, and had heard news from their fathers, following the recent incident at the Moon Orbiter. They had followed up their request for a meeting with Helena and Athena, and they were now being flown to home base in the morning. Both were apprehensive, but excited at thought of some time with them.

"Rob, how do we go about this, we must not upset the girls whatever we do, but obviously there are things we need to understand. I hope we can get more on their backgrounds anyway, where does all this ability come from? Their parents must be very interesting."

"We shall just explain what has happened and give them more details re this ECAW group and our concern relating to the recent attacks. We also need to establish what they know or suspect regarding the two Russian girls. Incidentally, I heard that they both have become friendly with two of our scientists working in Biosphere 2."

Robert looked a little apprehensive. "OK, let us hope they understand our concern. Ready to fly Chris, let us hope no more emergency calls today!"

****

Phoenix, Arizona, June 2075

Professor Devonshire, Colonel Somester, together with their wives were preparing for their trip to the USAFA base. Phillip had updated them all on the meeting that was to take place tomorrow. They had all agreed it would be better for their sons to have a private meeting with the girls before they all met together for dinner.

****

Edwards USAFA base, June 2075

"Chris, Robert, we are so pleased to see you, the trip was good, but long, we have to try and improve further on the time that these trips take. After our meetings, we have an idea for you to consider with your engineers."

"Helena, we also are excited to see you both again, how have things been at the Biosphere? Are you happy there?"

"We have not been detected by the Russian girls yet, and we have enjoyed working with Major Lancs on security matters. There is much to tell you. Are we going to meet with your families?"

"OK, first, we are taking you to our rented house in Vandenberg, where Robert and I will be able to talk to you alone. Then I am arranging for the family to be picked up from the Base here and they will join us for dinner, when we can give them a resume of our chat. Is that fine with you both?"

Helena as usual was first to speak. "We are both now ready to talk to you, and trust it will help you understand a few of the recent events."

****

Vanderberg, California, June 2075

The house in Vandenberg was an old, but large wooden house built in the previous century. It had been built for the senior officers of the NASAF units, but most of them had opted for more modern facilities near to the Edwards base, but Chris had seen it as a perfect retreat for them. Today, the weather was still warm, so Robert had made some cool drinks, including Chris's famous ginger beer cocktail, and they were all sitting in the big cane chairs on the front porch.

Helena now had a glass of the cocktail in her hand, and was looking over to Athena who was now nodding at her. The guys looked expectantly at Helena as they started on their drinks.

"Dear Chris and Rob, we first of all want to ask if we could have some white wine with some water added, as although your cocktail is lovely, it is too strong a taste for us."

Robert nodded. "Understood, we are not offended, it is a little strong even for some of our guys in the unit! Back in a moment."

Everyone was now settled and Helena again turned to them, and continued, "You should know that what we are going to tell you now is going to be very strange for you, but hope that you will continue to trust us, and understand that we have not had any wish to hide these things from you. However, it was necessary for us to do so until we both felt sure of your support, and that we understood the Earth's people a little more than we did before leaving our birthplace."

Chris and Rob were now looking very intrigued, and a little nervous, what was coming? Helena continued, "We should tell you first that Athena and I are not from anywhere on your planet, but from a planet that is known as Attica."

They both gasped. Chris could not help but interrupt.

"We always felt there was something different about you, but you are so like us. Where is this Attica, why can you speak our language?"

"Please be patient, we appreciate that much of this story will be difficult for you. The planet Attica is very small compared with your Earth, and if you know where to look it may be seen as a star, but to our knowledge it has not been detected over the years since it was first established in the universe. At the moment, we do not want to expand on that, just let us explain what our ambitions are, and how we can perhaps help each other."

"Certainly, we will try to understand and obviously we are fascinated."

Chris had actually put down his ginger beer and was looking towards Robert.

"Rob, I think we need something stronger before we hear more, there are a couple of bottles of Claret in the kitchen that we were going to open tonight."

Before Robert could rise, Athena intervened. "OK, but as you can see, we cannot drink raw wine, but if you bring some water, we can mix it to our taste."

Helena waited for them to settle again, and then continued, "So now let me resume the story, because it is just as difficult for Athena and I to relate, and we want you to give us every bit of your attention. This is now a serious matter affecting our future together."

Chris and Rob took a sip of their wines and now looked very concerned. They listened intently to Helena as she unfolded the story of how their planet was dying due to fertility problems that had been created by high mercury and methane levels developing over the last 20 years on the planet, and that had severely affected reproduction of the population, and even their animals.

She explained that over the last few years Attica authorities have been working hard on developing habitat on the planet Mars, and they had plans to move the younger people onto the planet over the next ten years. However, she explained, there is still the problem of reproduction.

"This is where we hope you will be particularly interested. Athena and I are here officially as the representatives of our planet, and have been given permission by our assembly cabinet to speak to you confidentially regarding our hopes and aspirations for the future."

Helena went on to explain that Attica had exceptional skills that had been developed over several hundred years. Based on their intelligence reports and sightings, they considered that their scientific knowledge was at least two hundred years ahead of the planet Earth.

"Please do not be offended by that statement, but we want you to know so you can understand why we have been able to obtain our university grades so easily, and to have the ability to detect things that you found strange. Let me now go on with the main theme of our plans, and then you must advise us if you feel you can work with our people to obtain results that are helpful to both planets. Athena and I do also want you to accept that we both are very thankful for your friendship, and we do want to develop our relationship."

Chris and Robert were looking still shocked, but this last statement brought on some happier faces.

Helena noted that, and was inwardly pleased, but she now continued…

"Now, to the proposal from our Cabinet. They have watched the Earth's problems for a number of years and know that you particularly now have a problem with this so-called ECAW group. We have been through all of our wars, but now there is peace because our people only see one enemy, that of extinction of the planet. Our final wish is that some of your younger generation will join us on Mars, and help us to create a new civilisation."

"We do know that our young female population are still able to conceive children, but to put it plainly, we need some of your males to help them. This of course creates a mixed race, but not one that should create any tensions in the future, as they will grow together in a place that will have other challenges that all the new population will have to continue to solve. There will be no time or case for division."

Chris put down his wine. "This is remarkable news, and it is like something from the science fiction books we read when we were in our teens. You will understand that what you are outlining is in theory something that could happen, but the decision to work together to this end, is of course, beyond our status, it would have to go to the heads of governments around our world."

Robert added, "Of course, we want to help, but do go on and give us more of your plan so that we can discuss it later with the elders. They will be as mesmerised as us!"

Helena put some more water in the wine, sipped it, and then settled down on the sofa as she continued…

"To achieve the aims that our Cabinet have outlined it would be necessary for very close co-operation. Attica has suggested that we help you with the update of your AI robot team, your space craft, and teaching programmes for future emigrants to Mars. However, first, they propose that we help you to extinguish, or nullify any warring groups. It is important that those who arrive on Mars are all of one ambition, so that the planet may develop in harmony."

Both girls now looked over at the slightly open-mouthed men.

"I think that is probably enough for you to digest for now, so please tell us if you feel we can discuss this further when we meet with your parents tonight?"

Rob recovered first, "Of course, we must, they will find it incredulous, and of course they, and other authorities, will need some more information as to how you think this would work, but, like us, I believe that they will have faith in you, and therefore would be very surprised if they did not want to follow up on this fantastic project."

Vandenberg, California June 2075 [Later that Day]

Josh, Ruth, Phillip and Dawn had all flown into Edwards Base, and had received the message from Chris regarding their earlier meeting with the Greek girls. They were now making their way down to the house in Vandenberg. The hydro tram occupants were very quiet, they had received an outline of the news, and were full of expectation, if a little nervous. The tram was now stopping, almost outside the house, and Josh turned to them before alighting.

"I am sure we all agree that whatever is said we are agreed that we take the news calmly, and decide amongst ourselves on how we deal with any matters arising, before talking to others in the ISPEG offices."

It was another warm evening in California, and all had agreed to use the terrace for dinner, there was as nice breeze, and they had all thought it a more relaxing place to talk. As the senior, Josh broke the ice.

"Good evening, Helena and Athena, we cannot tell you how interested we are in hearing all your news. You can be sure that whatever you discuss with us all will be treated with confidence and respect. Chris and Robert are treating us to dinner this evening, and so while they are preparing that, perhaps you could just outline your main story and your objectives."

Chris called from the kitchen, "When you make the drinks Dad, offer some water with the wine for the girls please, they cannot drink raw wine."

Helena was again the first to speak. "Thanks Professor, Athena and I appreciate your kind welcome. We are anxious to transfer as much news as we can this evening, so let me start the story. We were both born on the small planet which was named Attica by the founding Greek spirits who we believe came to the planet some 7000 years ago. Our gods are worshipped in the same way as the God we see being worshipped here, and our researchers further believe that human forms were first created on Attica at about the time that your God's son, Jesus Christ, was on your Earth."

"So, in Earth years, our creation is relatively new. However, it would seem that the humans that were formed at that time, we believe by the spirits, were born having already incredible knowledge that has allowed Attica to expand very rapidly. Today you will see a land that has many of the Earth's characteristics, and even some similar animals. Because it is so small, your scientists may have only detected it as a bright star in one of the galaxies, and taken little or no interest. It is in fact situated just a few days space travel from Mars."

The Professor interrupted as this was so interesting, but so many questions!

"Helena and Athena, are you representative of the people on Attica in appearance and voice, if so, that is incredulous. We have always thought that there would be other life out in space, but not in a form that we would recognise easily."

The two girls now looked out to the kitchen, and called out to Chris and Robert.

"I think you need to be here for our continued story, so we shall wait until we all sit for dinner."

During dinner, there was a lull in conversation as it was clear that the elders in particular were mulling over the news that they had already heard, and were wanting to ask so many questions.

It was Helena again taking the lead in the conversation as they now sat with their coffees and water. "As you can see, we enjoy most of your foods, but as Chris and Robert know we are what you call vegetarians and eat many vegetable, cereal and nut products. We know Chris and Robert made a special effort to make these meals for us, and really appreciate that, it has ensured our health since we arrived on the Earth. Now, to continue if you are ready?"

There was no doubt about that as all sat looking expectantly at the girls. Athena now was giving Helena a break, and she moved to the centre of the sitting room.

She continued to outline the whole events since they both landed on the Earth, and explained that they were sent as representatives of Attica to try and persuade the inhabitants authorities of their wish to create a new civilisation that would not only help their own planet's problem, but it was thought may help the Earth with its climate and population problems, which they had detected were becoming worse. In addition, they had witnessed a problem with terrorist activity which could not be tolerated if the two planets were to work together in the future. She went on to explain the fertility problem on Attica, and their wish to see this resolved by finding new partners.

Helena now continued. She could see the story had made everybody quiet.

"All of our plans are based on finding that partnership and developing new life on another planet, whether that be the Earth or Mars. We already have a small population on the planet Mars, and we have established a living environment. It is still a relatively small area, but with our skills and our new robot workers we are speeding up the expansion of this project. Time is, of course, of the essence as our people will not be able to reproduce, and age will become a factor. At the moment, we return all those who have reached sixty years of age to Attica. They know that they will end their lives on the planet, and not have the satisfaction of knowing there is a continuation of their family. It is this aspect that concerns us most. We must find a solution."

Ruth and Dawn had taken a liking to these two girls, but could also see the implications that were outlined if they were to become closer to their sons. Ruth spoke for them both.

"You are both extremely brave and intelligent girls. We can only guess at the powers that your planet has achieved in being able to take you and your people to this stage of the planet's development. Robert's mother and myself are aware that your plan will certainly affect us in some way as our sons are surely going to support and help you achieve your aims. They rarely stop talking about you! I know I speak for all of us when we say that whatever is decided we shall try to support you."

Helena was quick to respond. "We both thank you for that Dr Devonshire, you can see that we had decided that you all were professional people in whom we could confide. Although you may have the thought that we had ulterior motives for befriending your sons, you can be assured that we both have only admiration for them, and do hope that we can continue that friendship, even if we do have to eventually leave the Earth."

Chris and Robert were quietly delighted to hear this news, and now Chris spoke, "I can see that you have got our parents thinking about your remarkable story. On another subject, can you tell us all how you are able to speak to us so clearly, and why you are so like our own people."

Helena explained to them about the surgery that they undertook, both for their bodies and for their brain box. The latter they explained gave them ability to speak any language that was fed to them. Although their natural language was ancient Greek, the minute machine that had been installed when they reached adult age had enabled them to not only transfer thoughts between their own people, but had been adapted to pick up languages from any source and instantly translate. Many of the languages had been picked up by their satellite surveillance of various areas of the Earth.

"You had satellite surveillance of the Earth, that is incredible, for how long, and how?"

"Well Professor, we shall be sharing more of these matters with you, but in confidence we can advise that we had established for some time a satellite presence through one or more of the existing satellites used by your people. In this case, we are extracting information that is being picked up by satellites that were launched from a place you call Krulandistan, some years ago."

"Well, well, I can see that we have much to learn. However, before we leave tonight can you tell us your concerns about the two Russian girls who you believe not only tried to do you harm, but also may have been involved in the recent incidents that affected our ISS programme. Maybe the same source was responsible for the earlier laser incident in which we were lucky to escape with our lives?"

Athena took up the response. "One of the ways that Attica want to help, and by doing so, develop friendship and co-operation between our peoples, is to remove any factions that may destroy the peace if they are allowed to transfer to Attica or the planet Mars. We have suspicions that these two girls are agents for a group you have identified as ECAW, which, in turn, has been identified as an extreme communist group that may be existing in several areas of your planet. It is believed to be targeting your space programmes, no doubt hoping that they can establish their people on Mars with an ideology that we believe you are totally against, and that has created misery and bloodshed in your past."

"It is another ideology like the extreme Muslim culture that nearly brought your world to a catastrophic end when they threatened the use of nuclear weapons. The latter problem we understand was solved when the revered Imam's brought their people back to the true Islam and the masses turned against the terrorist factions. We have to obtain a similar result with this extreme group."

Helena was now sipping some warm milk instead of the coffee, and looked over to Athena as she now continued, "Here is a start to our thinking for a ten-year plan that would prepare us all for a new adventure and future for our younger generation."

"We are both able, with support from our Seniors in Attica, to assist you to eliminate potential enemies. The Russian girls are just the starting point. There are obviously many agents around your world who need to be identified, and then either eliminated, or captured, so that the leaders may see that their cause is lost. While this plan is being executed, we would like to help you with the advance of your science relating to spacecraft, robots, communication, etc. We believe that our experiences, and our sources of new materials, will enable you to meet the target of joining us on Mars, which by that time, with the assistance of the new robot team, we consider will be able to sustain a small city."

"We are already increasing our robot presence on the planet to assist with the heavier work involved, and gravity, atmospheric considerations, water and food supply are all being investigated, and some success has already been achieved."

"There is so much more, and you will have many questions, but first we want you to consider all that we have shared today, and maybe we can arrange our next meeting at the biosphere next week? In the meantime, you no doubt will want to talk to other authorities, and we know that you will ensure that our disclosures remain confidential. The element of surprise is essential, and of course we do not wish to create any panic with your population, who may see us as potential aggressive aliens."

Chris got up from the sofa.

"Dear Helena and Athena, you have been so open with us, and of course I am sure we all are still mystified and amazed at your backgrounds and your ambitions. I know I am speaking for Rob and myself when we would ask that you spend some time with us in these next few weeks. Maybe our parents can arrange for you both to join us on the Astronaut and Robot programmes while this is all being discussed and planned."

Josh again started speaking for the elders. "Let us retire now, but certainly it may be a great idea for you to be together while we look at the political position with the highest authorities. I speak for my wife, and our friends the Somesters, in thanking Helena and Athena for this opportunity. The science is a little beyond our comprehension just now, but we do understand the general plan. It is an amazing project, and we would love to be with you on that journey. As you say, let us meet up again soon, maybe at Edwards base rather than the Biosphere for reasons I will explain later."

They all rose and went to hug the girls as they prepared for a restless night thinking of the day's revelations.

****

Biosphere 2—July 2075

"We have been here for some months now Lara, and although it is interesting working with the astronaut programme and space health matters, we do not seem to be selected for other work that would bring us closer to the knowing more about the weapons and the ISS programme. I am going to make a play for a guy that I met in the Canteen, Lt. Terry Durham, he seemed interested in me, and it may get us closer to some of the more confidential work. I know he is involved in the laser programme for instance."

"Well OK Irina, but look out for someone for me, maybe he has a friend? We should be able to find out more about the ISS programme and the effect of our recent attack. Our cell is asking us for more news now. It would appear that the rocket attack has apparently not been attached to our organisation."

"Will see how this works out, and of course I shall look out for a partner for you. See you later."

****

Krulandistan, August 2075

"We have just heard from our Canadian cell that the ISS Venus programme is back on track, and they are preparing to send further important parts to the Florida site in the next few days. Within a week, there should be a new launch to the Orbiter."

"Well Kim Jong, that is not good news, we thought we had created more damage on the last attack. We need to think what our next move should be. Start looking at the French spacecraft for the possibility of re-using it for another attack. We could perhaps send it into space from the island or transfer it to our Chinese friends for launch. Check all the weapons and possibilities. The two astronauts we used last time were not that successful obviously, are we confident they can be trusted to this new plan?"

"Comrade Chairman, I believe so. The French astronauts that we released have not been able to identify anything, and the whole matter has died down as the West continue to no doubt investigate, but have little to trace the origins of the attack, and we do not think they know of the spacecrafts position. We did not detect any follow up to the spacecrafts return to the islands."

"Another point, the news from our agents in the ISPEG has been very sparse, any reason?"

"They have advised that they are trying to obtain a move into more confidential work, and are befriending some guys who they feel they can manipulate to obtain their goals."

"We shall watch carefully, and hope that works, we still want to know more regarding the laser developments."

Edwards Base, California, September 2075

The Devonshires, Somesters, General Edward Glen, and General Jason Worcester were assembled in the officer's mess together with the US Vice President, and the Deputy Prime Minister of the UK. The latter pair were listening intently as Josh and Phillip took turns to outline the story, and the Attica planet plan.

Senator Bill Styles and Sir Leonard Berks were unusually quiet, it was as difficult for them to comprehend as it had been for everyone else who had heard this tale.

As Josh and Phillip sat down, the Senator was the first to respond, "Ladies, gentlemen, that is a most incredible story, and very difficult for me to believe. It is only because I know the backgrounds of all the people here today, apart from Sir Leonard, that I know it must be true. You certainly have presented this plan in a first-class manner, and I would like to get this down on an official report so we can present it to the President. Your wish for confidentiality is noted and understood, and it will be dealt with by me personally. General Glen and General Worcester will I am sure be able to assist me in forming our approach to this report. We had always thought there must be some other bodies in the universe, but this is really incredible news."

Sir Leonard looked over his horn-rimmed glasses to see if the Senator was sitting down.

"Yes, what a fascinating and unbelievable story. The Senator has summed it up nicely. I have known the Devonshire's for some time as we had a US/UK alliance on a project that the professor lead involving gamma ray research for brain surgery some years ago. I certainly respect his view on this matter. As the Senator is going to report to the President, I shall liaise with him to agree how we present the report to the UK Prime Minister. We also have to agree on how many heads of governments we involve in some of the decisions that surely will have to be made in the near future to enable this bold plan. Perhaps we can all meet for dinner before I leave for London tomorrow?"

****

Attica, Earth Time, January 2076

The Cabinet council had just received news from their representatives that the US and UK governments had been totally convinced about the news from

Helena and Athena, and had agreed to meet with them. They were now very interested in negotiating a joint plan for working together. The assembly members had been called and were now eagerly waiting in the great hall.

"Assembly Members, we are now able to advise you that further progress has been made relating to the possibility of working with the planet Earth's people to form a new coalition. General Hermes and Captain Panomosis are making plans to send one of our Rotoships to the planet shortly, and we intend to land one more of our senior people for these discussions. We may attempt landing on this occasion, but still with stealth. We need to maintain secrecy until we know more about the Earth's plans, and that we may have full confidence in their intentions."

General Hermes now intervened. "Members, relating to the chairman's remarks, may I now confirm that Captain Efi Panomosis has volunteered to be our new representative, working closely with Helena Poulakis and Athena Balakakis. I believe this to be a sound plan as she has vast experience, is in excellent health, and is well known to our two agents. We do not have time for surgery, but in any case, we feel it is time that the Earth people should see our natural appearance. She is a fine example of our people."

Chairman Isis and the chief magistrate Panis Odysseus both then addressed the members, and asked for a support vote to the plan, Panis emphasising that he would have a meeting with the General and Captain prior to taking on the mission, outlining their main concerns and aspirations for the upcoming meetings. The voting was again unanimous, all were excited about this possibility for a new merger of their peoples.

****

California, Edwards Base, September 2076

Chris and Robert had been spending some months with the girls, and had now been introduced to Efi, who had arrived safely on Earth just a month ago. It had been no more a surprise seeing Efi and her long limbs, than all the other surprises that they had experienced over the last year.

She had also adapted remarkably well to the new environment. They were all now ready for the meeting with the higher authorities which had been set to take place in the Florida ISPEG HQ.

During the last six months, Helena and Athena had concentrated on the robot programme with Dr Devonshire, and Zikky and his team were now present on the base. However, after the first meeting in Florida, they were making plans to return to the Biosphere to confront the Russian girls. They had told the boys that they had further concerns about another attack on the new space station, or even that they were making plans to disrupt the laser programme. They were sure that something was not right. They were anxious to put their plan into operation regarding the Russian girls to see if they definitely were involved in sabotage, and if so, who were they reporting to?

Chris could see that the girls were really concerned.

"Sorry we cannot go with you all to the meeting in Florida, we shall miss you. It has been great having some time with you both. Hopefully we can see you again at the Biosphere after the meeting as we may be flying into Arizona with our new F95S soon, and testing the laser after the adjustments you helped us all with last month. The desert is a great area for these tests. In the meantime, we shall follow up on any information you are able to send us regarding any potential terrorist attacks."

"Good, thanks Chris and Rob, we shall go and find Efi so we can have dinner together tonight. We have loved our time here in California with you both."

****

Biosphere 2—September 2076

Irina and Lara were enjoying developing friendships with the two Lieutenant astronauts who were going through final training at the Biosphere. As expected, the guys had been more than ready to take up their offer of having some spare time together. The girls had used all their charms to seduce them, and the men seemed to be quite ready to ignore any earlier suggestions that they may not be trusted. At least once a week, when they all had some spare time, they would take the Hypolink train into Phoenix for a dinner-dance night, and in this relaxed atmosphere they would gently prod the guys to find out where they were going next, as they would miss them, etc. etc. The guys were also being asked if they would like to spend some time in the girl's apartment, and this had excited them and become too much of a priority in their thinking.

This week, both Terry Durham and Lance Warwick had been called for duty at the Edwards Base, and before leaving they had advised the girls that they were being asked to supervise the moving of the new ISS parts.

They expected to spend three days at the Base before going to Canada, and then onto Florida for launch time. After further prompting from Irina, they promised to keep in touch wherever they were.

****

Krulandistan, October 2076

"We have new information Comrade Chairman, our two girl agents working in the Biosphere have identified the route for the transfer of the new ISS parts, and have created a relationship with two of the ISPEG team that will be involved in moving the parts to the launch site in Florida. May I suggest that I alert Son Jing and Li Sue to be ready for re-launching the French space vehicle from our Iosha Islands. The craft has been checked and reloaded by our Chinese friends, and they say they have a suitable launcher. This time the target may be easier if we go straight for destroying the ISS parts on the Florida launching site? Instead of launching into space we could make a parabolic curve. It does mean that we will sacrifice the spacecraft, but I think it will have done its work, and it will leave little or no evidence."

"As usual, Kim Jong you have been thoughtful, and it is pleasing that our agents in ISPEG are again active. This plan does seem to be a better option than the uncertainties of the space attack, it does mean of course that we shall lose Son Jing and Li Sue, unless you have another idea for them."

"Thanks, Ho Chi, I think we shall try to use the spacecraft purely as a missile, but if we have to man it, then we shall also look for alternatives for them to leave the spacecraft before it enters the US air space. Please leave that to me, I am sure you will agree we may have to make some sacrifices in this venture."

Major Woo then picked up his transmitter. "Comrade Doctor Son Jing if you please, urgent."

"Hello comrade Kim Jong, Son Jing speaking. Good to hear from you, what can we do for you today?"

Edwards Base, November 2076

Chris and Robert were in the Officer's mess listening to Commander Glen and Captain Westmorland. The two senior officers had just returned from the meetings in Washington and Florida.

"Chris and Robert, we want you to be the first to know the result of our meetings in view of your involvement with the two representatives from Attica. May we first say that these young ladies, including their Captain, Efi Panomosis were outstanding in their presence and the way that they responded to all of the questions from our President, the UK Prime Minister, and their closest advisors. Captain Panomosis did of course create a little bit of a stir when first presented due to her appearance, but it did not take long for her to start making an impact on the meeting."

"We can go into more detail later when certain allies have been fully briefed, but you are the first to know that we have made an agreement to work with the Attican people, and you both are cleared for further highly confidential information. You will now be assigned to the project which has been coded 'Marsattica'. Before you ask, yes, you will be working with the Attica team."

Captain Westmorland had brought a champagne bottle into the room, and now he was pouring a measure into each glass as he spoke.

"I know your usual tipple is slightly more bizarre, but today we are going to toast this new alliance. Gentlemen, here is to a new dawn, the most exciting programme we shall see in our lifetime."

****

Attica, Earth Time, November 2076

The Attica assembly had just been advised of the outcome of the meetings on the planet Earth, and General Hermes was now already back on the planet. He was addressing them now.

"Chairman, Senators, Members, I can report a very successful trip. The Rotoships are working well, and with the new fuel source we are now able to reach planet Earth more speedily. Captain Panomosis was landed safely, and our spacecraft was not detected during the flights. It handled the transition from space to the high gravity pull onto the Earth's surface with relative ease, our new prolignic metals have given the craft ability to move through all temperatures and atmospheres. My team will be available for any questions in a few moments but just let me confirm that we shall be undertaking additional intelligence to ensure we all remain on target with this agreement. Priority will be to help the Earth to achieve peace within its own world, and this may mean our influence is needed in certain circumstances. I trust you will support us in this important time for our planet."

****

Krulandistan, December 2076

"We have everything set up Ho Chi, can you give us your approval for launch tomorrow? We are going for the missile approach and Song Jing and Li Sue will be posted back to our HQ for further work."

****

Biosphere 2—December 2076

Helena and Athena had returned to the office and were talking with Major Lancs and Lt. Kent.

"We have just returned from California, and they suggested we talk to you about our plan to talk to the Russian astronaut trainees that have been under your supervision. We are suspicious that they may have managed to get confidential information from the two lieutenants, Durham and Warwick, and could have been passing on information to your enemies. No proof yet, but we have instinct for these things. We believe we may be able to shock them, as they believe us to be dead, and if they are guilty, we can use them to establish the source of recent attacks, and then make a plan to remove these threats. It is part one of our joint plan for the Earth and Attica to develop a peaceful nation on Mars."

Tom Lancs looked very concerned.

"Thanks Helena, you are right, we have been advised to help you to achieve the objectives set out in the agreement, and we are pleased to do so. Gary and I are very upset to hear that our two trusted lieutenants may be involved in any leaks, we shall investigate further. In the meantime, the Russian girls are due to go to the simulator tomorrow for navigation training, and it would be great if you were there before them, and in charge of the spacecraft simulation. This should shock them considerably."

Edwards Air Base, December 2076

Chris had just returned from the meetings and was now with Robert, discussing the next moves relating to the new agreement.

"Rob, I have just heard from Helena, and they have set up a meeting with the Russian girls tomorrow. However, more worrying, she also said that they both suspected there was another attack imminent, and that they had learnt today that two of the guys who are involved in the ISS parts transfer to the Florida launch site have been seen regularly in their company. She advised that these two lieutenants are now being closely monitored by intelligence. They want us to alert all concerned with the launch immediately. In view of our previous experience, I am going up to the Commander's office to ask him to alert all parties concerned at HQ."

"These girls are amazing Chris, I do hope we can resolve these problems without too much bloodshed, and get on with the main objectives of the Marsattica Agreement."

★★★★★★★★★★★★

ISPEG HQ—Florida—December 2076

Commander Glen had just heard the latest news, and he was now on the phone to General Worcester.

"Jason, we have another message from our Attica girls that we should immediately take action to ensure safety of the ISS parts when they arrive in the launch area tonight. As a further security I am going to send our F95S, with our two top pilots, to look out for any suspicious activity coming into the atmosphere. I believe we can land them at the McDill base for further fuelling, if necessary, but please ask them to keep landing and take-off as secure as possible. As you know, this plane is top secret at the moment."

"Good to hear from you, Ed, sorry about the circumstances. We shall look out for them. Give them the following code to quote, and that will get my direct attention. ISP-EB-653. I shall speak to Major Delamare, you remember Tiny? He is now the head guy at McDill, so will alert him. Use the same code when in contact with him. I shall make sure that we both are alerted irrespective of time."

"Yes, I remember Tiny, that he certainly is not! Give him my regards."

★★★★★★★★★★★★

Biosphere 2 Mess—December 2076

Irina and Lara were sitting in the Canteen having lunch, congratulating themselves in having been able to find location times for the ISS parts, and having been congratulated by Kim Jong. They were just drinking some white wine to celebrate. They were also happy that they were being allowed into the simulator for training as they could see this being very useful to their cause. However, they were suddenly amazed to see two persons approaching their table.

"Irina Ivanov and Lara Gorinski, you do look very happy girls, what are you celebrating?"

The girls nearly choked. When they recovered a little, it was Irina who was first to speak. "We thought you were dead, where have you been, what is all this about?"

"Yes, we know that you both had plotted that end, but as you see we are both in good health. Athena and I have been monitoring your progress here at the Biosphere, and we know that you are not to be trusted. We do believe you were associated with the attacks on the Canadian plant, and that the two lieutenants you have seduced are good guys at heart and will be devastated when they know they have been duped into unwittingly giving away information that could lead to further attacks."

Irina was first to recover. "Well, you both think you are clever, but you will soon see that you are too late to stop us. There is nothing you can do, and you have to prove your ideas before you can arrest us. The laws here say that you are innocent until proven guilty."

"We shall see. We hoped that you would see sense in giving up your spying, and really start to enjoy the life that we are proposing for our scientists in the future. We can assure you that you cannot win, and your ideals are not conducive to a strong, healthy and wealthy community. Think about it before it is too late."

Irina and Lara looked into the deep dark eyes facing them, they were not feeling so confident somehow.

F95S Flight—December 2076

Chris and Robert were feeling much more confident. The F95S was a dream to fly, and they had just been advised that they were being promoted to the rank of Captain.

"Captain Somester, pleasure to fly with you!"

"Well, it is great Chris that we can still work together. The story so far has been amazing."

"Yes, you are certainly right there. Anyway, we better look at the latest news coming in from the Biosphere, and also check if we have any other info from ISPEG HQ, as we are nearing ninety thousand, and have a good chance to see any space activity from here."

****

ISPEG HQ—Same Time, December 2076

General Worcester and Major Fife were aware of the latest threats and news was coming over the transmitters.

"General, we have detected some activity in the South China Sea area. It looks like a projectile or space vehicle is being launched that we cannot identify."

"Thanks Hank, let us get co-ordinates and transfer them to the F95S just in case. It certainly is suspicious."

****

F95S—One Hour Later, December 2076

"Just had some better news, Rob. It has been reported that the Russian girls were given false information by our two young lieutenants. They may have been seduced by them, but their sense of duty prevailed. If this missile or craft is the enemy then it will be heading for our Florida airspace, supposing the girls passed on this info. This is still a problem for us if the craft is manned, but there is evidently reason to believe it is being used just as a missile. The problem for us is that if this is a missile we need to detect it before it reaches the coast. I will ask our admin office to track the projectile and see if we can get better identity and set some co-ordinates to intercept if our worst fears are founded."

Krulandistan, Same Time, December 2076

"Launch of the French spacecraft has commenced Comrade Chairman, we finally decided to go for high explosive head on the spacecraft, and use the co-ordinates sent to us by our agents to destroy the launch site in Florida, as well as

102

any evidence from this craft. We are using the parabolic curve equation sent to us by our agents."

"Keep me informed, Kim Jong, we may need to take our agents out of the US if there are any adverse reactions to our attacks."

The Normal Distribution

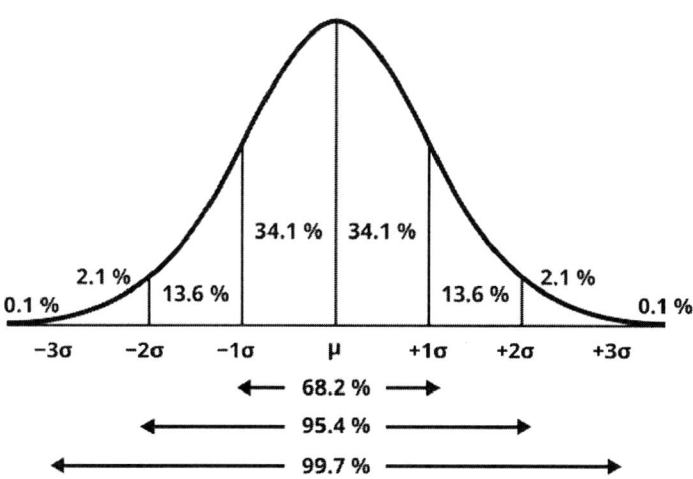

F95S—2 Hours Later, December 2076

"Info just in Rob, get ready to enter the following co-ordinates that our team have worked out. We must try to catch this craft before entering our air space if we are to avoid kickbacks. As far as we know they will be oblivious to the incoming attack and may detect it too late on their radar. If the craft is on the curve that our guys have identified, we should attack it over the Bahamas area…"

Robert interrupted, "Chris, I have it on the screen, it is too late for that, it is going to be with us in minutes."

"OK, Rob, I am going up to maximum speed to try to intercept. Get laser ready for firing now!"

They could see the missile craft now, and were getting ready to attack. Suddenly, a double red winking light appeared on the screens.

"Chris, we are going to have to be quick, fuel is very low. We must get in and out with speed, and then limp into McDill. We may just make it."

"Laser ready to fire, the craft is not responding to any calls, so we must assume the worst. On my count to three. One…two…three—FIRE!"

The laserGR5 had been upgraded several times since those early tests in the desert, and sure enough, this time it struck home in seconds. The space missile could be seen spiralling out of control. Was it going to explode before hitting the land? They watched hopefully as they prepared the plane for a new course to McDill, there was not enough fuel to go around again.

"Blow up, for goodness' sake, blow up!"

****

McDill Air Base, Minutes Later, December 2076

"Captain Devonshire calling KMCD. We are coming in on low engine power due to fuel shortage, please offer longest runway as we may not be able to use reverse thrust. Also, please alert Commander Glen at Edwards Base that we need to speak to him urgently."

"We have you on screen Captain, our Captain Fierra is in touch with Edwards Base. Please take runway 24 which you should set at latitude 28.4366, longitude 83.4422. We have emergency services on hand, but you have nearly 4 miles of runway, so take it easy."

"Thank you McDill, copied."

"Commander Glen here, Chris, concentrate on your landing, and I will stay on line to speak to you as soon as you feel comfortable. Passing you over to control tower now."

"Thanks Commander, I feel more confident now that we will be fine. I am just worried now about where the missile may have landed."

The F95S landed well, the runway was as predicted their saviour. Nearly all 4 miles had been used up, but they were able to slow her without the use of engines which had petered out a few miles from the base. Chris and Robert sighed, and sat back in their seats. It was time to hear the worst. Chris returned to the line to the Commander.

"We have safely landed, Commander, McDill were extremely helpful so please send them our thanks. We should take a note of the fuel problems so we can increase capacity for future flights."

"We are now very anxious to know if you have any news regarding our recent attack on the French space missile. We did attack it with the new laser, and know we hit the craft, but did not see any explosion. Our concern is that the craft fell to land and may have caused casualties. If they find the damaged French marked space missile, the locals will not be happy. They probably don't know what we suspect, that this was an ECAW group attack."

"Well, don't need to worry, guys, you did what you had to do, and we are delighted that the new laser is working well. You will be pleased to know that the missile, because that was what it was, did explode, but it landed in the Caribbean Sea, just off the coast."

"Our team did well to work out the parabolic curve, but again we have to thank your Attica friends for their early warning. When you have checked out the plane and re-fuelled, take a little break, and then take the new security hyperlink up to ISPEG HQ where we shall meet up. I shall also bring Helena and Athena with me as we need to talk to the Generals about our next steps to ensure the agreement clauses are met."

"Well thanks Commander, did not know the hyperlink connecting HQ and Washington extended to McDill, that will get us there in no time. After the meeting with the Generals, Captain Somester and I are requesting a day or two's break, we would like to take Helena and Athena to Miami where we can talk more unofficially, and I hear it is a great place to relax. We shall of course bring back any information that is pertinent to this agreement."

"OK Chris, you both deserve a break. Let us talk about it when we meet at HQ. Will call them now and tell them we are all on our way, and would like to meet tomorrow morning. You did not mention Efi, maybe I could take a few days break as well, and take her along, it would be good for her to see some of the everyday life on our planet, even if this is the better side of our life!"

****

Krulandistan, Same Time, December 2076

"Comrade Chairman, we have a problem. The French spacecraft which we set up as a missile, was intercepted over Cuba, and according to our US agents it was attacked by one of the ISPEG fighter planes. Worse is that we believe their plane was equipped with the new Laser GR5 which we are still trying to copy. The missile fell into the Caribbean Sea, and exploded, just missing the Cuban mainland. They are furious, but the one good bit of news for us is that they suspect the Americans were to blame with a malfunction test, although they were

105

mystified by the fact that French markings had been seen on the wreckage prior to it being picked up by a naval vessel."

"This is not good news though, Kim Jong. We have failed our main mission. The agents in the Biosphere seem to be out of control. Perhaps it is time to terminate their employment, and try to infiltrate with new blood, or blackmail an existing scientist if we can identify a potential weak link?"

"Are you giving me direct instructions to handle that situation Ho Chi?"

"Affirmative, and now can you get our Russian and Chinese contacts on the transmitter, I need to see how we can retaliate."

****

Attica, Earth Time, January 2077

Updated news had just arrived from Efi regarding her work with the robots and the Earth's astronaut team. She had also explained the recent problem with the two Russian girls and the consequent missile incident, which, although unsuccessful this time, was yet another threat to the peace that the new agreement was seeking. The assembly had been called to discuss this news and decide on action. General Hermes was first up to the dais. His voice boomed over the great hall.

"Chairman Isis, Members, we are at a junction in this story. Captain Panomosis and our representatives, Helena and Athena, have achieved a significant Agreement with the Earths authorities, but we still have problems with terrorist activity emanating from many areas on the planet. We now have to find a way of removing the extreme elements that are liable to prevent us reaching a full peaceful solution to our project. To understand what action is required from us I am proposing that we bring two of the Earth's representatives to Attica, so that we can hear their proposals, and then make a plan that incorporates our help. Please may I have your vote on this action?"

Chairman Isis rose to respond, as he could detect the excitement in the hall.

"General, Members, I have no hesitation in directing you to approve this action. We have now a great chance to meet our future allies, and as the General has outlined, we do need to understand them more, and to assist them where necessary on the first stage of the agreement, which to remind you, is to achieve peace on the Earth by removing or capturing these extremists."

After these two speeches, it was no surprise that the members fully supported the motion.

****

ISPEG HQ—January 2077

Following the December meetings, there had been continued attacks and although these were much more minor than the previous missile attempt, they were still worrying. Therefore, the latest news that the Attican authorities wanted to meet with two of the ISPEG leaders to discuss this, and other matters that would accelerate the objectives of the agreement, were most welcome.

It was decided that Commander Glen, with all his experience with warfare and astronaut activity should be selected, and that Colonel Phillip Somester join him, as he had been party to all the conversations that had taken place over the last year or so with family and the Attica representatives. Despite now being 64 years of age, he was considered more than fit for the voyage. They had all agreed that they would also send Zikky, as the girls had recommended a meeting with their own human robot team, who were very involved in preparing the planet Mars for future occupation.

Chris and Robert had taken the break with the girls in Miami, and they had been very happy. They had also been pleased to see Efi and the Commander enjoying themselves. Efi had said that she did not want to expose herself to the general public as she was concerned that this was too early to become headline news! However, the Commander had ensured they stayed at a private resort and this had worked out perfectly.

"Rob, that trip with the girls was fantastic, just what we all needed, and we keep learning from them all the time. Helena was obviously not too much into kissing, she said she found it a little strange, but she smiled, so it may grow on her!"

"Same experience for me Chris, but, as you say, early days, living in hope! For now, we better get our minds back on the job. It is great news that the Commander and my father have been selected to take the trip to Attica, I would have loved to go with him, but I can see the sense of the elders opening up the first contact with their government people. We must ask the girls if they think he will be able to take the strain of travelling in their spacecraft, it is after all about ten times faster than our current Starships."

"It is great news about your father, Rob, I know my father wanted to go as well, but he is needed more with the Biosphere programme, and the monitoring of the progress with the new agreement."

"However, my mother, with help from the girls, is evidently going to train Zikky to speak ancient Greek, and get her ready for meeting with the Attican robot people. There is no need for the Greek really, but it will be a good way for Zikky to impress them by addressing their human robots in the language that they have been taught."

"Agreed Rob, so let us now get back to the girls and plan what we do about the Russian girls. We must also plan how we can stop this ECAW group making further attacks, bring them to justice, and thus bring some peace to the whole world. It is a first priority of the Attica Agreement."

He paused. "It will be also great if we can get the resource and knowledge to replicate the Attica space vehicles, from what we are told they are amazingly fast and comfortable. This will also enable us to have more movements between the planets and build up closer co-operation. We shall see how the Commander and your father handle the trip. Let us hope that they are successful in building a strong relationship with the Attican authorities."

****

Biosphere 2, February 2077

Irina and Lara had been really shocked by the sudden appearance of the Greek girls, and had just heard that their plans for the attack on the ISPEG HQ had failed. They were sure now that the two lieutenants had obviously not been duped, and that was borne out by the fact that they had not heard from them for some days.

"Lara, should we ask Kim Jong what we are to do, our cover has obviously gone. We could just get out quickly and ask our Canadian contacts to hide us, what do you think?"

"I don't think Kim Jong is going to be very helpful somehow, maybe our US contacts will help hide us for a while until this all dies down?"

"OK, I shall put in a call tonight to them, but get ready for a quick departure."

****

At this time, Helena was in the science room with Athena.

"Athena, I just had a message through the device we left on the girls before we left them. They are planning to run away. I think we should let that happen, but will talk to the professor, and if he agrees, ask him to contact whoever is responsible for tracking them so we can find another one of ECAW's agents."

Krulandistan, February, 2077

Kim Jong was at one of his regular meetings with Ho Chi.

"We have suggested to our Canadian cell that they may be able to set back the ISPEG programme for the space race, if we help them to attack the Biosphere or the Florida space launch area. They are happy to work with us, but feel the easiest and safest way of retaliation would be to send another missile to the Orbiter station, which they could manage from their soil and would be possibly more of a surprise. We can leave them to it as this would not reflect on us. I will now think of a way of taking out the two agents in the Biosphere."

****

Gateway Moon Orbiter, March 2077

After the last failed attack, and Zikky's return to the Biosphere, Commander Hunter had set about reinforcing the station, and had sent for two more of the robots to assist his engineers with the further work on the ISS Venus structure. The final parts were now ready for assembly. They had also received the new laser gun that had been trialled on the F95S a month or so ago.

"Hi Professor, hope that you are all well, it seems a lot is going on right now. Just to let you and Ruth know that although Zikky has been selected for the trip to Attica with Commander Glen and Phillip, we need to take two of her robot team to accelerate the work on assembling the ISS Venus. I received instructions from HQ that we are to try to get the station ready so that we can use it as a holding station for the upcoming visits expected from our new friends from Attica. We only have a few weeks to complete. If agreeable, can you get them on the next launch leaving in the next 48 hours. If Ruth could get them briefed, our chief engineer will do the rest on arrival."

"Hello Norman, good to hear from you. Ruth and I are well, and trying to cope with all the recent exciting news. Yes, of course we must get ready for this amazing event. I am longing to see the new spacecraft that Attica are sending over. I cannot get up to the Orbiter I am afraid, but perhaps they will allow you to send pictures over to my secure screen in Biosphere 1?"

Josh continued before the Commander could respond. "On another more serious matter, we have reason to believe that you may endure another attack. Following our recent success in diverting a missile that was intended to destroy our HQ, we have been advised by our Attican friends that they suspect you may receive another attempt on trying to destroy you, or the Venus project. We are alerting Edwards Base, but you may also want to alert your defence system. I know it is new, but it has been trialled, and appears to be very effective. In the meantime, we shall continue to monitor any hostile activity, and deal with anything we consider suspicious."

"Thanks Professor, as you say we are going through an exciting time, but we shall remain vigilant, there are still people out there willing to destroy us. Will be in touch when we hear more from Commander Glen and Colonel Somester, who will be arriving here soon to prepare for the arrival of the Attican spacecraft. We are trying to get all the details we require for docking her. Not even sure if she needs any kind of fuel yet! Anyway, all will be revealed, I am sure."

****

Edwards Air Base—March 2077

Gary Westmorland, as the senior Captain, was taking charge of operations at the Base during the time the Commander would be preparing for his Attica trip. He had just heard the news that suspicious activity had been detected, and was awaiting further news from intelligence office. He was also made aware of the recent events surrounding the two Russian girls at the Biosphere, and was calling Captain Devonshire.

"Chris, can you and Robert get over here, we need to brief you and your team. Another storm is brewing!"

****

They were all now settled down in the mess room. Gary explained the recent activity to them. It was Chris who was first to respond, "Captain, we have been in constant touch with Helena and Athena since they returned to the Biosphere. They have challenged the Russian girls, and I think we can now be sure that they were passing on information to the ECAW group. There is no doubt that something is about to happen. The girls think that they may now try to abscond to one of their agent cells, and that maybe we should just let them. They believe they can monitor their movements which should bring us nearer to finding the main people behind recent attacks."

"Regarding the reported activity on the South China Sea islands, we would like to undertake a further surveillance with the F95S as soon as possible, I know you agree that we must not allow our enemies to thwart our plans for the ISS Venus, particularly with the imminent arrival of the Rotoship that is arriving to collect our Commander and Colonel Somester, and our first human robot, Zikky."

"You can be assured, Chris that I am with you both all the way. With my temporary authority, I can give you the go ahead on your plans. Please advise Helena and Athena that we agree with their recommendation regarding the Russian girls, and as far as using the F95S, you guys have shown you have her under control, so go ahead. I shall issue a release down to the Base controller now. Just check with him regarding the laser set up as it has not been checked since your return from McDill."

"Thanks Captain, we are on our way."

****

Krulandistan, March 2077

"I have just had news that our two agents in the Biosphere are in contact with our other agents in Wisconsin. This unit is near to the Canadian border from where we originally attacked the ISPEG factory. I am not happy for them to be there as they are obviously under suspicion, and it is possible that they will be followed. I think it is time to eliminate them. Ho Chi, have I your permission to contact our lady in New York?"

"Yes, I agree with you Kim Jong, they have had their chance, it is time to concentrate on how we can hurt the ISPEG programmes by other methods. We should put our thinking caps on. In meantime, let me know when you have contacted Yoko, and what plan she suggests for this job."

"OK Comrade Chairman. I can also advise you that we are going ahead with an attack on the Moon Orbiter very shortly. They are using the old Russian Soyez rockets which are cheap and expendable, but we asked them to paint them up with false insignia and codes. We have sent them a photo of the original spacecraft that we used for the other mission."

"Good, keep me informed as usual, Comrade."

New York, April 2077

Yoko Lin was enjoying her glass of champagne with her friend and lover Li Chung. The beautiful apartment overlooking the Hudson River was just one of the perks of being a top assassin for those who wished to pay her very substantial fees. Her freelance job with the New York Times allowed her plenty of scope to move around, and maintain a great life style. She heard her 'special' phone ringing in the next room.

"Li, I want to take that call, enjoy your drink and will be back with you shortly."

She listened quietly, and after a few minutes she put the phone down without comment.

"I told you I would be back soon Li, now where were we?"

On Board F95S—April 2077

"Rob, I have more definite news on the threat from the terrorist group. Apart from the South China Sea concern, they are evidently using the old Guantomino base in Cuba for another attack. They cannot have been aware that we bugged the base when our government decided to convert the site to more peaceful use some years ago. This ECAW group must have used a false company to purchase some of the land for space development, and a company linked to the space centre in Krulandistan has been on this site for a number of years. It may indicate that the two space centres are linked to this group. Anyway, we need to get some pictures quickly. Set the co-ordinates will you, and I will just check back on the laser and our fuel situation, so we are ready for a quick—"

He was interrupted by a shout from Robert, "Chris, get back here will you, we have a situation!"

"I had been looking at the monitored pictures ready to pin positions etc., but it looks as if we are too late to attack the site, a space rocket is already fired up, and looks as if it is ready for imminent take-off."

"OK Rob, I think the best solution is that we follow it into stratosphere and try to destroy it before it gets out into space. Buckle up Rob, and prime the laser, I am ready to take-off now."

****

The F95S was up in stratosphere, but the rocket was a now moving at its mid-speed, and they knew that soon it would reach a speed of 25000 miles hour ready for orbit. Chris was trying to line up the laser gun to a point that it would reach on a count of 10 seconds, otherwise it would be entering space. He signalled to Robert.

"Firing now, track beam on the screen, Rob."

"It is going out of our range so quickly Chris, the beam has just missed, but there was some reaction from the rocket, although it did not prevent it from continuing into space. Quick, send a message to the Orbiter."

****

Gateway Moon Orbiter, Same Day, April 2077

Captain Ann Broxbourne was at her intelligence post on the Orbiter and looking out the small windows at the work being completed on the new ISS Venus station alongside them, when her headphones suddenly crackled into life.

"Commander, we have an urgent message from Captain Devonshire. He believes a rocket craft is heading towards the Orbiter and may already be in orbit ready to strike."

"Thanks Ann, please try to identify on our screens, in meantime send out alarm, and advise all to go to action stations. Also, I understand our head robot Zikky has arrived already, so ensure she is protected."

All the Orbiter team were very aware that they had not completed the armoury on the new station and had only hand weapons which would be difficult to use against a rapidly approaching missile. The screens were being monitored very closely and with much concern.

Captain Broxbourne was back on the screens. "Commander, Zikky is with me now, but when I told her about the upcoming threat, she suggested a diversion plan. She is saying that with the new power supply they added to the Venus, they could move us all into a new orbit and this may not be detected by the rocket missile if it has been pre-coded to our current orbit position."

"Sounds as if it is worth a try, send her up please. Anyway, how long have we got Ann, is it on our orbit level yet?"

"It is not on our orbit as far as we can see at this moment, so we may have about 90 minutes assuming it is coming up to new orbit level on next time round."

Zikky had entered the commanders room as she finished speaking.

"Good afternoon, Commander, I hope you like my idea. As you know, I am involved in assembling the new power unit on the Venus, and thanks to Miss Helena and Dr Ruth there is a newly installed propulsion unit with considerably more power than you have in the current Orbiter."

"Hello Zikky, that is great news but we have very little time, can you power it up in time? We may have less than an hour before we expect contact from the missile."

"I am going right now, perhaps Captain Ann can prepare a space cord for me just in case I fall when working on the outside propulsion units."

"OK, go ahead, I will arrange that for you right now. Thanks, Zikky, your new IQ status is really working well. I know they will appreciate your new abilities when you get your chance to get to the new planet with Commander Glen."

Zikky had the Attican team of Efi and the girls to thank for her new status. Their knowledge had helped Ruth to push forward with the robot programme, and they were now nearly ready for her to meet with the Attican humanised robots.

****

ISPEG HQ. Later Same Day, April 2077

There was a huge tension in the ISPEG Boardroom. They were also monitoring the missile's orbit and final destination, and they could see that although it had been diverted from original orbit by the F95S laser attack, it was oncoming, and they appeared powerless to stop the pending disaster. Commander Worcester looked over to his right hand, Major Hank Fife.

"Hank, we are not able to intercept this missile now, and if it does hit the target, we shall have to not only put back our plans for Attica, but may lose some of our best officers and colleagues. In less than an hour we shall know where we stand, but it is surely time to ask Commander Glen to put the ECAW concerns to our new friends and see if they can help with steps to end these continuous conflicts and set about a world peace programme. We can then all concentrate on the Mars programme."

"Commander, there is some activity on the screen from the Orbiter which as you know is now attached to the partly constructed new ISS Venus, which is being prepared ready to receive the first Attica space craft. It appears to be moving out of the present position, although I did not think that possible without our support."

Commander Worcester picked up his transmitter to the Orbiter.

"Commander Hunter, sorry to break in at this critical time, but we seem to be detecting some movement of your station from the current set orbit. Can you advise position?"

"Yes, thanks Commander, we are still very much on alert, but I think Zikky has managed to power up the new ISS Venus propulsion unit and it is moving us all. I am now juggling with orbit controls to see if we can find a new stable position. We are hoping that the incoming missile has not identified the change in our position. We shall report back as soon as we can. Keep the line open."

****

Zikky was getting concerned. She was trained to detect danger and had been briefed on a number of emergency situations, but this was not something that the new ISS was ready for. She continued to work on the power source of the new ISS unit, and now could detect that there was definitely some movement taking place. However, she could also now detect on the phonograph on her sleeve that there was a large craft approaching, and it did look to be making directly for the Orbiter. She opened up the voice phone.

"Commander, I am having some success with the power unit, but the object still appears to bel heading towards us, please advise and prepare for possible contact."

"OK Zikky, you are doing a great job with that power unit, we are moving. I am trying to get us into a new orbit. Come inside now, and get back to the main

Orbiter room urgently, we only have minutes before the spacecraft reaches us, so we need to get into the emergency unit urgently."

Madison, Canada, April 2077

Yoko Lin was now settled into the Sheraton hotel with Li Chung. She was patiently waiting for the arrival of the two targets that Kim Jong had advised would arrive shortly from Wisconsin, thinking they were in a safe haven following the recent attack on the ISPEG's Moon Orbiter. The attack had not been a success, and only resulted in the spacecraft being destroyed as it missed its target and became broken up as it dropped into the Earth's atmosphere. However, the West had certainly detected the origin of the flight, and that it was the same type of craft that had been hijacked some months earlier. As ISPEG now had identified Irina and Lara as being ECAW agents, their superiors in Wisconsin had given them immediate orders to flee, and they were given names of two contacts in Canada who, they were told, would look after them until things settled down.

Irina and Lara were in fact just arriving at the hotel reception.

"Good evening, we are looking for Yoko Lin, who is expecting us?"

The hotel reception porter picked up the phone.

"Miss Lin, two girls have arrived and asked for you, but did not give their names, are you happy for us to send them to your room?"

Irina and Lara made their way to the suite that was room 930, and as they entered, were amazed at the luxury of the rooms, and the exotic dresses that the hosts were wearing. It was Yoko who opened the conversation.

"Please make yourself comfortable, shortly you will be able to take a shower and rest in the next room. First though, you may like a drink after your journey."

The girls were only too glad to take some white wine and were looking forward to the shower, it all seemed like another world, they had only been used to living in university style rooms, or the basic rooms at the Biosphere. Their accommodation in Russia had not even reached those standards. Yoko now turned to her girlfriend.

"Li Chung, will you see if our Canadian friends have arrived, because although I could easily arrange for these girls to disappear, I have been ordered to pass the girls over to them after they have rested and showered."

＊＊＊＊＊＊＊＊＊＊＊＊

Somewhere in Canada, April 2077

Following the recent attack on the new ISS station, Helena and Athena had agreed with ISPEG HQ that there was no doubt now that the Russian girls were agents and had been involved in passing on information and endeavouring to seduce the two lieutenants. They had asked permission to follow them more closely, hoping that they would now lead them to their handlers.

"Athena, I have found the girls, they are now visiting someone in the Sheraton hotel in a place called Madison. We know there must be other agents there, and they were probably involved in the damage to the ISS parts factory some time ago."

"I sense that these girls may now be in danger as their leaders will think that they are liable to be caught and questioned, thus giving away their HQ."

"Same sense is coming to me Helena, shall we devise a plan, it will need to be immediate if they are in danger. Do we really want to save them?"

"I would like us to try and save them so we can possibly extract information, or even convert them to work for us. It is part of our plan to bring a peaceful solution to the Earth's problems, so we can speed up working on the 'Marsattica' programme. Let us call Chris and ask to get us to this place without delay."

****

Madison, Canada, April 2077

Irina and Lara were feeling sleepy after the wine and the shower. Irina was a little concerned. She looked over to Yoko and Li, both lying on the couch and seeming to be in good spirits.

"Sorry we are not more fun; do you think we may go to our room to rest for a while before our safe house people arrive?"

"You certainly can, girls, don't worry, we shall wake you when they arrive."

****

Helena and Athena had been given priority transport and had already arrived in Madison. They were in time to detect two males whom they suspected were agents, and they were now approaching the hotel. Their sixth sense told them that they were not there to just talk to the Russian girls, and Chris and Robert had given them a good understanding of what could happen with these types of conflicts.

****

Irina and Lara had just taken a shower, but were still feeling drowsy. They could not appreciate the luxurious bedroom and the view. Irina went over to the mini bar to get some water before they took a rest. Suddenly a tap on the window!

Irina tried to focus. She stood there in disbelief.

"Lara, it can't be, that looks like those Greek girls have followed us, and must be on the balcony. How did they get here, and more important, why are they here? We seem to be already in trouble and I am still finding it difficult to focus."

At that moment, Helena and Athena pushed through the balcony doors. Before the girls could move to the door, they softly called out.

"Stay quiet, we are not here to hurt you, believe us. You are in serious trouble and we believe that two of your other agents have arrived to take you away, and possibly kill you, to prevent you passing on information regarding their leaders. You are probably already drugged? Do you feel any symptoms? You certainly do not look healthy."

"How do you know these things, and how did you get onto our 9 floor balcony? Why should we believe you?"

"More of that later, but we do not have much time if we are to save you. So, lock the door, and just listen for a few minutes, and we shall make a plan."

****

Larry Togue and Grad Mason were enjoying their drinks with Yoko and Li. They had been told that the two Russian girls had already been drugged, and were probably now ready for them to take away and arrange disposal of the bodies. Larry saw an opportunity.

"That gives us a little time for some fun Yoko, how about it?"

"Li and I are not interested. We do not go out with men."

"Well, what about the girls, can we have some fun with them before we complete the job?"

118

"I guess that may be possible, but be quick. We do not want any problems, the quicker you are out the better, otherwise the drugs may lose effect."

****

Helena was working on identifying the drug, and in the meantime was getting the girls to take large quantities of water to push the poisons through their systems. A knock on the door.

"Athena, check the camera on the door panel, I think that this is trouble."

"It is the two big guys that we saw earlier. Do you think Yoko sent for them?"

Lara spoke up. She had seen that the Greek girls were in fact trying to help them, and was certain now that they had been drugged, and were probably being set up for a disappearing act.

"They certainly may be after us as we are no longer trusted, or of value to the group. Can you really help us?"

Another knock. "Open up, girls, we are here to take you to our safe house in Winnipeg."

Helena gestured to Athena to get behind the door, and told her to put the girls on the bed. She then told Irina to call out to them, as she unlocked the door.

****

Krulandistan, May 2077

Chairman Ho Chi Dae was enjoying another one of his trips, and his yacht had just anchored off the port of Constanta after a leisurely short voyage with his escort girls on the Black Sea. He was just about to take dinner with his favourite girl, Sanya, when his satellite phone rang on the middle deck. He turned to the girl and told her to go to the dining area on the sun deck, he would be there shortly. One of the crew had already answered the phone.

"Chairman, it is Kim Jong, he says he needs to speak to you urgently."

Ho Chi did not like to be disturbed at this time, even by his own right-hand man. "Hello Kim Jong, what is so important that you need to call me at this time?"

"We have a big problem, Ho Chi, our two girl agents have disappeared, and Yoko Lin reports finding our two Canadian agents dead in the hotel room next to where she was staying. She had drugged the girls, but somehow, they must

119

have overcome the agents before leaving, although she did not hear anything, and only became suspicious when the Canadians did not return in the hour. I am very concerned that there is no sign of the girls. If they did kill the two men, then that would mean they may be trying to defect from our cause."

"It is hard to believe they could do that, as Yoko is saying that both girls were already drugged, and there were no signs of how these guys died. Also, these girls have been an invaluable source of information up to now, why would they suddenly change allegiance?"

"This is dreadful news. You must prepare a full search for them in the USA and Canada, we need to ensure that they do not talk. Get Yoko and our other assassination group together. This is priority. Also start alerting our agents and ask them to be prepared, we may have to move some of our bases. Do you think our business in Krulandistan is safe if there is a leak?"

"I shall get onto the search and alert instructions without alarming our agents too much. Regarding our base here in Krulandistan, I am not aware that the girls know of the actual address or nature of our business here, as they only made contact by a special phone, therefore I feel this is our best cover for the moment."

"OK, go ahead, Kim Jong, I am giving instructions to my crew to get me back to the Base, and should be with you in two days. Keep me advised."

Ho Chi had gone right off thoughts of dinner, and even his Sanya was going to have a restful night.

****

Edwards Air Base, California, May 2077

Irina and Lara had been taken back to California. Helena had called ahead to the base and asked that Chris and Robert could be there so that they could explain what was in their minds regarding the next line of action. The Russian girls had recovered and were now aware that they had indeed been saved, and were now sitting in the Commander's office, unusually quiet.

Chris and Robert entered the room with Captain Westmorland. Chris turned to talk to Helena and Athena.

"Rob and I are so delighted to see you both back safely. We have prepared rooms for you to stay over the next few days, but in the meantime, Captain Westmorland wants to question the Russian girls and hear what you are suggesting regarding their future."

"Miss Ivanov and Miss Gorinski. I am Senior Captain Gary Westmorland, the temporary head of this Base, and I have been authorised to question you regarding recent events where we believe you were involved."

"You are here under house arrest for being suspected members of an organisation that has been branded as a terrorist group, and we believe has been responsible for recent attacks on ISPEG and other Western property and persons. Our two scientists here, namely Helena Poulakis and Athena Balakakis, have bravely extracted you from a potentially nasty death because they believe that you can help us to track those responsible for these recent attacks."

"Before we hear from them, we would ask you to give your side of the story, and to advise us if we may rely on you now to assist us in ending these attacks, and thus restore a world peace which is important to our future plans. If so, you would be given every protection, and although you will be under surveillance for some time, you will not have to spend your time in one of our prisons."

Irina rose from her chair.

"We both can see that our extraction from Madison was indeed miraculous. We both had hated Helena and Athena because they were always ahead of us and getting in the way of the plans that we had been told to execute for the cause. We know now that this was cruel and are very glad that our original plan to exterminate them failed. They were so kind to us in Madison, and how they disposed of the two thugs who were sent to kill us was difficult for us to understand. We were already dizzy, and just remember that they used some kind of laser gun on them. How they got us to ground level is also a mystery, as we do not remember going downstairs through the lobby. It is clear that they have some ability that is beyond our understanding."

Lara then stood up. "Exactly, as Irina says, we were just amazed at what was happening. It is certainly clear that we are now considered a risk to the movement. Irina and I were taken from our homes at an early age and a commune in Russia trained us to be part of this worldwide communist cause. However, we are now starting to see, as we grow older, that some of our actions have been petty and of no value to the world generally. It seems that the only people who are benefitting are the party leaders and their cronies. We both now feel that this cannot be right, as we have been able to see how your country is run and how free the people feel, and how they can earn money based on their ability."

"We have spoken about this since the Canadian incident, and are ready to end this part of our life, and try to be better people. We have been driven into some bad ways in our lives, but trust you will forgive us, and give us an opportunity to move on. Maybe we can now be of some help in your plans."

Helena and Athena now rose together, and looked towards the captain.

"Captain Westmorland, we both feel that we need to discuss the girl's comments with you in more detail, so perhaps we could adjourn this meeting for now. In the meantime, we assume you will keep the girls under house arrest so that not least, they are protected until we have had a chance to review their comments and make our next plan."

The Russian girls were taken away, and Chris, Rob and the Captain were now alone with Helena and Athena, who now were ready to continue. Helena as usual was first to speak.

"There is every reason to believe we can start to rely on the girls for more information, although they do not know exact detail of the organisation's headquarters. I am sure we can deduct where the source is after some questions, but here is a suggestion for you all to consider."

"Your Commander is now in Attica with our people, and we are pleased to advise he has been well received. Ziggy has also been introduced to our robot team leaders, and we understand that they have been surprised at her quick understanding of the advanced programmes that we have developed in the last fifty years. Working on Mars has been an extraordinary learning phase for our planet. So, before they return, we have been thinking seriously of asking them to talk to our Cabinet about a plan to invade the Earth."

Helena was not able to continue as a gasp came from them all, and they all looked at her and Athena as if they had not heard this correctly. However, she smiled and looked back at them.

"Yes, it does sound as if we are terrorists instead of your friends, but, let me finish. Athena and I have been studying your history of the last two hundred years and looking in particular at the wars between the people. Many are not really settled today, and your extreme communist enemies are an example. One thing that stands out is that when one of your countries are under attack, the people are inclined to suddenly forget any differences they may have, and unite against a common enemy. Hope you can now see where we are going with our suggestion?"

Chris now intervened. "So, Helena, I think you are saying that although you will appear to be invading the earth, you will be threatening, rather than actually causing harm. By this means, you hope to unite the Earth's people to become more aware that they are vulnerable to an unknown force, and they better start talking to each other about uniting. If this is so, we may also be able to force out the ECAW cells, and rid ourselves of these extreme elements. I still believe we may have to eliminate leaders of these extreme groups, a tiger's spots don't change, and although they may give in, I think they are more likely to use whatever power they have left to attempt to destroy anyone they see as a threat to them."

Athena now took up the conversation.

"Helena and I are suggesting that we ask our Cabinet to prepare to send two of our Rotoships to the Earth and enter the atmosphere. They would be prepared to appear in various areas of the planet, and therefore will be seen by many people. This would lead to them being reported as UFO's. However, this time, the people would be told over news casts that these are not unidentified craft, but potential enemies of the Earth. We can at the same time ask Commander Glen, after speaking to your presidents and prime ministers, to talk to the world's press."

"He could then clarify that they have actually been in touch with the owners of these spacecraft, identified that they are aliens, and warn everyone that they may be preparing to invade. He will emphasise that these aliens have recently been identified, and all of our governments are uniting to find an answer to this threat."

After a pause for them to take this in, Athena continued, "To enable the Rotoships to move speedily in and out of the sky we need to ensure the two spacecraft can lock onto the new Venus ISS station, and become invisible while they are resting crew, and deciding on next move."

Gary now looked around the group, he had been stunned by this plan, it was so far ahead of anything they could have envisaged just a few years ago.

"Well, this is a remarkable suggestion of a plan, but I know this is part of a strategy that should lead to attaining Attica's aims, that of bringing our planets together in one cause, and when the time comes, to be able to live in harmony on another planet. Surely, we need to attain some final peace in this world of ours."

"OK, so let us now put something on our Krypton computers, and if we all agree, we can then send this proposal to our superiors in Washington and London, and to Commander Glen, so they are able to understand the motive, and give their blessing to this move."

They all nodded, and the girls smiled reassuringly.

Washington, June, 2077

President John Cable and the Vice President were sitting with UK Prime Minister Harry Sutton, the Foreign Secretary, Sir Leonard Berks, and Helena and Athena, who, following the conversation they had had with senior Captain Westmorland, were extended a special invitation.

They had decided to hold information to other leading G12 countries until they had finalised a plan, and maybe even after they had started action. They could not be sure of their support or even that they would be believed at this stage.

"Gentlemen, I have introduced the ladies to you. They have a plan to start the first stage of the Marsattica Agreement. Please listen carefully, and we shall take questions at the end of their presentation."

****

Part Two

Washington DC, February 2078

"This is NBC news on Monday, 20 February. Good morning. Abe Parato reporting. There have been worldwide concerns and some hysteria following the apparent sightings of UFOs in many regions."

"The world's governments have united in trying to identify the objects. In previous reports of this kind, the sightings have been put down to unusual cloud formations, or air force activity with new test equipment. The Russian and Chinese governments are asking the USA and European ambassadors to arrange immediate talks to discuss these reports and wish to confirm that these objects are not instigated by them. They have stressed that they continue to be firmly supportive of the peace agreement as signed in 2062 with the Western powers and wish to be involved in solutions to this apparent threat."

"There has not been any announcement made by any terrorist groups, who have been active recently in attacking important military sites."

"We shall keep you in touch with latest news, folks, so keep listening to our NBC special broadcasts throughout the day."

London, February 2078

A similar message was being broadcast some hours later from the BBC head offices in London.

"This is Gary Hutchings reporting from London. Over the weekend, there were several reported sightings of UFOs that appear to be more realistic than previous reports. Some photographs suggest that these vessels were very similar to the flying saucer concepts that have been reported in the past, but never substantiated. The government is to make a statement later today, but in the meantime asks that everyone remain calm. We shall be on the air at 19.00 hours for a special bulletin."

The BBC were not able to show the photos that day, but computer media around the world already had the pictures and the comments. There were definitely signs of fear in many of the comments, as most people really did think that the photos were genuine; in addition, many had seen lights emit from some of the craft.

Attica, Earth time, February 2078

The Cabinet were in full session. The assembly had been made aware of the plan for the Marsattica Agreement and were quite excited as they waited for the result of the first phase of the plan.

General Hermes was now talking to Chairman Isis and the main Cabinet officials.

"We can confirm that four of our Rotoships arrived to orbit the planet Earth two days ago and were able to lock onto their new Venus ISS orbiter thanks to some great work by our robot team, with good support from their head robot Ziggy, and from their Commander Glen and Colonel Somester. I trust the Cabinet will convey our thanks to them, and also advise them of how grateful we are for them making these long journeys on our spacecraft so that we could start this adventure."

Chairman Isis Parapoulis rose from his platform throne chair.

"Dimitris, you have been part of that first success, and we all thank you for your planning. We shall certainly convey our appreciation of the assistance we received from their representatives."

"We now have been asked to send a message to all the heads of the governments on Earth, which will hold a threat that we intend to invade the Earth if a certain terrorist group is still in existence by the end of one earth year. The friendly governments that we are already in contact with know that this is part of the larger plan, but will still respond as if the threat is real. They need to negotiate with the Chinese, Korean and Russian governments to assure them of the common goal of a world peace, and seek their assistance in overcoming any threat to that aim. Hopefully this will lead to identifying the terrorist cells, and either have them eliminated, or have them handed over to us. If they choose to fight, we are agreed that we shall have to eliminate them."

"However, our main aim is to capture them and bring them back to Attica where we shall put them through one of our conversion operations which we have used in the past to overcome our own problems with criminal activity. General, please ensure all involved are aware of that procedure, and check with Commander Glen that he agrees this to be a reasonable strategy. I assume Captain Panomosis and our agents already on the Earth are fully in the picture?"

"Thank you, Chairman and colleagues, our contacts on Earth are all aware of the plan, and are keeping our contacts fully briefed. We shall be making a further flight into the Earth's atmosphere in the next few Earth days and this time we are going to use our advanced laser to attack a false target that I have had set up by our American friends in their Atlantic Ocean. We believe this will help to frighten the terrorists, and show that we do have the strength to attack accurately and without response. It should also assist the governments to bring their people together when they later explain that they do have contact with us, and the main plan is to work together for world peace. We shall keep you updated through Spiros as usual."

****

Washington, London, Moscow and Beijing, March 2078

All of the news and social media were humming with the latest sightings of the flying saucer spacecraft and the news of the attack on a ship making a routine crossing of the Atlantic Ocean. There had been no confirmation of how many dead, but the pictures showed clearly that the ship had been totally destroyed. The report quoted that another support ship some 50 miles away had seen this flying saucer object eject a beam or flame in the direction of the damaged ship.

Their own ship had experienced technical computer interference, and were not able to respond. The US and UK Naval authorities were alerted but were not able to detect the offending plane or spacecraft. Worldwide alerts have been sent to all the major countries governments. Whereas China and Russia continue to be friendly, they have again insisted that they need immediate talks with the Western heads of state to identify the threat and agree on a solution.

London, April 2078

There were six countries represented in the cosy atmosphere of the UK Prime Minister's residence in the hilly countryside just 40 miles out of London. It had been decided it was an ideal place for East and Western powers to meet. Despite the comfortable surroundings, there was a high degree of tension in the room. President Xi Chun of China was first to respond to the UK Minister's reception speech.

"We are very concerned regarding this recent incident and need your assurance that this, and other recent incidents, were not instigated by European or American forces, as this would set us back on the 2076 peace agreement, which we do wish to continue and expand over the next years as we move to more joint work on inter-planetary travel."

Prime Minister Antony Cornish now rose at the table. "Ladies and gentlemen, I have spoken over the last few days with US President Cable, and all my opposite numbers in Europe, and can assure you that this is not in any way an attack on you. These recent incidents are certainly from an outside source, and we believe after studying them that there could be more attacks in the future. We need to unite our efforts worldwide if we are to succeed in stopping further problems. There is good intelligence information to believe that the UFOs are real and from another source, and we are following up on that theory. We promise to keep you fully informed, and trust that all here will share any data that may arise in their intelligence investigations."

At that moment, the Prime Minister's secretary entered the room looking very agitated. "Sir, I need to talk to you urgently on a matter affecting your meeting."

"What is it Peter, if it is affecting this meeting then we all need to hear, fire away!"

Peter Surrey was stumbling to get the words out fast enough, unlike his usual calm manner. "Madam, Gentlemen, we have just received a report from our intelligence HQ, and they have asked me to convey this message to you immediately. I have the recording as received by them today. Please listen."

"This is the planet of Attica calling the governments of the planet Earth. Over the last few days we have demonstrated our ability to enter your planet and create a hostile action. We have an ability to attack and destroy the Earth's cities. However, this is not our preferred strategy. It is our wish to create a better relationship. This cannot be undertaken until the Earth's governments remove the threat of terrorism between their own people. We have no desire to be associated with a planet that cannot achieve a peace with their people."

"We believe we may be able to help remove extreme groups that are making your task for peace difficult, and in the next few days we shall send a representative to you who will discuss this offer. In the meantime, we are monitoring all activity on your planet, and must re-iterate that we are in a position to take action if we see any movements that appears to be hostile to our representative, or to our spacecraft."

The whole room had gone very quiet. Russian President, Boris Cheknova, was the first to recover.

"How do we know that this message is genuine, where is this planet Attica? Certainly, we would be happy to remove terrorist threats from all of our regions, but if this is genuine, how can they help us?"

The Prime Minister now saw that he had to intervene before the Russians and Chinese became too suspicious.

"I am aware that our friends from Russia and China are finding it difficult to understand that these beings from this strange planet would contact us first, but we have been the targets of the recent acts of terrorism, and they appear to have identified that we have to be interested in receiving their help. We shall of course be checking all the message detail and origins, and looking for this representative that they mention. It is certainly very hard for us to take in at this time, but it does look as if this planet does exist, and over the next days we shall increase our search, and report to you."

"I think you will agree that this message, if proved to be genuine, should remain strictly confidential at this stage, as it may create worldwide panic if it is reported in the media. As promised earlier, we shall pass on any news relating to this mysterious approach. Whereas you will all probably wish to place your armed forces on high alert, I recommend not revealing the actual reason at this time. Can we all agree on this strategy?"

President Xi Chun now had risen. He had been very thoughtful throughout the meeting but now looked around him.

"Thank you, Prime Minister, we are of course very suspicious about this mysterious message, which apparently is from a planet that we have not even identified. However, although as you know we do have differences on our ideals for our people, we do not support extreme communism, and feel sure that our Russian friends agree. We both have spent the last forty years in repairing the damage of previous generations by installing a model that is similar to the original Swedish welfare state. We still have some communist ideals, but you can see that we now have more open trading and movements in our respective countries. After the Hong Kong fiasco and the Ukraine offensives in the 20s and 30s, plus the climate change difficulties affecting us all, we have moved on."

"So, if this planet is real, and they really do have advanced technology, then of course we should talk rather than fight. We shall watch developments with interest over next few days, and shall agree with your wish for this message and this meeting to remain confidential within our own top government officials. Please arrange for my transport so I can return to Beijing as soon as possible. On my return, I shall await your call for further news."

All the Europeans had listened intently to this, and just nodded their approval to the plan. President Cheknova also now appeared to be calmer after hearing from the Chinese President, and also nodded his approval. The Prime Minister rose again.

"Thank you all, as promised we shall be in touch as soon as there is more news. Have a good journey home. Please check all your coded contact details with Secretary Surrey as you leave."

∗∗∗∗∗∗∗∗∗∗∗∗

Edwards Base, California, May, 2078

Commander Glen and Captain Westmorland were in the mess room talking to Chris and Robert. The commander started the conversation, he was looking refreshed after a few days on the West Coast, following his recent demanding trip to Attica.

"Chris, Robert, please can you ask Captain Panomosis, Helena and Athena, to arrange to meet us here for a discussion with the ambassadors of the major nations, which follows the recent meeting of the heads of state in London last month? We are going to make the ambassadors aware that the Attica people are now in contact, and then introduce them. They are going to be a little bewildered at first, so our stories have to be solid, so that trust is built. We have to get on with the job of attacking the terrorist cells, and either eliminate or capture those involved. Those that are captured will be interrogated here, but then sent to Attica as promised so that they can be converted, as indicated in our first meeting. It is important that we continue to put pressure on the Eastern Block governments, as we shall need their help if we are to attain the first goal of the 'Marsattica' agreement, removing terrorism."

"If they are positive, we shall offer them the opportunity for a representative to visit Attica so that they can understand the formidable force that they represent in not only weaponry and space vehicles, but also in science and IQ. It may be also a time then to reveal that Attica has already established a city on Mars, that is working, and is ready to receive the first of the Earth's selected people who wish to be integrated with the present Attica population."

"However, if there is negativity from certain quarters then we may have to prepare some more convincing arguments, and not even rule out making a special demonstration of the Attica spacecraft in their regions, so that their citizens have no doubt of the power and threat that this new planet would have on our whole world. Peace can come with fulfilling the agreement that has been accepted by all those senior figures who attended the London conference last month."

Chris rose from the table. "OK Commander, we are having dinner with them all tonight, and will liaise with your secretary on timing when we have discussed this further, and agreed a strategy for the meeting. On another point, may we talk to the Russian girls again, we are anxious to start work on identifying these ECAW cells."

"You have our support in that goal Captain, you and Robert may discuss this further with Helena and Athena, and of course Captain Panomosis. First though, we look forward to hearing about timing for the ambassadors meeting, you will appreciate there is much to be arranged in a short time."

****

Ho Chi was back in the office, and he was deciding on action following reports that he had received from his cells regarding the sightings of the UFOs and other world news. He shouted down the office.

"Kim Jong, can you come here, we have much to discuss!"

"I am here Chairman Comrade, I have also seen the news, what are your instructions?"

"I am not sure about these UFOs, are they a hoax, was the film of the attack on the un-named ship real?"

"We cannot be 100% sure at this point but what we have seen so far leads us to be suspicious. If there are unknown spacecraft able to enter the Earth's atmosphere, they would need an orbital docking area somewhere that enables them to come and go, including any form of re-fuelling, not to mention astronaut's requirements for sustenance, etc."

"Good point chairman, and if that is so, it can only be a space station, and we know where they are. We have failed to date in our efforts to eliminate the Venus station, but let us take a closer look at the latest surveillance from our satellite to see if we have missed anything that may be happening that relates to these stories. In any case, we should prepare for another attack which may be more intense. If the captured Russian agents do give any more information to the Western authorities, then we should think about moving our base. I suggest we look at using all the facility we have here to launch a last effort of defiance, and then plan a move to the Chinese Islands where we have some protection."

Kim Jong was already thinking ahead as he was speaking, and a plan was already forming in his mind. If they had to move, they may have to sacrifice some of the staff on the airfield, and he would prefer that these people were not his staff. He continued, "I am going to set up a plan to close the airfield for a few days, advising clients that we are making safety checks on the site and facilities. In that time, I am going to try to employ a few of their staff to help us. I hope to persuade them to give me and our staff access to their spacecraft on the pretence of checking out that they all comply with our newest strict field regulations. I then have a plan that I believe will meet your wishes for a worldwide eye-catching event that will hit the front pages of the international press."

****

Chris had recently moved to a larger home in Bakersfield as he had been seriously thinking of possible prospects with Helena, and at the same time had plenty of space for his parents and Robert when they visited, which was much more frequently since the recent important meetings with world figures. He was now feeling happy that he had made the move as there were now a much larger number of people in the house this evening than he had expected at any one time. Apart from his family, and Robert and his family, he was delighted to see Helena and Athena sitting comfortably with them as he entered the main sitting room.

He crossed the room to Helena and gave her a quick kiss on the cheek. Was this the first one? He thought so. She and Athena looked at him. Yes, it obviously was! He changed the subject.

"Hello again everyone, how do you like the new house? I hope you will come more often now there is more room. However, tonight I know we all have a more serious topic to discuss. So, I have arranged a dinner to be brought in so we can relax and talk and not worry about the cooking or cleaning."

Chris's father now responded. The professor was looking very good for his 60 years and was still very much involved in the Biosphere major works, not least in bringing their knowledge up to date following the regular discussions with Helena.

"Thank you, Son, as usual you and Robert have been busy, and in turn that has made my friends Phillip and Dawn, and of course my dear wife Ruth, very involved in this new venture. I would like to take this opportunity to also say how marvellous Helena and Athena have been, not only fitting into our way of life, but bringing us such new knowledge and help. Although she is not with us tonight, we should also thank Captain Panomosis for her courage and help in establishing that Attica is a live planet, and for her assistance with the ISPEG space programme."

Helena, looking very happy after the surprise of something she had not experienced for a time, the thing they called the kiss, but was nevertheless recovered, and turned to respond in her usual professional manner.

"Thanks Professor, Athena and I have been surprised and delighted with our time on your planet, and hope we can now move on to completing the Marsattica agreement. We shall certainly pass on your kind remarks to Efi, she will appreciate your comments. Before we start our main meeting, we both are a little concerned that the ECAW people have not all been detected. We did obtain information from the Russian girls, who incidentally are now back in the Biosphere under our surveillance, and that should enable us to find the Canadian and Cuban cells. The New York assassin team that they encountered must know of the headquarters as they do receive direct orders from that source, and we have asked the NY police to arrest those two agents so that you can interrogate them as soon as possible. Our sixth sense is already indicating that there is a further imminent threat from the main ECAW source."

"OK Helena, we shall take immediate steps to transfer your concerns and put all our satellites and contacts on full alert. Now, Chris, if we are ready for dinner?"

They could all see this being a long evening.

****

New York, May 2078

The New York police had been very quick to see the opportunity to help the ISPEG authorities, and be involved in the press headlines. They also hoped that ISPEG would share more information regarding the recent reports about UFOs, so they could prepare for any emergency that may arise. Captain Dan Plymouth had his best team down on the job. He was also in liaison with his Canadian counterparts, hoping that they could capture all the ECAW agents in one consolidated swoop.

He was now briefing his men, and on the large screen in front of them, they were transferring this information to the Canadians who were intently watching and listening back in Toronto.

"Tomorrow, 26 May, we shall enter the premises of the Sheraton hotel and surround the area to ensure the two agents cannot escape. We shall not give any warning to the management as we cannot be sure they are not protecting these people. Our colleagues in Toronto have the two addresses that we have received from ISPEG and we are asking them through this briefing to endeavour to make their entry without any pre-warning, and to hopefully make arrests without gunfire. In all cases, we have been asked to capture and arrest these suspects and try to keep them alive and ready to be interrogated by the ISPEG security team. We shall all be in transmission contact throughout the day. Please advise me if there are any concerns, or last-minute changes needed for the outlined plans."

The voice of Canada's head of security, Captain Ronald Germand, was now heard as he came to the front of the screen.

"All fine Dan, we have all the information and will be in touch with you constantly throughout the operation. We, like you, would love to make this operation work as a joint effort and pick up some better press—we need it."

****

Krulandistan, 2 June 2078

"The plan is in place, Chairman. We have convinced our clients that we need two days for security and cleaning operations and the field will be closed from tomorrow so that we can prepare the satellite rockets for action. We shall use mostly our own staff but have also taken on a few more technical people from our client's staff advising them that we may need second opinions, etc. We shall actually be asking them to set up dummy flight data for at least six of the rockets, the detail of which we shall retain as we may have to eliminate these people after the work and launches are complete."

He continued, "I have another plan to discuss with you relating to the two Greek girls that captured our two wayward Russian girls. They have been a considerable nuisance to our plans, it is time to take them out. I feel that somehow, they are also involved with the recent threats that allegedly are coming from another planet."

"I shall be happy to hear final plans, Kim Jong. In the meantime, I am alerting all our cells in the world to be prepared for demonstrations against our cause and to seek cover until we can assess our next move."

****

Beijing, China, June 2078

President Xi Chun and his senior military staff were looking at satellite pictures taken over the last few months. Their top general, Chao Feng, had indicated to the President that he thought there was some truth in the recent press releases, and the message from the new planet could actually be real. They had detected movements in space that were vague, but never the less had concerned them, as they could not identify what had caused them. Strange noises and ghostly shadows had been detected, and now the pictures of the alien craft had been analysed there was good reason to believe them authentic. Chao was speaking now.

"My President, I respectfully seek your permission to undertake some action relating to the above. I believe the breakaway groups that named themselves ECAW after our transition to our new age democracy are behind recent attacks on the West, and these attacks are increasing. We have identified some unusual activity in Krulandistan, where our people have been asked to undertake some work for the owners of the satellite launching centre, and it does look a little suspicious. We already believe there have been launches from this site and others in our South China Sea that tried to upset the balance that we have achieved with the West over the past 20 years."

"The message from the planet Attica, that we now believe is real, indicates that they are interested in helping not only the West, but also all of us with our Mars project, depending on our ability to bring some world peace. In that regard you are aware that Russia, Korea, Iran, and ourselves, have already established good relations with our Western counterparts, and trading and political meetings are set up on a regular basis. What I am now requesting is that I meet with our counterparts in the USA and UK and plan with them to make a strategic assault on this final threat to our world peace order. I believe that at such a meeting we shall also find out more about Attica from the American authorities, as there are indications that they already have some communication with them."

"Go ahead, General, we have already discussed this with our elected chamber, and your comments are welcome. Ensure you keep us informed of all actions. We particularly wish to pursue our Mars programme. As you are aware we have a base, but our technology is still poor, and we cannot yet sustain any regular habitation. This planet Attica has yet to be confirmed, but if real as we suspect, the inhabitants must obviously have advanced technology if they are able to transmit these messages, and send undetected space craft to our atmosphere."

****

California, June 2078

Helena and Athena were now in their own apartment in Bakersville and were having the opportunity to discuss recent events in their own language. They had sent for Efi to join them, and they all were relaxing after the very hectic days they had all experienced in the last months. Helena as usual started the conversation.

"Efi, before we ask you a few questions, we have been asked to tell you how much the ISPEG personnel, under Professor Devonshire, have appreciated your work here, and how you have adapted to the different conditions. You have been a great help to all of us. Now you have had some time on the space station, and met many of the Earth's military people. How has it been, and what do you think about the final plans for the Attica Agreement?"

Efi did not rise from the sofa, it was so comfortable after the time she had endured on the space station. She did find her arms being a little hindrance in this new environment, but she felt content.

"Well, it has been a little harder for their people to understand me, my language box has of course enabled me to converse quite well, but my appearance has surprised many, and it takes a little time for them to accept me as 'normal'. However, I am impressed with all the people that I have met and am sure they all want a closer peaceful relationship. The idea of speeding up our plans for Mars, and helping with our fertility programme, all appear to be attainable."

Helena then was ready to respond. "That is good, Efi, but we have some real problems to solve to enable us to ask our leaders to go to the next stage. We are lucky that Chris and Robert, and of course their families, are all very helpful, and it is clear that Athena and I are feeling particularly close to Chris and Robert. It would be great if we can develop a new life together, but first let us look at the problems ahead. What do you see, Athena?"

"You are right, Helena, we are moving to a close relationship with Chris and Robert, but it will only make sense if we can remove the elements that are unsettling the Earth's peace. I have just heard that the Chinese are sending a contingent to Washington to meet leaders of the USA and UK, as they are sure that the group known as ECAW is again behind the recent attacks and disturbances. They want to assist in removing the cells that are evidently based in areas close to their country. They say that they are now believing that there is a planet Attica, and that they have enough evidence to indicate a potential alien presence. I suggest we speed up the support plan by allowing representatives of the Chinese, Russians, Koreans, and the new Iranian government, to take a trip to the Venus station, where we can demonstrate, with some care, the advanced technology of our Rotoships."

Helena was obviously in agreement and now looked back at Efi and Athena, "OK, let us enjoy today together relaxing with our own company, and tomorrow we can ask the Commander and the boys to discuss the Chinese move, and other matters relating to catching and stopping this ECAW group forever."

****

Caesars Hotel, Las Vegas, June 2078

"How far is it to Bakersville?"

Yoko Lin and Son Ming were settled in their luxury room and looking at the task ahead. Yoko had escaped the attack from the NY police by disguising herself as a housemaid, but the police had caught her partner and she had to believe that she was being interrogated and therefore time for this task was of the essence. Kim Jong had made it clear that there was going to be a big event that would upset the Western powers, but her job now was to work with the local cell to eliminate the Greek girls who had kidnapped Irina and Lara. Her new contact Son Ming looked up from the bed.

"It will only take two hours to Bakersville, as our cell has managed to procure a heli-taxi, and are busy now getting a weapon loaded. We have identified the apartment area where the targets are located, and so be ready to take off in two hours."

Yoko looked over to her new accomplice. "Just a little time for a cuddle then." She had already dismissed Li Chung from her mind.

****

Chris Devonshire's Home, Bakersville, Same Evening, June 2078

Chris and Robert were also resting after all the recent activity, knowing that they had a very busy schedule coming in the next few weeks. They sat comfortably looking at the 49ers playing the Diamonds on their huge wall monitor, and sharing Chris' usual ginger beer concoction. It was good to have some time to reflect, and just enjoy each other's company. However, the house intercom system suddenly buzzed.

"Commander here, are you both on your own?"

"We are indeed Commander, how can we help, we are just watching the game."

"I just had an initial chat with the Chinese general who has come over to discuss the ECAW problem. He believes that one of their goals is to take over the satellite and missile field in Krulandistan, and possibly make further attacks with missiles from that base. I have also just heard that apparently the owners of the Field have approached some of our technicians with a request for them to help with technical matters relating to some of the spacecraft, and I have agreed for them to take up the offer so we can watch over their movements more closely. The general also advised that his intelligence team had been made aware of the escape of Yoko Lin, the NY cell assassin, and he is aware of some of her previous work. He strongly suggests that she and her other cell contacts may be planning to assassinate some of our key people."

Chris was quick to respond, he and Robert were looking stunned.

"Wow, that is very bad news. That may include the girls, Helena and Athena are at their new apartment relaxing with Efi right now. With your permission we will take some arms over to them and advise of your call. However, they do seem to have other defensive mechanisms that work that we do not yet understand. The main thing is to put them, and indeed all our ISPEG seniors on their guard."

"That is OK Chris, you can both pick up any extra arms or clothing you need at the base. However, tomorrow we all need to meet to discuss the whole project and our next move. If there is something going on in Krulandistan, then we need to get out there quickly and ensure there are no further deadly attacks on our properties or people."

"Noted, Commander, we shall be over to your office with the girls tomorrow at 9am."

****

Overhead Bakersville, Later that Evening, June 2078

"Usain, prepare to fire the missile. The co-ordinates we have been given are already in the computer."

Yoko was enjoying this, no more chances taken in facing them with their fancy tricks, we can eliminate them from here. She already had an exit plan, and it was not to include the Driver of the Heli-taxi!

She was watching the computer screen as she called out to him. "Fire now!"

Same Time, Bakersville Apartments, June 2078

Helena had just had the call from Chris, and even as she turned to talk to the others, she detected a danger signal in her sixth sense box.

"Athena, Efi, they are right, I hear something that I think is not normal, get out into the garden at the back of the apartment now!"

A few minutes later an enormous explosion rocked the apartments.

The girls were thrown to the ground as they ran out of the door into the garden. Debris was flying around, and as Helena thought they were clear of the building, she heard a noise from Efi. She was down, and not moving.

****

Bakersville Apartments, Minutes Later, June 2078

"Rob, quickly, that was a missile explosion! Let us hope our warning was in time."

They both had taken just minutes on their hydro-cycle to reach the USAFA apartments, and could already see the damage. They rushed towards the area and were met by Helena, running towards them with a face that they had not seen before. It did not look good.

"Chris, Robert, so pleased to see you. Athena and I seem OK, but we are worried about Efi, she is alive but your oxygen levels are insufficient to sustain her as she is in what you call a coma. Can you help quickly? Also, we spotted the small craft that we believe fired on us, and it seemed to be turning back towards the SE area, can we detect it in time to catch those responsible?"

"OK Helena, we shall arrange to get Efi to the Base, we have accelerated recovery rooms which should be able to help her. Rob, will you take Efi to the Base while I take the girls to see Commander Glen?"

Chris called the Commander's hot line and advised him of the situation. He asked for a rocket aero-taxi to be ready to search over the surrounding 200 miles to try to detect the source of this attack. He explained that he thought the craft as described sounded like a public heli-taxi, but it must have had some weaponry fitted for this to happen.

"Commander, I believe there is a centre for these type of flying vehicles in Vegas. Anyway, it is worth a quick reaction. I am on my way to the Field with Helena and Athena."

****

Krulandistan, June 2078

"We have all the systems in place for attacking the space station, and the Florida base for ISPEG. The technicians that we paid were very helpful with technical detail, and we are sure that they were not aware that we made late changes to the co-ordinates for the proposed attack flights. We shall try to persuade these technicians to go with the spacecraft, so that they are eliminated when they crash into the targets. The money up to now has been a great incentive for them. The three spacecraft are fully loaded, and are now ready for your instructions."

"Well done, Kim Jong, you have my authority to launch them at a time that fits your target programme. We must now prepare to leave our business here, and transfer to the yacht for a while to avoid any detection or repercussions. We should take any useful staff with us, and dispose of the rest. Assumedly you have appointed some of the less useful staff to be aboard one of the non-returning space craft?"

"When we have seen this through, I am looking at how we can put a presence on the Mars ISPEG programme, which we are advised is well advanced. It would be useful to have a further target to delay the Western democracies plans for the new world. We can then look at taking power on the planet before they are able to understand what has happened. We must also further check the stories relating to an outside force, who are apparently trying to support the West in removing our operations."

Attica, Earth time, 27 June 2078

Chairman Isis and the senior Senators were reviewing the recent news from Earth.

"Senators, we have come to a critical stage of the Marsattica programme. Our agents and our Captain Panamosis have been attacked. However, help is

141

under way for them, and with our unique recovery ability, we expect a good recovery. Following this news, our intelligence head, Spiros Altemis, has been in conversation with our General Hermes, and with the Earth's representative, Commander Glen, who you will remember from his recent visit. We have decided that we have to take immediate action to set back the plans of this terrorist group ECAW who are determined to enforce their philosophy in countries of the Earth that were originally known as communist States; as described to you on the Commander's recent address to the Senate."

"These countries you will recall were named as Russia, China and Korea. The Commander explained that all of these countries have changed their regimes over the last 30 years, and have moved away from strict communism. There is another country on their planet known as Iran, that also was formerly hostile to the Western countries, but since their people revolted against the strict Muslim regimes some 25 Earth years ago, they adopted a free society policy, and have developed good relations with the democratic countries. Senator Altemis will now explain the plan that he has agreed with our Senior General."

****

Edwards Base, California, 27 June 2078

Commander Glen and Captain Westmorland were now ready to launch starship 5. Their plans had been confirmed by the President and the Senate, and by the UK and Chinese government's top representatives. They had decided to liaise with the Chinese government heads in view of their recent sympathetic approach to the USA regarding their concerns about the ECAW group disrupting the peaceful work they had established over the last 20 years. They had also passed on other intelligence information concerning the possible headquarters of the group.

They were now seated at the controls ready to lift off, destination space station Venus. They would be locked on to the station within hours.

Chris and Robert had acted speedily after the attack on the girls and Efi. The latter was now recovering in the Base hospital, the oxygen levels had been corrected, and minor wounds had mended surprisingly well; the doctors were amazed at the speed of her recovery.

As soon as they had established that Efi was recovering, they all rushed to the airfield, as the Commander had requested that the F95S be prepared for immediate take-off.

"Rob, can you and the girls take over on the intelligence centre, we don't have time to take on more of our ground crew?"

"All OK Chris, under control, the girls have looked at the equipment and seem totally at ease. I shall set the scanner for the size of craft we are seeking, and be ready with the laser. Are we able to fly low in this area?"

"Yes, I have alerted our control to warn off any commercial or domestic craft in the immediate area for the next 4 hours, giving reason of national security. Ready, we have clearance now."

****

Space Station Venus, 28 June 2078

General Hermes large figure was a welcome sight. Both Commander Glen and Captain Westmorland had locked on safely as planned, and had now transferred to the Rotoship. This was Gary's first sight of the craft, and he was amazed at what he was seeing. Apart from the General, there were three robots at various controls; controls that made little sense to him at this stage. The robots were very lifelike, although not in a form of Ziggy, or their other humanised robot team. Dimitris then addressed them.

"Commander, good to meet you again, and welcome Captain, I can see you are deeply interested in our Rotoship. We shall go through the control and attack procedures when we lift off from the docking station. The Commander will tell you that there is nothing to concern you, there will be normal pressurisation in the working areas, and although we shall be moving at speeds that are unusual for you, you should not feel any discomfort. We do have individual care cabins on board if you should encounter any discomfort. These are sealed units and are fully controllable for any conditions we wish to adopt to aid recovery. Now, we have our plan, let me introduce you to my favourite robot crew."

As they prepared for lift off from the space station, Commander Glen heard a message coming in from Commander Hunter.

"Ed, we have an emergency. We have been advised by the Chinese and the Attica agents that we can expect an attack from several manned rocket type craft from a place called Krulandistan, and maybe other sites near the Chinese mainland. Can you help to detect, and maybe take some action if we identify the source for certain?"

"Thanks Norm, we already have been alerted re the source, but if attacks are imminent, we shall ask General Hermes if we can amend our journey now to try to detect any incoming missiles or rockets before reaching our planned destination. Keep us advised your end, and we shall do likewise."

Dimitris had been listening to them.

"Yes, I heard that; we shall start the detection programme. Now, all ready for lift off, so please take stations we agreed. Our robot team have the craft under control. We shall talk to them when they have achieved target orbit, and again prior to entering the Earth's atmosphere."

****

Las Vegas, June 2078

The girls had detected and somehow identified the heli-taxi, but it was now down on the ground in a residential area. Chris and Robert decided to alert the Delta force, asking them to investigate any suspicious activity that they could detect around that area, and to specifically seek out the two agents who were suspected of being behind the recent attack in Bakersville. They could not land the aircraft in this area.

After the message to the Delta Captain, Brad Snyder, they had received another message from Commander Glen, advising them of the further intelligence regarding potential attacks on the space station, and maybe other important ISPEG sites. They had been advised to transfer their flight to the McDill base in Florida, and to be ready for action if they detected any suspicious activity én-route.

A call was coming in as they changed direction.

"Captain Snyder here Captain, one of our officers has managed to retain two girls who match descriptions, and they are under arrest, but one of the girls shot down the guy with them before we could stop them. We believe he was the pilot during the attack on your associates. Where do you want these girls to be sent for interrogation? One of them is really nasty."

"Thanks Captain, that is good news, the nasty one sounds like Yoko Lin. Please send a report to our ISPEG HQ in Florida, and the girls can be kept in the local jailhouse for now, it will bring them down to earth. However, please isolate them, as they have ways and means of bending the men's resolve. We shall advise Edwards Base, and they will pick them up in a day or two for interrogation at the Base."

****

Rotoship 2—June 2078 [in Earth Orbit]

"Zeus here General, we are ready to go into atmosphere and have detected three rocket type shapes on our scriptor. Orders please?"

"Zeus, set course to the following Earth co-ordinates as directed by Commander Glen. 43.4513 latitude x 34.3044 longitude. Prepare lasers and be ready to operate the ships magnetic field."

"Understood General, our team will be ready soon; please take your positions for action."

****

Edwards Base, 30 June 2078

Major Tom Lancs and Lt Gary Kent had been sent over from the Biosphere to interrogate the ECAW agents, who were now in solitary confinement at the Base. They had extracted information from Irina and Lara, without much difficulty, and had a good picture of the other two imprisoned agents. One, Yoko Lin, was certainly the ring leader, and a known assassin. They believed that her accomplice was just a scapegoat, and was used as a plaything for Yoko.

Accordingly, they decided to separate them for interrogation.

"Yoko Lin, you are accused of not only several attacks on our organisation and personnel, but for the attempted murder of your own two agents, Irina Ivanov and Lara Gorinski, and for the killing of your pilot Gorgan Browski."

"They had to be killed, they know too much. I had direct instructions, and will not be giving you any information. You will never keep me imprisoned, our movement has many cells and they will find me and destroy you."

"Well, you are to be isolated from other prisoners, and we shall be monitoring you 24 hours. You can improve this position by giving us some information relating to the ringleaders of your organisation."

"I only know that my instructions are sent from a place near the Russian border, but no precise detail. All instructions are in coded message by satellite phone. I have already disposed of this."

Tom and Gary looked at each other, the news did tie up with other intelligence. However, Yoko Lin was not to be trusted at this point.

****

Rotoship 5 in Earth's Orbit—Late June 2078

"We have detected missiles or spacecraft in the outer orbit General, they are on a course that will take them over the Florida ISPEG launch sites in a short time. We have also detected two spacecraft that appear to be under control by humans but are speaking in another language from that of the Commander and his colleagues."

"This is General Hermes. We have received intelligence regarding further possible attacks on the Earth's Florida area, and on the new ISS. All Rotoships are to be prepared to attack rocket craft or missiles that are detected; details of which are coming over to you now from our transfer unit. We are aiming to disable their auto systems, rather than destroy, and then our advanced auto-lock system can be adopted to re-direct them back to a landing area at the following co-ordinates in Florida, where our ISPEG friends will be waiting to land them safely and then confiscate the craft. However, if any missiles are released, you have permission to destroy these completely. Please send confirmation of these instructions back to me immediately via the transfer unit."

Somewhere in the South China Sea, Same Time, 2078

Kim Jong had just arrived on the yacht by the company Helo-copter and was now reporting to Ho Chi.

"I am sorry to report, Chairman, that the attacks on the ISPEG headquarters have not been successful, as the missiles were destroyed, we think by new laser systems that we have not seen before. They were directed from spacecraft that were not detected prior to the attack. We are also still waiting to hear from the spacecraft personnel, and what has happened to the crews. We therefore must assume that the planned attack on the space station has not gone to plan. There certainly was a relayed message earlier saying they had seen what appeared to be the UFO type craft mentioned in earlier reports. We must look at how we can destroy these new craft. Are they beyond our understanding?"

"Very bad news Kim Jong; it would appear that we are outflanked by these new craft. We are safe on the yacht for a time, but we must think how we can get you, or one of our best agents, onto one of these new vessels so that we can continue the quest. Our Chinese contacts seem our best bet as we have heard that their government are in talks with senior figures from other major countries regarding an agreement, which I think must relate to a new Mars programme, and some peace deal with these supposedly alien people. See what you can do Kim Jong."

Neither had mentioned loss of their people, or shown any concern for anyone connected with their wasted mission.

Washington DC—Office of the US President, August 2078

The president's secretary, Al Cummings, was busy receiving the heads of state, ambassadors, and their translators that had been requested to attend an extraordinary meeting to discuss the future of the 'Marsattica' agreement and to assess the terrorist threat, if any, after the recent success of the Attica Rotoships. Chris, Robert, Helena, and Athena had also been requested to attend together with Commander Glen, and much to the surprise of all, Captain Panomosis, now fully recovered. She had been specially invited by Commander Glen as he wished to introduce her as a senior representative of the Attica advance team.

President Cable now opened the meeting. "Ladies and gentlemen, thank you all for coming to this very unique meeting. Today we are here to discuss the next steps towards arriving at an agreement with the people of the planet Attica. Some of you will only have heard the name of this planet in previous meetings, or correspondence, but today we are grateful that we have three Attican citizens in our midst."

There were murmurs through the meeting room as most attending had noted the extraordinary, but elegant presence of Efi—but three! The President continued after the room settled down again.

"Yes, Captain Efi Panomosis is the second in command of the Rotoships that were deployed in a recent successful action, together with our own forces, that prevented severe damage and loss of life on our new ISS Venus, as well as several other critical targets. She was also recently targeted by the ECAW terrorists, together with our other two Attican representatives, but due to their very fast reactions, which are due to advanced warning systems that we may term futuristic, they are, as you can see, fully recovered, and indeed, want to address you all today."

"Their natural language is an ancient Greek, but due to other advanced systems that they have developed, you will hear the speech in English. Translators in the room, please note. So, first we shall hear from Commander Glen, who heads the USAFA and has had personal experience of what opportunities lie ahead if we can all agree on final steps needed to complete the Marsattica agreement. Commander, please?"

"Mr President thank you. Ladies and gentlemen, I recently was fortunate enough to be selected to travel to the planet Attica with General Hermes, head of their space programme, and therefore can assure you that all you may have heard, or had told to you in previous meetings, is entirely with basis. What you are going to hear today is extremely confidential and all of you attending will be signing a pledge to secrecy until we hopefully sign a final deal with their Senate. Before I continue, are you all able to comply with this request?"

The Chinese and Russian representatives looked across at each other. Chao Feng spoke, "President Xi Chun and President Cheknova have discussed this, and we are here to assure you that we do wish to exterminate all terrorist cells and build a better relationship with the Western countries, particularly related to the Mars and planetary projects; and so, we confirm our acceptance."

"Delighted to have you with us Chao and Egor, and please convey our thanks to your Presidents; we are ready to welcome you. If all other parties are now happy with the document, I may continue?"

All the representatives in the room nodded.

"First you should know that the Attica people are extremely advanced in scientific matters, the Rotoship being just one of the marvels of their knowledge. However, they are a dying planet due to an atmosphere that has created sterility in their male population, as well as affecting many food resources. Therefore, they have been searching for solutions. Their first thoughts took them to Mars, as this is the nearest planet to them, where they have been operating for some time."

"Many of you will wonder why they have not been detected by your own operations on that planet? The answer is that despite our great strides over the last 30 years, we are all still many years behind the technical ability of the Attican people. They have already built a small community on the planet, and this place will be revealed to us in time if we can all meet the terms of the Marsattica Agreement."

"In particular, they request that all terrorist activity is to be halted, so that they do not experience any influx of unwanted personnel. Apart from this plan, they do see that joining us on the Earth would also be a possibility, despite differences in culture and IQ; as you have now seen there are also physical differences, although the latter is not considered important, and may be addressed, as proven by the appearance of our two Attica agents in the room with us today."

Ed hesitated a moment while they took all that in, and saw they were looking curiously at the girls, but then who wouldn't he thought.

"We consider that working closely with the Attican people would certainly help the Earth's people to progress at a faster rate, and help to ensure continuity of peace on our planet. Helena and Athena [we shall not give other names at the moment], the two official Attican agents, will address us after your questions. They actually started this venture by first, going through surgery to attain a likeness to us, and then travelling by the Rotoships to our planet, yes, flying saucers if you will; finally dropping through our atmosphere from the spacecraft

149

in very technically advanced suits, before finding refuge in a Californian university."

"This is where they made themselves known to our people, even managing to take up university placements. It is a long and amazing story, but for now you should all know that they are helping our Intelligence centres to track the movements and the expected attacks on our persons or properties by this ECAW group. We should be very grateful to them as they have already shown us the future possibilities for our people in achieving peace; and how our joint efforts will enable Mars to be a new home to many."

"There is of course another aim. As explained, they do have a male sterility problem. They, and we, are hoping that we can achieve an answer for continuity of their generations by ability to provide them with fertile male samples, developing new lives living on a different planet, where due to new technologies that Attica have developed, they will have a real chance to build a future."

"They could also have the same opportunity if they chose some of their people to settle with us on our planet. Helena and Athena have proven that all this technology is real; by so quickly adapting, and living and working in our environment. I am going to now ask them to address you, and questions will follow."

As she looked around and saw that they were all still open-mouthed, Efi took up the conversation.

"As my colleagues here have been on your planet for a considerable period of time, I shall defer to them to answer any questions. I speak for our assembly and General Hermes when I say we are certainly ready to work with you all, to combine our forces and intelligence, to make the Marsattica agreement a reality."

Everyone in the room was applauding her as they had seen that here was a very brave and highly intelligent person that they could relate to.

Helena now took centre stage. She started to talk to them slowly in English so that the translators could clearly interpret for the Chinese and Russians who she felt were the key to moving the agreement forward. She explained, with short additions from Athena, the background of the Attica aspirations, their happier relationship with the people that they had met, and the hope that Attica could develop a much closer relationship with all the people of the planet Earth.

The two Majors in the room looked at each other. This was great news! They liked the bit about happier relationships!

Helena continued, "Now, we come to one of the most difficult parts of this venture. Final removal of any terrorist cells. They have proved to be very clever, and have caused much disturbance to our aims. We are suggesting that we make a time frame of five Earth years to complete this task, but we shall of course need all your co-operation. To this end, we intend sharing our new technologies with you all. This will enable us to accelerate our plans for the city we are developing on Mars."

"After discussion with our General Hermes and Captain Panomosis, backed by our Senate Chairman, Isis Parapoulis, we intend to offer representative persons from each of the countries here today to visit our planet, and shortly after that, if the agreement is signed, we shall introduce you to our new city on Mars. We ask you to consider your selected representative, who should be of good health, and able to interpret your questions and concerns at highest level."

Helena paused, then looked out at her excited audience.

"We are setting up a 'Marsattica' centre here in Washington that will be a direct contact for you all, and in due course you will all receive a coded number for your contact. Please advise us that this is all clear for now, and let us start to put our minds to the first stage of attaining a world peace, where all the Earth's people are ready to engage with us in this exciting challenge."

The room was now buzzing, with interpreters trying to relay the message to their presidents, ministers, and ambassadors. Chris and Robert went over to the girls and hugged them, and this was met with surprise, but no doubt looking at their faces, with pleasure. The US President now stood up.

"OK ladies and gentlemen, we shall have the confidentiality document ready for your signatures on the way out, and shortly you will receive details of the new contact codes and persons for further information. Thank you all again for your support to this venture. We look forward to working together to attain the goals that have been outlined."

****

Somewhere in the South China Sea—September, 2078

The cell bud in Ho Chi's ear was sending him signal for an incoming message.

151

"Chairman, good news, due to my former training for space travel, and my knowledge of languages, our Chinese agents managed to get me an interpreter's position with the main contingent for the Washington talks. I have taken a hotel room in Washington and advised the Chinese ambassador that I am ready to assist him with the next stage of the agreement that the Western powers have set up with the alien people we now know as Atticans."

"I shall have to be very careful as we all had to sign a confidentiality paper and we no doubt will be watched, but I now understand fully their intentions, and can see how I may be able to get myself, and maybe one of our cells, onto the Mars programme. They say they have a city already developing, and it would be a great setback for them if we can now infiltrate and set back their plans on Mars. I cannot be in touch again until the first trip is completed, but please confirm that you are in agreement with this plan, and if so, can you find me one or two reliable trained persons who we may use."

Ho Chi turned on the responder.

"Kim Jong, I did not know of your language talents. I am very pleased with this plan and I shall start to consider who we can use to help you in this mission. I shall maintain my position on the yacht and wait to hear further from you."

****

Bakersville, November 2078

Chris, Robert and the girls were now together in the house preparing for the trips to Attica with the countries representatives. They were mainly discussing the programme, but also Helena had raised another concern.

"I think that there was someone in the room in Washington acting as an interpreter, and our brain sensors were being alerted to a possible danger. Can we investigate again those who attended and try to identify this person?"

Chris and Robert were astounded, if this was the case it would be very serious indeed.

"OK, Helena, I will talk to the Commander so he can make some immediate investigations with our security people."

****

Somewhere in the South China Sea—Same Time

Ho Chi Dae was sitting on the lounge deck of his yacht thinking over the conversation with Kim Jong. He had not got this far in his infamous career without using information to his own benefit. His survival, and the cause, he considered were above all things. What were the chances of Kim's scheme? He thought odds were not high, because of the new information that had been coming in relating to the Attican agents, who had thwarted all their plans to date. What was their secret? What enabled them to have this uncanny insight into things that were going to happen?

No, it was time to realise that if they had this ability, and it would seem proven, then he must now think how he could not only survive, but perhaps lead his supporters into a new world. If Kim Jong's plan worked then all to the good, but he was expendable like his other agents. He looked up at his beautiful yacht.

"I will miss you, but will be back if my plan works, and maybe with some good company."

Washington DC, January 2079

Commander Glen was sitting around a large table with the heads of intelligence from all the countries that had been represented at the special meeting last August, to disclose and discuss the Marsattica Agreement. He was outlining to them the news that there was a strong chance that the content of that meeting had been infiltrated by a source close to the ECAW movement.

"Ladies and gentlemen, our Attican agents believe that this person, or persons, are possibly looking to travel with the contingent we are planning to send to Attica and Mars as part of the plan that was outlined in the meeting. This would of course give them insight into how they could extend their activities in the new world that we all hope to create with the Attican people. Please take immediate steps to try to identify this threat, and send back to us any information you may obtain. We shall make you all aware of any action we intend to take when we know the source. Although we may have mis-read this danger, we have to accept that the Atticans have been very accurate in their proprioception, sixth sense as we understand it. Thank you."

The representatives were all talking in the room, but then the Chinese intelligence head, Chao Feng, rose from his chair.

"I can advise you all that we have been concerned about activities in Krulandistan for some time, and we recently heard that our technicians in the rocket launch station were duped into an activity which would have had a grave result for the plan if it had succeeded. We did lose two people in that scam, but due to the quick actions of your people on the new space station and from your USAF HQ, the scheme was unsuccessful. We do admit that after the new government in our country, which has taken the road to bring world peace and understanding between East and West, there have been dissidents who wish to return to the old communist ways. We are constantly investigating, and now will increase our surveillance. We pledge to bring to your attention any information that may jeopardise the Marsattica Agreement."

Commander Glen was thinking how things had changed in the last 30 years!

"Thank you General, that was very gratifying to hear, and we all thank you for your help in this matter."

****

China, February 2079

Ho Chi had made land, and was now with his contacts in Shanghai. The Krulandistan operations had made him a very rich man, and he was now with people who he understood, just as rich and ruthless.

Mao Ling, the head of the Chinese cell, now listened to her old colleague.

"OK Ho Chi, we have the picture, and have heard of some of the recent activities. It does look as if we need to change our strategy in view of the increased intelligence that the alien people have supplied. As you know, I am on the countries defence board, and we are planning to send our new spacecraft to Mars very shortly, together with our robots, to develop the centre that we have been establishing there in the last few years. I could get you on that flight if you are ready, and can pass the fitness test that all human traffic must undergo. It is still a long trip, even with our new power systems."

"Thanks Mao, I have been on the yacht for a few months and my crew have been giving me daily fitness tasks, so I am in good shape, I think. Let us now discuss details of how we can infiltrate, and take major positions in the new government of the planet."

****

USAF/ISPEG Meeting, Edwards Base, California, March 2079

Commander Glen was back at the Base together with the senior team, including Helena and Athena, who were now part of this group.

Ed Glen started the meeting by updating all of them with the recent feedback from all the countries involved in the discussions concerning the Marsattica agreement. He was able to confirm that intelligence from the Chinese had been successful in identifying some ECAW agents, who they believe are operating on a worldwide basis.

"We are in constant touch with General Chao Feng, who has been extremely helpful. Now, regarding the two ECAW agents that we interrogated, I am pleased to advise that two of our senior Biosphere team, Captains Gary Kent and Tom Lancs, have been successful in converting Irina Ivanov and Lara Gorinski, and we now have them under surveillance in the Biosphere. They are working well under the guidance of our Professor Devonshire. They are continuing to co-operate with us on identifying the ECAW agents who we are keen to bring to justice. So good news on that score, well done everyone involved."

Helena and Athena looked particularly pleased at this news. He continued, "We are now ready to set up the promised trip to Attica and Mars for all the representatives involved in the Marsattica plan. General Hermes and Captain Panomosis will be in charge of this operation, working closely with Majors, Devonshire and Somester. The operation will be top secret of course."

"We shall also need to remind those involved in the various administration centres that health checks will have to be conducted here, before final acceptance of passengers taking this exciting journey. Thank you everyone for your co-operation, we trust this will be the start of our long-awaited journey into a new life with our Attican friends on Mars."

Russian Embassy, Beijing, April 2079

Kim Jong Woo was back in China, sitting in the boardroom of the Russian Embassy, together with the Chinese and Russian officials who were discussing the recent trip to Washington. He had continued his post as interpreter, and his English knowledge had proven useful in this meeting as he was able to persuade them that he was a very useful candidate for the proposed trip to Attica. He was fit; he was younger; he could translate back to them on a daily basis as the main language to be used on the trip was English.

Xi Chun and the Russian leader Boris Cheknova had listened, and appeared to trust him. Xi Chun now addressed him.

"Kim Jong, this is a very special journey. Our countries need to be well represented in all talks on Attica. We both wish to develop our relations with all those involved on this trip, which we see will advance our plans for increasing our presence on Mars. Please liaise with our two ambassadors at the end of this meeting, and undertake the necessary medical tests as soon as possible, so we may clear you for this trip. It is essential that you maintain daily contact with us. We shall be providing you with an advanced telecommunication kit that enables you to transfer news from space. Any other questions to be put to the ambassadors who are in direct contact with Washington."

Kim Jong was excited, he could now see the way to not only expand the cause, but inflict damage on those who had thwarted the ECAW plans over the last few years. He also could now forget going with the Chinese craft, and instead go directly to the Attican's HQ on Mars. He quickly went to transfer the good news to his boss.

****

Attica, Earth Time, April 2079

Chairman Isis had called a special session of the chamber and all were eagerly awaiting latest news. The situation on the planet was still unaltered; although citizens were living longer, they were not reproducing, and the need for more population was acute. New younger technicians and farmers were now badly needed, although the growth of the human robot team was helping to maintain some stability.

"I have called you all together today to advise that the next step of the Marsattica plan is soon to be taken. This will entail receiving appointed representatives of the Earth on our planet in the very near future. This will be followed by taking them to the planet Mars, where we shall for the first time exchange some technology with their representatives. However, there are still some matters to be settled with regard to the agreement, not least, that there are still cells on the Earth who are not complying with the call for peace and continue to try to destroy or disrupt our plans for the future."

"General Hermes and Captain Panomosis will be returning from Earth together with these representatives, and after consultation with them, we shall

156

decide on our next move to finally remove these unwelcome cells from the Earth, before continuing to our main goal of living together on Mars, and expanding our population here on Attica, or the planet Earth."

Spiros Altemis, the intelligence head, now rose. "Chairman, I assume all these representatives have been thoroughly vetted? We are about to share our technical achievements with them. Should we ask our agents, Helena, and Athena, to be present when the elected representatives are being examined prior to departure from the Earth?"

All the chamber rose and showed in their usual way the approval of this proposal. Chairman Isis responded quickly, "We are all in approval, so Spiros, please transfer your thoughts to our agents as soon as possible. Thank you all, we shall advise you when the entourage arrives, and make a programme for their time with us."

****

Bakersville, May 2079

Helena and Athena are back from the Biosphere following the important meeting at the Base in March. They had continued the interrogation of Irina and Lara, and as advised, it was clear that they had changed their minds about the ECAW group, and were talking. They had stated that they were sure that they were disposable, and had asked for protection while the cells were still active. Helena had also received information from Spiros regarding his concern about the representatives that would come to Attica on the proposed upcoming flight.

The girls were now feeling very comfortable with Chris and Robert, and were meeting regularly at the house for meals and chats. A close friendship was developing much to the guy's delight. However, it was a serious Helena that addressed them now.

"We have heard from Attica that they are also somewhat concerned about checks on the representatives that we are sending. They asked for us to double check them prior to boarding. Will Commander Glen arrange this for us, we only need to be there, no need to interrogate."

Both the guys had seen the girl's abilities many times now, and could see that this was a good move.

"We shall contact the Commander tomorrow morning, and ask him and General Hermes to arrange for you to be around in the briefing room prior to the flight. We both are sure that would be a good move and address your people's concern."

Helena continued, "Thanks as always for your confidence; now let us talk about the ECAW cells. We have some new information from the Russian girls, and we need to set up a plan quickly. There are signs that the ECAW cells are lying low, but we know enough now to take action to catch the USA and Canadian cells, and that should lead us to the headquarters of this terrorist outfit."

New York, USA, June 2079

The American nation awoke today to read on their tablets a New York Times article that read.

'Last evening, a major action was taken by the army, police and the FBI in parts of Canada and the USA that resulted in the capture of several cells of an organisation that has been damaging not only important institutions in our country, but had been identified as a terrorist group that continues to pose a threat to world security. Two members of the group were killed during the operation. The joint action by our security services followed the interrogation of two of the group's members who had recently surrendered, after themselves being subjected to an attack from the group, who suspected them of having passed on information. They are now under the supervision of the FBI and other intelligence services.'

By the afternoon of that day, the news was worldwide, and certain persons were more interested than others!

US Space Centre, Florida, USA, July 2079

Kim Jong was now waiting, together with the other interpreters and secretaries, at the interrogation and health clearance unit. He was thinking hard. He had picked up the news regarding the capture of ECAW's American cells, and the deaths of two of his former colleagues. He had not heard of the recapture of Yoko Lin since her escape from the prison in Nevada. He wondered if he could find her; she could tell him more about the Greek girls that she had tried to exterminate. He also remembered the one happy time in her apartment in Manhattan, despite her reputation as an assassin…

He brought his mind quickly back to his position. Despite this setback, there was no way he could see that they knew of his association with the group. He was after all now with senior ambassadors, so who would suspect. He settled down, and waited for the checks to begin.

****

Washington, DC, July 2079

Commander Glen, Chris, Robert, and the girls were all in the same building, looking through the one-way mirror into the interrogation room. Helena and Athena had been studying faces and listening on the intercom. Helena spoke first.

"That younger guy with the short beard and blue eyes dressed in the khaki suit, who is representing the Chinese ambassador. Can we monitor him, our sensors are advising something is not right."

Chris was quick to respond, "Commander, as Helena has suggested, we should monitor him, but suggest we do not take any action now. If he is one of the senior members in the ECAW group he must be very important; maybe he could even lead us to the head of this organisation. If he plans any mischief we shall be watching, and if necessary, pass him over to the Attican intelligence when we arrive. He can then be retained there until they extract further information."

Commander Glen was quick to respond, "OK that is agreed. Let us start by putting one of you into the secretarial group, and that will ensure we are updated on every move. Robert, you are fluent in a few languages, and although they will mostly be conversing in English, you may catch them off guard when they are relaxing. Could you undertake that task for us? We shall of course all be going to Attica, but on another Rotoship; but we are all still in contact."

Robert looked across to the Chris and the girls.

"Of course, Commander, it is my duty, though I shall miss being with you all."

Athena was now looking straight at him.

"Robert, we shall still be close to you, and we have some more time together when we get to Attica. We shall remain together when we transfer to Mars, where we shall be able to show you all the scientific advances we have made on this once uninhabitable planet."

Robert broke into a smile; this was certainly something to look forward to…

The Attican Rotoships had all arrived and docked, and Colonel Philip Somester, Robots Zikky and Mary Ann were in the huge central briefing room on the new space station. Phillip addressed them now.

"Ladies and gentlemen, welcome to Venus, our new international space station. With the latest technology, much of which I should add having been passed to us by our new friends, we are now equipped to take on multi space ship dockings, and swift passage to and from other planets."

"All of you here today have passed health and security checking, so we shall soon be ready for take-off. Zikky and Mary Ann are going to assist you with your seating and directions that you must adhere to throughout the flight. You have already been advised of the Rotoship number that relates to your trip. You should not suffer any discomfort due to the unique atmospheric qualities of this spacecraft, and you will be surprised at the room you have for daily exercise, and the quality of the food you will be served in the main seating area. We are expecting good conditions for the journey, and upon arrival in Attica."

"When we arrive, you will be health checked, and attend an acclimatisation clinic, where you will find comfortable sleeping facilities. After your acclimatisation period and discussions with the Attican council, you will be selected for a short trip to Mars, where we have been promised a sight of some of the advanced work that has been undertaken by them over the last twenty years. This is a goodwill gesture from them, but understandably you will be under supervision during this tour."

Zikky and Mary Ann now came forward, and all were amazed at their natural appearance and movement.

"Hello, everyone. Those who have been allocated to 102 and 103 Rotoships are to go with Mary Ann please. Remainder to please stay with me until we have boarded those numbers."

Commander Glen, General Hermes, Captain Panomosis, Chris and the girls were already seated in the console of Rotoship 101, listening to the presentation. Commander Glen was updating Dimitris and Efi.

"Robert will be in number 102 with most of the ambassadors and their approved interpreters. The guy that is being monitored has been identified as a

Kim Jong Woo, and his movements over the last year do seem to be suspicious. Anyway, we are keeping a close watch."

Efi now responded, "Thank you, Commander, I am advising our intelligence people of the position. We are all ready for take-off. I am advising Zikky and Mary Ann that we are taking off now, as we have our navigation instructions. Number 102 is to follow us as soon as possible. Number 103 may follow one hour later. Our own robot pilots are aboard all the flights and they will fly the ships. Zikky and Mary Ann may be instructed during the flight, to assist with their further education. I am sure that Senior Captain Devonshire, I hope I can now call you Chris, will be able to go with Helena and Athena to the forward cabins. They will be able to maintain contact with Senior Captain Somester from there. When we arrive, we shall all meet up to discuss our next move."

Chris looked over at the elegant figure in her scarlet astronaut uniform.

"I certainly will be very happy that we can use our first names Efi. Thank you to Dimitris and yourself for all your advice; we feel very comfortable with you now, and so good to see you fully recovered from recent events. I am sure everyone is now very much looking forward to this great adventure."

****

Attica, October, 2079

All the Rotoships had arrived on the planet without any problems during the fast flight, and the Attican representatives were at the space centre ready to welcome the newcomers and their assistants. Chairman Isis Parapoulis, and intelligence head, Spiros Altemis, had arranged for an initial briefing at the globe meeting rooms, which was fitted with engineering techniques that adjusted the atmosphere and temperatures etc., known as the acclimatisation centre.

Spiros and his team had been watching the people carefully as they stepped out of the spacecraft, and were now more than sure that the person in the Chinese contingent, calling himself Kim Jong, was the potential enemy that Helena and Athena had mentioned. But it was time to wait, to see if they could establish his aims, and deal with them accordingly. There had to be more people involved, and this may be the opportunity to also find them.

All the visitors had now been checked, and were amazed at the 'acclimatisation' facility, which was several years ahead of any of their country's technical developments. They were adjusting to the differences in the Attican people's appearance, who were now standing before them on a large glass looking platform. The atmosphere was incredibly comfortable, and they had all relaxed by the time Chairman Isis rose to speak. A language control system had been installed in the huge room, and they had been advised that this would record to them in the English dialect.

"Welcome to you all, and thank you for making this long journey to meet with us. I am Chairman Isis, and my colleagues and I on this platform are members of the Attican assembly, the equivalent of your governments. We are elected by census every ten years. You will meet many of them over the next few days, but now I just want to outline our plans for you while you are our guests. Our aim is for us to work together so that we may establish a new civilisation on Mars, and retain a close relationship with your planet."

"Isis, and other members, continued to give them background of the formation of the Attican planet and how Attica had remained undetected for so many earth years due to their position on the 'other' side of the planet Mars, and their small size. However, the conditions on the planet Attica were very unlike Mars, and over several hundred years the planet had developed quickly. The people had originated from an ancient Greek background, and had inherited many of the skills of their ancestors."

The various major country representatives looked at other in disbelief; During all their explorations, how could they have missed a planet that was so near to Mars!

However, the chairman was continuing. "Today, we are facing a large problem as the population is shrinking due to the impotency of the male population, for which we have not been able to establish a cure. Although we still do have sperm banks, reserves are small, and they are now over twenty years old. Therefore, we have not been greatly successful with new births. We have a belief that we can still develop a new generation with people from other planets, and we are hoping that our relationship will help that cause."

Chairman Isis paused to allow this news to be understood before he continued, "I think it is time to conclude this first meeting, there is much to digest, so time for some rest. You will be allocated special sleeping areas in the vicinity of this centre, and our members will now take you in groups, and help you settle. I would finish today by especially thanking agents Helena Poulakis and Athena Balakakis for all the work that they have undertaken over the last few years, for without their courage we would not all be meeting here today. Thank you from us all."

Chris and Robert looked on with much pride, and they were not surprised to see the girls looking very much as if they were going to cry, but they knew by now that was not actually going to happen! They had not met anyone with such resource, and continued to hope that they could spend more time together.

MAOXI-Space Vessel, Mars, October, 2079

Ho Chi Dae was in the recovery capsule after the long trip from Earth. He had handled it well, and the girl that his hosts had arranged for him had made the trip more relaxing. He was pondering the next move. He was due to meet the Chinese in the new small biosphere town that their engineers had worked on for the last twenty years. It was going to be a good base to find out more about the whereabouts of the Attican city on the planet, and hopefully Kim Jong was going to make that even easier for him. He just had to wait for the next message from him, and he would make plans accordingly.

Attica, October 2079

"Chairman, I have good news. I am now getting ready for the flight to Mars with the Chinese and Russian Ambassadors. The Attican authorities do not appear to have any suspicions, and are all very friendly. I have also met an Attican female who is working with the ambassador's group, her name is Panayiota, and she has this special instrument in her head which is unbelievable. It reads all the languages and translates in milli-seconds, so that not only can she converse with you, but seems to understand the meanings associated with the words."

Ho Chi was a little perturbed at the excitement in Kim Jong's voice as he talked about this female, but he saw this was a great opportunity to extend their cause on the planet.

"OK Kim Jong, take care that you do not make any moves that give away your real aims. I shall await your report."

"I shall be careful, Ho Chi. I shall be on Mars in the next few days, and if we can communicate somehow without any suspicion, then I shall be able to advise you where the Attican city is being developed, and we can make our plans for our next move."

He signed off the inter-planetary special communication unit which the Atticans had set up for all the delegates to use for calls back to Earth. However, his call had been detected by Dimitris Artemis at his intelligence centre in the assembly forum, and he was aware that this was a call to another planet, and what is more he was certain that the planet was Mars!

He adjusted his instruments, ready to send an urgent call to Helen and Athena, and the Attican intelligence team.

"I have just detected a communication from a Kim Jong Woo, who is a delegate with the ambassador's group, representing the Chinese and Russians. He is in communication with someone who is already somewhere on Mars. I suggest it may be the Chinese unit that we have detected there, who fortunately are not only some distance from our city, but also still considerably behind in technology. We shall maintain silence on the matter for now, but can you consider how we deal with this development?"

Helena was first to respond, *"Dimitris, I am with our group at this moment. We did have some strong suspicions, and you have confirmed our worst fears that someone from this ECAW group has infiltrated the contingent we brought to Attica. We shall form a plan, but can we agree to keep this news confidential for now, until we have more facts? I shall speak to Panayiota Fronimos, who we know has made contact with this Kim Jong, and make her aware of our concerns; she may be able to give us more information."*

"Understood, Helena, I shall await your thoughts and we can then finalise a plan if we agree there is a real threat."

Helena and Athena were in the main cabin of the Rotoship 1 with General Hermes, Chris, and Robert.

They had all heard the message from Dimitris and were now discussing how to deal with this new threat. Helena was relaying her latest news.

"I have had a quick conversation with Panayiota, and advised her of our concerns. She says this man has shown an interest in her and does not think it is purely to extract information from her, although that is possible. She has said that he is attractive, and she would have no difficulty in maintaining a relationship to see if his interest in her is genuine. I have thanked her for that and asked her to be extra careful. She is willing to transfer any information to us that may be relevant."

Chris intervened, "That sounds a good solution for now, but please emphasise to Panayiota that this guy may be attractive, but is obviously dangerous."

The General now spoke, "I shall advise Dimitris of our conversation and decision, and ask him to keep a close monitor on the Mars team generally. He will be able to see most of the movements of the visiting group, and listen in to unusual communications. We all need to get to the head of this ECAW organisation, and maybe this is our best chance yet."

Attica, November 2079

Since the first talks between Helena, Athena, and Panayiota, there had been a surprise development. Kim Jong was appearing to be in awe of Panayiota and her people, and not only that, he was evidently enjoying her company. She was aware due to her high level of perception, that despite their differences in their bodies, her arms had been something that Kim Jong seemed to want around him. She was speaking to the girls again.

"I understand that this guy may have a bad background, and may even be involved in a plot to harm us on Mars, but somehow, I believe there is something else in him that I may be able to develop. He is very likeable when he is in our company. Maybe we have found a better side to him."

"We are leaving this to you Panayiota, you have our support if you need it. We shall however continue to monitor his movements when he is not with you; we have to be certain that he will not cause any harm. We shall leave soon for Mars, and we need to decide if you both will go, so give us a further assessment in the next few days. We have completed our acclimatisation programme for the delegates, the Rotoships are being prepared for the trip, our human robots have linked up with Zikky, and all is now ready for their trip to our new Mars city, Acropolis."

****

Attica, Late November 2079

Kim Jong's mind was now in a turmoil. He had spent some days on Attica and seen the extraordinary people, and some of their amazing achievements on this small planet. It was obvious that they had many resources, and their people were far more advanced in technical skills. This woman he had met, Panayiota Fronimos, had been his companion throughout these short trips, and there was no doubt that, despite her unusual appearance, he had feelings that he had not experienced before. Maybe the ECAW cause was not suitable for this new world. However, how would he survive if Ho Chi and his colleagues saw him thinking this way. What to do? He suddenly rose, he was a man, wasn't he?

His mind was clearer now, he would let the next few days decide, if there was a chance of a new life, he may just take it. He would play along with both sides for now.

Mars, December 2079

The Rotoships had made good landings on the new Mars space station, that had been developed to access the Acropolis city.

The Earth's representatives, together with their secretaries and translators, had been again amazed at the fact that the flight was so short, but also that they had not experienced any discomfort during the changes of atmosphere or gravity, either in Attica, on the Rotoships, or now in this arrival station.

General Hermes was now addressing them in the huge domed reception area.

"Welcome to Acropolis. We shall soon be taken on the transfer drones into the centre of our mountain city. The reason for choosing this area for our centre will be apparent when you see how we have used our technologies, and our human robot friends, to create all the amenities necessary for permanent life on Mars."

The Chinese ambassador interrupted, "General, as you must know, we have a very much smaller development in another part of the planet, but we do not yet have any means of sustaining life, other than through using artificial means, and therefore the people we have in this development are only able to stay on the planet for a short period. We need water, we need atmosphere adjustments, we need protection from the solar winds etc. We are a long way from believing that Mars is ready for sustainable life."

General Hermes looked across to the representatives. "This trip is to show you the very advanced systems we have established to ensure that life can be sustained in our city, and that secondary cities will in due course be developed with that knowledge. Some of this information will be made available to you as a sign of our goodwill, hoping that future relationships may be peaceful and productive in every sense. We have used the natural ice caps, the solar winds, and minerals that we found on Mars to change the whole atmosphere and standards in our new mountain city. You will know more as your tour continues. For now, get ready for boarding the drones. You are about to have a whole new experience!"

Chinatown, Mars Village, January 2080

Ho Chi was getting restless. His female companions were very few in this isolated little village, and the conditions were somewhat short of his lifestyle aboard his yacht. He was just thinking of taking a chance on contacting Kim Jong when his communication cells advised a message was waiting in the main reception area. He exited the small bedroom, and ensuring his suit was oxygenated, started down to the reception area.

"Ho Chi, I am now on Mars with the other representatives, and seem to be accepted. No problems have arisen. I do not know the precise co-ordinates as we were taken on a drone into what looked like a huge volcanic mountain, but as it has ice caps that they use for part of their water supply I am assuming that it is in the North of the planet. Have you any plans that I may help with before I am told to return to Attica, and then back to home?"

Ho Chi listened to the recording carefully. He would make some calls back to Earth, and start planning how he could infiltrate or take over this new site, with Kim Jong's inside knowledge.

Attica, Late January 2080

Kim Jong and the representatives had been astounded by what they had seen on Acropolis and were further realising the tremendous advances that the Atticans had made in turning this area of Mars into a huge habitable area. The human robots were also astonishing, their work ethic and abilities far beyond anything they had seen. The Earth's human robots, led by Zikky, who had accompanied this trip, had certainly needed updating to make the journey. He was now being advised by the ambassadors that he should be getting ready for his trip back to Earth, and that they would brief him regarding a statement that was to be presented to their people on their return home. Kim Jong sat and pondered. He felt he must see Panayiota before he left. He called the reception area and asked for a connection.

Attica, Assembly Room, Early February 2080

Chris and Robert had been called into the assembly room by General Hermes, together with Helena, Athena, and Commander Glen. He was in his full uniform, he looked even bigger each time they saw him. His strong voice now addressed them.

"I wanted you to be the first to hear that one of our junior captains, Panayiota Fronimos, who has been one of our escorts on the visitors' trip, has been to see me regarding an association she has had with a man named Kim Jong Woo, a senior translator for the Chinese and Russian Ambassadors. She believes he has been involved in some of the troubles that upset the Earth's peace programme. However, he has asked if he can stay here for longer, and she feels that we should give her a chance to assess him. If he has changed, maybe help to develop a plan that will finally bring his masters to justice. He is due to leave for the return journey to Earth tomorrow, so I need you all to advise me if you are comfortable with this move?"

Commander Glen was first to respond. "General, I am sure that we think, that like Helena and Athena, Panayiota has the same natural sense of good and bad. If this guy is genuine in a desire to be with her and to start a new life, we perhaps should at least give that a chance. I would prefer we let him return with the representatives for now, and thus have a further time to consider the position. Panayiota will still be able to keep in touch, and could advise him that they will meet again soon. If he is just using her, we could test that by giving him some information regarding your Mars site to see if his colleagues take that up, and use it to try and damage your new city. I am still suspicious of his intentions."

Dimitris was first to respond, "Commander, I am so pleased we have you as a friend, that advice sounds good to me."

All in the room nodded their approval, and they agreed to meet again when the representatives were back on Earth.

****

Black Sea, August 2080

The representatives had all returned to Earth, and Kim Jong had just called Ho Chi. He had formed a plan in his mind.

They were now back on the yacht, which had become the only base Ho Chi could trust after recent events. His trip back had not been anywhere near as comfortable as Kim Jong's trip on the Rotoship.

"Chairman, I have been thinking of the possibilities for ECAW on Mars, and following the recent attacks on our worldwide cells, it seems to be our only chance to make a final upset in the West's plans. As you know, I am in contact with an Attican girl, who now thinks that I am going to return and settle with her on Mars. I should go back very shortly, but in the meantime perhaps you can still raise enough of your contacts to make a final push."

"If you are to succeed, it should be with destructive missiles that would penetrate a strong mountain type structure. When I return, I shall be trying to get the co-ordinates from my contact, so advise me when you are ready. I assume there are missiles that you could take over from the Chinese Mars station? I understand that they do have weapons already in place as they were not sure what they would meet when settling on the planet."

Ho Chi was just recovering, the recent journey had been hard and he had found it more difficult to find some solace with his girls as their numbers dwindled after the recent attacks on the cells. He pondered, sipping his iced Saki drink.

"OK, enough. I am ready to make this final push, and leave the world with memories of my great achievements for the real communist world. If our struggle is to end, then let it be such an event that all will remember. I shall start preparing with my contacts, and Kim Jong, as soon as you return to this Attica, find the co-ordinates for their Mars city, and send them to me in detail. I shall advise you when we are ready to strike, so you may join us to enjoy watching the destruction of the Earth's dreams of a new city on Mars. It should be easy for you to get over to Mars, you can always advise this Attican girl that you need to go and look at where you would live, and generally use your charm. I assume she is expendable, and you will eventually join back with me after the attack. I will have the yacht ready to take us away from the limelight. We can disappear from the authorities, and live on with our cause."

****

Bakersville, CA, August 2080

The last few months had seen an even closer relationship developing between Chris and Helena and Robert and Athena, and they were now back in Chris's house. They were all now seated with a glass of Californian white wine in their hands, which the girls had found very similar to the Attica wines, although they continued to add water.

Some months had passed away since the eventful trip with the Earth's ambassadors and their entourage. The feedback from the countries had been very positive, everyone being so amazed at the achievements that were visible in the Acropolis city. Therefore, the world's authorities were making even more efforts to pursue the ECAW cells in all the countries, and this had been successful to the extent that they had captured several terrorists, and were starting to extract information that would hopefully take them to the leaders of this extreme group.

Helena had also just heard from Panayiota that her new friend, Kim Jong, was asking to return to Attica to be with her, and was asking her if they could visit Acropolis again soon, as he was so impressed with the new city.

Athena had been listening intently to them all.

"Helena and I are now some 40 Attica years old, which is slightly older than you both, but our life span is normally well over 20 years longer than that of the Earth according to our studies, and we believe we are still able to produce a child. The infertility of our male population, and some animals, has mostly led to the present position where our diminishing population is looking to develop a new life on Mars or Earth."

Helena looked over to her friend and quickly added, "Athena, you are right, but we must not give the impression we have spent our earlier life with men trying to produce a child!"

Chris and Robert laughed, and nearly spilled their wine at this very unusual touch of humour from their very much-loved girls. Robert this time spoke first.

"We are both very sure that whatever your life has been, it has been full of service to your people, and we both have no problems with accepting that a future life with you is going to be very different, but it is one that we both hope you will allow us to share with you. Let us finish dinner, and then make some real plans for us to return to Attica. Priority is now to finish off the terrorist threat, and then look at the feasibility of either developing our lives in Acropolis, or even here on Earth. I suspect that with your skills there may be a need for you to

170

commute, but we may also be on that list of people who can continue to assist the space programmes."

****

Attica, January 2081

Kim Jong was grateful that he was now able to ride on the regular fast Rotoship trips that had been set up by the Attican people, and he was now back in Attica with Panayiota. He was now reasonably sure what his next plan would be. He started to explore the co-ordinates of the Mars city and those of the Chinese and American's positions on the planet.

He would call Ho Chi, in a few months, after working out the final plan and ensuring that Ho Chi could be back on Mars in time. Time now to learn more about the Attican people.

The South China Sea, March 2081

Ho Chi was getting bored waiting for the call, even although he was being well entertained by two girls that the main Chinese cell had sent him. He was just thinking how he could contact Kim Jong when the pilot called up to him to say there was a strange link coming through on the auto printer.

He sent the girls to their room and rushed to the upper deck. At last, this must be the information that he needed.

Sure enough, Kim Jong had all the information that he had requested, and he felt more at ease now.

"Well done comrade, we shall now make plans to get our team to Mars in the near future, after I have set up the necessary attack plans. Will you be able to get to Mars with that Attican girl? Keep me advised, we have a few months to get it right."

He turned to the satellite transmission centre, and called his contact in the Chinese cell.

"Mao Ling, we have an opportunity to make a real impression on our enemies. I shall give you all the news when we meet, but can you arrange for an urgent trip to Mars by a few of our colleagues, and be ready for some critical action. We are in danger if we do not move quickly as these Attican people have detection methods beyond our understanding, and we need to strike first."

"OK Ho Chi, I will look at transport arrangements, and speak to others, but it will take some time to arrange the armaments and the necessary robot support we shall need. I shall give you some dates for you to leave in due course, and I shall of course accompany you."

Bakersfield, June 2081

The last few months had been busy at the USAFA base, and at the ISPEG centres around the world. Several meetings had now taken place with higher ranking government officials, looking at information that would lead them to the ECAW cells, and also arranging the start-up of regular traffic to and from Attica and Mars. The Rotoship technology was being shared with Professor Devonshire and the astronaut senior team, led by General Hermes and Captain Panamosis. More training was needed, and they envisaged it would be a year or so before they were ready for a prototype test of a cloned Rotoship, as some of the parts were having to be brought from Attica. In the meantime, a search was being made in Australia and Alaska for new metals that had been identified on Attica. Mars samples were also still being evaluated, some 40 years since the first new materials were found there by the 'rover' research team.

The robot team were also being 'upgraded' with the help of Efi and Dr Ruth Somester. Zikky and two others were being prepared for a long spell on Mars, working with the Attican human robots to further prepare the city of Acropolis for a larger population.

Chris and Robert were now regularly meeting with Helena and Athena, and today they were in the house assessing information and deciding on their next moves. Chris opened up the conversation.

"Well, we have now a good idea from where the ECAW cells were receiving orders, but it appears that the ring leaders are not in Krulandistan at this moment, according to our special forces. They have a few suspects under arrest, but they believe that these guys were just engineers, and had not been involved in planning, and so would have little knowledge of others in the organisation. They will continue to search for clues as to who was running the group, and where they may be now. China and Russia have added their help to our intelligence team, so we are now very hopeful of bringing this aggression to an end."

Helena now intervened, "I think that we shall find they are hiding for the moment so that they can re-group and try another assault. Athena and I think that may be related to this guy Kim Jong, we certainly know that he has been in touch with someone here on Earth, and our Intelligence people think that it may be the head ECAW guy. We are watching him very closely now, since he befriended one of our associates, Panayiota Fronimos."

Chinese ECAW cell HQ—August 2081

Mao Ling was pondering the conversations with Ho Chi. Since the capture and death of most of her assassin squad in America, her numbers were dwindling, and many were concerned about the latest threat from this new planet. They had made so many blunders in the last year. She realised she was alone now in making decisions, and her mind was racing. She spoke out loud to an empty but luxurious room.

"Is it time to join Ho Chi and his team for a final push? Would they together be able to make any impression for the good of the cause if they made a final assault on the Mars city that Ho Chi had mentioned?"

She now turned to her process monitor and started to call the few good contacts she had left, again speaking to herself, "OK, one more chance!"

Acropolis City, Mars, October 2081

General Hermes and his astronaut team had decided to visit Acropolis to view the latest work, and particularly the systems that they had installed for prevention of detection, and to ensure the systems, including the latest laser were in ready state. They were also here because Spiros, in the Intelligence centre, had received information from Helena and Athena, as well as Captain Panomosis, that concerned him. The Atticans had not experienced war, or even simple conflicts for many years, but he knew of the Earth's problems, and there seemed to be a real chance that something was brewing that did not help towards the goals that the two planets had set. Spiros turned to them now.

"Senators, we are here today to discuss preparations for the upcoming visits from representatives of the planet Earth. As we have discussed, we are endeavouring to befriend these peoples; hoping to build a new life together, both here, and on Mars, as well as some integration with them on their own planet. As part of that programme the assembly voted to also offer the visiting representatives a certain amount of our advanced scientific knowledge, that will help them advance their own society and systems. As this information is sensitive, we do need to thoroughly check all those listed for this visit, including their advisors. My team will be checking this list and will report our findings to you all. I expect these visitors to arrive early next Mars year, so I hope to make final arrangements for the visit very shortly."

****

Paracel Islands, South China Sea, October 2081

Ho Chi had arrived on the islands to meet Mao Ling as he was advised that the next spacecraft was ready to be sent to Mars. He was now awaiting final instructions for loading of armaments and personnel.

"Comrade Chairman, we welcome you, and trust you are ready for this important trip, which we understand will enable us to find, and then attack the Attican city on Mars. This would then hopefully destroy the agreement that we understand is about to be signed, that would have brought the two planets together."

"That is correct, Mao Ling, but of course we still need to plan our retreat if we are to survive after this action. We shall have to find the timetable for their Rotoship shuttle service that we understand is now operating on a regular basis. We may have to capture one with those robots on board, so that we can easily navigate a return to Earth. If we are successful, we shall still need a safe place to hide, as there will be a worldwide attempt to find us, to capture or kill us."

"Let us take one thing at a time, Ho Chi, our people have already started preparing the spacecraft, and we should soon be ready for take-off. We therefore expect to arrive at our city on Mars in about fourteen weeks. Have we heard yet from Kim Jong regarding the co-ordinates for the Attican's city location?"

"Yes, Mao Ling, I believe he is landing on Mars soon, and has said he will try to send the location details shortly after arrival. The representatives will only be there for a few days, but Kin Jong is trying to establish a relationship with an Attican girl, which may enable him to stay there for a longer period, hopefully until we arrive. I shall now prepare myself for the journey; I assume you have arranged some company for me for this long trip?"

Mao Ling had already anticipated her Chairmans wishes, she had known him a long time!

****

174

Attica, January 2082

Panayiota and Kim Jong were both discussing the upcoming visit to Acropolis with the other representatives, who had now arrived on Attica. They had all spent some time exploring this surprising planet with their Attican guides, and Panayiota had stayed close to Kim Jong throughout.

Although she was very attracted to this guy, she was hoping that her sixth sense was wrong, for it was indicating some concern. She was trying to maintain a calm conversation with him until she could more fully understand what the problem may be.

"Kim Jong, we are all agreed now that we are ready to make the trip to Acropolis. Do you, or the representatives here, have anything else you wanted to know before the trip. You will appreciate that all of you have been our guests, but we have been open with you, showing you technologies that are beyond your understanding at this time, and meeting some of our people, giving you all an opportunity to experience our lifestyles."

She continued, "In return, our assembly authorised this trip on the basis that you will all help with the finalisation of the Marsattica agreement, which includes removal of all warring parties on your planet, and the peaceful integration of our peoples."

Kim Jong felt he had to respond, "Thank you, Panayiota, we shall all discuss with the ambassadors, and advise if there are any questions before we leave. For my part, I am looking forward to having more time with you, and hope that this trip will be successful."

He turned to the representatives and suggested meeting in their rooms the next day so he could give them a briefing of what they may expect on this trip. However, his mind was still whirring, and thoughts of love and hate were in equal balance. He had to find a solution for both!

****

ISS Venus—January 2082

After the earlier attacks, which had set the project back a few months, the huge project of building the new space station was now completed. It now housed astronauts under training, as well as robot instruction centres. With the new technologies that had been learnt from their Attican contacts, the station also had six giant docking stations that would allow the free movement of the Rotoships, as well as the commuter space vessels, that were now a regular feature, taking personnel and visitors to and from various launch centres based on the Earth. The overheating problems related to returning to Earth that had been experienced for many years, were now overcome. Attican help was increasing, and the Earth's governments were now realising how they could improve the lives of their people with this joint relationship.

Commander Hunter was contemplating these events as he sat in the main control room, awaiting the arrival of Chris and Robert, as well as Helena and Athena, and was looking forward to seeing them all again. There were now two Rotoships in the dock, and the robots were preparing them for their next journey, which he understood would take them to Mars directly, so that they could link up with the representatives currently being briefed on the Mars trip by the Attican authorities. His monitors were tracking the space shuttle as the vessel arrived on the orbit that he had determined for them.

"Commander to Shuttle Isis, are you ready for docking procedures?"

It was Chris's voice he easily recognised.

"Hello Commander, we are all ready, approx. 37 minutes to dock area. Please open port."

"OK Chris, we are all looking forward to seeing you, and Zikky is here and anxious to show off the new software on the Venus. We confirm port 12 is open and ready for your arrival."

****

Acropolis, February 2082

Kim Jong, Panayiota and the representatives and secretaries were now on their way in the Rotostar shuttle craft, which, although not as huge, and technically not as advanced as their Rotoships, were never the less comfortable, and certainly ideal for the short journey between the two planets.

The representatives were being given last-minute instructions by Zeus, the head of the robot team, which they found fascinating in view of his likeness to the human form. It was particularly interesting that the body had been formed without the long arms associated with the Attican people. As usual the language was a broad English, and Kim Jong and the other secretaries were busy translating to the other languages as the robot spoke, one of the translators for the Korean and Russian contingent suddenly shouted out, "Look at the monitor everyone, we are approaching the red planet, how clear it looks. Zeus, how do we land, will we feel any discomfort as we enter the low atmosphere?"

The representatives looked towards the screen, and suddenly were very silent, it did seem very difficult to see how a landing could be made in a normal docking procedure.

Zeus, and Spiros Artemis, who as head of intelligence had decided to join this trip, turned to them. It was Spiros this time who addressed them.

"Please be calm, Zeus and his team have undertaken this trip several times, and you will soon understand how we can make a comfortable landing. All take your allotted seating where you will be strapped automatically by shoulders and waist, when we signal our descent. Do not be alarmed by the automatic systems, they are standard security procedures. You do not have to do anything but sit comfortably. We are going to allow you to watch the monitors that will appear in front of you during the landing process, as I think you will then understand why we are so secure in our Mars city."

All were totally fascinated, and after the initial excited exchanges with other representatives, the cabin became silent. Zeus's voice was now the only sound.

"Ladies and gentlemen, we are ready for entry to our destination, take your seats as directed."

****

ISPEG HQ—Florida, February 2082

General Worcester and Major Fife were consulting on latest intelligence reports coming in relating to the concentrated efforts now being made to find the ECAW agents and their source.

"Hank, I have a report here of some interesting activity that recently took place in the South China Sea. There were an unusual number of ships around the Paracel Islands, and intelligence say they suspect they had armaments aboard, including what looked like the latest miniature hydro-cell missiles. They say that they also detected a space ship departure some few months ago that they now think could have been the Chinese departing for their Mars base. Their concern is that some of these missiles were already at this island base. If so, what are the Chinese up to?"

"They have been very friendly for some time now and their President seemed to be fully supportive of our attempts to remove these terrorist groups. Anyway,

177

can you pass that on to Ed Glen, who is now on the Venus ISS awaiting transportation to Attica with our guys, and the Attican agents, Helena and Athena. They are following up on the representatives visits to Mars, and preparing for a more concentrated movement of approved people to that planet. This information may want them to urgently talk to the Chinese."

"OK Jason. I envy them this trip somehow, but I guess we shall have our chance later."

****

Acropolis City, Mars, March 2082

The approach of the Rotostar shuttle had been spectacular. There was no anticipated high heating of the shuttle as it descended towards the ground area, and as they watched the monitors, and saw their craft heading for the ground, they had been amazed, when seeing a mountain ahead, which they must surely hit at this speed, but no, a large cavity suddenly appeared, and they realised they were now heading to the inside of this mountain. As they slowed, huge lights outlined a similar docking station to that of the type used in the Attican space stations. There was the usual clicking sound as they came to a halt on the dock. They all had the same thought, no wonder the earth's probes had not been able to detect this city, and exactly where could they go inside a mountain? They were interrupted by Zeus.

"Please stay in your seats for a few moments until we adjust the conditioning room for your arrival. This will ensure you are able to move freely without wearing special clothing or needing oxygen. Acropolis has been acclimatised to the Attican atmosphere by means of pressurised air created from a type of unit you would possibly call a compressor, but a little more sophisticated than that; later we may be able to discuss the technologies that are involved in this technical achievement."

All of those aboard were looking at each other, obviously thinking that this was yet again remarkable; they had spent years trying to find a solution to the oxygen supply needed for living on this hostile planet.

The Rotoship doors had opened, and now they saw the huge figure of General Hermes approaching.

"Welcome to you all. I believe most of you know me already. My astronaut team, led by Panayiota Fronimos, who you met on this journey; Zeus and his

178

colleagues, and a few of our assembly members, are ready to take you to your rooms. We are allocating a small team for every two representatives and their interpreters. Please direct any questions to my team, and not to any of the other people you may meet. You will be here for a week, before we return you to home, which we shall again arrange on one of our Rotoships."

"It will be a direct flight this time back to Earth. So now, rest in your rooms for a while, food has been arranged that should suit all tastes, and there are satellite entertainment consoles as well as communication equipment for your use to enable you to continue your work during your stay. We shall start the working tours tomorrow morning."

The visitors continued to be overcome by all the events over the last few weeks, and they were very ready for this news. Through the interpreters they conveyed their thanks for the welcome, and slowly moved as directed to the exit, to be met by their respective Attican hosts.

Kim Jong was with his Russian and Chinese representatives, but had noted that Panayiota was not going to be in his group. He waved across to her, and she gave him a look that suggested she would be happy to see him alone soon. He had commitments though that meant he would probably be better alone for a while as he debated his next move.

Acropolis, Mars, March 2082

The Rotoship had arrived on the Mars Acropolis station, breaking previous records for the trip from the Venus space station.

Chris and Robert had spent some comfortable time on the craft with the girls enjoying their free time together. However, they also knew that there was still a job to do. They were experiencing their first trip to the planet, and were very excited.

The entry to the mountain city had been spectacular, and even the girls were enjoying this new experience.

They all awaited the instructions from the robot team as to procedure once they left the comfortable surrounds of the Rotoship. They had been advised that the representatives and interpreters had been in the city for some time and were nearly ready for their trip back on the same Rotoship that had brought them to the planet.

Chris was first to speak. "Well, this is an adventure for sure, but our priority must be to see Panayiota and Spiros to ascertain if we do have a spy amongst the representatives. Let us see what they have learnt."

Helena as usual was first to respond, "I think Panayiota does have some concern about the interpreter Kim Jong, but she is also very keen to be with him, and hopes that she will be able to change any ulterior thoughts he may have in him mind. I believe we should let him stay here with Panayiota for a little longer, so we can monitor him ourselves. I shall ask her if she is happy with that arrangement. It will give her an opportunity to show him some more of the city and its wonderful technical achievements."

They all nodded agreement, and were now being advised that they could leave to the acclimatising room, and that transport was being arranged to take them to their lodges in the city.

China Town, Mars, May 2082

Ho Chi was relaxing with one of his female companions who he had brought over with him, and was now in the comfortable but small room allocated to him inside the complex that the Chinese had been able to establish on the planet. Despite some of the pleasures he did not want to be here any longer than necessary, and was anxiously awaiting news from Kim Jong as to the whereabouts of the Attican city. Mao Ling, as promised, had ensured the armaments had arrived, and he had been able to persuade the Chinese who were based on the complex that these were necessary. He had convinced them that he thought there was a distinct chance that the new aliens, or others seeking a base on the planet, may try to attack.

Anyway, they had taken the bait, not least because they were aware that other countries had made some small bases on the planet over the last 40 years, and historically there always seemed to be conflict. So, a missile site was being set up as a security deterrent, or so they thought, but of course Ho Chi had other ideas for their use. It was a pity, but some of his people were expendable, he could not have them around after the attack. He would have the spacecraft manned by those who he could bribe or trust, ready for an early departure back to the Earth.

He now sent the girl back to her temporary quarters, and marched down to the main control room. Time to decide who to bribe for access information to the missile area.

Acropolis, Mars, May 2082

Kim Jong was easily persuaded to have more time with Panayiota; he had to admit that this Attican city was incredible. He had been overwhelmed to see the size of this city, totally enclosed in the mountain. Layers of comfortable lodges were being erected in the mountain, and there were overhead transport services, and even sports centres, which were designed like the original Greek Olympic stadium that he had read about some years ago; but most impressive of all, he had been taken as a special visitor to the heart of the engineering centre, which was totally enclosed in the top of the mountain, where he had actually seen water running, much of this being converted to power by turbine type equipment. He was advised that the water was melted ice that they had been able to melt with solar and wind power equipment.

Although the formulae were still top secret, they had told him that their engineers had developed a system to convert carbon dioxide, and other elements on the planet, into a high level of oxygen, thus enabling them, for the first time, to breathe without suits or other apparatus. These levels were lower than the planet Earth, but still easily controlled within the mountain, which was sealed from outside influences such as dust storms and radiation etc.

As he reflected, his mind buzzing with all he had learnt, he realised that he had still to call Ho Chi. He had managed to extract the destination co-ordinates now for Acropolis.

"I must make this call; my life is surely in danger if I go against the cause."

He wandered off to his lodge and started thinking of Panayiota, but he was still very disturbed.

Chinese Base, Mars, June 2082

Ho Chi had finally had the news from Kim Jong, and was busy finalising the setting up of the missiles for what he saw as a final attack that would thwart the aspirations of the ISPEG people, and thus end the so-called Marsattica agreement.

He now turned to Mao Ling who had joined him in the monitoring room. She had been his main helper to date, and he was aware that her support was essential in getting the sites engineers to follow their instructions. He could see that she would be more helpful, and possibly more enchanting than the girls he had around him on the yacht.

"Mao Ling, there is an engineer called Tao Sin who I have identified as someone who we can trust to help us, provided we pay him the sum of 50,000 yuan into an account he has in Korea. I have told him that his account will be credited when he has completed this task; he can arrange for the return spacecraft to be manned and ready when we are ready to return home in the next week or so. He has no need for money while he is here."

"If you can use your charm when you meet him, that will be all to the better to ensure he is with us on this vital last effort to destroy some of those who have been involved in attacking our cells."

"OK, Ho Chi, I know that guy, and have already had a few approaches from him since I arrived. I shall now bring him over to the control room, please be ready with the directions that you have from Kim Jong. After you have set the co-ordinates, I think we should get him back to normal duties for a day to avoid any suspicion, before setting off the missiles on the target. I assume we have taken into account the change in the air density, etc. but check with Tao."

Acropolis, June 2082

Kim Jong was clear on his mission. He now walked down to the lodge where he knew he could find Panyiota.

"Hello, can I talk to you about some serious matters?"

Acropolis, Two Days Later

Chris, Robert and the girls were now talking to Panayiota, having asked to see her following an incident some 20 Mars miles away from the city. It had been agreed that Helena would open the conversation.

"Panayiota, we have asked you here to help us, you are not a suspect in this incident. However, we do believe that something was instigated by the interpreter called Kim Jong Woo; Athena and I had definite vibes concerning him. Evidently missiles were launched in our direction from what we believe to be the Mars site for the Chinese, some 300 miles away on the other side of the mountain. We are not sure why they hit one of the mountains about ten Mars miles from here, but we do have a strong feeling that it was meant to hit Acropolis. Can you tell us any more concerning this? Do you know where this Kim Jong is right now?"

"I can assure all of you that I know nothing about this incident. I am really upset to think that it may be instigated by Kim, he has been very friendly with me for some time now, and I had thought he may want to be closer to me. However, he has disappeared; a few days ago he asked about what transport we use to go to other areas of the planet when we undertake our regular investigations, looking for new minerals and future sites for development, etc. Perhaps we can check with our robot engineers to see if any transport has been requested by him, or is there someone he has managed to persuade to show him around?"

Chris now took up the conversation. "OK Panayiota, we do need to find him and get to understand what is going on. It is strange that anyone wanting to hurt us would send missiles so far astray. In any case, we were not aware that anyone else on Mars had the facility to send missiles. It could only be the Chinese base, although they have been friendly to us for many years now. We can speak to their representatives who are still here, but as their translator is Kim Jong, we will have to ask you to use your special skills to talk to them in their language, and maybe they will be able to help us solve this incident. Not least, your people here know the exact position of their base here, so we could make arrangements to visit. Do we need any special clothes or apparatus? I appreciate it is OK for your human robots, but how do we travel in this atmosphere?"

****

China Base, Mars, 2 Days Later

"What has happened Mao Ling. We did hear the missiles strike, even if it was some distance away?"

"Well, Ho Chi, the base has just had a message that Kim Jong to say he is on the way to us; he has evidently managed to get away from the Attican city on one of their land craft. It will be interesting to hear what he has to say about this."

****

Mars Desert, Same Time

"Chris, look, there is the base, and what is more I can see one of those Acropolis transporters parked outside, it must be Kim Jong, who else could it be?"

"You are right, Rob, so it now looks as if our suspicions were correct, he must have been involved in whatever happened. Helena, Athena, what do you think we should do now, we do not want to upset the Chinese."

"OK, Chris, we understand, but we have to extract him from that base. If there are any of the ECAW group there, they must be captured. We shall use all of our skills to make this attempt without upsetting anyone who is not involved. Let us see if we can get past the entry gate, surprise is another effective weapon."

China Base, Mars, 1 Hour Later

"Kim Jong, how did you get here and what is going on? Where did you get that special suit, we have not seen anything like that here? Anyway, down to business. We do not think the missiles reached the position that you gave us; I cannot think that it was our mistake as we followed your instructions with our engineer, and all appeared to be on target. You have been on that new planet, and here with these Attican people over the last few months, I hope you are not starting to take sides because of that Attican girl you mentioned? We are now in a volatile position due to you, and are making plans to depart back to Earth tomorrow, as it is only a matter of time before the Attican people, and ISPEG, work out what has happened."

"Ho Chi, I am sorry, but I have made a decision. I know that the ECAW people took me away from my parents at an early age and educated me, but also indoctrinated me with the extreme communist ideals before you then you took me under your wing. My whole life has been dedicated to that cause because I knew no other. However, in the last few months I have been mixing with other people representing many countries on the Earth, and have also met some of the Attican people. I particularly have been affected by one person. I have had very long hours thinking about my position, and it is now clear that I want to start a new life away from the ECAW group."

"So, I am here only to say, go on your journey, but I shall not be returning to Earth with you. I promise that I shall not be the instigator of any action against you in view of our long association, but I must now be free."

Mao Ling had entered the room and had heard the end of this conversation.

"Ho Chi, this is disaster, he will be interrogated, and eventually these Attican people will extract information from him, we have seen how advanced they are in their techniques."

"You are right of course Mao Ling, it is with regret Kim Jong that you cannot survive to tell the tale, I am so sorry after all our times together, but as you grew older, I always wondered if your parent's genes were still in you, and so it has turned out. Goodbye!"

A small weapon suddenly appeared from his tunic.

Just as he was set to fire, there was a very loud noise, and the automatic entry doors to the base opened. Four suited figures burst into the room.

"Put down that weapon now…we are here to arrest you for not only the recent attempted attack on the Acropolis city, but many other suspected cases of terrorism."

Robert had been first through the door. Ho Chi all looked at the strange suits on the intruders. They were identical to the suit he had first seen on Kim Jong. He slowly lowered the weapon.

"Who are you may I ask? We are just discussing an internal matter with this colleague who has been caught spying."

"I do not think so. As to who we are, we are representing ISPEG and the Attican people, and have reason to believe you are here to create problems for us on our Mars city development. We have been watching this Kim Jong Woo for some time now, and realised he was linked to you in some way."

"Well, I am sorry we cannot help, we were just arranging to leave after settling this internal matter with this man here. We only wanted to knock him out, and take him back with us on the waiting spacecraft."

Helena now moved forward to Mao Ling. "That is not what we sense, Mao Ling, your boss was going to kill this man I am sure if we had not intervened. We cannot allow you to leave. You are all to be taken back to our city for interrogation."

Another internal door had suddenly opened, and one of the Chinese engineers was coming in. "We are ready, Ho Chi."

Ho Chi turned abruptly as if to leave, but before anyone could get to him, he turned again and there was a sudden flash…

Kim Jong had fallen. Chris was the first to get over to him as Robert and Helena overpowered Ho Chi, and Athena saw the chance to arrest Mao Ling and the engineer.

The engineer shouted. "I am not part of their plan. I am only the engineer picked to set up the spacecraft for their return to Earth."

Athena still moved towards him, and as she went to ensure he was not armed, Mao Ling, who had been standing passively, now turned, and too late Athena saw that she had a heavy instrument in her hand and now it was heading her way.

Helena had sensed all was not well in the room, and she quickly left Chris, who was now trying to assess the damage to Kim Jong. Robert had command of Ho Chi, who was now bound and had stopped struggling. She called out in her language.

"Athena, are you OK? I am coming."

Mao Ling heard the strange language, "Who are these people, they are so strong for females?"

Next thing she felt was a sharp pain in her chest, and she fell to the ground, her mind now completely blank.

Helena now looked at Athena. She had a bad gash on the side of her head and it looked as if she was concussed.

"Don't move for a moment, Athena, I want to assess the damage. As you know we have good recovery units in Acropolis, but we must make that open journey first, and your suit has been damaged as well, so let us see if that is possible."

Chris and Robert had both seen the incident, and Robert now came over to her.

"Dear Athena, we shall soon have you back for treatment; let Helena help you for now, and we shall deal with these other two. Unfortunately, Kim Jong is not moving and we fear the worst, it will be a shame if we lose him, apart from information he could provide us, I feel that Panayiota will be very upset."

****

Acropolis, Earth Time, 20 June 2082

General Hermes and Efi had just heard the news from Helena regarding the recent attempted attacks on the city, and their recent visit to the Chinese base. They were now waiting for her in the intelligence centre, so that they could decide on next action. Helena did not keep them waiting long.

"General, Efi, we are pleased to advise that since our report, Athena has shown great recovery after the recent attack on her, and the surgeons are just now checking out her head monitors to ensure that she is fully operational. I was really

186

worried, because the brain attachment containing the translators is our most vulnerable point as you know."

"Good news, Helena, we shall go over to see Athena after the meeting, but what about this Kim Jong, and this Ho Chi Dae, and his accomplice? Also why were the Chinese not aware of what was happening on their base?"

"First of all, we are very concerned about Kim Jong, and Panayiota is with him and our surgeons at this moment. With all our skills, we do hope to get some recovery, but he is in a severe coma."

"Regarding the Chinese, they were advised incorrectly that these two people were senior diplomats who were here to look at setting up defence mechanisms at the base. The information was obviously a scam by one of the ECAW people who had infiltrated their space centre in Shanghai. The Chinese engineer who helped them has been taken into custody as he was instrumental in not only helping them with the missile set up, but had the exit spacecraft readied for their quick departure. He had been promised a large sum of money to help them. The Chinese will deal severely with this man so that is not our concern, we are sure he was not actually belonging to the terrorist group."

"Finally, Ho Chi Dae was also taken prisoner after using a laser taser on Kim Jong; his accomplice Mao Ling was electrocuted by myself as I saw her attempting to murder Athena. We have asked the Chinese to allow us to keep Ho Chi Dae, as we are now certain that he is one of the leaders of the terrorist group, and was responsible for the financing and planning of the many attacks that have occurred on the planet Earth."

Efi now rose to speak. "Thanks Helena, you have all been very brave and very clever in catching these people, and we must hope Kim Jong Woo recovers so we can get a better picture of their activities. I think he will be more likely to talk to us if we save him. This Ho Chi Dae will no doubt be a little more difficult to break, but we do have some good surgery options to use, if we have any difficulty with him. Can I suggest General, that we now go to meet with Chris and Robert, who have also fully recovered from the recent events at the Chinese base. They have been with us all the way, and would like to think that any plan we make is made with their full support."

The General nodded. "Well said, Efi. Let us all set up a meeting with them for tomorrow and get down to how we deal with this Ho Chi Dae, and how we make our final offensive against this ECAW group. Only then will we be able to finalise our plans for the joint agreement with the Earth authorities."

Acropolis, Earth Time, July 2082

Chris had been pleased to hear the news that Kim Jong was evidently slowly recovering. Panayiota had been able to hold him in her long arms, and this had certainly speeded up his recovery. She had been so happy to hear that it had been established that Kim Jong had deliberately given false information to his boss, and that he had taken his life in his hands by going to them later, to try and extricate himself from further activity.

He was now in the intelligence centre with General Hermes, Efi and Helena.

"General, thank you for inviting me into your meeting. I speak for Robert and myself to say how very much we appreciate having your confidence. Before we start though, Robert has been with Athena for the last few days, and we are pleased to report that she is doing really well, and in fact, Robert feels he can leave her to rest now; he will be with us in a few minutes."

"Chris, we had no hesitation in inviting you both into our intelligence meetings, you both have shown tremendous ability and resolve in our efforts to attain the signing of the Marsattica agreement, and now we at last appear to have the opportunity to extract the information we need to pursue these terrorists that you have endured on the Earth. When Robert is with us, we shall outline our plan for your approval. We should then all return to Attica, and start the interrogations, before we all return to the Earth to complete this task."

Helena looked over to Chris and he saw for the first time that this was a look of real affection. His heart was beating just that little bit faster as he sat and waited.

****

Attica, Therapeou Healing Centre, Earth Time, July 2082

Kim Jong was feeling very ill, but at the same time a kind of happiness that he had not experienced in his life was beginning to overcome the pain. Over the last weeks his brain had been working overtime, and for some reason he had been drawn back to his childhood and memories that had come flooding into his brain. Why had he never had any parents to go and visit? Why had he become a member of the ECAW group, who had brought him up to believe in these communist ideals; why had he always had the wish to eliminate people who did not have these same ideals? He thought he maybe now had the answers.

Panayiota had told him that their healing centre surgeons had considered that he had at some time been what he would call, brainwashed. They had detected things in his brain structure that indicated something dramatic had happened to him during his formative years. They had added that they believed that the recent shock had re-phased this area of the brain, and it was possible that he could return to a more normal way of life. He closed his eyes, and waited for the interrogation to begin, for surely that was the next move from his former enemies.

****

Attica Intelligence Centre, Earth Time, August 2082

Chairman Isis, Spiros Artemis and the senior senators were all assembled in the room. They had been advised of latest developments relating to the events on Mars and now were eagerly awaiting the outcome of the interrogations of the terrorists. General Hermes, Spiros Artemis, Helena, Athena, now fully recovered, and Chris and Robert had all been invited. Dimitris was first to address them.

"Chairman, senior senators; Spiros, as head of our intelligence unit, and all the people here in my group have been instrumental in bringing us two of the people whom we believe to be the leaders of this so-called ECAW group. This is our report and plan for the next moves towards finalising the Marsattica agreement."

"Dimitris, we are happy to see the full recovery of Athena and major Somester, and you are all to be congratulated on your bravery in bringing these terrorist people to us, so that we may get further leads to enable us to assist the Earth's governments in eliminating all terrorist activity. You are all particularly welcome, as we have heard many good things about your help with our cause. Now, please continue Dimitris."

"We started with interrogation of this Ho Chi Dai, who we are now sure is either the head, or one of the heads of ECAW. He has been more fascinated by our women in the Desmoterion where he is being held, and we therefore decided to ask our head female officer to conduct the first interview. This was partly successful as he had been advised that the other prisoner being held was Kim Jong Woo, and that he was making recovery from the recent incident, and starting to talk to us. Although he tried various attempts to persuade her that she would be a very happy woman coming away with him, and sailing around the

Earth on his yacht, that was as expected rejected, and at her recommendation he is now being sent to our surgeons at the Theropeou centre, who will make inspection of his brain, and then we shall make a final analysis of what to do next."

Helena now stood up and moved to the front of the room.

"First, thank you all for your kind comments, and yes, we feel we are ready for the final thrust to complete our plans."

"Athena and I have had further words with junior captain Fronomos, following the interrogation of Kim Jong Woo. There is no doubt that he was the right hand of the suspect Ho Chi Dai. He has realised now that his actions over the years were due to him being abducted at an early age, his parents killed, and then being taken into the ECAW cause by Ho Chi Dae, who treated him as a son, but was actually brainwashing him into the ways of the extreme communist world."

"With his permission, our surgeons are now looking at restoring his thinking to normal matters. There is no doubt according to the initial reports that Kim Jong has a very brilliant mind, and could become a very useful member of our society. However, we shall soon receive a full report from the surgeons."

Spiros was next to stand, his long arms reaching out to them from his long robes.

"Helena, Athena, thank you for updating us; after some discussion with Panayiota Fronomos, I concur with your appraisal. At this time, I have been given permission by the chairman and the Cabinet to address you today regarding your outstanding work over the last few years, and for bringing us hope that we may now find another partner in our quest to preserve our race and find peace between our planets. In addition, we have noted the supporting role played by Majors Chris Devonshire and Robert Somester during this period."

"We are delighted that this has resulted in not only offering Attica the opportunity to survive, but that all four of you are considering a life together on our respective planets; I include Mars of course, because that is set to be our second home in the future. So, today with great pleasure and honour, I am authorised to present you all with the newly forged medals, for services rendered to your people. Please step up to our dais."

All four were stunned, and it took a while for them to realise what had been said, and what to do next!

Helena, as usual recovered first, and turned to them, "come on, this is a great day, let us enjoy it."

Chris and Robert looked over to the girls, and saw their happy smiling faces. This was really happening. Their dreams were really coming true!

****

END OF PART TWO

Part Three

Washington, DC, December 2082

"This is NBC news, Dan Burger reporting. Following the recent visits of our own representatives, and those of the major countries of the world, to the recently discovered planet Attica, it has been announced that a new agreement has been signed between the two planets authorities that will lead to joint operations against all terrorist groups that may impede the peace agreement. In addition, this agreement will provide new scientific information to us that will allow the peoples of both planets to be able to regularly visit the planet Mars; that hopefully will eventually lead to a new population being sustained on that planet."

"Our President, and the heads of the world's major countries have now all signed to this agreement. The agreement is very significant in as much as for the first time we have two planets working towards a common goal, and this should lead to the removal of further terrorist threats such as we have experienced over many years. During the summit meeting in Attica, all the representatives announced their support, and it would seem we at last have full détente between the East and West. Guys and dolls, this is amazing news!"

"You will be able to listen to more about this in our later bulletins, and of course, our national blog posts on your personal head computers. I am privileged to bring you this news, good morning, America!"

Krulandistan, December 2082

The astronauts and engineers at the site had realised that the head of the space centre was missing, as was his side kick, and those who had been part of their plans were now considering their next move. They had not yet heard of the fate of any of the other cells, but they were thinking how they could make an impact before leaving.

However, one of the senior engineers working for the Chinese satellite area on the base had become suspicious of certain people on the site, and he was sure now that they must have been involved in the recent approach to their engineers that resulted in the unannounced firing of rockets and missiles that were fortunately intercepted by the Americans. Further, he had seen the report from his country regarding the new agreement with the Attican people, and the need for world peace. He turned on his satellite transmitter.

"Calling the President's office, this is Kapitan Ming Shang. I have some important information relating to the recent announcements concerning the terrorist group ECAW."

His conversation was being listened to with growing concern.

****

Edwards Air Base, December, 2082

The Rotoships had again broken new records on the space trip from Attica, and Chris and Robert were now back at the USAFA base. The American President had just called them personally to request that they come to the White House, following their successful trip to Attica and Mars. They were delighted to also hear that he wished the Attican girls, as he put it, to attend with them, as well as Captain Panomosis.

Helena and Athena were also now in the mess room with them, where they had all decided to meet to discuss this unexpected call with Commander Glen and Captain Westmorland, who were now entering the room.

"Major Chris Devonshire, Major Robert Somester. I am addressing you formally because we have some more news for you both. When you all go to the White House, we are going to be with you as you have both been promoted to Wing Commander status. This will be confirmed at the ceremony that will include you receiving, not only one medal for bravery in action, but three, which are to be awarded for your service to our USA security and armed services. You will also be pleased to hear that the President has accepted the nomination of Helena and Athena to be given the highest recognition of their services to science, and for their bravery in making the exploratory trip to our planet; that of the Silver Star medal."

"Finally, you will also I know be very happy to hear that our own Senior Captain here has also been chosen to receive the rank of Colonel in appreciation of the support he has given to you and our country over the last two years."

All four of them were looking at each other. Chris recovered first.

"Commander, we are overwhelmed. This will be such an honour, and for the President to also acknowledge the girls tremendous work and their bravery, is a real bonus. I know we are all looking forward to continuing to work with you and our new Colonel. There are many tasks ahead, but working together, and with the knowledge that we now have regarding the terrorist networks, we are hoping that the Mars programme will be in operation by the end of next year."

Helena now stood.

"Dear Ed and Gary, if we may be informal with you. It seems incredible that we are now so much part of your lives, and our thanks for all the friendship and support that has been necessary over the last few years. Athena and I look forward to attaining these final goals with you. We both feel very lucky that we met Chris and Robert in the early part of this campaign, and hope that we can continue a future together."

Chris and Robert looked at each other, did they just hear what they thought they heard, they hoped so!

****

Following the meeting at the Edwards base, Chris and Robert were now visiting their parents at the new human robot centre, that had been established by Josh, Ruth, Helena and Athena, with the help of Zikky and the head Attican robot, who was called Zeus. The latter had been flown over on the last mission from Attica to especially work with Zikky and the human staff at the Biosphere, and he was already much loved by all for his abilities.

Chris was now talking to his father while the others were talking to the robots.

"Dad, Uncle Phillip, we have some good news. Robert, Helena, Athena, and I are going to Washington next week to see the President. You may not have heard yet that we are all to be presented with some medals for our work over the last few years, leading to the Marsattica Agreement, which evidently has now been signed by all parties. I just wanted you to know that you both have been such a part of this success, and we all owe you a great deal. I know that the advanced work you have completed with our Attican friends on the laser and scientific programmes will allow us to not only find and terminate those who have persisted in terrorising our people, but now can be put to a more constructive use."

"Dear Chris and Rob, your mothers, and both of us, are so proud of your achievements. Your acceptance of Helena and Athena from the start has been a large factor in helping us all to come to terms quickly with these exceptional times, and we do hope that you will all find some happiness when this is all over. I think I speak for Phillip as well in saying that both of us are getting older, and it is probably unwise to make regular long journeys in space, but maybe once or twice if we are fit enough to enjoy it. Now, we also have a surprise for you. The President has also called us and invited us to the presentation, and of course, your mothers will also be there on this momentous day."

Robert had listened intently for some time, and now decided he had to respond, "Wow, that is so good to hear Uncle Josh, but come on, you are both still strong; we shall be reserving a prime place for you on the new Attican Rotoships, hopefully next year if we can get rid of these terrorists quickly."

****

China, December 2082

General Chao Feng was sitting in the Congress building of the Chinese Republic in Beijing together with his intelligence officer Li Zhanshun.

"Li, this information you have brought me must be shared with our new American friends. Please alert our Congress to the fact that we need to take some urgent actions if we are to be in a prime position with the Allies. It is important that we are strongly involved in this new venture with the Attican people. Let us not make the mistakes that were made in the 20s and 30s."

"I share your views on this Chao, I shall also call President Xi Chun with this news. In the meantime, can you prepare us for joining our Western allies in this important venture. They will want to know that we have intelligence of use to them, as well as knowing our intentions regarding the news from Krulandistan."

Attica, Earth Time, December 2082

General Hermes was back in the assembly, and he was on the dais with Spiros Artemis.

"Chairman, Senators, before I speak on other matters, Senator Artemis has some information that he wishes to share with you that may affect our next move."

"Yes, thank you Dimitris. I have now received a report from our medical team regarding the recent capture of the man called Ho Chi Dae. Many of you may remember that some years ago, when we also experienced some disturbances on our planet from thieves, and those opposed to our form of democratic government, that we took these people in, and our medical team put them through medical and psychological tests to identify reasons for their behaviour. After diagnosing these results, the professors decided to create a new machine that enabled them to adjust certain parts of the brain, which took away aggressive, or other anti-social motivation. This in turn led us to our work on the present brain implants that all of us have found so useful, particularly recently when talking to our new friends on the planet Earth."

"I can advise you now that the old system was used on this man, and following this surgery, he is now talking to us, and we believe the treatment has been successful. Although he still has maintained an interest in the other sex, as vouched for by our female medical team, he is no longer considered a threat to us. We shall detain him until we have concluded our task, but then we shall discuss his future with the Earth's authorities."

Spiros stopped and took a sip of his drink as he looked over to Dimitris.

"To continue, the Earth's representatives, together with our own agents, have compiled a plan that will take us to the finalisation of the ideals of the Marsattica Agreement. Dimitris will now take you through that plan, and we trust we shall receive your support in the usual way when you vote at the end of this presentation."

Krulandistan base, December 2082

Three ECAW members were sitting drinking snaps and cafinata in their room, situated next to Ho Chi Dae's office, and going over their position, after one of them had overheard the transmission from Ming Shang.

Song Jing To was looking very angry and suddenly banged his cup down, pieces and liquid scattering the room.

"Song Jing, calm down!" Li Sue Kwang had jumped up; the hot liquid having just missed her.

"We must plan to retaliate, but also to find a safer place for us to re-group. It is obvious that Ho Chi Dae, and it looks like Kim Jong, have been captured, and this place is not safe for us anymore. It cannot take long for them to identify us if we stay. We have missiles here, and a spacecraft with the new engines and fuel source. Let us see how quickly we could persuade some of the staff here to help us to get it ready before the balloon goes up. We should head for Mars where we may have a chance of persuading our fellow Chinese engineers that they need us. We may then even be able to penetrate the Attican's base, and inflict some damage to their ambitions."

Haoyu Kai had picked up the cup pieces and had been listening.

"Li Sue, you are right, and Song Jing, you should listen and plan, not throw things around. We need to stay calm. The plan may work, but in any case, we cannot stay here, so I think we should give this a try. Maybe we could also kidnap Kapitan Shang and use him as hostage if necessary for any negotiation later."

Song Jing was now sitting quietly again, but looked over to them both.

"So sorry for my outburst. I am worried. Yes, you are right, and thanks for seeing a possible solution to our problems. I shall, of course, be with you, and will take the responsibility of capturing Ming Shang."

****

ISPEG HQ, Florida, Late December 2082

The presentations in Washington had gone well, and Chris, Robert, Helena, and Athena were all in happy mood as they made for the meeting with General Worcester and Major Fife at the new admin building, that was set up at the same time as the new space centre in 2082. It was built to accommodate the new spacecraft that were expected to arrive from Attica via the Venus station in the very near future. They entered their codes at the door and the recognition cameras appeared. They were now entering the new 'missions' room, especially built for future meetings between the two planets authorities, and for secret service missions within the planet. They were pleased to see that Commander Glen was also in the room. He was first to speak.

"Well, congratulations to you all on your fantastic achievement, the President advised me that you all had a great day, and he was so pleased to meet you again."

He paused before going on. "Now to today's business. General Worcester is going to head this meeting, for we now have good intelligence on the ECAW positions, and hope to make final plans for attacking the cells in the next month."

"Thank you, Ed, first, I add my congratulations to you all, we would not be in this advanced position without all the work and help we have received from you."

He paused, looked over to them, but now with a more serious face.

"We do have some good information on cell positions, and Commander Glen and his team will be heading the USAFA attacks, in conjunction with our British, Chinese, and Russian friends, who are now assisting us in this project. Krulandistan space centre has been identified by the Chinese as the headquarters of the ECAW group, and the leaders have also been identified by our Attican friends after the recent operation on Mars. Ho Chi Dae is being held in Attica, although now believed to be harmless, and Kim Jong Woo is under surveillance, but following his recent change of heart, he has permission to stay on Mars. You will also be pleased to hear that junior astronaut Fronimos, who has befriended Kim Jong, has been elevated to senior status, and will head the team that monitor astronaut movements to and from the planet."

"Ho Chi will be closely monitored but the surgeons advise that they are confident that he will not now be of any danger to our citizens. He will remain on Mars under the direction of Zeus, our senior HR."

Helena now interrupted, "That is good news General. We shall keep alert for a while on this new partnership between Panayiota Fronimos and Kim Jong. On the subject of our upcoming strategy to remove terrorist cells, may I suggest that you allow Athena and I to talk again to the Russian girls, Iranov and Gorinski, as we plan to use them in our operations in USA and Canada. They are now very friendly with Captain Lancs and Lieutenant Durham, and we have received news that they are working together on the new robot programme at the Biosphere. I believe we can speed up the operations with their help."

"You have been able to read situations far better than us Helena, so of course we shall go with your wishes. No doubt Commander Glen will talk this through with you at the end of this meeting…"

However, suddenly Athena was interrupting, "Helena, everyone, I have just received a message from our intelligence centre via my head transcriber that there is suspicious activity taking place at the Krulandistan space centre; our people say the satellites have picked up movements that indicate that a person was being visibly attacked on the site. No more can be established from Attica, but in view of recent reports from this site, they want us to treat this as highly suspicious, and want us to investigate further as soon as possible."

Commander Glen looked over to Chris and Robert, "Sorry, time to go, we shall prepare the F95S for this mission. This site is on our target list anyway, so we may as well start there. Fortunately, the plane is down at McDill having just been serviced. I shall call Tiny Delamare right now; we can be there by the hyperlink by 17.00 if we start now. Chris, Robert, say your goodbyes to the girls, we are off!"

Helena and Athena ran over and kissed them both. "Good hunting guys, we shall go to the Biosphere now and will wait to see you at Bakersville when you return."

"Wow, what happened there, Rob?"

****

Krulandistan Space Centre, 29 December 2082

Song Jing was back in the pre-flight room with Li Sue and Haoyu Kai.

"I have managed to overcome Ming Shang, he was not expecting me and I was able to inject him. He is now in the spacecraft where the water osmosis plant and energy production unit are located, and it is locked."

"OK Song Jing, good, we can now plan the trip, and check with the engineers that the spacecraft is ready for take-off tomorrow. They have all been told that the Chinese authorities require our presence on Mars within the next four months to help with a major improvement to the base, and they have been very helpful, so it does not appear that there is any concern about our movements. Let us get some rest, collect our suits, and make our safety checks in the morning. We leave about 20.00 on the 30th."

Aboard F95S, Same Day, 2082

"Rob, that was a great take-off, these new fuels combined with the solar energy plant that our Attican friends helped us with have made such a difference. Do we have all the co-ordinates for this space centre?"

"Yes Chris, we are locked on to the site, and expect to land about 17.00 local time. We are now at 70000 feet and cruising at Mach 2."

****

Biosphere 2, 30 December 2082

Helena and Athena had linked up with Major Lancs and Lieutenant Durham. This time Athena was first to speak.

"Tom, Terry, are you satisfied with the progress of Irina and Lara? We have been given the go ahead to start our offensive against the North American cells, and we believe they know exactly where they are hiding. We need to start the attack tomorrow, although our main aim is to capture the terrorists so we can get them back to Attica or Mars. We can then put them through the same treatment that we have used on their leader."

"Well Athena, we have got a lot closer to them over the last year, and they do appear to be free of the terrorist thoughts that have been a large part of their lives. They certainly feel insecure and have suspected that they would be targets once the leaders had identified that they were not to be trusted anymore. Terry and I are now willing to take a risk on their loyalty, so yes, we are ready to seek their support. They are actually waiting in the science room at this moment."

Helena and Athena looked at each other, and Helena responded, "OK Tom, we both feel that is the right move. Bring them in and let us talk to the others afterwards about our attack plan, so we co-ordinate on all destinations. This should ensure that one cell does not have the opportunity to warn any of the other sites before we strike."

Krulandistan Space Centre, Evening 30 December 2082

The F95S was sitting on the landing site, the helic-engines having been used to bring the plane down horizontally as it approached the short runway. The local engineers were standing around admiring this wonderfully shaped plane. One of them now walked over to Chris as he alighted from the cabin.

"Wing commander, welcome. What a great plane, any chance of a ride sometime?"

Before Chris or Robert could respond, he continued, "We all received instructions yesterday to help with the new spacecraft that is over there ready to take off for Mars tomorrow, but were a little concerned about the three guys who gave the order, as they have been acting suspiciously here for some time, and then we heard on the grapevine about this guy Ho Chi Dae, and his right hand, Kim Jong Woo, being arrested. Also, we have not seen the Chinese chief engineer Ming Shang recently. Can you fill us in as to what is happening?"

Chris looked at the badge sewn on the engineer's pockets.

"Thanks Francois Remerce, we very much appreciate your comments. Yes, we are here to investigate recent incidents. Do you think you can get us onto this spacecraft without any of these guys you mention noticing, we do believe there is a problem. As to your first question, let us get on with this task, but maybe before we take off again, we can take you aboard for a short tour."

Francois looked really excited, and turned to two of his colleagues.

"Rene, Paul, check out where those guys are now, and distract them if they come out of the accommodation area. I will get the Wing Commander's group onto the spacecraft. He has promised us a short tour of the F95S if we can get this job done quietly."

Chris and Robert saw their chance, and nodded to Francois. He took them over to a conveyor unit and as promised drove them quietly over to the spacecraft, which stood gleaming in the night lights.

Francois put his passcode into the door entry and it slowly moved back. The spacecraft was comparatively older in design when compared with those that were being developed in Florida, and Chris thought, not anywhere near the advanced Attican craft that we are using for the long space trips.

"Wow, it is an advance on our previous models but don't think I would want to make a long trip in this Rob, the technology is still a good way behind us."

Suddenly they heard some noises, and Francois called over to them. "Sir, there is another smaller cabin down here near the air-lock, and I think the noise is coming from there."

They both joined up with him, and sure enough there was no doubt, something was banging in the sealed compartment.

"Francois, can you open that unit?"

Francois just responded by taking out one of his tools in his belt and inserted it into the lock mechanism. The door slowly revolved open, and the noise stopped. The cabin was small, but Chris stepped in... "Captain Ming Shang, I presume! Do not be concerned, we are here to help you and investigate recent incidents at this site."

"I am so relieved to see you sir. As you can see, I am locked in this contraption, and I think the guys who put me here were planning to use me as a hostage, although I cannot see how they think they will get away when the authorities know of their terrorist backgrounds. Anyway, have you already caught the people responsible?"

"No, not yet Captain, but now I see what has happened I have a plan. First, let us get you out of here. Francois here will help you, and then we must re-seal this compartment and get you back out of sight. I shall discuss this more later. Francois, please?"

****

Krulandistan, 30 December 2082

Song Jing To and his colleagues were now in the spacecraft awaiting signal from the control area to take-off. He turned to Li Sue and Haoyu.

"We can take-off now, and then you can go to give the captain some food and drink, he has been there for some hours, and we do not want him to pass out at this stage. Anyway, for now, all systems seem to be in order, so get strapped in to take-off positions."

****

Chris and Robert were now in the control tower with Francois and the site engineers, and the very relieved Captain Shang.

"They are off, and now, as they have no hostage to negotiate, we shall be waiting for them on Mars. I think that we can safely say that the Chinese base will be more than happy to pass them over to our friends in Acropolis, and they will probably put them through the same treatment that they used for the conversion of Ho Chi Dae. They will surely be able to tell us of any other cell members first, and that should not be a problem when they see their predicament."

"Thank you so much, I am very grateful to you both. We shall seek advice from the respective authorities on taking over this important site, it obviously has no management now."

"Well captain, we would like the ISPEG people to discuss this with you before making any further decisions. In the meantime, we promised Francois and his team a short tour of our new F95S before we leave, would you like to join us?"

"I certainly would, what an honour, thank you."

All of them looked highly excited now. Francois jumped up. "I speak for us all, we are so appreciative, we cannot wait to see this wonderful plane. I hear that it also has a new laser attack system, is this still on the secret list?"

"It is Francois, but we can show you the laser room without going into detail. I am sure you will all enjoy that."

****

Edwards Air Base, 1 January 2083

"Commander, we have just heard that Helena and Athena have the full information on the cell sites in Canada, and a major centre in Wisconsin. The Russian girls have been helpful, and they have high hopes of converting them completely. Major Lancs is asking if they may now set up the attack plan?"

"Good morning, Chris, and Happy New Year to you both! First, great work on the Krulandistan site incident. We have alerted the Chinese to the position, and they have confirmed that they will advise us when they have these three terrorists in custody. Now, I am going over to the mess room; let us talk to Tom Lancs, and get ready for final attack plans on these remaining cells."

"Yes, sorry Commander, Happy New Year to you and Gary, of course. Robert and I must call our parents, there seems to be a lot going on, they will wonder why we have not called. However, we shall be in the mess room by 10.00 hours for updates."

****

Canada, 2 January 2083

Major Tom Lancs and Lieutenant Terry Durham were now in the ISPEG Toronto office talking to Helena and Athena. Irina and Lara had been taken to the local hotel with one of the secretaries, it was still too early to fully trust them while the attacks were being planned.

However, if they could overhear their conversations when they arrived in their room, they would have been that much happier.

"Lara, I do not think we have any choice now, and in any case, I am feeling very interested in Tom. I think he likes me also, so maybe they will forgive us. We have been useful to them after all."

"Well, Irina, I thought you were going quite soft. However, you are right as usual. The Attican girls have treated us well since we moved to the Biosphere with Tom and Terry, and I must say that Terry is very attractive. Maybe we can negotiate something with them that will provide a better life for us both?"

****

Edwards Air Base, Same Time

"Tom, Gary Westmorland here, we have just received the final co-ordinates for the sites that Irina and Lara outlined, and Commander Glen has confirmed that Edwards base has been in touch with the Canadian government, and we have permission to land the armed F95S team in Calgary or Toronto. Therefore, we shall use two planes headed by Wing Commanders Devonshire and Somester, and these will target the sites for you. Can you now get into position with your land team; we are to be ready to capture any persons that try to flee the areas after the attacks on the properties. We prefer to capture the terrorists, but there may be some casualties if they do not surrender immediately. Are your new helic-planes all equipped to take prisoners?"

"Thank you, Gary, we shall be ready, and yes, we can take prisoners on board. Ask Chris and Robert to send us the time sheet for their arrival and details of final attack plan. Also, Helena and Athena want to say hello to them before they leave the base, can you advise them?"

****

Wisconsin, 4 January 2083

Ivor Levinski was in his suite on the top floor of the Palace Hotel, sitting with four other men.

"I just heard that Ho Chi Dae and Kim Jong Woo are missing from the Krulandistan HQ, and news from our three remaining agents indicates that they were captured on Mars by these new alien people. They are now trying to escape to Mars before the balloon goes up. They have a man in captivity on the spacecraft that they intend to use as a hostage, hoping to strike a deal with the Chinese. Their engineering knowledge would certainly be of use to them out there. However, who wants to be stuck on Mars!"

Gregor Marosk, one of the four sitting in the room, and Ivor's right-hand man, now intervened, "Boss, we need to get out of here; not only is there that news, but do you remember the Russian girls we had based in California? They are known to have passed on some information that led to the break-up of our cell network. All in all, I suggest we need to get back to our warehouse facilities; take the money we stashed over the last years from our activities, and get into hiding somewhere nice until this all blows over."

"Gregor, you are right. OK you guys, make your way home, and I will follow you after removing any signs of activity here at the hotel. I need to get some new identity for us all, and I know the man for the job. I shall bring him down to our office with me shortly, and we can discuss how we do this."

****

Canadian Air Force Base, Calgary, Canada, 5 January 2083

"This is USAFX.95S calling Calgary, permission to land as per our recent application to your Commander Rolls. We are 100 miles out and our unit code is CA.001.24. We estimate arrival at 12.40."

"You have clearance Wing Commander, we are expecting you. However, we have just been advised by Toronto HQ that your targets are moving, and you may not have much time on the ground. Can you come to the operations office when you are landed?"

"Roger Calgary, we are coming in now."

****

New York, NBC World News Desk, 7 January 2083

"This is Dan Burger interrupting our correspondent reports with major breaking news."

"Following the news that we reported in December we have now received a joint communique from the world Alliance Group, who are currently meeting in Geneva. It is confirmed that major actions are currently taking place to remove the terrorist cells that were operating under the ECAW name. They have confirmed that all the world governments have now signed the Marsattica Agreement. This agreement is a base for our planet Earth being able to arrange a peaceful coalition with the planet Attica. On 10 January, there will be a further bulletin posted on the new satellite web which will explain the aims of this agreement, and the time frame for future actions."

"It has been emphasised by the alliance that this is an historic time; we now have the opportunity to expand our scientific knowledge for the benefit of the world's people. Shortly after this communique there will be a satellite address to all countries that will introduce our new Attican partners. Questions may be presented to them via the usual links. Keep your channels open for any further news folks.

Good morning, America, and salutations to all our friends around the world."

Krulandistan Space Centre, 8 January 2083

ISPEG had now heard back from the Chinese that they were preparing to arrest the three ECAW members when they arrived on Mars, and were happy to pass them over for interrogation. They had been given a contact at the Acropolis city intelligence centre, and following the recent world alliance announcement, they were excited about a potential first meeting with the Attican representatives.

General Worcester had been selected as the ISPEG representative, and he was now in the centre's office talking to Captain Shang, who, following his recent experiences, had been authorised by the Chinese delegation to negotiate a possible joint ownership of this important site.

"Captain, I have heard of your recent experience and am so pleased that you have made a complete recovery, and that we have the culprits identified. Hopefully they will soon be under our control."

"Many thanks, General, it is very good of you to come to talk to me and my colleagues. Your men were extremely professional and kind in the handling of that difficult situation. I know you are here on behalf of ISPEG, who we respect very much, and I am happy to report that my superiors are prepared to transfer Ho Chi Dae's assets to you. As we have so many of our engineers and astronauts based here, it would be good if you can agree to a 25% interest being held by the Chinese company, Mazrospace, which is now a private company, with engineering and science background."

"Thanks, Captain, I shall take that proposal back to our HQ, but it sounds realistic. Your government has been very helpful in identifying further cells in their country and on the Chinese islands, and as we speak there are joint operations ongoing to eliminate or capture these people and their weapons."

"I think that the staff here will be very happy under you as the senior engineer, and although it may be necessary for us to have a representative manager here, it is obvious that your skills, with our support, will be able to run the centre."

"Well General, that is good to hear, and look forward to your final decisions which I shall relay to Beijing to seek final agreement."

"I have also made some investigations here to ensure we have no other ECAW supporters. If we do unearth anyone, you can be sure that we shall advise you immediately. In the meantime, the news that was broadcast around the world yesterday is still sinking in, but I, for one, am looking forward to meeting these people. Perhaps you will put a good word in for me when we start more regular trips to Mars?"

****

ISPEG Centre, Florida, 10 January 2083

General Worcester was back from Krulandistan, and now in the office with Commander Glen and with senior captain Gary Westmorland, who had been recently promoted to Colonel.

"Hello Gary, congratulations, I am so pleased to hear the news."

"Thank you, Jason, I know you and the Commander here were my main sponsors, I appreciate it."

Gary now looked over to them both with a more serious face.

"Now, I have more news for you. Further to the successful trips to the Krulandistan space centre, the Chinese have confirmed that they have now identified the cells in the Shanghai area, and on the Paracel Islands. Action is taking place as we speak to capture those concerned, and to destroy any facility or weapons that are found at the sites. Commander, I understand that you have coordinated with Wing Commanders Devonshire and Somester, and that the operations in North and South America are going well. We are now waiting for some news from London and from Munich."

"Yes Gary, I can advise that we have eliminated the Canadian cell, the lasers from the new F95S destroyed the warehouse buildings used by this cell, and the terrorists have been captured by our ground forces after a brief struggle. The terrorists seemed to be resigned to their fate. However, after interrogation we found that there is at least one other member who managed to escape, since he was not at the address we attacked."

"We have asked Helena and Athena to use their special sixth sense powers to help us with detecting a man named Ivor Levinski. In the meantime, we shall start registering the prisoners so we are ready for shipping them out to Attica for interrogation and treatment, which I must say, having heard recent news, has worked miracles on Ho Chi Dae, the former leader of this group."

Attica, 12 January 2083, Earth time

Chairman Isis Parapoulis was sitting in the Cabinet room with his senior senators and General Hermes.

"According to Senator Artemis, who has been in constant communication with our agents Poulakis and Balakakis, the Marsattica Agreement is signed, and we have heard that very good progress is being made with the removal of terrorist groups on the planet Earth. I think it is now time for us to expand our activity on Mars, and extend our interests with the citizens of the Earth."

"Regarding the prisoners sent to us for treatment, I have received reports that our clinic for rehabilitation has been very successful with the first group of terrorists. So far, we have had complete success in reversing brain rhythms, to an extent that we may be able to employ these people on Mars in due course. The second in command of this terrorist group has, as you know, been co-operating with us since a close association developed with one of our own citizens, Astronaut Fronimos."

"We are monitoring this man closely, but so far, he has been helpful in exposing the group's leader, as well as other information now being used by the Earth's military to bring this whole group to justice. Eventually these persons will also be brought to our clinic for interrogation and treatment. Our goal is to change these people's thoughts and attitudes so that they can work with our robots, and other Attican authorities."

He stopped for a moment for this news to be absorbed, and then his long arms were raised again as he continued...

"On a more sober note, I have also news from our citizens bureau. Our population is continuing to fall and there are signs that acceleration of deaths is taking place. We have as you know vast resources that we have built over the last 100 years or so, but this serious news indicates that we should speed up our plans for Mars, and of course hopefully make new friends on planet Earth. Please all reflect on this and discuss with our engineers and scientists how we can further extend Acropolis to be a major city, with facilities that will be attractive to all the people who settle there."

"General, can you also please arrange further meetings with Commander Glen and relative authorities on the planet Earth as we must be now ready to work with them to meet our dream of developing a new generation."

"Chairman Isis, thank you. I shall of course leave the expansion plans for Mars to our more qualified senators here, but I can now advise the Cabinet that we have arranged to increase our number of Rotoships, and to make them larger, to enable us to transport larger numbers of people. We expect, that with the new space station facility Venus in full operation close to the Earth, we can now dock the larger spacecraft, and it will be possible for each to carry over 200 people plus our crew, which will of course include our human robot engineers. Zeus will be very involved in the training of personnel on these new ships. I am returning to planet Earth shortly and will meet up with their authorities and our agents again to explain our aims in more detail, and to ensure that we have eliminated all war risks."

"Captain Panomosis will accompany me on this mission as she has learnt a great deal about the Earth's people and is well respected there. We also believe that it may now be time for us to bring back our agents, Helena, and Athena, so they can develop a normal life again, although from my experience of our last meetings I feel they are becoming very attached to two of the people who have been working with them so closely over these last few years. I trust you agree that it must be their decision, they have been invaluable in bringing us to this point in our plans."

Isis nodded, and there was a distinct approving murmur from the Cabinet members.

****

Black Sea, 12 January 2083

Ivor Levinski had summed up the situation in Wisconsin correctly, he had no intention of following the others to the Canadian warehouse HQ. He had money and false passport already in a safe in his suite, and he had made his plan quickly. He had taken advantage of the news of the chairman's and the major's capture, and had made a call to a man in the country of Georgia who was in regular touch with the group. The result was good, because Volta Tomaski had advised him that Ho Chi Dae's luxury yacht had been confiscated, but he had been certain that he could negotiate its return to the Black Sea port of Odessa, where he intended to take control.

"Volta, that was a great job, what do I owe you? I am happy that you can join me on the yacht, she is beautiful. I must say our former chairman certainly knew how to live while we were all in action for the cause."

"You are right Ivor, but we must now find a destination that will take us away from harm. We have lost most of our members here, and you probably heard that your people in Wisconsin and Toronto were captured, and one was seriously injured, but that was what you expected, I suppose."

"OK, let us move on, can you get us a small crew quickly? We could make for the South Pacific Islands; I do believe we could build a new life there. It looks like you have decided to come with me, are there any other agents left where you were based?"

"Well, you have given me a good idea. There are two that are in hiding and have been my main support. I will contact them to see if they would be prepared to be staff on the yacht, after all their fate is in our hands, they are surely going to be detected soon by these new alien people if they stay."

"OK, Volta, and maybe they could bring a couple of those young Georgian women that we heard so much about?"

****

Bakersville, CA, 15 January 2083

Chris was back in his home after the various activity that had seen a considerable success for the joint operations against the ECAW group. He was looking forward to Robert and the girls joining him for dinner, which he had prepared himself. For the first time in a long while, he was feeling relaxed.

To his surprise, the video camera suddenly started up, and immediately he saw Helena waiting at the front door.

"Helena, you are early, but so pleased to see you. Are you OK, and Athena, is she still coming? Come on in and help me in the kitchen, and tell me your news."

"Chris, I have come early on purpose, because I wanted to ask you if you would be happy to be my partner for the future, and at this moment, Athena is with Robert, and will be saying the same things! I know this is a rather big step up in our relationships but we are now in our late-30s and frankly I would like us to be the first to create a new family between our two people."

She hesitated. Chris stopped cooking. He was now looking intently into her lovely large brown eyes, and saw that she was not joking. He took hold of her.

"My dear, Helena, what a wonderful surprise, I have thought about this for some months now, and have been trying to decide when to ask the question. I suppose your special powers probably already read this indecision?"

"Yes, it is true that we did detect your affection for us was getting stronger, but that you were finding it difficult to take this step, and that is why I could be so forward with this request."

"This is fantastic news! I shall be very happy to be your partner Helena, we must give the news to Rob and Athena when they arrive, and celebrate."

Chris was experiencing his first real close embrace, when they were interrupted by the video camera, which had started up again. Reluctantly, he broke away, but as he went to the door, he saw two very happy faces.

"Come in you two, I can already see that you must have been having the same conversation as Helena and I."

"Chris, I think you are right, Athena has told me of the plan she and Helena had discussed, and hope that you have given the same answer as me."

"Of course, Rob, there was no doubt, as you know. I was just going to ask Helena about the kind of ceremony that would be acceptable, and where are we to live? How do the Attican people celebrate these occasions?"

The girls were looking radiant, their olive skin never more shining, and really the guys had never seen them look so well. Helena broke the spell.

"Well, we must all have this ceremony together that is for sure. If we were in Attica or Acropolis, these occasions are celebrated by what we call Gamos, preceded by Proaulia, and finally, after the Gamos, an Epaulia festival! This is not necessary for us, and whatever you suggest will be fine. We are so looking forward to being partners with you, and starting a new life."

Chris was now moving back to the kitchen.

"I suggest we have a celebratory drink now, and after dinner perhaps we can talk to the Commander and see if he can give us his blessing for this unique partnership. It would be great if he could be the speaker at our ceremony, whatever that is. He has been so supporting to our roles and I know he has very high regard for all of us. After that, I shall put us all on a satellite link to our parents. On that note Helena, have you anyone that we should contact for you both? Do you have to have any permission from your parents or the Cabinet for us to be partners, in view of our different backgrounds?"

Both girls wanted to speak at once it was clear, but this time it was Athena first.

"Rob, Chris, we did not want to discuss this before because it is a very sad subject. We both were left without parents some years ago during the last of the conflicts on our planet. Our parents were Senators in our Cabinet, and were targeted by people who accused them, and many others, of allowing the planet to develop chemicals that were already affecting the male population, and very few new children were being born. They died from these cruel attacks. It took some years for our people to realise that it was not something that was controllable, and that we had to seek new solutions. It was after this event that the Cabinet decided they had to introduce the new treatments for people who were showing the signs of violence, or even malicious mischief."

"Helena and I were very young, but because our parents were senators, the cabinet undertook our welfare, and we were schooled by them to become their agents in the plan to seek another life on Mars. However, as you know, the cabinet had seen some other opportunities from their intelligence satellite readings, and the planet Earth was now a major target as they saw citizens with similar, but old-fashioned ways; not too different in stature, and speaking a language that they felt they could replicate with the implants that you know we have today."

"We both had been trained as astronauts and when time was right, we applied to undertake the first trip to your planet. Of course, we did not know what we would find, or how we could make any influence. I can say now that both of us have met many people in the last few years here, but I know I speak for us both in saying that we always thought that you were special. I hope that this news does not affect any of your thinking, but if it does, we would not want to place you in any position where you feel obligated to us."

Robert was quick to see the anxious faces.

"Athena, I do not have to ask Chris, we have thought of this day for a long time, and we guessed that you must have some difficult backgrounds for your people to send you on this crusade. We are very sad for you that you lost your parents, but hope that you will accept our families as your own when we undertake this next adventure together?"

The faces all round now looked more relaxed and Chris was anxious to change the subject.

"Rob, I need to finish up dinner now, will you go and get some champagne that has been waiting in my fridge for some time, ready for any success with our careers, but this is a much better reason."

"Helena and Athena, are you both happy with this drink if we dilute it with some spring water, or would you just like some of my special ginger beer concoction?"

∗∗∗∗∗∗∗∗∗∗∗∗

213

Commander Glen was gleaming. He was sitting with Chris, Robert, and the girls in the mess room.

"Well, Wing Commanders Devonshire and Somester, Chris and Robert, what can I say. It will be a privilege to speak at your ceremony, and congratulations to all of you. Would you like to talk to your fathers about the possibility of having one of the ceremonies at the Biosphere in view of how much it has been a factor in your development, and of course your time with Helena and Athena. I think it would be wonderful for all those who have been involved with you over these last few years to be able to attend. You can always have another ceremony in your church, or maybe the girls have an idea for something on their home ground?"

"We think that would be a great idea, Commander; we did talk to our parents last night after dinner and they are really excited about this. I think there would be no problem with persuading them that we can use the Biosphere. Incidentally, I know you will also be pleased to hear that Captain Panomosis is going to be coming over with General Hermes soon, so we shall of course be inviting them to the ceremony."

"Well, that is great news, I really want to spend more time with Efi, she is such a strong person, and we had such a good time when we went to Miami last year."

Helena now took up the conversation, "We are happy that Efi is coming to see us, and Athena and I will arrange for all of you to be included in our plans. We are thinking that it would be perfect if we have the first ceremony in the Biosphere, but then can we suggest that we think about a legal ceremony that we could hold at our new city of Acropolis? It would be such a big occasion for Attica, and I know the senators, many of whom knew our parents, would be delighted to be invited."

"That is a wonderful idea Helena, let us all start planning dates and venues as soon as we know all concerned are happy about our new union. In the meantime, we still have a few loose ends to tidy up with these ECAW people. Commander, we shall leave you now so we can get some updates from Attica intelligence and our own people over in Florida, and of course, not least, hear what Helena and Athena have to say. We shall all be more comfortable when we know that we have removed these troubling elements."

"Isis, our General Hermes and Captain Panamosis are now on their way to our new friends on planet Earth."

Spiros Artemis was in a private meeting with the chairman, and he now took a short intake of breath before continuing.

"On a more personal subject; we are the guardians of Helena and Athena as you know, and they are asking us if we have any objections to them becoming partners with the two Earth men that they have been working with for the last few years. They want to undergo an initial ceremony on the Earth but would like to have the main ceremony on Acropolis. They ask if you would be the Ceremonial head, and if those of us who knew their parents could attend."

"Spiros, that is our best news yet; of course, we are all happy to comply with their wishes. We met these men and are sure they will be a great asset to our future lives together. It is also an opportunity for us to show off our achievements on Mars. Hopefully this will be the beginning of our dream for a new generation to develop on the planet. Please relay the news to all concerned, and liaise with Commander Glen, our closest ally, to arrange final details. He has our permission to invite all those who have been involved in the creation of the Marsattica agreement."

He hesitated a moment as if thinking, and then continued, "I think this may also be the time for us to release more information regarding our scientific advances on the planet, and thus improve the Earth's knowledge. For instance, we can start advising them on methods we set up to avoid further internal conflicts."

"Good news Isis; do you think we can also release information on the work we are now undertaking in the second volcano, where we found the underground frozen lake some 3 leagues under the surface. Also, you will remember the work that we are planning to re-create atmosphere on the planet. This work is well under way, and we are aiming for 60% gravity initially by means of increasing the mass of the planet; work which has been secretly ongoing for some years is now well underway, and we believe we now have means to move the planet's orbit to be nearer to Venus, which in turn will increase rotation of the planet to be nearer to 700 leagues per hour."

"This will change solar wind speeds, and eventually provide a more normal weather pattern, and hopefully in time produce the rainfall that will regenerate the areas that we have designated for future habitation. Our chief scientists and the head robot are wanting to discuss this with the incoming contingent from the Earth as it will entail some uncertainties. However, the research says it is practical."

Isis was again looking thoughtful.

"I think we should hold on to that last piece of information for now, but certainly give them an indication that we are working on such theories, as this will give them confidence in settling on the planet. Now, on other news, the terrorist that was brought to us for treatment is now ready for release. I think we should ask our new friends how they would like to re-introduce him to society? Will you pass that on to Dimitris, so he can discuss it at his next meeting with the Commander."

"I shall Isis, and thank you for your insight as usual. I also have another subject. We have been advised that a spacecraft that is on its way to the Chinese base on Mars is being controlled by three of the terrorists that managed to escape from their Earth base. We are a little concerned as to its tracking route and will keep you updated, but there should not be a problem."

ISPEG HQ, Florida, 18 January 2083

"General, we have just been advised by Commander Glen at Edwards, that the Atticans are planning to bring four of the new Rotoships over to the Venus station, so we can now advise the respective government officials to be ready to move several people over to Mars in this current year. It will also mean that we can move more of the prisoners to Attica for treatment very shortly. We understand that General Hermes will arrive shortly and has had permission from the Attican cabinet to go ahead with release of certain scientific and medical information, that will help us to have a better understanding of their plans, including the expansion of their Acropolis city."

"That is great news, Hank, we are really moving on now. Our own new spacecraft will benefit from the Attican help, and we should be able to start on the first test flight in less than a year's time. I can see that we shall be able to ship many personnel regularly to and from Mars and Attica in just a few years, who would have believed that just five years ago? Now, on more immediate things, how is progress with the final assaults on the ECAW cells?"

"We have a small problem with the Wisconsin agent that escaped our attack on their Canadian headquarters, and the latest news is that he is on a luxury yacht with some other agents that escaped from European Georgia, we believe also of

Russian extract. Edwards base have advised that they are dealing with that particular problem. As to the spacecraft that escaped from Krulandistan, the three agents are known, and the Chinese are saying they will be under arrest when they land, and are prepared to hand them over to us. We shall advise the Atticans, as they are able to liaise with the Chinese base, and then we can make decisions jointly on their treatment."

"OK Hank, keep in touch, this is getting very exciting for us all!"

****

Edwards Base, 20 January 2083

Chris and Robert had just had a few days with the girls, and for the first time they had shared rooms at the house. However, Chris had now received a call from Commander Glen to say that the ECAW yacht had been located, and he was asking them to be ready to fly a F95S to the target tomorrow.

"Well, Helena and Athena, Rob and I are going to be sent to catch the Wisconsin guy that escaped, together with two other agents from the Eastern European zone, so while we are away can you talk to your people regarding the ceremony that you want when we get to Acropolis. We are so pleased that your two guardians have given their blessing to our partnership."

"All being well we should finalise our work on elimination of the ECAW cells in a month or two, and then we need to talk to our parents regarding the ceremony we all want in the Biosphere. That would mean we could possibly be in Acropolis by our September month."

"Athena and I are going to miss you even more now, so be extra careful as we still have some concerns running around in our heads. However, we shall keep in touch all the time, and as you say, we can start some planning for our Gamos, weddings, as you call them."

Both Rob and Chris looked at each other, they had to take notice of the girl's concerns, they had been so right before.

****

Spacecraft XI-MP—in Space, Earth Time, Late January 2083

Song Jing, Li Sue, and Haoyu Kai had been trying for some days to understand how Captain Shang had escaped. They had not found him elsewhere on the craft, so they could only assume he escaped before they left the base. This was not good news as he would surely report them, and now it was unlikely that the Chinese would accept them. They were on their evening meal of protein pills and dried fruit, and starting to plan how they would handle things when they arrived on Mars now that circumstances had changed for the worse.

A buzzer suddenly interrupted their conversation...

"This is Oranki sir, from the radio satellite room. I have picked up some conversations circulating in the Earth's news rooms regarding our spacecraft; they say that they believe that you are terrorists, and not on this trip just for testing this craft for the landing on the new Chinese base site. This base on Mars was recently involved in an aggressive act against the Atticans, and they seem to know that you, or your colleagues were involved. I do not want to be involved with rights or wrongs, just to get on firm ground again soon. On that matter, I am concerned about the oxygen generator on the craft, was it checked before we left?"

"OK Oranki, we had forgotten that you were there. I will open the entry to the cabin and you will then be able to come here and talk to us."

Leric Oranki had been one of the staff that had been taken on for his expertise on these missions, and was hesitant about this instruction. What if the news was true? Anyway, what can they do to me, I have experience that they need. In any case this emergency may mean we have to return while we can, and surely, I must keep out of harm's way. All this was going through his mind as he entered the cabin.

Song Jing looked at the worried face as he entered.

"Oranki, we are not going to hurt you, you are valuable to us all, so just tell us about your concern."

"My job is to check all indicators every day for any malfunctions, and the oxygen indicator is showing that we only have storage for some 30 days, and the generator is not working to restore our tanks to the level required for this long journey. We expect to be on Mars in late March, and it is now only the end of January. Can you come and look at it with me, and maybe your skills will show us a way to get us back up for this system?"

They all looked more alarmed now, and quickly rose to follow him through to the main engine area.

****

Luxury Yacht 'Ho Chi Min'—Solomon Sea, February 2083

Ivor and Volta had set the boat on automated pilot heading for the Solomon Islands, as they had been assured that they would be able to harbour there. Although the cost would be high, the island mayor would hide their identity. They had ideas of selling the luxury yacht and taking on a more modest, but still very liveable boat. They could surely have a good life.

They were now enjoying some drinks, watching the gannets plucking fish from the high waves around them.

"We must be near to the coast now Volta, in a moment we can start setting up the controls for arrival. The mayor has said he will be there at the port, and we must pay him. However, we can also try to entice him aboard on one of our trips, and probably we can persuade him to reduce the harbour rental if we give him a good time. Do you think the girls on the islands are negotiable?"

"OK, Ivor, if anyone can charm them it is you! Listen…do you hear a high-pitched sound or is it the waves intensifying as we move into the wind?"

A very strong light suddenly flashed across the yacht.

"Ivor, Ivor, what is that, what is happening, the boat is starting to change course. We are not in control!"

Aboard the F95S-2—Same Time, 2083

"Rob, the electronic beam is working, and the yacht is under our control now. Are you ready? We shall go for crippling the yacht, but allowing it to get into port, where I am now in touch with the port authorities. I have asked them to arrest those aboard, and our people will arrive soon to pick them up for further interrogation. So now I am setting the laser to bore a hole just above the water line, and then we shall turn the yacht into the wind so that it starts slowly taking in water. They will have no alternative but to seek refuge quickly in the harbour. We can then fly the plane over the harbour to ensure that it arrives before we return to the air base at Sydney, who are expecting us; all being well, we shall be back in California the next day."

"Chris, all systems go, settings for laser complete, I am opening up hatch for the laser in two minutes."

Luxury Yacht 'Ho Chi Min' Same Time, 2083

"Volta, get down to the engine rooms, we have been hit by some missile I think, certainly the boat is taking in water. We may have enough power and time to make the harbour before we go under."

Volta just stood there, and turned to Ivor with a grim smile.

"Ivor, I do not feel we are now in control of anything, that missile, or whatever it was, came from that plane that flew over just now, it looked like one of the latest USAFA fighters, and I think that was a laser that made the hole in the hull. We must expect the worst when, and if, we arrive. That mayor probably cannot help us now, no matter what money we give him."

"OK Volta, then we must go out in style. I know Ho Chi had this vessel fitted with some armaments, let us see what is aboard before we limp into the harbour. Maybe we can give our oppressors a dose of their own medicine!"

Aboard the F95S-2—Minutes Later

"The yacht is nearing the harbour now, so just check our guys are all ready to take those aboard into custody. The Chinese will certainly be pleased to get them back to the mainland."

"Chris, there are warning signals on the computer, I cannot believe it, but it looks like we may be under attack. Quickly, put the magnetic field ranger on, whatever this is should be destroyed before it hits us."

Chris could see the danger now—it was a missile. He rushed over to the console to engage the field around the plane, but just as he left the console there was a big explosion and the plane lurched suddenly…

"Chris, are you OK, the missile exploded some distance away, but we appear to have been taken some damage as the magnetic field set off the explosive on the missile, but did not defend some of the debris getting through. I can see we need to land more quickly than anticipated. Chris, can you hear me?"

Robert moved over to the control room, he was worried, Chris had evidently hit his head on something hard when the plane lurched and he was not looking good. He could also see that the yacht was now only a few miles from the harbour entrance. He made up his mind what he would do, he would ensure that this was the last terrorist act here, it had to be done. He looked at Chris.

"Chris, are you badly hurt, can you hold on for a moment? I am going to call HQ to seek permission to attack the yacht as it is obviously armed and dangerous. If it has other armaments aboard it could blow up the harbour, and the port personnel."

"Go ahead Rob, I hurt but can hang on. I only wish Helena was with me, she would know what to do."

Robert was already on the communication board.

"My colleague, Wing Commander Devonshire is badly hurt, and I need a new baring for landing as soon as possible. Before I do so, I am going to destroy a target that we partly damaged, but they then released a missile which was destroyed by our protective ring. With your permission, I feel I must put them totally out of action before they cause any more damage."

"General Worcester here, Robert, you have both had good judgement all through this campaign, so we leave it to you how you handle this situation. I am making a call now to our colleagues in Australia, and will confirm shortly if you can land at the Darwin air force base. It is only a few hours flight away, and top-class treatment facilities are available there for Chris."

"Thank you, sir, going into attack mode now, will advise outcome, and eagerly await your instructions for Darwin air base."

****

Biosphere 2, Nevada Desert—Same Day

"Athena, I am getting vibrations in my head indicating a problem. We have nearly finished our work on clearing out the terrorist group now, so what is happening, I am concerned it may be about Chris or Robert."

"I am calling through to Commander Glen now, Helena, maybe he can check for us."

****

Yacht 'Ho Chi Min'—Same Day

"Volta, the plane is still there, our missile appeared to be on target, but it is still flying."

"Can we speed up to Honiara port with the present water damage? If so, I can set the yacht on course and ensure it blows up on arrival, which should cause maximum damage to those who may be waiting for us. We can get off the yacht shortly and use the jet emergency boat to get away."

"OK Ivor, I will try to set the controls to top speed, will you pick up the cache of money we stacked in the hold safe, we are going to need it if we get away."

****

Aboard F95-S, 10 Minutes Later

"Chris, the laser has worked perfectly again, and the yacht is now on fire. I do not expect it to reach the harbour entry. I have also now heard from the Commander and we have clearance to land in Darwin in just over two hours, so hold on."

Chris was dazed, but he had been watching the action on the attack screen, and now he saw a large ball of flame and a cloud of debris was clearly seen in the air below them.

"The yacht has gone Rob; you have done it. However, it is good we are near to one of our bases, I am losing strength."

Honiara Port, Solomon Islands, 30 Minutes Later

"Commander, this is the mayor at Honiara, we can confirm that the yacht has been destroyed. There were a couple of survivors, but they are only minor female crew. They say that two men left the boat just before it entered the harbour. We are awaiting your instructions."

****

Darwin Air Force Base, 26 February 2083

F95-S3 was now in the hangar at the base with the S2. Commander Glen had immediately arranged for Helena and Athena to be transferred to the base when he heard the news. They were now with Robert in the medical centre at the base.

"Chris is not responding as well to treatment as we would wish Helena, but he keeps asking for you."

"Rob, ask the doctor to let me see him please, we must not delay. I hope I can make a difference."

****

Spacecraft XI-MP, in Space, Earth Time, March 2083

Following the problems that Leric Oranki had reported in January, Song Jing and his colleagues had not been happy. There was a problem with oxygen supply now, and it was looking unlikely that they could all survive the next few weeks. He turned to the others in the cabin.

"Well, we seem to have a big problem. I think we must accept that we cannot survive until we reach Mars. We will not advise Oranki of this as he may panic, but it looks like we must plan a suicide mission rather like our ancestors did in the earlier part of this century. We have all done our best for the cause."

Li Sue was quick to respond, "We must make one more check Song Jing, but if our fate is to be in this craft, then what can we do to let the world remember us; will the spacecraft continue on its journey without us?"

"It will, Li Sue, the craft has the new automated systems, and there is where we can make an impact. Let us arm the weapons on board so that they destruct when the craft lands; we do have a precise time for this on the systems monitor. It would be useful if we could find the co-ordinates for the Attican city, as we could change the landing instructions before we pass out. Perhaps Oranki knows someone at the base who may know that? Bring him in, but no words about our final plan."

****

Darwin City, March 2083

Helena was looking at Chris, but now in the more comfortable hotel room that they had transferred to from the base medical centre.

"Thank goodness that we were in time, when I heard it was a brain injury, Athena and I knew that we could make a difference. The surgeon at the base was marvellous in following the instructions that we had transmitted to us from our head Attican etymologist, who was responsible for all the work that led to our progress in making better use of the brain. You should be fully recovered in a few days."

Chris was still wrapped in bandages but he looked at Helena now, and he was starting to talk, when she just smiled at him and spoke, "Later Chris, get fully recovered and I shall talk to the Commander about having a few days here to recover. Maybe Robert and Athena can return now, and help us with setting up plans for our upcoming ceremony at the Biosphere. I am going to talk to them, so get some sleep, and I shall be back soon."

Acropolis, Earth Time, 15 March 2083

Kim Jong and Panayiota were sitting together in one of the new home units that had been built by the robots in the last month. Kim Jong was now seeming a different person. He had marvelled at all the technical achievements that he had seen since landing in the city. His life with Panayiota had opened new opportunities for him to work with the astronaut team, and they, and the human robots, had taken to this new personality. There was something in the back of his brain that seemed to be telling him that this is where he should be, and would have been earlier, if he had not been captured by the ECAW cells when his parents were killed. He looked over to her now, and apart from her beauty, he saw this intelligent lady who he could not believe was now wanting to be with him.

"Kim Jong, what are you thinking, I can see that you are a little sad, and you know we have this sixth sense trigger in our heads that tells me you are going over some old thoughts. I do hope that you will be happy with me?"

"Panayiota, I am only thinking how lucky I am to be this new person, and to have you with me. It is like a dream that may suddenly stop, it is so difficult to believe."

"You are here and hopefully we can make a new life together. However, we must first finish the job that started with the signing of the Marsattica Agreement. I have heard from General Hermes, and he advised me that very soon we can expect a spacecraft to land at the Chinese base a few hundred leagues from here; we must ensure that the occupants are arrested before they can do any damage. We are sure they are former cell members that you had under your control when you were with the ECAW people. Our premonitions are not good. The General and our Intelligence senator advise me that they believe there may be some problems that currently are not clear, but they want us to go over to the base and be ready to intercept them on their arrival."

Mars, China Base, Earth Time, 20 March 2083

Tao Sing was in the mess room with General Chao Feng, who had recently arrived at the Mars base to take control after the recent problems, and he was now listening intently to his senior engineer.

"General, we have a sighting of the spacecraft that we were advised would be carrying the engineers that we were needing for our new projects. However, the Attican people have made contact to say that we should be aware that they are probably terrorists, and they are sending someone over from their base to intercept them on arrival. Our government has advised us that we should support them."

"OK Tao, keep tracking them, and estimate arrival time. Have you been able to make voice contact yet?"

"No sir, they have not responded to our first calls. We shall keep trying and will give estimate of touch down shortly. Also General, we have received a communication from a Captain Fronimos, who is an Attican senior astronaut at the Acropolis city, which we now know is about 250 miles from here beyond the volcanic area. They are suggesting that they come here when the spacecraft arrives so they can take the prisoners away to their interrogation centre, before any trouble can develop."

"I am wondering though if they should land there directly if I get co-ordinates and advise the flight engineer on the XI-MP. Our colleagues who were able to go on the recent goodwill trip to the Acropolis city advised that the facilities there are amazing, as they obviously are taking in traffic continually from Attica, and now we believe, from Earth."

"That sounds sensible Tao, get in touch with Captain Fronimos and make the necessary arrangements. However, we would ask them to advise us when they are in custody as I would like to be there when they are interrogated, if they would be so kind as to allow me access."

Spacecraft XI-MP, Space, Earth Time, 22 March 2083

Leric was in a very weak state, but the good news was that the three suspects on the craft had died, and that meant that he had sole use of the meagre supply of oxygen. However, he was now on his own and had little oxygen left. He had managed to find a few emergency canisters that had been put in the storage area that had not been detected by the other three. His communication channel suddenly came to life, and his spirits rose. Could the craft land before he passed out?

"Hello XI-MP, we are calling the flight engineer for final landing instructions. Please acknowledge these new co-ordinates for Mars arrival."

Acropolis, Earth Time, 22 March 2083

Panayiota was relaxing with Kim Jong. She had just agreed with the Chinese that the suspects on the incoming spacecraft could land at the Acropolis flight centre. They would be ready tomorrow to receive them. Kim Jong looked over at her, he was looking concerned.

"This is sounding too easy. I know how these people think. Have we spoken to anyone on the spacecraft, or have we just given them our position for landing here? Would you like me to talk to them to be sure we do not have any trickery; I am really concerned."

"Of course, Kim Jong, you are one of us now, so do put your mind at rest. I will get the call sign for you, but make it quick as they land here tomorrow."

Spacecraft XI-MP, Later Same Day, 2083

Leric had just received the call from Kim Jong, and had been able to give him the news regarding the three suspects. He had been advised to check the spacecraft before landing as Kim Jong was concerned that these people would have set something up that still made an impact, even after their death. He knew them only too well. Leric was now very weak, but understood he had to check the craft, and particularly the armaments area.

Acropolis, Earth Time, 23 March 2083

"Kim Jong, this is Leric again, the co-ordinates that you gave me are set, I cannot change them. I must conserve my energy with water and the little air supply I have left. I suspect that I will not survive anyway as I noted earlier that the spacecrafts missiles have been tampered with, and it may be that the three of them decided to use these to detonate on arrival. If so, the blast would of course destroy the base, and those persons at the base. As this is more than a probability, please prepare, and advise the Chinese base of the possibility of attack. I must leave you now, I wish you all well…"

"Leric, Leric, listen! I will talk to the Attican engineers here and we shall discuss plans to intercept your spacecraft before landing; I am going to talk to others to find a way of getting you off that craft before this attack…keep listening…hold on."

Kim Jong hurried down to the hyperlink rail to get to the Acropolis space centre, and called Panayiota.

"I have spoken to Leric Oranki on the incoming spacecraft, and there is a big problem; can you speak to the General and the engineers to see what can be done to prevent the spacecraft arriving? There is a strong reason to believe that the craft is set to destruct on arrival, which would destroy the Chinese base, and all personnel in that area. I am on my way up to the space centre, so please meet me as soon as possible. I would really like to help Oranki, he has been very brave under the difficult conditions, and is in a bad way now. Can we get him off somehow? I know that is asking a lot, but your people seem to have so many answers to these problems."

"I am on my way, Kim Jong, we have a few hours to get this solved, one way or another. I am talking to the General and all concerned now. See you soon."

Acropolis, later that day

General Hermes and Efi were now speaking from the Rotoship which was soon to arrive at the Venus space station.

"Panayiota, Kim Jong, we have discussed this problem, and have also spoken to General Chao Feng at the Chinese base. He has agreed that we may take action against the incoming spacecraft as he agrees that the risks are too high to allow it to make land. He understands that Leric Oranki may perish, but cannot see a solution to save him. He says that in view of his service and bravery, their government will support his wife, and she will receive a posthumous medal in his name."

"Thank you, General, and Efi, so pleased to hear from you. Kim Jong was asking me if there was any way that we could get this man off the spacecraft before we destroy it, do you have any ideas or is this really one problem that we are not yet prepared for?"

Efi was first to respond, "Panayiota, as you know I have spent many months on the Earth with Helena and Athena, and we have continued to come up with new ideas revolving around space travel. For instance, all the craft are now fitted with the new jump suits that are based on those used for the first entry onto the planet Earth. It is possible that the Krulandistan space centre had some of the earlier suits fitted for their new spacecraft as safety measures were updated. Is Oranki strong enough to check, and if affirmative, can he get into one? We shall continue to think while you check. It is obviously urgent now."

"Good thinking, Efi. Kim Jong, can you get in touch quickly with Leric and see if he is fit enough to check, the safety gear must be easily accessible, it normally is close to the air-lock hatches."

Spacecraft XI-MP, One Hour Later

Leric had been able to take in the news from Kim Jong, and realised he had set himself up in the cabin closest to the exit hatches. Could he make the effort. His brain was telling him to move, and he crawled over to the exit hatch. He had to get into the air-lock, there was nothing to lose.

Acropolis Control Centre, 3 Hours Later

While the conversations between Kim Jong and the spacecraft were taking place, Panayiota had been thinking following her recent advanced astronaut training exercises, and now she suddenly saw a possibility to end this problem. If only this man Oranki was still strong enough to go through the procedures, she had in mind. Efi was still anxiously talking to Kim Jong.

"Efi, sorry to interrupt, but following your earlier comments re the space suits, I have an idea. We have one of the Rotoships locked on to our space centre that is getting ready to depart for Attica in the next hour. Do you think we could divert it, with me on board, as I would like to try and link with this alien spacecraft while it is in orbit. We have the ability now to spacewalk with our new suits and energy supply. I am thinking of taking the walk from the Rotoship to connect with Oranki before the craft starts it final descent. If we can get him out of the air-lock with just a standard spacewalk suit, I should be able to catch him, connect one of my air supply units to his suit, and bring him back to our Rotoship, or maybe make the full descent with the aid of the new suit. What do you think?"

Kim Jong was quick to intervene. "Panayiota, you are so clever I know, but this sounds extremely dangerous, I don't want to lose you now!"

Efi was listening intently and was first to respond, "Kim Jong, you must understand that we do have abilities that you are still to witness. I have complete faith in Panayiota, and she would only try this if she felt there was a chance of success. I suggest you renew your connection to Oranki, and get him ready by explaining what we are going to attempt, and calming him. I shall call our space centre now, and use my authority to get Panayiota aboard the departing Rotoship. I will also check that they have the new spacewalk suits on board, and adequate facility to treat Oranki if you should decide to bring him back to the craft. OK, get ready, I shall call back to you shortly."

Kim Jong still looked despondent. Panayiota now turned to him as she picked up her bag.

"Do not worry, Efi will guide me. Why don't you go down to the armaments centre to see what they are doing to destroy this spacecraft once we have completed this operation. We cannot allow it to land. You may be able to help them with your knowledge of this spacecraft, which was after all, in your care when you were in Krulandistan. Also, could you call the Chinese base and advise them of our plans. We are not allowing this craft to land, whatever happens."

****

Florida ISPEG HQ, 24 March 2083

Chris was now near full recovery, and Helena and he had been summoned back to discuss the final plans for the ratification of the Marsattica Agreement. Robert and Athena had been back for a few days and updated Commander Glen, General Worcester, and Major Fife, who were now in attendance. Jason was first to speak.

"Welcome back Chris, good to see your recovery, that was a close shave. Thanks to you Helena for bringing him back to us safe and sound. I have heard of your plans to marry from Robert and all here wish all four of you a happy time ahead. We can talk about that later. We are now making plans for us all to attend a meeting at the Attican assembly in the fall, Earth time. The Attican cabinet have agreed that we can use the Rotoships at any time by just organising timetable with General Hermes or Captain Panomosis, so we all need to finalise our plans over the next few months to be ready for this historic moment."

Chris was really starting to feel good now, Helena's care had made him so warm towards her.

"Thank you General, Robert and I are of course very excited, and know that we are so lucky to have found Helena and Athena. We want you to know that we appreciate the huge support you have given us over the last few years. We are hoping to have the first wedding ceremony with our parents present in the Biosphere 2 hall as this is really where it all started. Hopefully you will also all attend with your partners?"

The Commander had been listening intently as usual. "Helena and Athena, I have been in touch quite a lot recently with Captain Panomosis, and I am looking forward to seeing her again shortly. We are hoping to follow your good lead, and if she agrees, we shall be joining you when you plan the date for the Biosphere ceremony."

The guys looked stunned; and it was Helena first to speak.

"Commander, as you would suspect Athena and I are not surprised, but delighted. Efi has been such a strength and I can see you both being very happy. Will you ask her to stay here on Earth, or plan to be perhaps living on both planets? I think we are hoping to live on Mars and Earth at different times of the year, and as our duties direct us."

"I shall talk to you all again when I have spoken more to Efi, but with the new Rotoships now on a regular two-way schedule, it sounds appealing to be living on two planets!"

Jason Worcester just looked at them, but his face was grinning.

"Well, well, what a day! I could not be more pleased with this news, and certainly I know Hank and I will take you up on the invitations."

Jason hesitated, and then with more serious face continued, "Now, a catch up on the ECAW position. The last thing we heard was that we are still chasing the two who got away from Ho Chi Dai's yacht after your successful operation over the Solomon Islands. The more worrying event relates to the spacecraft that is about to land on Mars. There is an innocent guy on board who the Atticans are saying they may be able to save before the spacecraft is destroyed. It must be before it can land as there is certainty that the craft has been set up as a suicide bomb, with detonation on landing. The heading is thought to be the Chinese base on Mars. It would be a catastrophe."

"General, I have news from Acropolis." It was Athena who interrupted, "Helena and I have been advised that Captain Fronimos, our senior astronaut on Mars, is working on a plan to extract this guy from the spacecraft during its final orbit of Mars. That is going to be very difficult but we have faith in their decision. Efi is in regular communication from the Rotoship that is currently nearing arrival at the Venus space station. It is only right that we do try to extract this guy before destroying the craft, he is not a terrorist."

Robert had been listening to the news regarding the two terrorists who escaped from the ship.

"On other news; we are now sure that the two we lost in the Solomon Islands are seeking refuge in the South Pacific area, and maybe have managed to get to Australia. They probably have money, so let us start tracking that area, and see if we can finish that job. So, if the Mars bound spacecraft can be intercepted; and we can capture these two; then I believe that will be the end for this group, and we can start concentrating on peaceful plans for all our people."

Mars Orbit, Earth Time, 25 March 2083

The Rotoship had found the orbit co-ordinates for the XI-MP craft, and Captain Fronimos and Zeus were in the astronaut chamber. Zeus was at the controls.

"Captain Fronimos—I now have sight of the target—please start suiting up procedures and be ready to walk after 3 bells—I have made contact with Mr Oranki—he is in poor health—he understands that he has to get into the air-lock and await your appearance—I will get as close as possible to the craft to give you a good view of the entry point to the craft—He has been asked to put on the protective suit that should enable you to get him back here—Have you got the safety harness checked—is your motor fully charged for the free space travel. You will have about 300 metres to cover to reach him—we shall advise you distance coming back—expect a larger distance."

"Thank you, Zeus, as always looking after us. I am ready, open the secondary doors."

General Hermes, Senior Captain Panomosis, still in their Rotoship, and Kim Jong, now in the Acropolis control centre, were anxiously watching events taking place on the departing Rotoship. Kim Jong was amazed at how nervous he felt, something he rarely experienced in the past. He turned to them now.

"General, Captain, I know you will shortly be back to Earth, and no doubt are very excited, so I really appreciate you staying in contact with me until this is over. I have now spoken to the Chinese base and advised them of our intentions regarding the destruction of the spacecraft. They would like a call from you to confirm that I am working with you on this matter. They obviously still have some concerns about me, following our last meeting!"

231

Before they could reply, he continued, "I am hoping Panayiota can pull this off quickly, she has taken on a really tough challenge; have your astronauts actually done this kind of manoeuvre before? I am feeling so worried about her."

"Kim Jong, this is a new challenge, even for us, but we do have capabilities that you will soon fully understand, so keep calm, we shall do all we can to bring this incident to a satisfactory conclusion. You all need to be ready to attack and destroy the craft when it is in atmosphere, after ensuring that Oranki has been extracted by Panayiota. It must not land at the Chinese base."

****

Oranki was now more alert, he still was feeling a little faint, but he had managed to put on the suit; he was aware that the oxygen belt had a meagre supply once he left the craft. He wondered how this could work. Nothing to lose he told himself, I should be dead already. He looked through the site hole in the air-lock and into view came this fantastic vision, a flying saucer! His thoughts were interrupted by the communication transmitter on his space helmet.

"Mr Oranki, please look for me, I am space walking over to you now from the spacecraft you can see from your window; I need you to open the outer door of the air-lock when I give you instruction, it must be a quick action. When I arrive be ready for me to put a harness on you, before we lift off back to our ship. Speed is of the essence if we are both to survive."

Efi Panomosis was silently worried, it was not often that she had cause to feel this way. The suits and power unit had been designed to take on these kinds of possibilities in space. However, the indicators on the Rotoship's satellite screen were being relayed to her, and she had not been able to pick up a sight of Panayiota after she reached the alien spacecraft. They had seen her enter, but the screen was not picking up any sign of her returning with the male they knew as Oranki. She turned to the General.

"I am going into our main control room a minute; I need to find Panayiota; I will report shortly on progress. I hope that she has things under control but I cannot detect her for the moment, she has gone off screen. We need to be sure she is safe before our people set up for the destruction of the alien craft."

Zeus was also concerned; he went to the transmitter again.

"Captain Panayiota—please respond—Why have you not left the spacecraft?"

"Zeus, I have a problem, when I entered the spacecraft, my suit was damaged trying to get Oranki into position to attach him to my lifeline. I am not sure I can make the spacewalk. Can you advise alternative plan, or shall I try to land the craft? Please check with Captain Panomosis and our space centre control."

****

"Panayiota, it is Efi here. Zeus has advised me of the problem. The two options are; one, we try to extract you from the craft by Zeus getting another suit over to you; he does have a suit that was fitted especially for the human robot team; or, two, we try to get the alien spacecraft under control and land it. If the latter we need to advise our guys that we want the craft to land, and not to destruct as they have been advised. I must act now, what do you think is best option?"

"Efi, I think we must try and land; the first option is too risky and I still have a weak guy to control. Oranki is sure that this spacecraft is set to destruct on landing, so can you think how we get me out of here once we are inside the planet's atmosphere. I believe that the spacecraft can survive the planet entry and so that is not the problem. I am thinking of what would happen if I try using my suits power pack, together with the old type of parachute that I have seen is still in Oranki's suit, and jump the craft some minutes prior to landfall. It is worth trying as we need to get down fast now, as not much oxygen left. You could then destroy the craft after we depart, but before it lands."

"Panayiota, I am in touch with Zeus now, and I shall ask him to use the electronic brain on the Rotoship to take control of the spacecraft, but we cannot solve the detonation problem without destroying it prior to landing. So, I think your idea is good, it is very risky, but it is better than the alternative. Please start getting Oranki prepared for your ordeal, and explain to him clearly what he must do. He seems a very brave guy, so good luck."

Acropolis Space Centre Control, Earth Time, Early 26 March 2083

"Kim Jong, we are going to have a very tense situation in the next few hours, the alien spacecraft is going to start landing procedure under our direction from the Rotoship, but evidently it has been set to detonate on landing. The spacecraft is still set to arrive in a few hours at the Chinese base, and we cannot seem to change that destination. Therefore, we are going to try to destroy it just after it enters the planet's atmosphere. As we believe that you have now been fully accepted by the Chinese following the General's call to Chao Feng, please go immediately to their base with one of our engineers and advise them of the plan. They must be ready to fire missiles directly at the craft; it must be destroyed prior to landing so it does not detonate on the base."

"OK Efi, but you talk about destroying the craft; how do we get Panayiota and this guy out before that drastic procedure. Are we sure that the spacecraft has been set up to destruct on landing?"

"The guy on board, Oranki, has confirmed that. So, as we have explained before, we do have some advanced techniques that help our astronauts, so you will have to trust us. We shall do our best, it is risky, but Panayiota is ready and trained to take that risk."

Spacecraft XI-MP, Two Hours Later

"Mr. Oranki, you understand all I have said."

Oranki was scared, but he looked at this lovely woman with her long arms, then nodded.

"Here is the harness, and some of my oxygen supply; we shall be departing the spacecraft in a few minutes; wait for my signal, and then open the air-lock door. It may be very hot, so use the gloves in the pack I gave you. Do not panic; as I said you will be strapped to me, and my longer arms will be an asset in this operation. We shall be dropping quite fast due to the lack of atmosphere on the planet, but then we should slow down when I can get my power pack started, although it is low on energy, so do not expect to float."

"After that, I am going to open your parachute in your suit, and hope that together with the power I have left, it should get us down on the ground at a reasonable speed, so we should be able to roll over and avoid any serious injury. I shall give our control centre an idea of where to pick us up, so they should arrive soon; they will have emergency supplies for us to use until they can get us back to the safety of the Acropolis city."

Panayiota had quickly gone through the procedure again, just to keep him calm, because she knew it was time to go.

"OK, let us open the air-lock door Mr Oranki; be ready to jump with me…now!"

****

Chinese Base, Mars, One Hour Later

Kim Jong and the Attican engineer, Remus Achilles, had made the journey in good time, and were explaining the situation to Tao Sin and his crew at the base. Tao was responding, "Kim Jong, what a difference since our last meeting, I have heard from our Attican friends of your change of heart, and how helpful you have been since your arrival on Mars. Thank you for your warning. We have now monitored this spacecraft's position, and I will go to the missile room to be ready to destroy it, if the Attican authorities are certain that is necessary."

"Thanks Tao, yes, I appreciate I have been an enemy in the past, but now hopefully we can work together in the future, once we solve this problem. I am very concerned right now as my girlfriend is aboard this craft, and is trying to escape with one of the surviving members of the crew before it is destroyed. She is an Attican, and very experienced, but still, it is difficult to see how she can pull this off. I do not want you or your team to be exposed if we fail to take down the craft. I have experience of the missiles here, you will remember that they came from my former base in Krulandistan. Therefore, leave this to me please, I need to do something useful that will finally show everyone that they can fully trust me."

Mars Atmosphere, Later Same Day

Oranki would not open his eyes, this was amazing; this ladies' long arms were wrapped around him, and he knew that the harness was also attached to her suit. For some reason, he was feeling safe.

He felt for the button on his helmet transmitter. Captain, are you OK, are we going to your plan?

"So far Mr Oranki—you are doing fine. I have the power pack on now, and in a minute, we shall open your parachute, so be ready."

Rotoship 4—Mars Atmosphere, Same Time

"Zeus here Captain Efi—the craft is now out of orbit and starting entry to ground—confirm that we cannot change present landing co-ordinates—can confirm that Captain Fronimos has started her descent with the man she named as Oranki—please confirm that we are ready to attack—estimate that the craft is only minutes from going into landing procedure. We are now returning the Rotoship to base."

"Thank you, Zeus, we have advised all concerned and they should be ready now."

****

"Tao Sin, this is Captain Panomosis, I am currently in space and unable to be positive assist. We may have a problem, has Kim Jong arrived? We have detected that the two people in freefall are in a direct line with the spacecraft, and we must be sure that we do not hit them on the missile trajectory. Please pass this on to whoever is handling the missile attack."

"Hello Efi, this is Kim Jong. I have spoken to Tao and advised him already that there may be a problem. I am going to the missile bunker now; I am the most experienced when it comes to these types of missiles. Has Panayiota been able to get out of the craft safely?"

"She is on her way with Oranki, and I have alerted our medical team to go to meet them when they hear from Panayiota, who will I am sure be shortly giving them landing details; they will be in the best hands. If you have visual on the spacecraft, make sure that Panayiota is not in line with your attack as she descends. You should see the spacecraft now; it is imperative that the craft is destroyed before it reaches you."

"Kim Jong! Kim Jong! Are you there?"

Tao Sin had not been happy to be asked to go with the engineers to the emergency shelter, but Kim Jong was insistent that he should handle the missiles. He seemed to be aware of the danger to those on the base. The noise of the explosion had even sounded in their bunker, and Tao was now searching the missile room area which was in a terrible state. No answer was coming back to him.

****

Same Time, 100 Mars Miles from Acropolis

The Acropolis medical team were seeing a large fireball in the distance as they raced across the Mars desert to reach the two persons that should have landed. The noise of an explosion was travelling to them just a few seconds later. The head of the team was Latros Pericles, he was speaking on his transmitter as they sped along.

"Captain Panomosis, can you hear me? Have your monitors on the Rotoship detected the explosion that we can see from our vehicle? Is there any damage that we need to know about? I assume we prioritise the two people on the ground?"

"No Latros, we are now near the planet Earth and have lost visuals, but we know Captain Fronimos and a Mr Oranki have landed, but could be in serious condition; please do all you can to get them back safely. In the meantime, I shall make enquiries regarding the explosion, I hope that it is only the destruction of the alien spacecraft which was heading for the Chinese base. Will call you later if you are needed."

****

Chinese Base, Hours Later

Tao Sin had found Kim Jong, but it did not look good.

"Tao, I had the missile in line and fired…but it only diverted the craft…the force of the explosion was exaggerated by the very low atmosphere here, and thus blew all this debris into the missile chamber… I am hit somewhere…can you get some help… I feel I may not be able to move."

"Hold on, my team will come down and make you more comfortable Kim Jong. Here is my spare oxygen kit, I can put that on you for now. I must now contact Captain Panomosis to see what she can suggest regarding getting you urgently into their treatment centre in Acropolis, I am sure they have all the facilities to help you."

****

237

Mars Desert, 100 Miles from Chinese Base

Panayiota and Oranki were now both in a medic tent that Latros and his team had speedily erected, and were taking in the fresh oxygen mix. The few bruises they had experienced were nothing serious, and Latros had decided to deal with those later when he returned them to Acropolis. Leric Oranki was still dazed, and could not believe he was still alive. Panayiota was now strong enough to start asking questions.

"Latros, thank you so much for looking after us, that was some journey! The new suits power plant was our saviour; that trip was a great test for the equipment; we had never tested it under such conditions. Can I now speak to Captain Panomosis, please?"

****

"Panayiota, you must be prepared for some bad news. I have just been advised that Kim Jong is in a very serious condition at the Chinese base. Although the missiles struck the target, the spacecraft explosion was too near to them, and debris badly damaged the missile chamber. If you and Mr Oranki are well enough, I am going to ask Latros to continue to the scene to see if we can help, he has most of the supplies he needs with him."

"Efi, you are not saying he is dead? I must go with Latros, maybe Oranki can stay in the tent until we see what has happened. I must see him."

****

Chinese Base, 3 Hours Later

Kim Jong was now in Panayiota's arms, but Latros was looking serious.

"We have not been able to stabilise his condition, Captain. If we are to save him, I need to get him back to Acropolis urgently where I shall try to stem the haemorrhage in the brain. I am calling for the heli-rover so we have maximum speed. While we are on our way, I will ask one of our team to collect Mr Oranki with the hovercraft, and they can take him back to our medical base on Acropolis. You can come with me, that may keep him comfortable. Let me know if you see any change in him as we travel."

****

Darwin Seaport, Australia, 30 March 2083

Ivor Lerinski and Gregor Marosk were sitting on the deck of a new yacht drinking Australian beer. They had changed their attire, cleaned up, and now had found some girls to come and join them. After their escape from the yacht, they had negotiated to buy a twenty-metre boat with great accommodation, and most importantly it had given them quite a lot of extra cash.

"Gregor, we may have lost the cause, but we should be able to start a new life on the sea; stopping unannounced at various ports, we may escape being detected. We also can now afford to take on a couple of girls from time to time?"

"Great Ivor, but let us start moving soon before they catch up with us."

****

Bakersville, CA, 30 March 2083

The now regular meeting of the happy four was again taking place in Chris's house; he was now fully recovered, and was as usual in charge of dinner. They had all moved to the kitchen to be with him, and it was Robert who was pouring everyone a drink, the girls as always taking the white wine and water. They had all been continuing discussing personal plans for the upcoming ceremonies, but also their new status in ISPEG, following the recent successes against the terrorists, and the signing of the Marsattica Agreement. Robert was now voicing his concern about tidying up the terrorist threat.

"Following our earlier chat, we seem to have successfully ended the threat from the spacecraft that landed on Mars. It did crash, but was hit by a missile from the Chinese base just before landing. Some remarkable thinking by Captain Fronimos from the astronaut centre, enabled her to transfer from the Rotoship to the orbiting spacecraft, and she was able to save the life of the engineer who had been duped by three of the terrorists."

"We no doubt will hear more about that fantastic feat later. However, the bad news is that the former terrorist Kim Jong, now close friend of the captain, and who was responsible for the downing of the spacecraft, was seriously injured, and is in life support at the Acropolis medic centre."

Helena intervened, "Robert, that is sad news for Panayiota, I must get in touch with her urgently; they both had become very close in the short time they have been together, and certainly she has, more than anybody, been the catalyst in bringing Kim Jong back to reality. He has become a totally different person."

"However, as you say, we must also move on with the finalisation of all threats. Regarding the two or more terrorists that escaped in the Solomon Islands, it is fairly certain that they are now in your Australian area. As we do not want to have another incident as happened on Mars, I am thinking with Athena of another more peaceful plan to get them under our control. Athena, can you carry on while I enjoy this drink."

"Yes, as Helena said, we have thought about this quite a lot. We have been speaking to the Russian girls recently following their closer association with Tom Lancs and Terry Durham. They are willing to help us finish this job, and they feel that by doing so they will prove that they are ready to totally embrace a new life."

"How can they help Athena; these terrorists are on the other side of the planet?"

"Well Robert, the idea we have is to get them to Australia as soon as possible, maybe we can get permission for them to travel on one of your F95S planes to save time. They could be there by tomorrow night if we act now."

"They would be given a sum of money to allow them to track where these people are now, and then try to use their charms to get aboard the yacht on pretence that they can cook and clean, and maybe offer other services."

"They certainly have some charms as they have proven over the last few years, but are they really ready to take on this very risky task?"

Chris had been quietly listening while preparing the meal.

"OK, let us take dinner now, but I am going to make a quick call into the Commander and ask him to talk to us in an hour or so. Be prepared with our story. Also, perhaps we should ask the intelligence centre in Attica if they can help with their surveillance data, to give us a better idea of where to send Irina and Lara, if that is approved."

****

Brisbane, Australia, 2 April 2083

The 'ocean dreamer' solar motor launch had managed to navigate around the Australian coast taking in a stop at the Great Barrier Reef, which despite earlier century concerns, was now thriving under the 'World Nature Conservation' management. This was partly because the climate had not continued to warm as predicted, but in fact had started cooling, due to the influence of the melting glaciers in the early part of the century affecting sea temperatures. In fact, the glaciers had started to grow again. They were now in the port of Brisbane, situated in the Fishermans Islands, and were beginning to enjoy the life.

No identity pass had been requested, so they could see this life on the ocean being anonymous. Ivor was now in the town looking for food and drink to stock up the boat for the next trip. He had got downtown in a taxi to save using any of the stolen cards or having to give his identity to hire a car. He was close to the market when he spotted a new entertainment centre. He took note and thought immediately that this is where they may find a couple of girls who were interested in joining them, and hopefully they could also cook and clean! He would return with Gregor to investigate later in the evening.

Darwin AAF Station, Australia, Same Time

The F95S had made its second trip to the Darwin air force base. The guys at the base were delighted to see two lovely images emerging from the super plane. Irina and Lara had no shortage of helpers to show them to the temporary accommodation. They had again been amazed at the treatment they had received from Commander Glen and the Attican girls, the trip had been sensational, just five hours from the Florida air base.

The Wing Commander had been so helpful with his advice during the trip concerning their upcoming task. He really did seem to want them to be certain they could undertake the task, outlining the risks that were in front of them. Anyway, now they were enjoying this attention. They had been advised that they were going to be guests of the Australian air force for dinner that evening, but before that they were to receive a briefing in the mess room about 18.00 hours.

****

Biosphere 2, Nevada, 4 April 2083

Helena and Athena were back in the main hall with Chris and Roberts parents. They had been reluctant to stay home when it was decided that Chris and Robert were to take Irina and Lara to Australia, but they had given them all the news from Attica, and they all knew that there was a lot of planning to do regarding the upcoming ceremonies, not only for the weddings, but for the trip to Attica and Mars which was to be scheduled shortly, which would be for the final ratification ceremony of the Marsattica Agreement. This was to be held in the great assembly room under the chairmanship of Isis Parapoulis. All the Earth's senior government officials were expected to attend.

Professor Devonshire was first to open the conversation.

"Well, Helena and Athena, we know you are missing our boys already, but we must now get down to final plans. I am not sure if the Colonel and I can make the Attica trip, we shall have to undergo some medicals to check our stability; but I know that our dear wives will go no matter what, so let us see."

Phillip now intervened, "Josh, we shall all make it, I feel sure, it is such a celebration after all that has happened in the last twenty years or so. Also, it is about time that we let the girls call us by either our first names or just 'dad' if they prefer, it is good with me."

Josh, Ruth, and Dawn nodded, and Ruth now took up the conversation.

"OK, and we shall of course be happy with the same arrangement, but 'mum' I think is fine. What do you call parents in Attica?"

"We use Metera for mother, and Patera for father, but thank you, we shall use your terms, we feel so close to you now. We are really happy with this outcome after what started as a lucky meeting with your sons."

Phillip was now looking more serious. "I think we can say that everyone is happy with the upcoming event, and all look forward to you joining our families. We now must get on with setting these dates and making up the invitation lists. For the wedding ceremonies that should not be difficult, but for the Attica business trip we shall have to tread carefully so as not to offend those we have to leave out. I think General Hermes and Efi advised us that the new Rotoships here will take at least two hundred persons, but with the degree of comfort most diplomats are used to, we may have to reduce that number. What do you both think?"

"We shall speak to those concerned with the Rotoship organisation, and also speak to our Spiros Artemis regarding the arrangements being made for the agreement ceremony on Attica later this year."

Athena now added, "Regarding the earlier news from Attica, we have detected some activity in your Eastern Australian area. There is a new boat in the harbour that you call Brisbane, and Spiros believes that may well be the one we are trying to trace. Two men who had not been seen before in the area were evidently making enquiries about girls in a local entertainment centre and had been acting rather strangely. It is worth checking."

Brisbane Harbour, April 4, 2083

After the welcome dinner, where they had received a lot of attention from the guys, Irina and Lara had now booked in to the small hotel that ISPEG had recommended as not too ostentatious and were now ready for action. One of the pilots on the F95S that had brought them there in record time had taken lodgings close by, and he had already called to say that he had seen the two suspects when he walked down to the local harbour that morning. They had boarded a luxury motor launch, which, in his opinion, may well be the target.

Irina had now decided that they should go out to eat in the nearside cafeteria where they could watch the local action. They were half way through their snack meal when their patience was rewarded.

"Lara, get ready to go. We must follow those guys, and seek an opportunity to talk to them. They may have heard our names from the old cell, but they have never seen us, so we should be unknown to them. Perhaps we shall take on new first names just in case. I think Tara for you fits, and maybe Serena for me?"

"Sounds great, Serena! I have got the bill."

****

Brisbane, Flutter Entertainment Centre, Same Evening

"Well Ivor, this is some place, so many great looking women. Can we just ask some over for a drink, or how do you want to play it?"

"Calmly Gregor, we do not want to move too soon; there is some dancing, but I see there is also a gaming room over there. Maybe we can take a little gamble and at the same time attract some female attention. Remember, we are not just interested in the sex, we really need someone who is interested in coming on the boat, and then, we maybe have the best of both worlds?"

****

Irina had seen them going to the gaming room.

"OK Tara, this is an opportunity. Our guys gave us some money, let us take a seat near to them if they go to play Roulette. We cannot afford the Banque table, so hoping they also start with something a little more in our league."

****

Ivor was sitting at the Roulette, and was whispering to Gregor.

"See, I told you to stay calm, look how many girls have joined this table. Some are having to wait to sit. Maybe our first move is to offer two of them our seats, we can see what develops, we are in no hurry to play."

****

Irina had stood aside while she decided how they could make contact with the two guys, but that problem was solved very quickly.

"Hello, I am Ivor. My friend Gregor and I were wondering if you and your friend would like our seats as you seem to want to play. We are in no hurry, but happy to join you."

"My names Serena, and this is my friend Tara, we are Russian girls on holiday here. We do not have that much money but it would be good to try our luck."

"OK, both come and sit over here and meet Gregor, and maybe we shall watch you make your fortune."

Irina managed to laugh. Her experience in the ECAW had put her in a position to know how to deal with most situations. She had to think through how this was going to end.

The girls took their seats, and the guys as expected had already ordered some drinks for them; she could see that they were of a type that would soon make them sleepy. So, she thought, if that was the game, they obviously were hoping to take them home. Shall I let that happen? What would be the end scenario? They had been told that the ISPEG people wanted them alive, but what about us?

The evening was going as predicted, the two guys had taken over at the table and asked them to wait as they would like to take them to their yacht, show them around, have some cocktails. Later they would return them to their hotel. They had made plenty of money that was for sure.

Irina looked over to Lara. Good, she was in good shape, she had also watered the drinks while the guys were distracted.

"Ivor, we will be asleep if we don't move soon. Are you happy to go. We are looking forward to seeing your boat you have mentioned."

****

Brisbane, Same Evening

Captain Gary Kent had thought about the message he had passed on to the girls, and was not happy. If the guys he had seen were indeed the terrorists, then they were in a strong position to get away again. He had watched them all enter the entertainment centre, and so far, nobody had come out. He suddenly thought of a plan. He made a call to Florida; he was going to be delayed for a while in Australia.

****

Aboard 'Ocean Dreamer', Hours Later

It was now nearly one o' clock in the morning, and their plan was working. Irina and Lara had heard that they wanted to have them aboard for a longer period to help them as crew, and had offered them one of their superior cabins and some money as an incentive. They were both in the cabin now.

"We must go carefully, Lara, they are obviously expecting that we shall be easy prey. However, I do not fancy landing up in bed with them. I think they will try to dominate us. We need to get them to go easy tonight, play them along with some chat, and hope that tomorrow we can get in contact with the ISPEG people to confirm that these are the guys they want, and have them advise us how we should proceed."

****

Ivor and Gregor had just returned to their quarters after chatting with the girls. They had been disappointed that despite giving them drinks and offering them some cash for their trip, they had not been successful in attracting them to bed. They had decided that it was not time to use any force, they had them on board, and there was another day. However, Ivor had been thinking.

"Gregor, did you think there was anything odd about the girls, apart from them not obviously wanting to go to bed with us tonight, even after all the drink and chat. They seemed more nervous than I expected after the way they behaved in the town. Somewhere in my mind, I am wondering if this is a trap. Do you remember some time ago, that our colleagues in Krulandistan had mentioned some concern regarding two of our agents."

245

"They were I am sure Russian girls, and although the North American cells were asked to eliminate them, I do not think they were successful. Perhaps it would be wise to lock them in tonight until we can leave the harbour tomorrow. We can then interrogate them to be sure. If they do turn out to be these agents, we shall have to either get rid of them at sea, or use them as hostages if they prove to be working for the ISPEG group. We are not going to give up this opportunity for a new life."

****

Gary Kent was listening. He had followed up his suspicions by getting onto the motor yacht while the two terrorists and the girls were occupied in the town. He had found it easy to access the lower decks, and was surprised that on such a big boat he had not seen or heard any crew. He now was certain that these were indeed the guys they wanted. How to get them without endangering the girls. He quickly returned down the corridor to the boat's hold, and lay there thinking, before picking up his solar phone, and punching in his message.

****

Bakersville, CA, 5 April 2083

The initial wedding ceremony plans had now been set, and Chris and Helena were now back at the house following the news from Australia.

"Helena, we must help Gary, he is in a difficult spot. The news that the Russian girls may be taken hostage has made it difficult for him to take action against these two men. We need to either get them off that boat somehow, so we can get them to safety, or allow our team to storm the boat and take our chances. Whatever happens, we must end this. It is the last chapter in our long-term efforts to eliminate terrorism on our planet."

"Well Chris, I think that as we have some time before the Biosphere ceremony, I would like us to fly to this Sydney destination, where we know they were heading; between us I know that we can resolve this. Does Robert need to come? If so, you can be sure that Athena will want to be with him."

"I think he will want to assist me on the plane; I shall call him after I ask the Commander if we can take one of the F95S's tonight; the sooner the better. I

246

know it is a big expense, but we see this as the end play for the ECAW era, and hopefully the Marsattica Agreement can begin in earnest."

He picked up his transmitter while continuing.

"I am advising Gary that we hope to be on the way shortly, and he should prepare himself for a few days aboard, until we can get in position to help him. If the girls should be in any danger, then I have told him he must do whatever he thinks is necessary to protect them."

Sydney Harbour, 7 April 2083

Irina and Lara were now very depressed; they had been roughly treated since these men had interrogated them, but had not been assaulted. They had been forced to do all the cleaning and cooking duties, although it was seeming that the terrorists wanted them in reasonably good health, as they were receiving good food and drinks in their cabin. However, there was no doubt that they were now hostages. They had been locked in at night, and they were under constant scrutiny.

"Lara, we must get off this boat now while we are near the harbour. It is going to very difficult to get off when they start moving again. What can we do to distract them enough so that we can get on the tender? If so, do you know how to operate that?"

"I have an idea Irina, but it does mean some risk, are you ready to take a chance?"

****

Gary had received a new message. His trips to the lower deck toilets and to the garbage area had managed to help him survive the last few days. He continued his vigil on the girls and the men, but saw no problem yet.

****

Ivor and Gregor had started to feel safe again, and with the girls under their control, were now thinking of a more determined effort to keep them, they were after all very desirable. Perhaps later they would be more willing to share the new venture with them.

****

Irina heard the lock being turned in the cabin door.

"Lara, listen, I think those guys are coming in, what do they want now?"

The door swung open, and Ivor and Gregor went over to the girls and before they could resist, they were thrown onto the beds.

"We have waited patiently for this time girls; we expect you to stay with us for a long time, so we may as well enjoy ourselves. You will be given more time and we promise to get some more help on the boat if you will be nice to us."

Irina was so angry.

"We have no wish to be your whores, you will be caught soon, and if you harm us, you will certainly be sorry."

****

Gary was just in the corridor and had heard some of the conversation. He was about to take a chance on jumping into the girl's cabin when his solar transmitter vibrated. He looked down, it was his Wing Commander. He made a quick decision.

The girls had stunned Ivor and Gregor by their fierce response, and they could see that they were not going to enjoy any romantic romp while they were so angry.

"OK, we are going to release you now, but you will be kept in the cabin until you see sense and join with us on our venture. You would be much more comfortable. You will only be released if the authorities agree a deal with us that does not involve several years in jails, and that, at the moment, looks unlikely."

****

Sydney Airport, Later that Day

"Gary, well done. Do you think that they had any idea that you were on the boat?"

"No, Wing Commander, after your call, I got out as soon as I heard them tell the girls that they were locking them in, but was sure no harm was coming to them for that moment. Fortunately, the waters here are warm, and as promised, you were at the harbour to get me; I am now fully refreshed, thank you."

"Gary, we are all on first name terms for this mission. We really appreciate your efforts and bravery in watching over the girls. You did take a big chance."

"Anyway, as you can see, apart from Wing Commander Somester, Robert to you, we have brought along Helena and Athena, who you will remember from earlier tasks. We all need to finalise a plan now to get Irina and Lara back safely, and at the same time try to capture these two terrorists alive. Helena has a suggestion, so listen carefully. We expect the boat to leave the harbour tomorrow, as they will believe they are safer at sea."

"Well, at least we shall know where and when they are going Chris, because my last job before leaving the boat was to place a tracker in the hold."

✶✶✶✶✶✶✶✶✶✶✶✶

'Ocean Dreamer', Whitsunday Islands, 9 April 2083

"The girls have been calmer since we left them alone for a while, and I have put them back on cooking, and other light duties. However, thank goodness this boat is so automated, even without crew, it is so easy to navigate."

"OK Gregor, we are now on our way to the harbour on these lovely islands; the weather is great, and I have looked up places of interest to us that we can go to on arrival. We shall have to lock the girls back in their cabins shortly."

✶✶✶✶✶✶✶✶✶✶✶✶

"Gregor, get up here quick, there is something strange in the sky and it seems to be coming this way."

✶✶✶✶✶✶✶✶✶✶✶✶

The Rotoship had been called on by Helena after she had noted that it was waiting at the Venus ISS for a return trip to Attica after recently landing General Hermes and Efi. She and Athena had explained their plan to the Commander, and now Chris and Robert were looking at the monitors on the F95S, following the action. There was a further surprise for the terrorists coming soon.

"Robert, they are about two miles from the coast now, I can see that the Rotoship has got their attention. Shortly, one of the robot team will be sending out a message to the terrorists to distract them. Are our guys ready with the diversion tactic, so we can get one of them on board?"

****

"Gregor, we are near to the harbour now, but what is this all about, how does that huge thing suspend like that? It is really a flying saucer!"

He was still goggling at the craft above them, but then a huge echo type voice was heard.

"This is Rotoship 2 from the planet Attica. We have you under surveillance—you will be destroyed, if you do not return to the harbour you call Sydney—We shall give you one hour in your time to turn round."

The terrorists were stunned, and then as they were trying to take in this new event, another distraction…

"Ivor, look, there seems to be some guys out there who are paragliding on those new jet skis. Are they anything to do with this, there must be at least four of them."

"I am more concerned about this object above us. Those guys look like they are just having fun; after all we are close to land now. 'More importantly, do we use the girls now? Do they know we have them as hostage? Do they care?' How can we communicate to this craft to warn them off if they do know these girls are aboard?"

"Let us go down and make sure they are locked in their cabins. I wish we were having fun like those guys seem to be having. Look, some of them are waving, perhaps they have just seen the object above us. Many would not believe this object; it is so big. It must be like the one reported a few years ago when we first heard about a new planet. I am worried, let us hope we can negotiate a deal."

****

Captain Don Martin had seen the spacecraft, and as planned, he was now breaking away from his team to his planned designation. It was time to go, the fun had to stop now!

Ivor had decided that the best course of action was to start the trip back to Sydney so that the alien spacecraft would at least leave them alone after seeing they were complying. He went down to the control room with Gregor to set the autopilot once more.

"Gregor, we have the girls locked in, put some food and water in there, and keep them secured in that cabin until we can negotiate with whoever is waiting for us in Sydney. We cannot get away now I feel, but we may be able to do a deal if we promise not to harm the girls. They must know we have lost all contact with our group, and maybe we can get a short sentence, and return to a more normal life. After all, the cause is finished, we have not been able to contact anyone for the last few months. The alternative is not good, they may storm the boat, and even if we threaten to kill the girls, they will surely finish us off."

"You know I will follow you, whatever the outcome, but the girls are certainly our best chance in a negotiation I feel."

****

Don was now on board the Ocean Dreamer, it had been easy to board after ditching his jet skis and parachute, and he had all he needed in the pack on his back. He could see his colleagues continuing to circle the boat to continue the distraction. He had told them to return to the harbour in ten minutes. The boat was quite big, but the loading bay doors on the lower decks had been easy to access. He was sure that he had not been detected. It was obvious that the boat

251

was on autopilot because there was no crew visible. Maybe, apart from the girls, there were only the two guys aboard? He unpacked the bag, and moved to the stairs to reach the upper decks.

****

Irina and Lara were aware that the boat was turning, they had been in the cabin now for 2 days and were getting restless.

"We cannot let them keep us like this Lara, if they come with food soon, it will probably be the one they call Gregor, we must try to overcome him. We can then decide how we can control this boat, and how to get the other head guy. He may be more of a problem?"

****

Helena had contacted the Rotoship, and advised them to return to the Venus base, but to fly as low as possible over the 'Ocean Dreamer' before doing so.

"Chris, Robert, we are ready now for next stage of this operation. Captain Martin has advised us that he is aboard. How do you want to proceed?"

Chris had been pondering on the journey how they could get this all finished.

"Captain Martin is fully skilled in hostage situations, so I think we can leave him to proceed as he sees fit. He can call us if he has any need of our backup services. I did think of you and Athena being dropped onto the boat, as you know the girls, and with your amazing abilities, would no doubt overcome the two men without bloodshed. However, it is risky getting you on board, and we do have a good man there already, so let us wait. I admit being a little selfish in that decision, we do not want to risk you both at this stage on what should be our final showdown with these terrorists!"

It was Athena who responded first. "Chris, we know you are looking out for us, but you must let us go if this first plan does not succeed, we promise to be extra careful, like you, we do not want to be parted, but we are still in service."

****

Don heard the footsteps—it was the one they called Marosk. He quickly opened the nearest cabin door and waited for him to pass. He would take him to where the girls were being held.

★★★★★★★★★★★★

The girls could hear the lock turning again.

"Hopefully, this is that Gregor with some food. Get ready to pounce if you see an opportunity and then if we can overpower him, we have a chance of getting that Ivor guy, and although I am not sure about the boat controls, we should be able to contact Helena to help us get back to safety."

Gregor entered, and saw the girls were in their bathrobes, but revealing a lot of body.

"Here is some food, we are returning to Sydney. You will be kept here while Ivor is negotiating with the authorities. Let us hope that we can get a good deal, because if not your lives are pointless to us."

"Well Gregor, don't you want a taste of what you have been seeking since we met?"

Irina moved up from the bed and approached him, her gown revealing even more of her body. As she approached, Gregor was not certain what to do; he started to panic; are they trying to get me off balance? He realised what he had to do. He opened his coat to reveal an electronic weapon. The girls had seen these before, they were lethal to the nervous system…

At that same moment, a shot rang out, and Gregor went stumbling forward, He grabbed Irina's robe, and held on, turning towards where the shot had come from; there was blood coming from his weapon arm.

"I am Captain Martin of the Australian ISPEG forces, and I am here to take you and your partner back to stand trial for the atrocities that your terrorist group have bestowed on our peoples over the last twenty years. You had better call your friend down here, or we can make you suffer a little more if you prefer."

The girls were astounded, Gregor was whimpering, and muttering to himself. Just when it looked as if he was going to speak, there was another shot…

"Captain, you had better put that weapon down, I have you all in my sights, it is a good job I came down to see what was happening, Gregor was far too long down here. Gregor, come here, we shall leave the girls to attend to the captain. I am locking you all in again, and this time, if the authorities do not comply with our wishes, you will all be dumped, and we shall go into hiding, which will of course hold up this talked about agreement with the alien planet."

＊＊＊＊＊＊＊＊＊＊＊＊

Lieutenant Winslow was an experienced air force and space navigator. When his colleagues were para-jetting back to base, he had held back at the harbour, he knew the captain had taken on a tricky task, and had not heard back that he had detected the hostages. He wondered why he had not had this confirmation, and came to a decision.

"Wing commander, this is Lieutenant Winslow, Captain Martin's right hand. I am concerned that he has not confirmed contact with the hostages and the terrorists. We know he was aboard the target. We should consider that something has gone wrong."

"Lieutenant, thank you for your prompt call, you are right to be concerned, they are tricky customers. I do have an alternative plan, so leave this one to us now, I shall ensure that you are kept up to date with events as they unfold. You all did a good job in distracting those guys, we were impressed with your para-jetting. Let us hope the captain is at least safe, maybe he was detected and is now another hostage?"

Helena and Athena had been listening to the conversation.

"Well Chris and Robert, it seems we do not have any alternative now. We must get on board that boat when it docks. No doubt the senior guy is this Ivor Levinski. It is our opinion that he will come down to the harbour to undertake the negotiation, while the other guy, Gregor Marosk, will have to stay with the hostages; he will no doubt be prepared to take action if he does not see Lerinski return to the boat. In any case, they will have some form of communication. Athena and I are going to use one of our favourite toys to try and get aboard while Levinski is off the boat. If we are successful, be ready to hold him prisoner."

"OK Helena, we both know better than to interfere with your ideas, we shall be ready to take any action you want from us, but Rob and I will be in pain until we know you are safely back. I shall now call back to the lieutenant as promised to tell him the plan, and put them all on standby. We shall call Levinski shortly after we have set up the negotiation team, and get him to come ashore."

"Gregor, that was a close shave, it was as well that I was concerned. Anyway, I am certain that there is nobody aboard now apart from our hostages. I have been in touch with the Australian authorities regarding our wishes, and they have agreed to negotiate when we land. You will have to stay here to be ready to take action against the hostages if I run into any difficulties. If you do not see me returning after I have called you, then you can assume they are holding me. You will then have to warn them that if they do not release me, the hostages will be shot one by one. We have nothing to lose."

****

Sydney—AAFS Centre, 11 April 2083

"Mr Levinski, we understand that you are here to negotiate a deal for you and your colleague in exchange for our colleagues being held under duress on your boat, the Ocean Dreamer. Exactly what do you think you can achieve?"

****

Ocean Dreamer, Some Hours Later

Gregor was getting bored, he had checked on the hostages and had seen that the captain had recovered, and he and the girls were now securely locked inside their cabin. Just as he was going up to the top deck for a drink, his transmitter was buzzing. Well, that was quick he thought, the hostages must be more important than we thought.

"Ivor, have you some good news for us, your discussions did not seem too long."

"Before they will make any deal, they want you to bring the hostages to the top walkway of the boat so that they can be sure they are all alive and well. They are sending a female representative to talk to them, so look out for her. After she has seen them, you can return them to the cabin while we continue our negotiations."

"Ivor, your message was a little bit scratchy, but understood. I shall call you when I have seen their representative."

Gregor wanted to get this over. He finished his drink and started down to the girl's cabin.

****

Athena was now in position at the harbour alongside the Ocean Dreamer, waiting for the appearance of the hostages. She did not have to wait long. She saw the captain first, and then the girls, who were being ushered forward by the guy she knew must be the one they called Gregor Marosk.

Gregor looked down on the harbour from the mid-deck walkway. He had some kind of weapon in his hand. He started to shout.

"Well, if you are the representative for this negotiation, please confirm that you have seen the three hostages, so we can get this…"

Gregor could not understand what was happening, his voice had suddenly gone, and he was feeling very shaky.

"Marosk, you will drop your weapon or we shall increase the volume of the laser, which we can assure you will be difficult to recover from."

Gregor groggily turned round to see where this voice was coming from. Helena stood there with her full ISPEG uniform, a beautiful girl, but not in a beautiful mood he could see. He still could not speak, and slowly put the weapon on the deck, almost falling as he did so.

Captain Martin was well enough to march over to him, and picked up the weapon.

"I think our new friends are cleverer than you think Marosk, you will hear more when we take you to meet your colleague."

Irina and Lara now rushed over to Helena. It was Irina who spoke first. "Helena, you have both saved us again, how did you get on the boat, none of us saw you? That laser thing of yours is amazing."

"Yes, all will be revealed when we get this guy back to the authorities. The other man, named Levinski, is already there thinking that he has you still as hostage, so he is going to have an unpleasant surprise. Now, join Athena down at the harbour, and the captain and I will pick up this guy. He will not be difficult to handle now."

****

Ivor Levinski could not believe what he had been hearing. They had lured Gregor out onto the deck with the hostages by somehow mimicking his voice over the transmitter, and then overpowering him. They were both now sitting in the interview room and it was obvious that the game was up. They must try to persuade these people that they were willing to give up all activity associated with the ECAW cause, and were ready to become good citizens. They could tag them if they wished with the new 'tracer chips' that they had heard about.

"Ivor Levinski, Gregor Marosk, you are now under detention, and will be charged with terrorist activity leading to the deaths of several civilians, as well as damaging property of several countries of the world. If you wish to say anything in your defence, then this is the time for us to consider that, so we may prepare a final case for the magistrates. You will be taken from here tomorrow under guard, and we expect your initial trials to take place in two weeks' time in Washington, DC."

"We had no alternative but to take the hostages if we were to try for a better life or sentence. We really did not intend to harm them. We believe that we may be the last of the ECAW people, and that means that the cause has failed. We understand that you must make us pay for our past activities, although like many of us we were following orders from a higher regime. It is now obvious that with the support of the new alien people like these ladies here, the future is going to change. We do not understand how you could mimic my voice so easily, and not least, how the new weapon you used on Gregor works. However, I trust we shall have a fair hearing in due course."

Gregor was still groggy, but just nodded to them all.

Chris and Robert and the girls had listened to all this, and now Chris spoke, "Well, you certainly have changed your tune. We shall see what the magistrates say, but I think you will join your former colleagues eventually on one of the rehabilitation centres that the Attican people have for re-training former criminals. Your former boss is already there. So, Lieutenant, please take them away, and get them ready for the trip back to London or Washington tomorrow. We are awaiting final instructions on where the prisoners will be taken for first assessments. Also, can you arrange to take possession of the 'Ocean Dreamer' yacht. I feel sure that authorities will approve you selling this boat and putting proceeds towards more productive ventures in your beautiful country."

Robert had been listening intently, and as the two were escorted from the room he turned to them all.

"Another great achievement from Helena and Athena. That was remarkable. A good peaceful ending to this long saga. These guys were right of course in one thing; I do believe they are the last serious threat from this ECAW group."

"Anyway, it is now time for us to think about ourselves, and Captain Martin, Lieutenant Winslow, and all those who helped us to get to this position. Perhaps we can invite them to the ceremony in the Biosphere, or more exciting for them—Acropolis?"

"We shall all take the F95S back to California tomorrow, Robert; we do not have much time to prepare for the ceremony in the Biosphere, but at least we do not have other problems for the moment. Helena, can you both think of anyone back at your home that you want to be at the Acropolis ceremony, and what date should we aim for? You may also want to check out how Efi is progressing with her plans? Hopefully she and the Commander are already in California when we get back, as I think we are all looking forward to a ceremony that includes them."

****

Bakersville, CA, 14 April 2083

The Australian authorities had been more than helpful in arranging for the terrorists to be transported over to England, where there was now a good number of the terrorists being held, pending discussions with ISPEG and other groups affected by their actions. There were now three major holding sites around the world, including the major one in the McDill base in Florida. Over one hundred were being held there.

Chris and Robert were back in the house together with Commander Glen, who had been happy to join them at home rather than the formal mess room at the base.

They were out on the back deck with one of Chris's drinks. The Commander was looking very happy.

"Chris. Robert, this is such a great time for us all. I have been in touch with General Hermes and he is on his way here, he said he would not want to miss our ceremony. Efi has been his right hand for some time, and he thinks very highly of her."

He paused to take a sip of the gingery concoction.

"On a more sombre subject, he also asked me to convey a request to all those concerned with the round up of the ECAW terrorist group. The Attica assembly have asked if we would transfer all those who are now in custody to Attica, where they have special facilities for such people. You know I think that the head of the organisation, Ho Chi Dae, was put through this facility, and is now working with the human robots on Acropolis. He has no recollection of previous events. With our support they see that these people will also be able to be put to good use, working with the human robot team on Attica and Acropolis. The robots are evidently able to give them all work, male or female, and will take into account their individual abilities and strength. It is very difficult for us to understand at this stage how advanced they are with this work, but no doubt Efi, Helena and Athena will bring us up to date later."

"Commander, we are so pleased to see you here, you have been such a great support to us all and we are particularly looking forward to the ceremony in the Biosphere later this month, and I hope Efi will persuade you to join us for the Acropolis wedding if your commitments allow? Helena and Athena are at this moment in the Biosphere arranging the ceremony details with our parents. You may have also heard that Irina and Lara are safely back and well, and it has been rumoured that there could be another ceremony coming up with two of our top astronauts, Major Lancs and Captain Durham."

"That would be something; the girls have changed completely under their influence, and the experience in Australia will have knocked out any lingering thoughts of returning to terrorism. Helena and Athena have also taken to them, and there is a good chance that they will want them to continue to work for ISPEG."

"OK, I will have a chat with Tom and Terry, it would be good for all concerned if they do go ahead with this plan. Now, it is time to go and meet the General on his arrival, but first I must talk to Washington, London, and Sydney, to check if all agree to releasing the prisoners to the Attican authorities as requested. I do not see any problem, but we need to have everyone on board with our plans from now on. This is a momentous moment for all of us on our planet. Our new friends have taken us to a new era, one that could not have even been dreamed about thirty years ago. Thanks again to you both. See you at the ceremony!"

****

Attican Assembly, Earth Time, Late April 2083

Chairman Isis was with his senior senators and Spiros, his trusted intelligence officer.

"General Hermes is now on his way to meet with Commander Glen, and other planet Earth authorities, to discuss our request for the persons who have been detained as being former members or associates of the terrorist group they called ECAW, to be sent to us for rehabilitation treatment. As you know we have hopes of restoring them to useful lives on either our planet, or on Mars. In view of the fast reduction in our male line, there is already need for labourers to work with our robot team. I am confident that this will be accepted."

He paused, looking over the great hall, before continuing, "Senators, this is a wonderful opportunity for us. We have achieved many things, but to have the planet Earth's people with us to work for a future that looked very uncertain just a few years ago is due to some outstanding duty by the General and Captain Panamosis; our team here; and of course, the bravery of Helena Poulakis and Athena Balakakis. Spiros has advised me that these two are going to marry two of the men that they have worked with since landing on the Earth. You may remember Christopher Devonshire and Robert Somester."

"I believe we should all be delighted with this union, and as they wish to have a ceremony of their marriage on Acropolis, I would like us to make a major effort to ensure this is a day to remember. One that will be recorded to show all those people on planet Earth that we are their friends. This can only entice more of their people to come to us, and thus our hopes for the continuity of life on Attica and Mars may be accomplished."

All the senators and Spiros rose, and with their long arms extended, shouted their approval.

****

Acropolis, Earth Time, Late April 2083

Panayiota had resumed duties having taken time to be with Kim Jong. He had received treatment from the medic centre that had basically renewed parts of the brain, and there was now no sign of his injuries. During the operations the Attican surgeon had taken some readings from the brain as a precaution, having been advised of the patient's background. He had decided that it would not be necessary to undertake any more work on the brain. Surprisingly the results of

260

the readings indicated a calm and intelligent person. He could hardly believe the information that had been sent to him prior to these tests.

They were now back in their apartment and taking in the news from Earth.

"Kim, you know that my senior is Efi Panomosis, and have just had confirmed that she is to marry that nice Commander that came here to negotiate our new agreement with planet Earth. That is great news, she is such a wonderful person. Also, it is reported that our two agents, Helena, and Athena, who you may remember, are going to marry the two wing commanders who had been leading the activities to round up your former colleagues. This must be very strange for you; how do you feel?"

"I only know that you have saved my life Panayiota. I have seen tapes of some of the activities that I was involved in during the past few years, and I cannot recognise that person. The brainwashing must have been severe for me to be so dedicated to such a cause, that involved destruction and killing. I understand that people will still be somewhat suspicious about me, so it is up to me to prove that I am not that person anymore. Do you think you can trust me enough to marry me now?"

"Look my love, all the young Atticans have this sixth sense thing, me included, so when we met, I just thought this is a man I could spend a life with, so the answer is obviously yes."

Kim Jong was sobbing now, but she continued talking as she went over to him, putting her long arms around his body.

"This is not the time to weep Kim, we must look to the future together. I have heard that there is to be a big ceremony here in Acropolis in a few months' time. The marriages that I mentioned are first to be celebrated in the area you call California, but then they are all coming to Attica, and then on to Acropolis. We should ask the authorities in Attica if they would agree to us being part of that ceremony. What do you think?"

Kim Jong looked up at her, and brightened.

"I think that would be like a dream come true. Would we stay on Acropolis? For me it is fine as I feel I must give something back to the community; starting afresh, I could involve myself with Zeus's team, and maybe help them to establish a working Rota for the people that were former colleagues. I understand that they will be vetted first, and some will have to undergo surgery, that has been explained to me, but some could be useful labour for the human robot team, and some others, including the female prisoners, could be put to work on administration matters, thus allowing your people more time for the more scientific thinking, and forward planning. Eventually, they may be able to be released back to the main community; they may even feel like I do now, I suppose I hope so."

****

END OF PART THREE

Part Four

Attica, June 2083, Earth Time

The Atticans had started taking in prisoners from planet Earth. Their Rotoships had been a source of amazement to the passengers, and they were already subdued by the overwhelming feeling that they now had no escape. Among the first batch was the old Korean ECAW cell terrorists, Son Jing and Li Kwang. It was Li Kwang who was the first to speak.

"Son Jing, this place is unbelievable, we had no chance. It is obvious that their technology is so far ahead of us. That spacecraft got us here in 8 weeks, how do they get that speed and yet have everyone on board in not only a 60% gravity level, but able to eat and drink and even sleep normally…and just look at this control room! Anyway, look out, here comes someone. Just look at his build, those arms are like you would expect on an animal."

The voice was strong and clear; they had no problem understanding.

"Please pay attention. You are all now in the hands of our intelligence office. My name is Spiros Artemis. We shall shortly be taking you to holding accommodation, where you will fully adjust to our atmosphere, and then you will be taken to our medic centre. We have, as you have experienced on your journey, all the types of food and drink that you will need to sustain you here, and that will be given to you when you arrive at the centre. Over the next few days, you will undergo some treatment, which will be painless, but you will be allowed to rest for some days after that. This will all be arranged for you."

"We then plan to transfer you to the planet Mars, where you will be assigned to the local security team. Be under no doubt that whereas you will be treated humanely, you will now be our prisoners for some time. Those of you who show outstanding abilities, particularly in technology subjects, will have the opportunity to progress, and will be returned here to work with our scientific team in due course. Those of you who do not have these abilities will be assigned other lighter duties."

Spiros paused to look around, he saw for the first time some fear in their eyes, they no longer looked like terrorists!

****

News Stations—Washington 13.00, London 18.00, and to All Major Cities Around the World, 10 June 2083

"The White House have issued a statement today that is being broadcast throughout the world to confirm that, following the capture of the ECAW terrorists, an agreement has now been signed by all parties that unites our world with that of the Attican people. There will be further details in the coming days, but this is a unique opportunity for peace in our time, and considerable acceleration of our knowledge to enhance the lives of our people."

Buffalo, NY, 11 June 2083

Miss Yvonne Lourdes was booking into the Reikart House Hotel. She had lost little of her looks, and Guy O'Mahony at the reception desk had taken in a long look.

"How can I help, Miss?"

"I would like a room for two nights with a view of the river, and are you able to book me rapid private transport to California on the 13th?"

"Of course, please give me your details and it will be arranged. Do you want to return?"

The identity pass looked rather new, but Guy was not particularly interested in the paperwork!

Biosphere 2—14 June 2083

What a turnout! Professor Devonshire and Colonel Somester, and their wives, looked across the great hall, and through the windows, where you could see Biosphere 1. Josh was the most in thought.

"Was it really 21 years ago that we were in Bio 1 addressing our new intakes? So much has happened, and today we are here with our sons, and all these dignitaries for this unbelievable ceremony. What better ending could you have even if you were writing a book?"

Phillip looked over to his friend.

"Josh, we are all blessed. The boys turned out to be wonderful ambassadors, and a credit to Ruth and Dawn. Our future daughters-in-law are amazing people, and we look forward to our journey with them for the Acropolis ceremony. We must save all our energy for that experience; I am sure we shall not have too many chances for such a trip."

Ruth was also thoughtful.

"The whole day will be brilliant; what a pleasant surprise to see Commander Glen and Captain Panomosis together, and who could have predicted that the two Russian girls would be so changed that they seem part of us. I think Tom Lancs and Terry Durham may have a lot to do with that. Anyway, I am looking forward to a wonderful ceremony. I am so happy for them."

The university chancellor, Dr James Riband was to perform the ceremony. He had received special dispensation from the authorities after they had been advised that several of the persons were former pupils of the university. He was also a former colleague of Josh Devonshire, and he was talking to him now.

"Well Josh, this is something. I could not anticipate all those years ago, when your son and Robert would meet these alien girls, that we would be here ready to celebrate a unique ceremony. People from two planets coming together as one."

"Yes, remarkable. Do not forget you are also blessing the Russian girls who would have been considered our enemies for so long. The transformation in them since they met our Major Lancs and Captain Durham is similar to the news that their former boss, Kim Jong Woo, has evidently completely converted after meeting with the Attican, Captain Fronimos. Indeed, he has shown to be brave and worthy; we understand that they may also marry when the second ceremony takes place on Mars next year."

****

The biosphere was looking wonderful, Ruth having had the main hall decked with the flags of each nation attending, and the Atticans had sent over a large statue which took centre place on the podium at the top of the hall. Flowers were abundant and filling the whole area with scent.

"Irina Ivanov, are you ready and willing to undertake a life with Thomas Peter Lancs, for good or for worse, so long as you both shall live?"

"I am."

"Thomas, are you ready to undertake a life with Irina, for good or for worse…"

The Chancellor stopped in mid-speech; what was this? There was a huge commotion in the hall.

"Irina Ivanov, Lara Gorinski, you may recognise me. Did you think you could get rid of us so easily?"

Chris had seen the problem first, unusually Helena and Athena were distracted as they waited to go up for the ceremony. He rushed to the front of the hall, but as he did so, he heard the soft sound of the laser gun.

Helena had been so entranced, but now she also saw the danger.

"Chris, be careful, that is Yoko Lin, how did she get here; I thought our people had killed her?"

"Yes, well, you are not as smart as you think you are. I duped someone who took a fancy to me in the prison, and I also promised her some money to get me out. She was rather nice, but of course she could not live to tell the tale."

As she was speaking, Tom Lancs had seen that Irina was hit, but not critical. His tall powerful figure had been quietly moving towards Yoko Lin as she was speaking and bragging, her weapon now pointed towards Chris as he approached her.

Before anyone could stop Tom, he grabbed at the weapon, and turned it towards her. Yoko started to hit him hard, but Tom sent a crashing blow to her head, and Yoko fell to the floor. He now looked at her and raised the weapon… Chris was now shouting…

"Tom, no, get back please, we want her alive; this time we shall make no mistake and send her for treatment."

Chris and Helena now both ran over to him, and Helena picked Yoko up, she appeared to be in a coma.

"I am sorry Chris, but I just lost it when I saw my Irina being attacked. She is pure evil."

"OK Tom, we understand. Go to Irina now and check how bad the injury is; then we shall all decide if we can go on with the ceremony. I will arrange for Yoko Lin to be taken to our hospital. She appears to be dead, but we shall take no chances this time. This must be the end. I really did think we had already got there."

Helena and Athena had gone over to Tom and Terry, who were attending the girls.

"Chris, Robert, we have looked at Irina's injury, and it is not too serious. They are in shock, but after some treatment here, they should be ready to complete the ceremony. They certainly want to. They say this incident must not affect this special day."

Chris and Robert were now already moving over to talk to the Commander and Efi, who had watched the whole affair unfold from the back of the hall.

****

Hotel California, Bakersville, Same Evening

The newlyweds, and General Hermes, who had arrived especially for the ceremony, had all agreed to stay their first night at the hotel, and all of them were now around a large oval dining table ready to relax after an exciting day. Commander Glen, as the elder, felt he had to be first to rise.

"First of all, I am Ed when we are in private like this, I know Efi would like that. What a day! That woman was certainly evil, such a charmer; she turned out to be one of the worst of our enemies. We still do not know how she managed to switch identity with that woman prisoner in Nevada, and why we did not hear of the escape? Anyway, our people are double checking now on what happened, and now let us ensure that this is really the end of the road for this terrorist group. I do believe this was a one off. Let us hope that if Yoko Lin recovers, she will receive punishment for her atrocities; as Dimitris is with us tonight, perhaps we can talk about that matter, without spoiling our day too much."

Dimitris had just had his first full day on the planet; He had been expecting a happy day watching his second in command marry this great guy, whom he had come to admire.

"Commander Ed, you really gave me some concern today. I did not know how to react; it is so long since we have seen this type of primitive behaviour on our planet. I had heard many things from you all, but never witnessed such an event. As you know from your visits, we have eliminated all war like tendencies in our people, and even minor troubles such as theft are rare now. Everyone on Attica is focused on saving the planet, and hoping that they can, in time, rebuild the population. I trust that the Earth's people will also now see the way forward is to work together for the good of the planet, wars and terrorism are not productive, as has been proven by both our planets…"

He now rose from the table, his long arms extended, and continued…

"Anyway, we have managed to come out of today in one piece. Irina and Lara look remarkable after their experience at the ceremony. I am sure Major Lancs and Captain Durham have much to do with that… Efi, I know you are going to be so spoilt by the Commander, but you deserve it. Now, I trust we can all enjoy the evening, and talk more tomorrow."

"Dimitris, you have summed up our feelings and our aspirations, we are so pleased to have you as our friend, and promise we shall remain diligent to ensure the next century is one of growth and happiness for our peoples."

They all raised their glasses, the girls still mixing some water with their wine before drinking.

Helena and Athena just nodded, and continued to look lovingly at their new partners. This story has just begun they thought.

****

Acropolis, Earth Time, September 2083

Panayiota and Kim Jong were settled in their new lodge on the side of the mountain, their toughened glass windows looking over the red landscape, which although still bare, had many rock formations, which in the varying light from the sun and stars gave for an interesting landscape. Both were now fully recovered from recent events, and had been tasked by the Attican cabinet to start preparing for the arrival of the terrorist prisoners, who had been interrogated, and where necessary, had received surgery like the treatment given to their leader.

The job was immense, as they had to organise facilities for housing over one hundred people, ensuring that they had fair treatment, and feeding them.

In return, the new migrants would be assigned to various tasks, and Kim Jong had been given the job of deciding where they would be used. He had already made friends with Zeus at the human robot centre, and he was thinking that many of them could be useful with the work that was now underway on the adjoining mountain, where, still unknown to most, a new city was being built for the future growth on Mars.

The food banks were another area that still needed labour, including the building of new laboratories to produce protein and carbohydrate tablets. He had seen the work that had been undertaken on Attica to supplement the planets major food supplies, which were becoming affected by the fast decline of animals, due to the sterility of many of the new-born.

"Panayiota, apart from this project with the migrants, we also have to plan for the upcoming ceremony in December, when I hope we shall be formally made partners."

"Yes, it is a lot to do, but let us start planning this project first, and then we can think of happier times ahead. For now, let us get some rest—the first arrivals will be here in a few days and I know you want to see Zeus and others tomorrow to get your plan together."

****

Acropolis Human Robot Centre, 12 September 2083

Zeus and Plato, his right-hand HR, were in discussion following the recent news.

"I have been talking to Kim Jong regarding the former Earth's terrorists— When they arrive they will be under surveillance for some months while undertaking the tasks that we shall assign them—Let us talk about the most important projects—a training programme for them to understand the robotic machinery that we are using to extend the living quarters and services—The increasing supply of oxygen and water to our city—We are also preparing to build inside the second crater that our scientists have deemed suitable for a second city—we have discovered underground ice lakes some five leagues below the surface areas—When this development begins it will be dangerous—I see some of these people being used in this area—They will help us until we can

eventually install automated machinery—It will be a long project—Those who are weaker will still be able to work—We have the food farms to maintain and expand—Also for the new arrivals from Earth we shall be looking at new food production."

Zeus stopped for a moment, but before Plato could respond he turned his antennas to look out over the internal city from the huge quartz polymer windows.

"Plato—I have some other news which I wanted to share with you—I have been in contact with HR Zikky several times—She is the Earth's senior robot— she is very intelligent. I am seeking permission for me to approach her when she arrives shortly on our planet to ask for us to be made a couple—so we may be working together for the years ahead—I do not see why the humans should have all the fun!"

"My goodness Zeus—that would be a first for us—I hope we shall all have that opportunity in the future—I know you will advise me if you are successful— Regarding the plans for the incoming persons from Earth—I have some ideas to share with you—we should be ready to start this project in twenty Attican days."

****

Attica, Earth Time, Early October, 2083

The assembly was once more amassed in the great hall, and Chairman Isis was about to speak.

"General Hermes will be returning from Earth shortly. I am advised by Spiros Artemis that he will also be bringing a further contingent of the people that were involved in the terrorist activities on the Earth, and had prevented the signing of the Marsattica Agreement. The latter is now complete, and we are about to enter a new phase in our lives. First, all these new arrivals are being taken to our medical centre, where they will be interrogated, and sectioned according to risk. As you know from our success with surgery on previous prisoners, we expect to normalise all these people in due course."

"In that respect, I can advise you today that plans have been made for them to work with our human robot team on Mars. Captain Fronimos and her new trusted Earth partner Kim Jong Woo, together with our senior HR Zeus, are at this moment planning a programme for them that will enable us to proceed faster with our plans for expanded food production and the development of a second city on Mars."

Takis Fotopoulis, the house speaker now intervened, "Chairman, this is good news, but are we sure about our ability to change their brain to a more normal thinking. I have heard from Spiros that there are women in this group who have been very difficult to capture, and have used what they call 'women's whiles' to escape capture a few times. Will the surgery work on them, to my knowledge we have not experimented on them before?"

"Thank you, Takis for those comments. They are good points and I shall ask Spiros to speak to the medical centre for some assurances. We shall of course monitor them after the surgery, and they will be working in areas under the control of our HR team…"

"Now, a happier announcement, one which I trust you all will join me in celebrating. Captain Efi Panomosis and Commander Glen, who you have all met, have announced that they are now married, a service of partnership recognised on the Earth. They both now wish to fulfil their vows here, together with others, at a special ceremony, our first in the new city of Acropolis. To add to our excitement, I know you will all be happy to hear that our agents, Helena Poulakis, and Athena Balakakis, are now married to the two men who have been so helpful in bringing our two planets together…"

"Finally, another surprise; we have been approached by our senior HR Zeus. He requested that the Earth's HR Zikky be placed with him for all their future, working together. Furthermore, he asked if they could be part of the same ceremony that we are undertaking later in the year on Acropolis for the other couples!"

"This is indeed a remarkable time, Senators. I have agreed to this request; we are in times when we must appreciate the work that Zeus and our human robot team perform. They will oversee many of the new prisoners that are arriving, and after treatment, these people will be under their control, sometimes in dangerous areas, for instance in the unknown territory that we are developing on the second volcano, to be known as Hermitage City."

The assembly all rose and their long arms raised above them, started a loud clapping of approval.

****

Rotoship 4—In Space—Mid-October 2083, Earth Time

General Hermes, the newly married couples, and several dignitaries, including the American and UK ambassadors, and other senior diplomats who had been invited for the Acropolis ceremony were aboard, some experiencing their first trip on this magnificent craft. They had been advised that arrival time would be in about ten days' time. They had all been able to work and transfer messages via the sophisticated satellite system set up by the Atticans after the new association with the Earth's scientists, following the signing of the Marsattica Agreement.

A new set of apartments had been prepared for them for their stay on Mars. Furthermore, they had been given freedom passes to use on what was now a Rotoship shuttle service to and from Attica, with shuttle connections to Mars. They only had to book in with the Rotoship centre, now set up on the Venus ISS.

Dimitris had assembled them all in the spacecraft's mess room, and was now talking to them all regarding the upcoming plans for the Acropolis ceremony; everyone was looking excited.

Chris had taken this opportunity to have some time with Robert and the girls, and they were enjoying some relaxing time in their cabin.

"Helena my love, do you or Athena have any concerns about our future plans, this is a big change for you as well as for us?"

"Athena and I could not be happier Chris; and we have just heard from our Senate assembly that they are going to also give us freedom passes to come and go as we need, using these lovely Rotoships. So, if you are homesick, or we are, then we can easily transfer and work for a time on whichever planet we choose! On another subject, are you both concerned about any children that we may produce? I do hope we can…"

Helena was interrupted by the emergency transmitter in the cabin…

"Please will General Hermes join us in the control room immediately."

"Athena, we should go and see if we can help, we do have some good training on the Rotoships. We shall be back shortly boys; do not be too concerned, the robots occasionally worry too much if there is the slightest deviation in the controls."

Rotoship 4 was indeed having some problem, and as the General left the mess room, there was a distinct change in the atmosphere, and those not seated were starting to lift off the floor.

"Everyone, get to the seats at the table and belt in, there has been a change in the rotational spin of the craft which is affecting the gravity." It was Efi who had spotted the problem.

The English ambassador, Sir Leonard Berks, was now looking at Efi, and asking what was probably in all their minds at this moment.

"Is this usual Captain?"

"No, Sir Leonard, it is not normal, but please do not worry. We should wait for the General to advise us after he talks to the robot team. Let us stay in our seats until we get a new message."

****

Dimitris was now a little anxious; there was signs that some sabotage had taken place on the craft, and this was affecting the rotational spin, and this in turn could affect their ability to control the navigation. In speaking to the robot team, it was considered that someone had been on board at some time before this trip started, and had managed to damage one of the energy cells that fed power to the rotational system. Dimitris decided to set them duties that would include scanning the system, and re-setting if necessary. Then he could decide how dangerous the situation was if they remained in this position. He bounced back to the meeting room; he could feel the gravity change taking place on the craft.

"I have now looked at the problem, and our team are going through a reset routine to try to stabilise the system. It is obvious that one of our important power cells is damaged. Efi, come with me please, we should be at the controls for a time until we can sort this problem."

"Let the Commander come with me please Dimitris; apart from anything else, he needs to see how these machines work when he is involved in the future."

"Ed, you are of course welcome, but I must tell you this is an unusual situation, and we trust that we can find the answer soon."

He now addressed Chris and Robert, who had quickly joined them all in the mess room.

"Can you ensure everyone on board is aware of the problem, but do not give any other information at this time. We need to discuss later as to how anyone could tamper with the systems."

****

Attica Medical Centre, Same Time

"Well Gregor, we may be in trouble, but I think one of their spacecrafts is also in trouble. I have seen some pictures on their monitors as I was being brought here, and it did seem there was a lot of urgency by the people in astronaut suits. I am hoping this upset is the result of one of our colleagues getting into the control room when we were on the space station. She said she had been a friend of a Yoko Lin, and she thought that person was trying to make a last ditch stand before they found her. Evidently, this woman seemed determined to get her own back on those who had captured her. I think the women prisoners were put on Rotoship 4, and if I remember correctly that spacecraft was reserved mainly for the top brass."

"I am not sure Ivor, but anyway I think we are about to be called for this treatment they spoke of; let us hope we are still in one piece when that is over. We have done all we can, I do not see any way out for us now!"

****

Rotoship 4 in Space—Earth Hours Later

"Ed, this is the result of an attack on the power system. While we are checking the solution, can you advise the authorities that there is still a rogue element somewhere who has managed to get into the system at the space centre. We must ensure we have no further terrorist activity; it is crucial to our agreement."

"I am onto that now, Dimitris, we shall tighten up the security at the space station. There were too many people being taken in at a time, and it maybe that one or two may have had more freedom to roam than we had prepared for. However, I thought all the prisoners were on the other Rotoships ahead of us. I will check with Venus now, and ask if they did get all of them away; otherwise, we must face the fact that someone slipped on board with us?"

"That would at least let us know what we must deal with. In the meantime, we are in poor shape as the craft is not responding and we are a little out of control. I am going to slow all systems down, and Efi, and the robot team will go through everything again. I do not want to frighten your people, so perhaps you and your team will look quietly for the possibility of another rogue person on board. Is someone here in disguise as one of the ambassador's aides, do you think? We had that problem once before, you will remember?"

Following her capture in the Biosphere, and subsequent hospital treatment, Yoko Lin was taken to the Venus space station. As she had been some weeks in treatment, she had been sent with the last few female prisoners. They were escorted by two senior armed female astronauts throughout the journey; They were then advised that they would be travelling on a spacecraft called Rotoship 4, and would be working with her escorts in the galley area during the trip. The Venus personnel had not been concerned as there was no way to escape. The Rotoship was huge, and even she had to marvel at this fantastic craft. When she got her bearings, she had been able to move around the craft without too much attention being taken of her movements. Where could she go without being tracked anyway?

She was now back in the small cabin which was clearly locked. However, she smiled. She had just started to feel the gravity change in the cabin.

****

Commander Glen was now sure that there was nobody left in the Venus station, and had been assured that all prisoners were now accounted for. The last sentence from Captain Ann Broxbourne stated that there had been a couple of late arrivals, four females who were accompanied by two of our astronauts. They should have been on earlier flights but these four had been injured and had just been released from hospital. They were put on duties with their escorts on Rotoship 4. She had then written their names; Marylin O'Reilly; Justine Baker; Son Ming Jo, and Yoko Lin.

No, he could not believe it!

Ed hurriedly bounced his way back to the meeting room. The gravity was slightly better, but it was still very bumpy.

"Listen everyone, can you believe this? I have just been advised by Venus control that a few female terrorists arrived late, having been under escort after leaving hospital in California. They were put to duties with their armed escorts. Guess who was one of the names on that list?"

"Yes, Yoko Lin!"

Chris jumped up, only to nearly fall as he lost gravity. He quickly sat again and strapped in.

"Helena, Athena, this is crazy. That woman has too many lives. We must find her quickly and see if she is the cause of this problem with the spacecraft. How could she do that, she has no knowledge of spacecraft navigation?"

The ambassadors and top politicians were all looking very concerned, surely one prisoner could not cause such mayhem.

Helena saw the frustration and slight fear in the room.

"Please stay calm everyone; as you have experienced in the past few months, we do have some advanced knowledge that will I am sure help us to solve this problem. I am going with Athena to the galley where I am sure the four prisoners are working. I shall extract information and then talk to General Hermes and Captain Panamosis, who are up in the control room trying to correct this fault."

****

"OK Yoko Lin, we thought this is where you would be. What have you been up to? It seems you are not aware of your position? You have no chance now of escaping again, this is it…"

Athena was interrupted by a deluge of language that she was interpreting in her brain box. Yes, it was translating from a language that they called Japanese. She could see Yoko was in a rage, and now she spotted her going towards the knives clipped to the galley table. The stability of the spacecraft was still poor and all of them were having some difficulty keeping balance. Helena then shouted out to everyone in the galley.

"All stay sill and hold on. Yoko, if you go anywhere near those knives your life is ended. You know we have the powers to really hurt you. I have no more patience. Tell us what you have done and we may be able to give you better conditions during the time you will spend on Mars."

"Nobody said anything about going to Mars, what is all that about? Do you think I cannot escape if you take me to this remote planet, the guards will all find me…"

She was stopped mid-sentence as the laser gun buzzed into her. She looked across in horror and then gently floated in the galley as she lost grip.

Helena had moved across the galley to grab hold of her before she hit anything else.

"OK, Yoko, you are not dead yet; we just gave you a mild dose; give us the information we need and you will be back to normal in a few hours. Otherwise, we are ready to take more drastic action. There is no way we are going to allow you to damage the future of the new agreement we have with the Earth's people. We can also confirm that all your former colleagues are now under our control. Over to you, this is your last chance."

****

Dimitris and Efi had been busy talking to the robot team in the control room; they had established the fault. Sticky nut substances had been detected, and these had affected the solar feed. There was no doubt it had been done deliberately, and the robots had been questioned on how someone could have entered the energy source area without detection. They showed running pictures of the last 24 hours, and sure enough, in one of the change-over periods the shadowy figure of a human was seen entering just behind one of the robots.

The robot had not been programmed to detect unauthorised humans on board, and Yoko was somehow aware of this; she had the chance to throw the liquid over the solar system, before making a hasty retreat to her quarters, where she must have given some excuse to her handlers that they accepted. She was very charming when needed!

"Efi, now we have detected the problem, I want you to programme the robots with new information for our flight into Attica. I think we can bypass the solar system with the new hydro engines. It will not be as comfortable for the passengers, but we should get back on track and arrive just a few days late."

"Thank you, Dimitris, send the new information to my scripter and I will deal with that; perhaps you can go back now and assure our friends that we should be able to continue without worrying about the gravity level. However, the rest of the journey will not be as smooth as before, so keep strapped in when seated."

"I think they will not be the least worried about that. They must have thought this journey would not end well!"

****

Attica, Earth Time, 29 October 2083

The space station on Attica had been put on full alert following the news from General Hermes, but Rotoship4 was now in orbit ready for final landing. They had been relieved to know that the new power source was effective in an emergency. They had made plans to immediately take the female prisoners off after docking, as they wanted them to go for immediate treatment at the medical centre. They were told to ensure that only senior male personnel were to be used for this transfer.

Kim Jong and Panayiota had also now been returned from Acropolis, having been requested to oversee the final operations for the transfer of the prisoners to Mars, after the interrogation and surgery process.

"Panayiota, I am going to watch this landing, and I want to talk to this Yoko Lin before she goes for treatment. I need to know that all these former cell people are now in our hands. I had a list of many who were under Ho Chi's control, so I need to check that out."

"Well Kim, I trust you; if you feel that is necessary you must go ahead. I am going to start making up the lists for Zeus and his team so they may allocate these persons to their respective duties when they arrive on Mars. They will soon have all been through the treatment process."

****

Rotoship 4 had made the landing, and all the passengers were now being made comfortable after the long and somewhat hazardous journey. Chris, Robert, and the girls were now back at the temporary accommodation near the space centre.

"Chris, I just heard from Panayiota; she says Kim Jong is going to meet Yoko Lin at the medical centre. He says that he wishes to interrogate her to ensure that there are no other people left in the ECAW cells. Would she know that? It certainly seems a little strange; I hope he has not started having some sympathy for them. That would be disastrous after all we have gone through. Panayiota would be distraught. I think I should go to check what is happening?"

"Of course, you must go Helena, we are a team. You have a sense for these things that we still do not have. However, please be careful, I do not want to lose you now after all we have been through."

Athena had listened. "I will go with her Chris; I am sure Robert will understand as well."

****

Attica Medical Centre, Next Day

Kim Jong's mind was in turmoil; of course, he knew Yoko, had not she used her charms on him those years ago when they first set up the cells. Even Ho Chi had not suspected that he had a romance. He thought it was over a long time ago, but now having heard that she was here, he had to see her. His thoughts were suddenly interrupted, "Kim Jong, we meet again. What are you thinking? We do not understand why you need to talk to your former colleagues? We thought you were now happy with your new life here and were even planning to marry our Panayiota Fronimos?"

"Helena, and Athena, where did you come from? I heard you had arrived on Attica but did not know you would come here."

"We were concerned that you may still have some yearning for this Yoko Lin person, and what is more you may still not be fully convinced of your new life? You can understand that we have fully trusted you after the events earlier on Mars when you showed much bravery, and you did appear to be in love with Panayiota—what is happening?"

"You are right of course; you always seem to be. I do want to be with Panayiota, but I was drawn somehow when I heard that Yoko was here. We were together for some time and you will agree she is very attractive. I just wanted to see her again."

"I am sorry, Kim Jong, that indicates that whereas your old ways of terrorism may have gone, you still have some thoughts that could take you back to those ways. I think you must go back now to Panayiota and discuss if you need some treatment. It would not be as severe as the treatment that your former colleagues are undergoing but will help you in forming your new life in these very different circumstances."

"I am not sure I want that. Perhaps Yoko was part of the brainwashing plan set up by Ho Chi. She certainly seems to have some hold on me… Maybe it is better that I end my life here…"

He suddenly brought out a laser weapon and turned it towards his body… "Tell Panayiota I am sorry; I do think I loved her, but my mind is split."

Kim Jong was on the ground, his words coming slowly as they stood over him. "I am so sorry; I felt so good these last few months…but something has happened since my injury at the Chinese base… This has shown me I cannot escape my past…"

Helena looked down at him. "He seems to have gone, Athena; this is such a tragedy, I am sure we could have done something to convert him entirely in time, he had so many good qualities. I do not look forward to having to tell Panayiota what happened here."

****

November, Earth Time, Acropolis, 2083

Helena was now talking to Panayiota, who had been distraught following Kim Jong's attempted suicide. They were all assembled in the new lodge that had been allocated to them, where there were three bedrooms, each with their own living rooms and hygiene areas. They were all in Chris and Helena's suite now, feeling elated at being together, but at the same time wishing that they could give their colleague better news.

"Dear Panayiota, you should not give up hope yet, the news is better than we first thought; we have him in the Attica Medical centre under sedation, and although the first reports are not looking good, you know we have some wonderful surgeons and medical team, who have performed miracles before. Just look at how quickly we repaired Chris, and others that you know."

Panayiota looked over to them all.

"I must not spoil this happy time for you all; it will be wonderful if I have some better news, but I must be realistic and help you now with all the work we are undertaking in the next few months. I can see now that Kim Jong's injury a few months ago at the Chinese base was the start of something in his head that was not helped with our surgery. He seemed perfectly fine with me, but once he was on his own, his brain was working differently. Anyway, as you say, let us hope for a miracle!"

Chris and Robert now came over to her for a hug in her long arms. Chris spoke for them all.

"You know we shall be checking each day for some good news. Now, if you can help us with the itineraries for these people that have undergone treatment and are ready for work, then that will help you to take your mind off the present for a while. Can we take you back to your lodge now Panayiota?"

Panayiota decided to take the inner-city rail-elevator down to her home on the next floor. She always loved the view of the city from the elevator as it wound down the various levels, she marvelled at what had been achieved in such a short time—it was a good distraction for her, she started to feel more optimistic…

✶✶✶✶✶✶✶✶✶✶✶✶

Biosphere 2—30 November 2083

Josh and Phillip were back in the Biosphere with their wives, having just given the astronauts, scientists, and students an update of the Attica Agreement, and forward plans for working in conjunction with the Atticans. They had been an excited audience. They could see that the knowledge of the Attican people had already accelerated their work on many things, including spacecraft design, power sources, and not least, the huge improvement in human robot behaviour, and working ability. They had also received the news that Zikky was to be partnered with the Attican HR, Zeus, and Zikky had received several congratulatory words from the assembly. As they returned to Josh's office, he was first to speak.

"I cannot believe that it was twenty-two years ago that I was addressing a new intake in Biosphere one. Today's assembly included many of those who stood in that hall all those years ago. We were worried then about many things, and our laser work nearly finished me. However, we have steadily moved to this point where all things are possible now that we have this extra expertise. What a time for a scientist, and indeed an astronaut!"

"Josh, you are right, it is fantastic outcome for all of us. Now, we are being asked to visit Attica and Mars, and have been offered a suite on Rotoship 6, the newest of the Attican's spacecraft. Do you think we are all fit enough for this journey? It is now a journey of about eight weeks, it seems incredible when you think of the speed that they have accomplished with these new designs and power sources."

"We certainly are, Phillip." It was Ruth who had been sitting quietly with her friend Dawn.

"We are all now only in our sixties and our exercise routines and good eating have us all in good shape. With Dawn helping we shall undertake some tests over the next few days, but in the meantime ask Chris or Robert to arrange for us to leave shortly. Is the Rotoship at the Venus station now?"

"OK Ruth, Phillip and I want to talk to Chris and Robert anyway. We have not spoken since they left for Mars after the wonderful ceremony here, even if it did have some moments of concern."

****

Attica Medical Centre, Earth Time, December 2083

Dr Pericles was in the assessment room with his surgery colleagues. He had been asked to assess Kim Jong as he had previous experience of his treatment after the Chinese base incident.

"Amyryllus, do you think that I may have disturbed his mind with the treatment that I had to give him at that time? He was nearly dead then, it had to be a quick decision."

Dr Amyryllus Koulouris was a specialist in brain behaviour, she had been a leader in developing the systems that most of her fellow citizens now had implanted to help them with everyday matters. One of her most cherished achievements had been the development of the brain box that enabled them all to understand the languages that were being relayed to them, and having the ability to speak in that language.

"I think it is likely, Latros, but it is nothing for you to be concerned about; there was already something I had identified in the brain pattern that would have been triggered at some time, and that would have given rise for concern. Anyway, shall we all go into the operations room, I want to go through something with you. He is still unconscious, and not responding to present treatment."

****

Acropolis, Late December, 2083

"Rob, I have just heard from Dad. We missed Christmas with them, but the good news is that they are all ready to board the new Rotoship that Dimitris and Efi told us about. They will be here in about eight weeks. We can now start planning the ceremony. Let us all meet up later tonight to discuss this? Also, I have just heard from Helena that Panayiota is organising the new intake, and they now are working well under the direction of the human robot team. Acropolis is beginning to buzz!"

Acropolis, Evening of Same Day

After the news earlier in the day, they had all agreed to meet up in Chris and Helena's living room in their new lodge. Dinner was a different experience from those they had been used to in California, but non the less nutritious, and the wines from Attica were now easily available. Chris was making up the nut and dried fruit roast with some gravy that was made from vegetable proteins that he had seen being grown in the new vertical food farm down at the base of the city. Volcanic rock had been pulverised and watered enabling plants and small nut trees to be grown under artificial light and heat.

He had been pleased to see that the new intake was already making a difference to that important area, with labour, administration, and assistance to the robots in the engine rooms. He could also now understand how the city was going to grow and prosper. The technologies were such an advance on the work that he knew the Biospheres teams had been working on for some fifty years.

His thoughts were interrupted by Helena.

"Chris, I have just had some extraordinary news that even we did not anticipate. Dr Pericles has called me to advise that he has established something that explains some of the problems with Kim Jong. He is still unconscious, but he and Dr Koulouris have been undertaking regular tests that indicated that the brain had been, as they called it, separated. To try to understand this more, they decided to look at results of tests that had been undertaken on the incoming former terrorists to see if there were other examples of this phenomenon."

"Here is the amazing outcome. A female who he says had been taken in more recently, and is due for surgery soon, was tested and found to have not only a similar brain pattern, but when APH graphs were read, which is our advanced personality history test that is an advance on your original DNA idea, they came up with a match for a male who had been in for former treatment, and was now lying in their intensive care unit...yes, Kim Jong!"

They all wanted to talk at once, the question was on all their lips. Chris was first.

"Helena, you are not going to tell us that this female is Yoko Lin, surely? I know they are similar ages but did not Kim Jong have an affair with this woman, and apart from that they were from different nationalities..."

"Well, everyone, just wait while you hear more. Further investigation was then undertaken by Latros's team, and it was established that these two are from the same family. The mother had been born in a country you call Japan, and the father was from a country called Korea. The parents, as we know, were killed in an Earth war earlier your present century; they were very young. We also already know that Kim Jong was taken by the ECAW group at that time, to be brought up as an assassin for the group, eventually coming under the wing of the man we know as Ho Chi Dae. Maybe the same thing happened to Yoko Lin?"

"She is being interrogated further now, and we hope to get more background to this incredible story. It is obvious that they do not know of this parentage, and it is fortunate that any affair they may have had did not result in an offspring. It is likely now we know this background that Kim Jong's feelings for Yoko Lin were not actually what he believed, his was probably a love that draws a brother to a sister!"

Chris had listened from the kitchen which surrounded the main living room, and suddenly stopped what he was doing.

"This gets more and more intriguing, Helena, is this relevant to what is happening now to Kim Jong?"

"We certainly must consider that. I am going to ask Latros to take this information into account, and when safe to do so, operate on Kim Jong. I shall advise him that we feel he is needing a brain cell injection, which although this will possibly give him some problems, will eventually restore him to a normal life. I am sure Panayiota will understand that is better than him losing his life. Later, if Kim Jong is with her in a working environment he may regain a fondness for her, and who knows all could end well, even if a little later than she had hoped."

Latros Pericles was making his monthly report to the assembly, the senators were seated but the buzz in the great hall was unusually loud. He now went up to the dais and the noise subsided.

"Chairman, Senators, I can hear that you are excited and may have already had some news regarding recent events. I am here to today to advise you that Dr Koulouris and I have undertaken one of our most sophisticated surgeries to date, and that it has been successful. The former terrorist Kim Jong, who was believed dead, has been fitted with a new brain section, and is responding very well to the treatment."

The assembly all rose and applauded with their long arms extended above their heads, but Latros wanted to continue.

"As you know, this man had apparently converted from his former ways, and we were impressed with the bravery he showed on several occasions. However, there was a fault in his brain caused by earlier contamination of the brain cells by persons unknown, but thought to be undertaken by members of the ECAW group, who have been terrorising many of the Earth's people for many years."

"During the tests that we undertook, not only on Kim Jong, but on all the incoming former terrorists, we found an extraordinary result. One of the most wanted of this terrorist group was a female named Yoko Lin. She was interrogated on her arrival here, and we found that she had the same APH graph, and similar contaminated brain cells. It is now certain that she and Kim Jong were related. However, in view of the severe damage to her brain rhythms, we may have to undertake a brain transplant as soon as we have a suitable one available."

"However, we are reluctant to do this; we still believe that a person is born with a clean brain, it is their life history that changes that brain; in this individual it is obvious that there is still something of that original brain that we may be able to save. If you are agreeable, we shall undertake a similar operation to the one we performed on Kim Jong."

"If these two treatments are successful, they will have a higher IQ than they would normally expect, but may lose much of their memory."

"When Yoko Lin has recovered, we must consider if she should work with her brother? My advice would be that we find a position for her here in Attica. She is a very good-looking woman and she should find a new life with one of our own men. Maybe, with some support from our surrogate stocks we shall see a healthy new-born for the first time for many eras. I appreciate that sperm stocks are very low now, but this case is certainly worth giving priority."

Chairman Isis now interrupted by standing at the dais next to Latros.

"Latros, first, our congratulations to you and Amyryllus for this remarkable achievement. We had the technology, but I believe this is our first trial on a human. Provided we can find brain cell donors, or develop our own artificial brain, there is no reason why we cannot apply this treatment to many of the incoming prisoners."

He hesitated as again the assembly applauded.

"Latros, please stay with us for the moment. I have further good news. Yesterday, several of our friends from Earth arrived on Attica, and I have asked Professor Devonshire to address us all here shortly. He is on the way to us, together with Colonel Somester, and our old friend, Commander Glen. After their flight, they were checked at our medical centre, and they all have been confirmed as fit for the upcoming tour of Attica. This will be followed by all concerned joining them as we travel to Mars for the upcoming wedding ceremonies that will take place in Acropolis next week."

"When the professor arrives, I ask you all to give him a great reception, he has been a very key element in the development of the Marsattica Agreement. His son Christopher is already known to you, and he, and his colleague Robert, are now partners with our esteemed agents, Helena, and Athena. Following their Earth ceremony some months ago, they will be celebrating their marriage here in the new Acropolis Greek church. This is our first major building within the volcano; it is built from Martian stone, and is situated at the very top of our volcanic city. I think all those who can attend will enjoy this special occasion."

****

Acropolis, Later that Day

Panayiota had just received the news from her friends who had attended the assembly. She was not sure what to make of the incredible story that had unfolded regarding Kim Jong and this former assassin, Yoko Lin. It was fantastic that he had recovered, and she now easily could forgive him as he obviously had not been in control of his feelings, and had not done any harm. However, the news regarding his treatment indicated that he may not recognise her now, and any feelings he had for her may have disappeared! She started to sob, but then her head transmitter was taking in a message.

"Panayiota, it is Efi, we are coming over to see you tomorrow; we want to talk about the upcoming ceremony, but also the role of Kim Jong when he returns."

****

Acropolis, Earth Time, 30 March 2084

Chris and Robert were now fully conversant with the city, and had spent several hours understanding the remarkable achievements of the Atticans in building this vast city inside the volcano. The sunny daytime light was like they had experienced on Attica, and the gravity control was allowing them to move to any part of the city without any assistance. They both had marvelled at the work that was continuing with the robot team, and now, the new workforce, which were the former prisoners who had received training after they had all been through the medical centre treatment. All these thoughts were going through their minds as they made their way to the new church, to meet up with Helena and Athena.

"Rob, this is so exciting, and I feel that I want to be part of this growing new city. I am sure the Atticans have more up their sleeve, they are so technically advanced."

"Yes, I have the same feeling. Most of all I am looking forward to our ceremonies in this new church, the design is so much like the churches you find in Greece or Macedonia, even today. When are the others coming over to go through the pre-ceremony routine? Do you think the wedding ceremony will be similar to those we have watched over the years?"

"We are here now Rob, and I see Helena and Athena are already waiting for us, so we shall soon find out!"

****

Acropolis, Earth Time, 20 April 2084

Chairman Isis had arrived on Mars together with the older senators from the assembly. They had travelled on the private shuttle with Josh, Phillip and the rest of the people who would be involved in the upcoming ceremony.

"Professor, I am so pleased to welcome you all to our new city on this otherwise barren planet. We know that for several Earth years you and your colleagues around your world have tried to establish a site on Mars, and indeed we have followed your exploits closely. However, we do have to admit that we were pleased when most of your countries decided that you were not ready for such expense, and proceeded to make a deal with the Chinese, who by your year 2035, had become a friend rather than a foe. As you know we had some contact with the Chinese but have not to date invited them to our city. With your permission, we would like to invite two of them for the ceremony in view of the recent events, where they were very helpful to all of us. We have in mind, General Chao Feng, and head engineer Tao Sing."

"Chairman Isis, we all thank you for your hospitality on Attica. The journey and the things we have already witnessed are a testament to your wonderful achievements. I feel sure we shall continue to be amazed over these next few days in Acropolis. I still cannot believe we did not detect you during our 'Rover' explorations. However, the entrance to the volcano is not exactly clear, the docking procedure is fantastic, we really believed the shuttle was going to hit the mountain until that last-minute opening appeared."

"Concerning the Chinese people, I know I speak for us all in saying we concur with your thoughts, and look forward to thanking them for the help they gave us recently. The Russians and the Chinese have been good friends since the changes of their regimes some years ago."

****

Acropolis, Next Day

Following Efi's earlier visit to see Panayiota, she was now back talking to her new partner, Commander Glen.

"Ed, I think we should try to persuade my assembly people to bring Kim Jong back here. I feel that Panayiota may still be able to attract him, and maybe start a new life with him. I know he is being considered for a task on Attica where he would meet other females and they think that with his new brain cells he will soon be able to readily converse and socialise with them. I think we can make better use of him here, and at the same time give her a chance to re-ignite their friendship."

"Well, Efi, we know he was trained as an astronaut in Krulandistan, so that knowledge should still be with him. With Panayiota's, and Zeus's help, we could propose to Dimitris that he joins the space expansion group that I have heard is being formed at the SCC to investigate further alien activity in the universe, and to investigate and test improved spacecraft technologies?"

"I knew I was attracted to you for more than your good looks, Ed, I will follow that up."

****

Acropolis, Earth Time, 23 April 2084

Kim Jong had arrived from Attica, and was feeling surprisingly well. However, he was still having difficulty remembering anything from the past. He had been told that when he was transferred from the Earth to the planet Attica, after what they had called the Marsattica Agreement, he had been taken seriously ill, but after his treatment he would regain full strength. As he was a single male, and had no apparent family, they had suggested that he stay in Attica to join the astronaut team; but then he had received an urgent message saying that he should talk to the space centre control, as they wanted him to now join the newly appointed astronaut team on Mars, where he would hold a higher position working under the direction of a Senior Captain Fronimos. He was approaching her office now.

"Captain Fronimos, my name is Kim Jong Woo. I have been asked to report to you by General Hermes. I understand I shall be working with you at the new SCC?"

Panayiota was just about holding back tears, but realised that this was no joke, he really did not recognise her.

"Welcome to Acropolis. Can I call you Kim Jong? My first name is Panayiota. We are going to be working closely together so I would like us to have an informal relationship. Let us start by going down together to the new SCC, and I shall give you a tour on the way, so that you may see all the facilities in our wonderful Mars city. I have also arranged lodge accommodation for you on the same level as mine so we may travel together to and from our work."

Kim Jong was thinking, this is some reception, it is as if she had already known me. Is that possible? I do feel warm towards her already, but that is probably because she is beautiful as well as obviously clever.

"Thank you, Panayiota, I appreciate all you have planned for me."

Acropolis, Earth Time, Church of Aphrodite, 30 April 2084

The great day had arrived. All the dignitaries from the various countries of the Earth together with the chairman and selected senators from the Attican assembly. Two of those senators, Spiros Artemis and Takis Fotopoulis were there for a very much more personal reason.

The huge roofed stone church was brilliantly decorated with ribbons and some flowers and plants that had been grown in the vertical gardens on the lower levels of the volcanic city, close to the water reservoirs. These were being highlighted by strong light which was flooding in from the huge insulated windows at the top of the church. The gravity level had been set to levels comparable with the Attican planet, and temperatures were set at a perfect 24 degrees Celsius. Ruth and Dawn were now entering, dressed in flowing pink robes which had been supplied by the assembly as a gift for this special day.

They not only looked wonderful; they were glowing. Their sons were going to be the first to marry Atticans, and what lovely girls they were. Their time together in the Biosphere had been so productive, and they had already developed a great friendship. Now they were to be their daughters-in-law! Ruth stopped at the top of the moving stairs and turned to her friend.

"Dawn, this is surreal. Here we are millions of miles from California, yet I feel calm, comfortable, and happy. The Attican people have proven that their culture has survived, and this church is proof of that. The whole city is incredible; the thought and technology that has gone into making this a real place to live is hard for us to understand. However, our new couples will no doubt fit into the future here, and hopefully they will come back to us from time to time."

"Yes Ruth, I feel the same way… Look, people are coming in carrying what looks like the Bouzoukis and Harps. I think we are nearly ready to start the ceremony so let us look out for the girls as we are supposed to be behind them as they walk up to the dais. Where are they all?"

****

"Takis my old friend, we have a very important day ahead. Helena and Athena will be ready very shortly. Shall we take our places?"

"You and I have seen these girls grow since we took them into our care all those years ago. They look fabulous, and they have done so much to bring us to this happy day. We should be proud, Spiros. Let us make it a great day for all those involved. Attica is now going to be officially linked to the Earth's people."

As they were talking the music started, it was resounding around the huge building. They started to line up at the entrance to the dais waiting for the girls to appear. They could see the male celebrants had already taken their place, but wait, there appeared to be five of them! Also, what was Zeus doing here?

****

Helena and Athena were suddenly aware that the two senators were alongside them, their long arms around their waists. Spiros looked warmly at them.

"Please don't be alarmed, we are here to take you to the dais. We owe that to your parents. We have been your appointed guardians since their untimely death.

We cannot miss this opportunity to say how proud we are to have been in that role, but now we are here to see you happily join with your future partners."

"Spiros, and dear Takis, we had heard that the assembly had taken us in when we lost our parents, but so pleased to hear that it was you both who have been watching over us all these years. Athena and I will surely be honoured for you to take us to the dais."

Athena turned to face Takis and kissed him on the cheek. "Yes, we are delighted to see you both."

The men at the altar were waiting patiently, dressed in the robes of the Attican senators, which had been requested by the girls. What Spiros and Takis had not known was that this ceremony was going to include the marriages of their Chief Astronaut Captain Panamosis, and two more couples who they did not recognise, but obviously were well known to Helena and Athena.

"Where are the other partners, Helena, we have seen five men waiting down at the dais and two ladies dressed in pink robes with flowered hair pieces, who look beautiful I must say? Also, we spotted Zeus down there; I do remember our chairman saying something about a partnership with another of the Earth's human robots, could that be?"

"You will see, Spiros. You remember Commander Glen of course, well, he is to marry Efi today after already having undertaken a partnership ceremony on her last visit to the Earth. There are other surprises. The Russian girls who were so involved with the ECAW group were captured some time ago and then put under the supervision of two of the senior astronauts at the Biosphere that you have seen on our satellite pictures. They were attacked by the terrorists after they found out that they had been helping the ISPEG people to identify their cells."

"Over the last two years, they became very friendly with their supervisors and today we will see the outcome of that. Major Lancs and Captain Durham are two of those men you see at the dais, and they have now complete confidence that the girls are totally converted from their previous roles. Now, you are right about Zeus, he is going to go through a civil ceremony to unite him with Zikky, who you did meet when she accompanied the first contingent from the Earth to our planet."

"Yes Helena, you are right, I do remember. This is a unique partnership, I think, but very happy to see this forward thinking. Now, regarding these girls, Irina, and Lara, I think you called them. I am delighted to hear of their transformation, but as head of intelligence, and knowing their backgrounds, you will understand I must continue to put them under surveillance if they are to stay on Attica or Mars. However, let us not spoil this day, Takis and I are ready to take you and Athena down to the dais. We should not keep your partners in suspense any longer!"

****

The music from the balalaikas and drums was rising and the church stone seating was being filled by a number of the senators and Earth officials, as well as the astronauts and scientists based on Mars. The celebrants were moving towards the dais rails, with Chris and Helena leading. They were quite surprised to see Isis Parapoulis, the Attican chairman, had taken a position at what looked like a font, situated behind the dais. He was dressed in green robes with a large domed hat.

"Helena, why is the chairman here, is he part of the ceremony?"

"He certainly is, Chris, he is going to officiate as is our custom for these occasions. You are all regarded very highly, and he is the equivalent Attican official to your Archbishops. This is his way of showing you all that the assembly greatly appreciate your peoples link with us, and all that was done to bring that about."

"Commander, Rob, Tom, Terry; did you hear that? We must all feel highly honoured by this tribute from the chairman. Incidentally, I believe there is water in that font, and I am thinking this will be more like our baptism ceremony."

"Yes, you have guessed, Chris, I hope you will enjoy it?" Zeus and Zikky will not have water on them of course, but will be blessed by a programme being added to their systems that allows them to think alike. "We thought that would be very apt."

The music 'Samera Gamos Ginetai' was now heard as they approached Isis.

Isis ushered them all to the font, his long arms raised above his robes as he started to speak,

"In the authority given to me by the Attican people, I hereby declare that Christopher Devonshire and Helena Poulakis are life partners, please step forward for your blessing… Robert Somester and Athena Balakakis…"

Isis continued one by one to bless them all, but then the celebrants could hear a gentle sobbing coming from the seats leading down to the dais. They all turned to look.

Efi was first to see what was happening.

"It is Panayiota, we must bring her up with us and let her be part of our happiness."

Ruth and Dawn had also seen the girl crying. "We shall go over to her. She could join us for the party we have arranged back at the astronaut room at the space centre if you agree?"

"That would be very kind, Ruth, please do bring her. In the meantime, I will check where Kim Jong is. I know he is still not aware of his past, but maybe she will be happier if he is around."

The sobbing had stopped, and now the music had started again, and the celebrants all started to file out of the church with Ruth and Dawn looking like bridesmaids; and now Panayiota following in their wake. The inter-city elevators were opening as they ascended the steps to start their new lives.

Chris's mind had been racing, he was so happy, and he had just realised that this was the first time that Robert and he had been able to go through a meeting or ceremony without having to think about ECAW!

****

Acropolis, Earth Time, September 2084

The celebrants had settled in to the new life, and had already been back to Earth with their parents and friends. At the same time, the Earth's officials had also returned. The latter had been astounded by the things they had experienced on Attica and Mars, and were starting their duties with a fresh hope. They could not wait to tell the people about the new opportunities and the new science that should bring a new prosperity to the world's people.

Zeus and Zikky had been appointed heads of the workers control centre, and had been busy setting up schedules for the newly imported labour force. The prisoner's treatments had obviously been successful, and although they were all being monitored constantly, the former terrorists were now a viable work force; some in manual work with the robots, starting the development of the new Hermitage City in the volcano close to Acropolis, that had been identified for future habitation. Others working in administration and many working in the vertical food farms, now an increasing necessity as the population of Acropolis was growing.

Chris and Robert were now heading the training programme for astronauts and inter-space travel, their work enabling them to be in all three centres at various parts of the year. They were together now in Chris's and Helena's lodge, preparing for another trip to Attica, when they would update on the latest technology from the Attican space centre authorities. Their work kept them in constant touch with Spiros Artemis, as the Atticans continued their intelligence work in space.

Panayiota had now been added to their team, and Efi was their main Attican contact, due to her vast experience. She, and the Commander had really settled well, and although they both had to spend several months apart it was obvious that the partnership was strong.

Helena and Athena had been given posts at the new science centre on Acropolis, which was starting to take in students from Attica, and were proposing to be ready to take in students from the Earth's best universities, from America to Russia. In addition, they had identified some of the prisoners as being worth further education, and Helena had been particularly instrumental in pursuing this with the Attican assembly. Today, they were working in the new centre, and looking forward to taking the ride with the boys on the upcoming trip to Attica.

Chris was as usual deep in thought.

"Rob, I think we have everything planned now for this trip, but I was just thinking about Kim Jong and Panayiota. She has been a great asset for us in this new job, and I would love to see her happy. What about us taking Kim Jong and her on this trip. They would be useful anyway, and I think we could put Kim Jong on the training programme. That way they will see a lot of each other, and who knows?"

"Let us speak to the girls and get their view, but it sounds a great idea to me."

****

Attica, Earth time, October 2084

The trip from Mars was now just as the guys remembered a trip to the moon in the early days, when we ISPEG were exploring Pluto. They passed the moon in ten hours. The shuttles had also become larger during the last year to enable them to cope with the increased traffic, not only human, but the larger machinery that was being required for the building of the new city of Hermitage. The Attican assembly had authorised their request for Panayiota's visit, and all had considered that Kim Jong could now be trusted in the training centre on Mars. Kim Jong was beginning to absorb his new life, but still was not showing any particular recognition of any of them.

Robert was first to express their feelings.

"I am sure, we all feel this is another step in the right direction, we can already see that Panayiota has forgotten past events. Spiros was very helpful in getting us to this point, let us go and say hello before we go down to the astronaut and science centres."

****

Intelligence Centre, Attica, Earth Time, October 2084

Spiros was in great spirits, his plans for the prisoners was going well, but mostly he had just received some news that he had been waiting for. A remote small planet close to Mercury had been sending out signals for some time that indicated that there was some life there. They had called it Mercury Regulasis. His team had now heard a language that they had identified as Brittonic, their historians advising them that this was a language used in ancient times on the planet Earth by those calling themselves Gaelic or Anglo-Saxon. This was an area of the Earth that he knew was now part of Western Europe. Could there be the possibility of their origins coinciding with that of his own people?

He was just digesting this news and thinking how they could make an exploratory trip when his head transmitter buzzed.

****

Attica Assembly, Two Days Later

Isis was back addressing the assembly having just received the news from Spiros. He had invited Helena and Athena as well as their partners into the chamber as he was increasingly aware of their contribution to the present situation, and had become very attached to these younger people who he saw as the foundation of the new life on Attica and Mars.

"Senators, we are very happy to welcome, our planet Earth agents, Helena, and Athena, and their new partners, who are to be leading our new astronaut team on Mars and on the planet Earth. They are invited here today to share with us some more good news that has just been confirmed by our Senator Artemis and his team."

"A small planet close to Mercury has been sending out signals for some time, and now we have heard transmissions in a language that is strange to us, but we believe is a tongue originating again on the planet Earth many years ago. It is early days, but of course we are very excited, and plan to explore the possibilities that this planet has human life, and is habitable in some way."

There was much excitement in the chamber, and it was difficult for Isis to continue; he realised that there were many questions. Chris and Robert were looking at each other in wonder, but the girls seemed to be looking a little sad.

Isis interrupted all their thoughts as he raised his long arms again, and the chamber quietened.

"Our astronaut team under General Hermes, Senior Captain Panamosis, and Captain Fronimos are to link with our two new commanders here, Christopher Devonshire and Robert Somester to pursue this opportunity. We shall be giving out more details in the next few days but in the meantime, this is a confidential matter not to be discussed with our people at this time. We need more information, and to be sure that we do not get involved in another war, or another terrorist situation as experienced by our friends on the planet Earth. As they appear to be attempting to contact someone in space it is hoped that they are friendly aliens."

There was applause now in the chamber, and Isis sat again waiting for the senators' responses.

Helena was quietly talking to Chris as the proceedings continued, "Well Chris, this is a gigantic moment for Attica, and although one part of us is happy to see the possibility of yet another planet opening up, Athena and I are concerned about your roles in this venture, and the fact that we may be parted for some time during these exploratory trips."

"But, dear Helena, we shall not be away that long, the new Rotoships are as you know amazingly fast; we have no idea yet if this planet is habitable, or if we can enter its atmosphere. I think we shall undertake a few orbits with our intelligence team aboard, and decide if we can actually enter their territory without being attacked. We can set up satellite pictures for you both so you can follow our progress."

"Well Chris, when the assembly closes, we need to all return to our rooms so we can talk more and you can see the reason why Athena and I are concerned."

Attica, Executives' Accommodation, Same Evening

The four of them were back from the assembly, and getting ready for their light meal and drinks. Chris had found a ginger plant on the planet, and had been showing the locals how to brew his ginger beer concoction. They were drinking this really before meeting up with Efi and Commander Glen at the new eating house that they had named 'Steak Nuts'. An idea of Robert's as he saw the Atticans love of nut products, and the fact that they had no meat steaks to offer. A little roast goat being the only animal protein on offer. They had all agreed that the recipe was a winner.

Chris opened up the conversation.

"Rob, Helena gave me some concern with some comments she made today that seem to affect us all. She is concerned about our new roles, and being away from them for long periods. I have explained that we expect these trips to be fast and exploratory at this stage. We shall involve several other personnel if this survey proves successful…"

He was interrupted by them both trying to talk to them at the same time…

"Chris, Rob, you do not understand, we are both going to have children."

"Well, of course we sincerely hope so, both of us."

"No, Chris, Rob, listen. We are going to have a child very shortly."

They both looked stunned.

"But, neither of you are showing any signs of being pregnant, are you sure?"

"We have both been through tests. When the Attican planet was not afflicted as it is today, it was normal for us to have very short pregnancies. The babies were taken by surgery and taken to a special chamber, and after about two months they developed to a stage whereby the mothers could take them back, and start to feed them. We hope that will be the procedure this time. We have already spoken to Latros, and he is preparing the facilities for us both."

"We do both have some concerns about how these children will develop, will they be like us with olive skins and long arms, as we had until our surgery, or like you both. We are hoping the latter."

Chris, as usual, was first to get over this news.

"I know Rob well enough to say that we think you are both fantastic. You have already taken on many things in your lives that most of our people would consider impossible. We are so excited that I feel sure we shall not care what colour or shape they are; they will be our children! This will be such good news for not only your people, who will start to see things in a new light, but our people, who will see peace and future growth potential with the Attican nation… Now, can we both get a big hug before we leave to join the others!"

****

Earth, December 2084—World News Centres

"This is Abe Parato reporting. What excitement there will be around the world as we digest the news just arriving from our new alien friends in Attica!"

"They have confirmed that two of our esteemed American ISPEG commanders, and their Attican partners, have announced the birth of Joshua Takis and Phillip Isis. These are the first natural births to take place on the planet Attica for many years, and of course there will be considerable interest in how these children will develop. We have been advised that the first pictures will be shown in about three months when the babies are fully developed, so we shall have to just excitedly await that day."

"2084 has been some year. It is clear that the ECAW threat has gone, and our people around the world are starting to work together to ensure a

better environment, and a more prosperous planet, thanks to the new technologies arising from our work with the Attican nation."

"Good day to all our listeners around the globe, Abe Parato signing off until next week."

Attica, December 2084

Chris and Rob had been talking to their parents on the newly established communication channels with Attica and the Earth. The delay factors were now almost gone as the new link had opened. The Atticans had seen that they needed better communication now that the agreement with the Earth was working.

"Dad, Mother; Rob and I are here with the girls in the medical centre, and we have just seen the new arrivals. Dr Pericles has been fantastic and allowed us to watch the procedure in a viewing room alongside the surgery. The boys are of course very small and at this stage hard to identify, but they all have assured us that this is normal and will now be looked after by the specialists here for the next few months until they are strong enough to be returned to us. It is unusual, but then, everything has been like that since we first met the girls! We are confident."

"Chris, Rob, first, I trust the girls are well and not too exhausted by this experience. It must be quite a concern for them; Dawn and I would love to be with you all at this time. Second, Josh and Phillip are here and were so thrilled to hear the names you all selected for these two boys. We are all thinking of you."

Rob was thinking, but now interrupted the conversation. "You know Auntie Ruth, you, Mother, and of course our fathers, should all try to get on the next flight by the new Rotoship 7. It is a fantastic machine and will get you here in 6 weeks and is fitted with every comfort in the new executive wing. Our new positions here allow us to use this facility, and we can speak to Efi and Panayiota to arrange that if you can find some dates. Your arrival could coincide with the two babies being released from the medical centre. Apart from that we shall update you first hand regarding our new venture into space, whereby we are hoping to find life on a newly found planet. Maybe another Attica!"

Chris nodded over to Robert…

"What a great idea Rob, please all think about that, folks, it would be such a great way to start the new year. We had better sign off now, let us know your plans… Oh, before we go, we should tell you that Panayiota has been working with Kim Jong the last few months and we heard that he has asked her for a date. It is amazing news as his brain, although changed, retained something that obviously told him that this girl was something special. We are all delighted for her, she is such a great worker and person. Now, goodbye from us and the girls, who have just waved to us, and look fantastic…"

****

Biosphere 3—30 December 2084

Professor Devonshire, and now newly promoted, Commander Somester, were at the rostrum in the great hall of the newly built Biosphere, which had been developed with the assistance of the human robot team, and the Attican scientists. They had both been appointed senior advisors to ISPEG and had been asked to address a new contingent of scientists who would inhabit the biosphere for the next two years, working on new food and water sources that could be developed for Mars, and to meet future needs for the planets of Attica and Earth.

"Ladies and gentlemen, Commander Somester and I are so honoured to be able to address you today. Some 22 plus years ago, I stood in the adjoining Biosphere 1, and could not have even thought about the amazing progress we would make in these last few years. We are just closing on the most progressive year in our history, 2084."

"We shall shortly be flying on what we all called in 2060, a flying saucer! We shall fly to a new planet that was only discovered a few years ago, and arrive in just six weeks! We shall experience these craft being flown by human robots who have such high intelligence they can converse with us! We have even lived to see a partnership between a male and female robot!"

He paused as the young scientists and trainee astronauts were taking all this in…

"Following this remarkable period, you will now be seeking even further advances in our technology and understanding of the planets. There is a priority for us. Due to the success of moving humans to Mars and who knows, soon to other planets, where water and food supply are essential, we must find new ways to sustain this growth in population."

"When we started here several years ago, we were just looking at survival methods on alien planets, supposing we found them. We looked at spacecraft, we looked at protective clothing, we looked at laboratory samples from the moon, and we spent several years developing new armaments. The laser gun research nearly killed me and did kill some of our best scientists. However, we now have laser armaments that are ten times more powerful than when we started, mainly due to the assistance of our new Attican friends."

"Our next priorities will be energy and atmosphere control. Already there are plans being made by the Attican nation to increase gravity on Mars, having established a city on that planet that is stable enough to allow its citizens to move around without special clothing or masks, and where you will see all the comforts and facilities that you may experience in your hometown."

"So, my friends, the commander and I are here for another hour before leaving you to take on the next era; if you have any questions do come up and say hello. Our time here is at an end, and you are our new hope for the future… May it be as exciting and fruitful as our time here. Good luck!"

One of the young scientists had already stood up. She could easily be heard above the hubbub in the hall.

"Sirs, my name is Yoko Lin. Do you think that we have now seen the last of the old communist ideals?"

Phillip and Josh looked at each other…no way, surely!

THE END